The Arthur Moreau Story

Guy Booth is a gifted designer maintaining a keen interest in the history of architecture and related design disciplines ranging from fashion to technology. He has worked in London, Belfast, the Sudan, Hong Kong, Qatar, France, Italy and Switzerland on projects as diverse as churches, private palaces and the design of cities. He has devised a simple method of understanding the complexities of design that everyone can grasp. In 1983 he set up his own practice in London. He was asked to write the biography of the Victorian architect Sir Charles Barry, creator of The Palace of Westminster. Enthused by this task, and later inspired by the majesty of the Swiss Alps, he decided to write full time. *The Arthur Moreau Story* is fiction that fuses philosophy with fabulous experience. The author's potent imagination sees life as a gorgeous story to tell.

The Arthur Moreau Story

Guy Booth

Arena Books

First published in 2011 by Arena Books

Arena Books
6 Southgate Green
Bury St. Edmunds
IP33 2BL

www.arenabooks.co.uk

Distributed in America by Ingram International, One Ingram Blvd., PO Box
3006, La Vergne, TN 37086-1985, USA.

Guy Booth
  The Arthur Moreau Story
   1.   Antiquarian booksellers – Fiction. 2. Private
   investigators – Fiction. 3. Power (Social sciences) -
   Fiction. 4. Good and evil – Fiction. 5. Suspense fiction.
   I.   Title
   823.9'2-dc22

ISBN 978-1-906791-74-2

BIC categories:- FF, FL, FHP.

Printed & bound by Lightning Source UK

Cover design
by Jason Anscomb

Typeset in
Times New Roman

This book is printed on paper adhering to the Forest Stewardship Council™
(FSC®) mixed Credit FSC® C084699.

Prologue

During the Nineteen-Seventies the World heard the news of a macabre event; *The Marriage Island Case* - a mass murder.

The atrocity involved two hundred young men, all around nineteen. In the sumptuous ambience of a French château, in an elegantly furnished *salon*, the victims had been branded, partially flayed and their eyes put out.

The butchering was done at the Summer residence of an American billionaire. Police from three nations were called in as the Paparazzi hammered home the sleazy facts. The billionaire was a compulsive gambler, drug addict and sadomasochist pervert: an old fashioned all-rounder.

Just before the Second World War, we read, he had purchased an island off the western French coast not far from La Rochelle; the *Isle des Noces* – that's "Marriage Island" in English. During the 1950s and '60s the billionaire's guests included an impressive list of film stars and politicians who were ferried to the electric-fenced domain in a luxurious yacht. After his death the property was rented to a rag-bag of rock stars, diamond dealers and ancient movie queens. When the murders were discovered the château was silent, open and empty.

Autopsies revealed that the two hundred victims had been under the influence of a strong narcotic, but nobody could agree on a motive. A well known German daily that I happened to take in those days leaked three startling facts. The alien substance found in the victims' tissues defied analysis; the bodies were physically perfect, like classical Greek statues: all were identical. There was an immediate, top level clamp-down on this report and nothing more was heard of the case.

So we never knew that the billionaire was called Emanuel Blaisedale II, that his father had made a fortune in the Nineteenth Century elevator boom, that his business empire was based in Minneapolis, USA.

♠

Why should I have been the only one to make the following observation?

Two hundred souls had endured an unspeakable death that had been reported round the World, yet there was not one cry from a mother or father, wife or lover, relation or friend. No appeals on television, no audiences with The Pope, no monument: nothing.

Nothing makes sense if you think about it.

Consider the following unlikely scenario; a hundred identical sets of identical twins - all friendless orphans - are murdered in peculiar circumstances simultaneously. No attempt is made to conceal the victims' bodies or the murder weapons. The case is examined by experts from France, Great Britain and the United States. No conclusions are published, the murderers are never found and the authorities behave as if nothing has happened.

Almost twenty years later *The Marriage Island Case* arrived on my doorstep.

♠

My step-father had left me his grand old house in Winfleet, a Buckinghamshire village not far from London. Recently divorced, I asked my sister, Celia, to help redecorate the main rooms. We were upstairs hanging pictures when the door bell rang. Laurence, the butler - in his youth my step father's batman - announced Sir Frederick Appleby and my brother-in-law, Peter Tyndale. Celia went down to greet them while I leaned over the landing balustrade.

"What brings you from London on a grey Monday morning, Fred?"

"To squeeze information out of you, Johnny." Fred heads the Government Bureau of Sincerity. What this vast organisation does he will never divulge, but colleagues in Whitehall murmur over their gins that Frederick controls the country.

We went into the tangled garden and sat under a rotting pergola while Celia prepared drinks. Fred wasted no time.

"When did you last have anything to do with Arthur Moreau, Johnny?"

"Arthur?" I paused. I had to think. "Years ago."

"I have it as thirteen years. Does that make sense to you?" I looked at his wise face. Beneath the iron grey brows one eye is glass, occasionally he dabs it with a silk square. The good eye observes you with penetrating, humorous knowing. A bastion of intuition, Fred guts mysteries with the skill of a master fishmonger, laying the facts before his customers in a row of neatly filleted solutions.

I glanced at the tepid smile glimmering on Peter's lips. "Peter? . . . What's all this about?"

"Don't wriggle, Johnny! Answer Fred's question." I confirmed that it was thirteen years since Arthur and I had our business bust-up.

"You've never seen him since?"

"No."

"Categorical?" Of course I was! Wouldn't I have told them if I'd seen Arthur?

"Do you know where he is?"

"France, I suppose. Yonroche. I never think about him. Don't want to know."

"You retain no contact with his circle?" This question was absurd. One of the main reasons for resigning as Arthur's co-director was that I had never felt included in his *circle*, as Fred put it. "What is so important about Arthur that brings you away from lunch at the Club?"

"Never mind the Club, Johnny." His eye fixed me with an imperious glance, "I will remind you of one monumental principle, my friend: never ask any questions, it is the surest way of getting to know the answers."

"You've been asking me questions since you arrived, Fred." He brushed a drop of dew from the sleeve of his impeccable Aquascutum jacket.

"Do you remember that French murder? The Marriage Island pantomime? A pack of partygoers skinned two hundred young men, spooned their eyeballs out and shoved red hot door chimes up their arseholes. Remember?"

How did I know that Fred was going to mention The Marriage Island Case?

"Yes I do. I found the whole thing fascinating."

"*Really*, Johnny! Most folk were revolted." He puckered his mouth, expelling his breath with a hiss. "You followed the case? - as far as press coverage permitted?" I told them what I'd read. Fred got up and stood by an ancient, rambling rose.

"What made you different from everybody else, Johnny? What was it about The Marriage Island Case that particularly fascinated *you*?"

"The fact that the victims . . ."

"Two hundred young men ... go on."

". . . were identical."

"And?"

"And . . . they didn't have any origins. They came from nowhere. It was bizarre, if you see what I mean."

"Bizarre is a refined word, Johnny. The actual word for The Marriage Island Case is *shit*. The case stank so badly that it had to be buried. I was one of the undertakers." He pointed to the rose, "A thorny problem, burying the truth, Johnny. You see, *politically* it had to be done. I did not agree with the Prime Minister, I did not agree with the French President, and I certainly did not agree with the American President. But we had no choice: they were three very embarrassed people."

Celia came across the lawn carrying a tray of drinks. Fred was immediately affable, plucking his glass of Chardonnay with a word of pleasure. Peter passed me my gin and Italian, then took his mineral water. Fred mused for a while, picking-off gigantic thorns from the snake-like rose stem.

"I have a suspicion, Johnny, and it is - alas - a lasting suspicion, that Arthur Moreau - *your* old business partner - was involved with The Marriage Island Case."

7

"*Arthur?* ... involved in the ... that's *impossible*, Fred!"

He ignored me. "Was Moreau interested in your ex-wife? Sexually, I mean."

"Arthur was interested in men, Fred. Young men and old books. You know that." Frederick tapped the pollen of a late daffodil from a burnished toe-cap.

"You never saw Moreau in the company of an American gentleman who spoke with a German accent?"

"No."

He stared towards the great, brick house, pensive. I took a swig of my drink, "How on earth can you think that Arthur was involved in The Marriage Island Case?"

"I don't *think* anything, Johnny."

"It's crazy! Arthur was devious. He was a liar in business when he needed to be, but he was hardly a murderer. I knew him well enough to tell you both that."

"I believe you were completely deceived by Arthur Moreau, Johnny."

I stared at them both, incredulous. "*Deceived*? By an antiquarian book dealer? By a harmless, charmingly camp homosexual?"

"By a man *you* chose for a business partner, Johnny!"

"Yes! Because he was damned good company and a master of his trade. I was bloody lucky he took me on. I didn't have to show my appreciation in bed, either!"

"Male love is not at issue here, Johnny." He put his glass down on a damp bench and began to walk briskly towards their waiting limousine. "Nor, by the way, is The Marriage Island Case. That is done with." He was handed into the night black Rolls by his chauffeur. "The case was part of something larger, Johnny." The door clicked shut. Peter got into the front as the rear window purred open revealing Fred's august face framed in polished steel. "Arthur Moreau is very important as far as we are concerned, Johnny. What he does, who with, and where."

"What has all this got to do with me?"

"If you hear of Moreau, hear *anything* you understand, please tell Peter at once."

Leaning towards the car window I made a final plea, "The bust-up with Arthur was terminal. I don't ever want to see him again and I'm damned sure that he certainly doesn't want to see me."

"You never know, Johnny. You *never* know!" The window shut noiselessly as the battleship sized car eased itself down the drive.

That was how the interview ended. The subject was never spoken of for two years. Then, one morning in the post, a shocking-pink envelope arrived.

It contained a card inviting me to Arthur Moreau's funeral.

PART I

I am the Chairman of an internationally renowned company dealing in rare books and manuscripts: *Limited Editions Limited*, known to the trade as "Johnny's". My headquarters is housed in a row of picturesque historic properties on one side of St. Damian's Square in Aylesford, a quintessential English country town.

Now we have the Internet, making it possible to buy so much from home. At the time of this memoir there was nothing like it. Bibliophiles came to St. Damian's Square from all over the world. They paid up to five million guineas for a single item. Our best clients were entertained to lunch in a panelled room unchanged since the time of Charles the Second.

I employed a staff of three, I still do. The youngest, Thomas, was my trainee. On the day of my departure for France to attend Arthur's funeral, Thomas had to catalogue a superb collection of books I had bought at a bankruptcy sale. I needed to tell the boy what I wanted him to do but he was late. When he finally arrived I was in no mood for a young man's impudent repartee.

"Where the hell have you been?" He stood at my desk looking like a fallen idol with his jacket collar raised and his hair untidy. "You're a mess! What's that revolting stain on your shirt?"

"From dinner last night, Gov'ner."

"With your girlfriend?" He gave me a furtive, twenty-one year old glance.

"How many times have I told you that sex and business don't mix! You know damned well that I have to be at Peter Tyndale's office by noon, and then I have to catch the Eurostar. Bloody irresponsible! . . . Have you *shaved?*"

"No."

"For God's sake, Man!" He stared at me with clear, very beautiful eyes. I smiled, I would have been the same at his age. "Go downstairs and ask Melissa to make some coffee, then I'll tell you what to do with the Ashbin Collection, it won't take long. And comb your bloody hair while you're at it!"

Thomas! Fresh to life, loving every moment of being young and strong and blessed with faultless English looks. His beauty draws a breath of pleasure from all that set their sights on his deep hazel pupils and dark chestnut hair slopping in masterly strands over a sensual, bronze-cream complexion.

"Black or white, Gov'ner?"

"As long as it's not powdered, I don't care if it's green."

♠

Half an hour later, just before London begins to mantle the rural scene with the hem of her grimy cloak, my car climbed into the Chiltern Hills. I considered Arthur's typically unsuitable funeral invitation. A card in Chinese yellow, his favourite colour, its deckle-edges in gold leaf, the text done in candy pink and glow-green inks - all dusted with silver. At the top, in a flamboyant shield, a rampant adolescent cherub of sixteen - elderly as cherubs go. Wearing a rakish sailor hat and a gold bow tie the cherub poses lewdly with the Keys of Heaven.

Sacred and profane: the Moreau touch.

Arthur was, I have to admit, a breathtaking queen. He had a captivating personality but his melodramatic bouts of bad taste and brash, 'Roman' vulgarity (carillon farts and falsetto whoops) took a lot of getting used to. A brilliant conversationalist, an accomplished antiquarian, a deft socialite, Arthur at his best was an orchid of a man. But like an orchid, a taint of dank decay hung about him.

London traffic was moderate, I made it to the City well in time. Negotiating the narrow turning off Threadneedle Street that leads to Peter's office building, I drove into Eve's Court and parked in a pre-arranged space below a super-expensive stainless steel tower shaped like an Hour Glass corset.

Peter was no longer a merchant banker. I never understood what he did, nor did Celia. All we knew was that Peter worked for Fred. We had little in common and I often wondered what my sister - trained in Fine Art - saw in this suave, standard issue, English Public School, five-star hero. I walked into his Pent House office suite marvelling again at the icy luxury of it all.

"Life being kind to you, Johnny?"

"Can't complain. Yourself?"

"Thrilling." He spoke without emotion, staring indifferently into my eyes. Wearing pinstripe trousers and a Jermyn Street shirt, he lolled on the back of a sofa upholstered in sheet-steel. He wore crimson braces – fashionable in those days, his oil-slick thick, matt black hair was immaculately groomed. With a cricketer's hand he gestured to an industrial glass chair studded with antique golden dollars.

"Make yourself comfortable, my friend."

Beneath the shirt his immensely broad shoulders and superbly honed torso rayed bestial power, erotic, fractionally brutal. I did not much care for Peter's brand of thrusting virility. Maybe my sister did.

Giving the glass chair a miss, I wandered over to look at a painting by Picasso. Genuine (of course), it was hung - ridiculously - on a wall-high circle of cut-crystal mirror-glass. My reflected image confirmed that Peter's world of executive status symbols was far from my own. A creased, cream linen suit; a jade green, Russian style tunic shirt; tan leather Italian slip-on shoes; carelessly combed corn blond hair. Definitely "not cricket" at Number One, Eve's Court, EC3.

Fingering the Picasso, I was wondering when Peter was going to get round to Arthur's funeral, when he strode over the gleaming Japanese onyx floor and pulled my hand sharply from the canvass like a primary school teacher pulls a little boy's paw from a glue pot.

"Moreau's funeral, Johnny. Sit down and tell me who you will meet there."

"I haven't the first idea who I will 'meet there', Peter." A bronze door slid open and Liz, Peter's leggy, 'Essex Girl' PA, sashayed in with a tray of smoked salmon sandwiches and two bottles of Krug '66. Her cheeky, raucous laugh made a welcome contrast to the insipid vulgarity of the hideous "Designer" interior.

"'Ello, Johnny, darlin'. You're lookin' a dish today, luv – isn't he, Boss? That *gorgeous* shirt!" She put the tray down and popped me a lipstick-smarmed kiss. "Oooh, I could have that shirt orff of 'is back, Boss." She shot me a smile bright as the bars of an electric fire while Peter put a sandwich in his mouth and deftly opened one of the bottles, pouring out three glasses. It was as if they chucked down smoked salmon sandwiches and Krug '66 every hour.

"Johnny's off for a dirty weekend in France, Liz. Staying with his mistress. Suppose you and me go too?" He gave her a slap on the bottom.

"*Oooh*, Peter! Warra bleedin' liberty! In front of yer brother-in-law an all." She slid her hand down his back, resting talon-like false nails on his sumptuously muscled, tundra-shaded buttocks. "An innocent girl like me in France with a married man!", she darted me a piquant, pert smile. "*Peter*! Think of your position!"

"I am. It's lovely." He said this almost without a movement of his lantern jaw.

"Are we expected to drink that lot, Peter?" I spoke with the grim satisfaction of one who has taken The Pledge, noticing Liz's hand ease into the gap at the top of Peter's thighs. "Why don't you and Corinne marry, Johnny? Celia and I want you to be happy after those bitch years with Dawn."

"Yeah! And so do I, Johnny. An 'ansome bloke like you. An' she's a French *countess*! Bleedin' 'ell, darlin'! What are you bloody-well waitin' for?" Caressing the inside-leg of Peter's left thigh she raised her glass, squealing, "'Ere's to you and Corinne! Gawd bless yer both."

"What am I going to do with a French Countess and sixty thousand hectares?"

"Live it up, darlin'!" She poked Peter's left pectoral with a dagger-sharp nail, coachwork crimson. She caressed his nipple, erect beneath the shirt fabric. I flicked my gaze away.

"Pour another glass for yourself, Liz, and get back to work. Make sure nobody disturbs us." Peter hitched his balls generously at the crotch of the beautifully tailored trousers. His expression softened, the mouth breaking into a charming smile, the sort of "Alps over Lucerne" smile smooth operators like Peter flash-up when they want something from you. He pressed a button on the wall beside me, activating the lock on the bronze door, and I smelt the rich, male musk of his armpit.

"Celia tells me that Moreau was a revolting little man."

"Celia was always afraid that Arthur would corrupt me."

"And did he?" He eyed me with the purity of a Sixth Form prefect. I knew he had always suspected that my relationship with Arthur was homosexual, conventional men did. Dawn, my ex-wife, had not dispelled the illusion. She was married to Show Business; we lead a zany life. When she did night club contracts we never saw one another for months. People often wondered if I compensated with a lover on the side.

"Arthur didn't corrupt me. He represented a stimulating, exotic world. He was bizarre, sometimes impossible, finally intolerable, but I'm glad I knew him. I owe Arthur my success. If he hadn't turned up at that Oxford undergraduate dinner, I would now be running father's law firm, pretending to be something I'm not." Peter opened the second bottle and took my upper arm in one hand, pulling me down close to him on the street-length sofa. With the cunning gentleness of an experienced interrogator he murmured, "Go on."

"There is nothing I can tell you that you don't already know. Arthur taught me my business, together we made a hell of a lot of money, we enjoyed ourselves doing it. I was not obliged to be his lover. What more could I ask?"

"That you note all the people at the funeral you can remember from the past and get the information to Sir Frederick without delay."

I took a mouthful of champagne. "Who *do* I remember, Peter? It's been a long time. My business contacts have altered completely. I'm no use to Frederick." Seeing that he ignored this last remark, I continued with staccato emphasis, "All the people I now come into contact with, day-in, day-out, Peter, are antiquarian *book* dealers, *not* mass murderers!"

"What about Switzerland? He had a place in Geneva, didn't he?"

"Lausanne."

"And France? There are bound to be faces you recognise, Johnny. We are relying on you." He was sitting so close to me that I felt the intimate heat of this body surging with mine. Uncomfortable, I stood up. It was my turn to pour champagne.

"When Arthur and I were partners I had nothing to do with the French side. I now deal with two firms in Paris, one in Lyon, but they never knew Arthur." I grabbed two sandwiches.

"Sir Frederick, Johnny, is no fool."

"What's all this *Sir Frederick*, Peter? You sound like a flunkey! Fred is my mother's second cousin . . . remember? Your wife's God Father!" Peter butted his rock-like torso back into the aluminium gauze cushions of the sofa.

Resting his hands behind his head, he threw his long legs out, one foot crossed over the other.

"What about Alexandre Laborde?"

For an instant I was stunned. How did Peter know this name? I had to search my mind before I answered. "Alexandre Laborde died about twenty years ago. His partner, Alain Remondet, was the only link I maintained with Switzerland. Alain retired … I can't remember exactly … certainly ten years ago. Well into his eighties. That ended my Lausanne connection. If Remondet is still alive he will be too old to attend the funeral." Wiping salmon oil from my fingers with a napkin I perched on the arm of the sofa. "We are talking of the dim and distant, Peter. Arthur must have been well into his nineties when he died. I hardly think he was concerned with business. He was a millionaire. Did he need to work himself into the grave?"

"He was worth two hundred and sixteen million US dollars, he was ninety-one when he died." The sharpness of Peter's response concerned me.

"Not as old as I thought." Instinctively, I changed tack. "Who else should I recall? The pack of snarling queens at Poppets' Corner? I don't think Frederick will thank me for lining *them* up in his office."

"There's Jo."

Jo! . . . Half-brother Jo! Did they *have* to remind me of Jo? "I don't want Jo near me. If he's there, which I doubt, I shall leave at once."

"Arrive late, sit near the back amongst the uninvited. When they file round the coffin you'll see everybody. When they are all seated, listening to the priest, sneak out. It's a big place, isn't it, Yonroche basilica? Plenty of doors." He upturned the second bottle into my glass. "You had better catch your train. I'll have them put your car into the Chairman's space, he's away for a week."

"Why choose me?"

"Nobody knew Arthur Moreau as you did, Johnny."

"Fred told me I didn't know Arthur at all."

"Perhaps."

Non-plussed, I took a champagne-pink, sanded glass elevator to the main lobby where I was handed into a taxi for Waterloo International.

♠

Corinne, *La Comtesse de la Breuse*, had been my mistress, lover, confidante, and friend since we met at an Élysée Palace garden party and fell fatally in love. She traces her line to Clovis, which beats the Bourbons. She is a Countess in her own right, far more senior in the French aristocratic pecking order than Adrien, her first husband, a mere Baron.

Corinne's official residence, the Château de la Breuse, is twenty kilometres from Yonroche, the town that Arthur chose for his final business

13

venture. There he retired, served - and serviced - by a swarm of extravagantly good looking young men.

I left the Paris TGV at Angers where, as usual, I hired a car for the last leg of my journey. It was dark when I pulled-up in front of the great, open doors of La Breuse. In silhouette against the light from radiant chandeliers was Corinne's pencil-slim figure. We took each other in our arms, dawdling over a sizzling kiss.

"Was the train comfortable, darling?"

"Not as comfortable as you!"

"José has spent all day preparing your favourite dishes."

The evening progressed in style.

♠

Morning's gilt light sprayed through the four shuttered windows of Corinne's bedroom, painting lacy patterns amongst the Rococo plasterwork of the ceiling. I gazed at my shirt strewn on a canapé, at Corinne's stockings gauzily slopped over a Louis Quinze fire screen. A bottle of Margaux '63 stood empty on a mantel piece, there was the aroma of fresh coffee. A clock chimed nine.

"The *funeral*!" I jolted myself out of bed, "I'm going to be late!"

"Don't go, Johnny!" I sat down, nestling in the curve of Corinne's warm body. She dawdled her fingers over the blond hairs of my thighs.

"I can't miss it, darling." I kissed her shoulder, feeling the force of desire. Of course I could miss it. Silently I cursed Fred.

"I have to be there, Corinne." This time I got up with purpose, though my half-way erection made me look slightly farcical.

"Moreau was a *lurid* little beast, darling. He ran some sort of pornography business. I don't mind what you say in his defence, he collected filthy old books and all sorts of creepy people came to buy them." She got out of bed, traipsing into the adjoining boudoir to pour coffee. "They came from all over the world, Johnny. It was *lurid*!" I loved the way Corinne said 'lurid' in English. "He had strings of boyfriends. Adrien might have been a bastard but he couldn't stand queers. Moreau was barred from our circle and for once I agreed with Adrien. There was something nauseating about the man. That awful, *awful* laugh!"

"Ridiculous! Tell me one time when Arthur misbehaved in company? You were all being horribly stuffy. You talk about manners, what about your husband? Adrien was one of the rudest men I've ever met."

"Moreau never attempted to speak French, Johnny, not two words! He must have lived here for the best part of twenty years."

I stood naked by one of the windows, wrenching a croissant to bits. "I might have known! My sister, Fred, my brother-in-law, and now you. All against Arthur. I was the bloke who knew him. Would Arthur deceive *me*? Impossible!" I wound my arms round her waist, massaging her breasts with buttery fingers. We looked at our reflection in an ancient mirror. She turned in the circlet of my arms and kissed my chest. In a few seconds I would be a powerless slave.

"I'll take a shower and go. I shall be back for lunch."

"He betrayed you! You owe him nothing. Stay with me." She ran her tongue down my belly; I put in a last plea, "Arthur never sold filthy books when I was his partner." She sprang out of my arms and stood confronting me in a fit of girlish anger.

"*Johnny*! You were so romantic a moment ago! Forget Moreau!" She took a cigarette from a silver box, lit it, and sucked hard at the tip, propelling the smoke from her mouth with a short gust of breath. "He was tawdry and vulgar. Where on earth did you find him?"

"Oxford. He was invited to a college dinner by one of the dons. I think Arthur's family made their money in Canada."

"I've never heard such rubbish, it sounds like The Great Gatsby!" As I darted towards the shower she called, "If you must go, I can't stop you. But be careful. I have a very bad feeling about this funeral."

♠

The day was chilly and clear. At eleven I parked the car three blocks from the Yonroche Basilica. I could hear a crowd shouting; like a football crowd. Walking briskly towards the main square I enjoyed the Neo-Classical buildings that typified Napoléon's ideal of a combined new town and military base: what Yonroche was created to be.

The streets were lined with scores of black limousines, like an army of dung beetles. Once in the main square, that is large, with one end dominated by the twin, squat, domed towers of the basilica and the centre by an equestrian statue of Napoléon, I realised that the noise I had heard was the screech and jeer of a rioting mob. In front of the basilica about two thousand people were on the point of mass hysteria.

I stopped by a Plane tree at a safe distance from the crowd and considered what to do. This was clearly a demonstration well out of control. Placards, many in shreds, waved and drooped with the sway of the crowd. I could make out the daubed slogans; MOREAU! - SALAUD! - CONARD! . . *Moreau! - The Bastard! - The Shit!* Mounted police had forced a way to the steps of the basilica that were littered with a dross of burnt-out television equipment. Vans had been overturned and set on fire, bulky television cameras lay in the wreckage of snaking cables that smouldered and sparked. Riot squads were operating water cannon. A tear gas canister was thrown.

Common sense told me to get back to the car and drive like hell to La Breuse. But I couldn't let go, not now. If there was a chance to get into the basilica, I would fix Fred and Peter once and for all.

An official car screamed into the square behind me. It rasped to a halt where I stood. The rear door opened and a very senior French Army officer walked over to me. He had a pistol in his hand; a body guard covered him from the car. For an instant the man scrutinised me. I was, after all, very elegantly dressed.

"May I ask who you are, and what you are doing here, Monsieur?" I explained only that I had been invited to the funeral. When I mentioned the Château de la Breuse his face betrayed concern, "Monsieur Debrett, please be sensible and leave the area at once." He indicated the pistol, "We may have to use these."

"I have a duty to get inside the basilica." His eyes narrowed.

"An official duty?" I decided to take the risk that he would know who I was talking about. "Sir Frederick Appleby has asked me to investigate the funeral."

There was a pause. "Get in the car!" It was a command murmured with demure. I sat in the back next to him as he rapped out an order to the military chauffeur, adding an equally brisk order to the body guard. We thrashed down a one-way shopping street the wrong way, sirens wailing. "Despite what you see, Monsieur, the riot is ninety-percent under control. I have come from Bordeaux by helicopter to ensure order is restored. Those who resist will be shot. The President authorised the use of firearms at nine this morning."

"You are telling me that the event is being followed at the Élysée Palace?"

"Certain matters in this region have been under observation for some time."

"Since *The Marriage Island Case*?" He turned to me with a faint smile, I could tell that he was impressed. In beautiful French he said, "You are very well informed, Monsieur! So I might tell you that I have known Sir Frederick for thirty years. A remarkable man." He turned towards the car window; a side of the basilica was already looming into view. He smiled to himself, almost secretly, coming out with a quaintly expressed compliment, typical of the French upper class, "As for the Countess, Monsieur ... a most beautiful woman. You are favoured by Venus." Immediately, his manner became clipped and business-like. "The south entrance to the basilica is now secure. We are approaching the porch." The car stopped. "I shall set you down here, and leave you to your task. If anyone in London should ask, I am Colonel Jean-Claude Descartes." We shook hands, and I got out of the car to face a morbidly classical portico.

I walked briskly to the bronze doors inside the cavernous porch. One leaf was open just enough to let a single person pass through the gap. I was about to pull the door open a little further when a hand shot out and grabbed my waistcoat. I was hauled through the gap like a mail sack to find myself inside a dimly lit vestibule staring into the face of an unusual young man.

Whatever else Western funeral convention demands, the one sure thing is sober dress - most of it black. The young man confronting me in that dusty, early Nineteenth Century vestibule - that smelt of mildew and damp stone - was wearing a shell pink drape suit, an iridescent green silk shirt, and a silver bow tie. He wore oyster pink lipstick, reeked of scent, and his tan came from a bottle. He was film-star handsome.

"What is the colour of your invitation card, Monsieur?"

His guttural French accent was terrible. I looked blankly at his cupid's bow mouth.

"What?"

I glared at the ruby studs in his shirt front, at his shiny, blue-black hair that was combed straight back from a high, white forehead in the style of a Silent Movie star. The hair was oiled and reflected the lamps above in two shimmering, silver slicks.

"*What*?"

"What is the colour of your invitation card, Monsieur?"

"This isn't a party-game! Get me into the church! I'm late!" From his left, clenched hand I heard a click. Calmly, he held a knife blade to my face and I had time to notice the thicket of blue-black hairs on the back of his wax-white hand. This was certainly not a party-game.

"Yellow!"

"*C'est pas vrai, Monsieur!*" . . . Not true? *Ridiculous*! I repeated that the card was *yellow*. The knife touched the skin of my right cheek. "It's damned well *yellow*!" The cupid's bow mouth pursed as he shook his head, looking steadily into my eyes. His pupils were the deepest amber: arrestingly lovely. He ran the blade of his knife lightly, harmlessly, down my cheek, as all gangsters do in the movies.

It occurred to me that I was to give him some sort of password. A password to get into the basilica. Arthur's favourite colour was not any yellow, but *Chinese* Yellow. So I said, "Chinese Yellow."

I found myself pushed towards the inner vestibule door upon which my usher knocked. The door was opened by another young man in exactly the same garb, with identical jet black hair and features. He too was film star handsome. I judged both were around twenty. This boy gripped my arm painfully, then frog-marched me into the basilica, down the central aisle to a row second from the front. So much for Peter's plan that I sat unrecognised at the back!

I was forced to sit in a pew and my usher vanished. Stealthily, I looked round. The basilica was enormous, a barracks of a place. It must have sat over a thousand people, yet there wasn't an empty pew in sight. I had just enough time to notice that the congregation consisted of blocks of young men with jet black hair and that each block was punctuated here and there by a brilliantly cerise, broad rimmed, fashion-plate hat. A priest was droning through the public address system while an organ growled throatily at the back. Everybody began to stand. I did likewise, facing quickly front, looking for my service sheet which had been purloined by the woman standing next to me.

I turned to this woman, who was smartly dressed in a cerise silk two-piece with a Bolero top. She wore a pearl necklace and broad-rimmed cerise silk hat. I gave her the faintly polite smile one adopts at funerals and weddings when you don't know a soul. She leaned towards me. I thought she was going to return my service sheet, but she said, in a deep whisper, "Try to clear out of here and I'll fuck you with steel."

Incredulous, I looked her up and down. The woman wore long white gloves and carried a small, white, envelope-shaped leather pocket book in the end of which I noticed a perfect steel hole: the muzzle of a gun. The woman was tall and slim, but her hips were too lean and her shoulders too broad. Her muscular neck had the girth of a domestic drain pipe and her pan makeup did not quite conceal the faint black stubble of a five o-clock shadow. The lady was a bloke in drag.

'She' suddenly put his mouth close to my ear and spoke in a whisper that was just audible against the swelling volume of the organ. He spoke awkwardly in English with a heavy mid-west American accent, "Listen good, Mister. They're gonna bring the body in any moment, OK? So I'm gonna pose you a riddle. Like it's a quotation. I'm gonna say the first half an' you got two seconds to chime-in with the second half. If you fuck-up, you're dead, OK?" Sharply, he shoved the muzzle end of his handbag into my side.

"Go ahead." I was galvanised. How many million quotations are there to choose from? With painful slowness the bloke repeated a short phrase he had been made to learn by heart. Learning by heart was not my man's forte, *"Woman governs America because . . ."*

I knew it! *". . . America is a land of boys who refuse to grow up."*

"Wow! Ain't that *somethin'*! You got it!" To my relief he tossed the handbag down on the pew. "Now listen to me, Mr Dove."

Mister Dove? Was this a code name?

He was just starting to speak when the organ went wild and the lights went frantic. A Cardinal came forward up-stage centre wearing diamond earrings and false eye lashes. He was flanked by a bevy of acolytes. These boys were models of adolescent beauty, exactly the same height with Marcel-waved, platinum blond wigs. They each wore an *Eau-de-Nile* see-through tulle tunic held together at the waist by a gold chain. Beneath the tulle I could make out a gilt jock strap and a girdle edged in black Chantilly lace with suspenders that held aloft - stretched over well muscled thighs - fishnet stockings of the "Show Boat" variety. The place reeked of incense, hair lacquer, young males - and baby oil.

The officiating priest stood in front of an altar sluiced with silver lamé and loaded with Capo di Monte figurines amongst which I failed to recognise any member of the Holy Family. The priest's ecclesiastical collar was a diamond and ruby choker. He wore an ash blond wig *en bouffante* with a saucy black bow over the back-combed crown. For a cassock he sported a gauzy Naughty Nightie. When he raised a monstrance above his head, telling us that a piece of Arthur's heart was inside it, the Naughty Nightie lifted to expose his genitals. These were enormous, floodlit, and painted deep ultramarine blue dusted with silver.

Baboons came to mind.

The transvestite next to me bawled, "When they done the ceremony, we move. This row files left, you an' me go right." He motioned a strangler's hand in the direction of the north aisle door. "We make for a car ..." but it was useless to continue, the tumultuous crescendo of organ, choir and chanting prelates drowned all sound. I nodded assent, and for the first time he smiled brilliantly, like a school boy.

I turned to my left: the funeral procession was directly at my side.

Floating by at a stately pace, supported upon a bier that must have been electronically powered for its sides were hung with huge wreaths of sizzling blue, purple and white fluorescent tubes; preceded by five magnificent naked men each sprayed bronze with silver-gilt crowns of thorns on their shaven heads; guided at each corner by four naked Asian boys selected, I suppose, for their girlish beauty; followed by three nude Negros of gigantic stature, each dusted with gold, who had genitals the size of prize-winning vegetables - was a huge, rectangular, lavishly furnished, awesomely proportioned, clear glass sarcophagus. In the American fashion it was a casket, not a coffin. In this glass casket, floating in clear formaldehyde, his flesh already turned to the fungaloid transparency characteristic of preserved organs in a biologist's laboratory, was the body of Arthur Moreau.

♠

He was brilliantly illuminated from below. I could make out his shadowy skeleton through the jelloid flesh. The massive scale of the solid gold funery furniture annealed to the outside of the casket - each component encrusted with diamonds and inky sapphires - struck a wan contrast to Arthur's shrunken, naked corpse. The rock crystal crucifix riveted to the summit of the lid, for all its attendant precious stones, only served to convey more poignantly the pathetic quietude of the cadaver within. I noticed that the casket lid had a thick brown wax seal round its perimeter joint - as do all specimen jars.

It was a gruesome sight. Yet he rested peacefully in death. Despite my revulsion at the glass casket and distaste for the general scene, sad reflections glimmered. I forgave Arthur his actions that had destroyed our friendship.

♠

When it was all over, Arthur's body processed to the West Door and the congregation began to follow. My man jabbed me sharply in the back and we made our way smartly through the north aisle door. Outside all was tranquil, no sign of the riot remained. I was motioned to the only car in sight, a huge white Cadillac. It was a long out-dated model with spiky tail fins and chromium plated trim. It had white-walled tires and velvet curtained rear windows. I was pushed onto the back seat between two grey suited young men while my guardian perched himself on a drop-seat with his legs apart, revealing stocking tops and a white patch of underwear. On the other drop seat sat a magnificent boy in a grey military uniform. In front there was a driver and a flunkey. Not one of these six young men was more than twenty-two.

Carelessly, the transvestite hauled off his hat and wig and slung them over his shoulder into the front. He smiled at me, telling his companions in bad French that my name was Monsieur Dove. They nodded shyly but nobody spoke, so I murmured, "Bonjour".

Suddenly the driver whipped a packet of cigarettes from the dashboard, snatched two with his lips (the flunkey took one of them), then chucked the packet over to the lad on my right who proffered me one with a dumb-show of shy courtesy. I seldom smoke but judged this was not the moment to refuse. The cigarettes were a Moroccan brand.

Exhaling smoke down his nose, the flunkey said, "We stay here for another five minutes, Monsieur. Is that OK with you?"

"As you like." They began to chat amongst themselves in a strange language, giving me the opportunity to examine them.

As with the crowd in the basilica these young mens' features were uncannily identical: pretty-boy face, white skinned complexion, luxuriant jet-black hair, deep amber eyes, rose red lips. The soldier sitting on the drop seat interested me most. He seemed to be bigger than the others, though it was hard to tell when they were all sitting down. He matched the transvestite in shoulder width and leg length; I judged the others to be shorter, less elegantly built but more stocky, like rugby players. The soldier's uniform was a silver-grey battle tunic belted round his lithe, slender waist. A neatly rolled grey beret was tucked in his left epaulette. His feet were shod in a pair of calf-length, silvery leather Commando boots.

As I watched him talking to his companions, I saw that his features were animated by intelligence. He possessed an heroic, Ulysses-like, icy male beauty. The only unusual thing about the others - I could not judge the transvestite because of his makeup - was their handsome similarity, otherwise they were average young men. But the soldier spoke with enthusiasm and expression, his eyes sparking with the electricity of an extraordinary personality. Every ten seconds or so, he furtively glanced at me with the curiosity of a young adult and I sensed that he was burning to know about me. Suddenly he decided to overcome his shyness. Facing me, he crossed his arms and shot a penetrating, smiling look directly into my eyes. He was powerfully charming, unashamedly alluring.

"My name is Kyla, Monsieur." His French was perfect, and when his smile broadened he was exquisitely beautiful - more beautiful, in his way, than a woman.

Their language was as enigmatic as their appearance. I could not recognize any linguistic clue amongst the rapid, guttural, softly enunciated sounds of their speech. The style was declamatory, as if they spoke in verse, like Ancient Greek bards.

"Where are we going?" My question brought the chatter to a dead stop. Six pairs of respectful eyes gazed at me. After a moment Kyla said, "To Paris, Monsieur. To the Hôtel Bradford." and he gave me a tiny secret wink, followed immediately by a half-seconds frowning speaking look. What was he trying to convey? Did he know something that the others didn't? They thought I was 'Mister Dove': did Kyla? It was vital not to betray my absolute ignorance of their circumstances so I decided to act the part of an affable small town bank manager for whom nothing is ever a surprise, and life is an eternal Bowling alley.

"The Bradford! Good *heavens*! I haven't sampled the luxuries of the Paris Bradford for years!" I clapped my hands together, wiring-up a smile that didn't crack me apart: no small town bank manager would get within ten miles of the Bradford. A long weekend there with Corinne had cost me half a million francs. I wagged an index finger, "Do you know, driver, if you put your foot down, we can be there for a late supper!" I grinned at them all, vicar's tea party style, "By George, won't *that* be a treat?"

As the Cadillac turned into the main boulevard of Yonroche I rapped, "I need to stop at my car. It's parked over there."

"We will drive you ..."

"I know that, boys. I need some things out the trunk." We pulled-up and when I could see they were talking and not looking at me, I discretely stopped a passer-by. "Madame, I have to leave this car here overnight, can you telephone the Château de la Breuse and have them pick it up in the morning?"

"Is anything wrong, Monsieur?"

"No. Here are the keys, and my card. The Countess is a …"

"I know who you are, Monsieur."

"Tell the Countess that I have to go to Paris." She eyed the ancient American car, then puckered her mouth in that typically French way they have, "You could drive to the château now, Monsieur. I can easily keep those young men talking." We looked at one another. "I remember the War, Monsieur. People being taken to Paris in strange cars. Driven by Nazis in those days, Monsieur, if you see what I mean."

"You are wise, Madame. But I must put myself in the hands of Fate."

♠

During the five hour trip to Paris the six lads behaved like gentlemen, well - almost. They talked laconically in their own language, I learnt "Pass the cigarettes!". They asked me the usual tourists' questions about England, but they had nothing to say on subjects that normally interest young men; sport, beer, clubs, girls. I wondered if they had much idea of what was going on in the world for they seemed innocently vague, like royalty.

We sped along the A11, making one stop at the *Chartres Bois-Paris* service station where the transvestite got a kit bag out of the trunk and kicked-off his high heeled shoes.

"What are you doing?"

"Changing, Monsieur." He ripped off his pearl necklace, skirt and top.

"You can't do that on the car park!" I turned to see a group of horrified French people pointing at us. "Get in the car!" He removed his suspender belt, stockings and a pair of beautifully brassiered falsies while Kyla sorted out a battledress tunic identical to his own. "For God's sake keep your knickers on!"

"They are cute, Monsieur, don't you think?"

"On my girlfriend, yes. On you, I have my doubts." Whipping open a tin of theatrical removing cream he wiped off his make-up and was into his uniform in a flash. He now looked very much like Kyla. Not quite as heroic, but with the same deep agate hair, arresting male beauty and magnificent build. We trooped off to the gents where they queued for cubicles. Only Kyla and his twin stood alongside me at urinals. I was intrigued, but asked no questions.

Kyla brought a tray of coffee to the table where we sat, "You will meet an old friend at the Hôtel Bradford, Monsieur."

"Who?"

"We do not know."

"I have lots of old friends, Kyla, but none that live in Paris. Male or female?" He was handing round tablets to each man to wash down with their coffee. "A male friend, Monsieur." He flashed me a naughty grin, turned to the twin and gave him a kiss on the ear lobe. "*Please!* Not in here!" I glanced round to see another group of horrified French people pointing at us. "Why not? Don't you think he's cute, Monsieur?"

"No!" From one of his tunic pockets Kyla whipped out a powder compact and lipstick, made himself up as deftly as a woman, finishing off with a spray of scent from a tiny gold vaporiser. He winked at me, took the twin's hand, and lasciviously kissed the tips of each finger while eyeing me provocatively. The travellers on the table across the aisle ostentatiously walked out.

This time I thought it better to keep my mouth shut: I had the feeling that 'Monsieur Dove' was supposed to know all about the habits of these enigmatic young men.

♠

Fifty minutes later we scorched into the centre of Paris.

The Hôtel Bradford lurks on the Avenue Franklin D. Roosevelt like an Art Deco monster. The building is a riot of Movitone reinforced concrete and bronze statuary that only the French can create with panache. We parked amongst a litter of limousines by the main entrance. A flurry of nattily liveried attendants opened the car doors.

Kyla accompanied me into the greenish reception hall, its brown marble floor zigzagged with malachite. Where the others went with the Cadillac I shall never know.

I was invited to sit on a fake Louis Quinze *fauteuil* by a footman. An impeccably discrete Assistant Manager, decked out in white tie and tails (unnecessarily, in my opinion) placed a ruby encrusted fountain pen at my disposal. "Please, Monsieur, your signature will be all that is necessary." I dawdled the nib above the parchment reservation form,

"I trust that everything ..." I gave a discrete cough "...has been arranged ... in advance." I avoided the words, *paid for.*

"Of course, Monsieur. You are one of our regular celebrity guests." I gave Kyla, who stood majestically by my side, a speaking look. "Quite so ..." I glanced at the man's lapel badge "... Antoine. Nice to be back." I was about to sign *J. M. Debrett* when Kyla stage-whispered, "Monsieur Dove."

"Thank you, Kyla!" As I quietly cursed Frederick, we were taken in an exclusive elevator to a floor of penthouses frequented by film stars, footballers and deposed Royalty. The apartment was caked, I could say gobbed, with vulgar luxury, as if the décor had been done by an Interior Designer recently released from a lunatic asylum. Standing by a life size, frosted glass nymph that was illuminated from the crotch, was the General Manager. She was dressed by Chanel, her scent obviously Creed. She greeted me with the hammy formality normal on these occasions.

"When is my friend due to arrive?"

"At eleven-thirty, Monsieur." She reached into a disgustingly tasteless silver-gilt wine cooler supported on three polished teak monkeys where six bottles of champagne loitered in the pack ice. "A Welcome Cup, Monsieur?" She snatched a bejewelled, cut-glass, horn shaped drinking vessel from a Connemara Marble tray held by the nymph. Sloshing champagne to the object's silver-gilt brim she handed it to me a touch too briskly. I felt like the Juvenile lead in a musical comedy by Ivor Novello.

Glancing at my watch I grimly noted thirty minutes to the *rendezvous*.

"Is anyone else coming? There's an awful lot of champagne for two." Appearing not to have heard my question she rapped, "Is this your first time at The Bradford, Monsieur?"

"Yes." I turned to give Kyla another speaking look, but he was nowhere to be seen. "Your servant, Monsieur, will attend you at the half-turn of the right nipple." She indicated the nymph's right breast. "Her left nipple dims the lights." I saw that the nipples were of ivorine, like oven controls. In that carnival of kitsch anything went.

"Supper will be served through there, Monsieur. Staff are presently arranging the table." She pointed to a closed, glazed partition at the end of the salon beyond which I made out an oval dining room bloody with crimson damask. Twenty-six minutes to go.

"I really must change. Will you excuse me." Her plastic *politesse* failed as the woman shot me a withering look, rasping, "The bedroom is that way!". She vanished through a service door in a mural where a brilliantined Pan played a set of Nineteen-Twenties pipes.

The bed was the size of an Olympic swimming pool. My overnight bag had been seen to, my clothes were laid out beside a garish silk kimono. On the kimono was a box of twenty-five contraceptives: "Atlantic Brand: Force 8". Definitely, there was something of Arthur in the plan. Glad that Corinne had the feminine intuition to put a *mallette* - French for overnight bag - in the car, I quickly washed and changed, ignoring the kimono.

Returning to the salon I poured myself a stiff gin and Italian from a bar stocked with just about everything except milk. The screen to the dining room was now open, candles were lit, the table shimmered with silver and crystal. Standing by the nymph I glanced at a repro Louis Seize wall clock. Twelve minutes. The burning question was: "Do I stay, or get out?"

♠

I was going to be murdered, of this there was no doubt. I had no weapon, a dinner knife would have to do. If more than one person arrived, maybe with guns and silencers, I was in trouble. There was no calling the management, no involving the French police: I was on my own. I made a lightening inspection of doors, windows and telephones. Not surprisingly the entire IT facility was dead, the fire escape was padlocked, the door to the vestibule would not budge. Where was Kyla?

The nymph possibly enjoyed my rough handling of her right nipple, but I wasn't enjoying myself at all. I slammed my hand hard on the Adam green panel of the vestibule door. Wrenching a bronze bust of Louis the Fourteenth from a console, I was about to ram it into the lock when Kyla opened up. Furious, I took the kid by the shoulders and banged him up against the vestibule wall.

"What the hell's going on, you little bastard!" He began to cry, it was pathetic. I took his jaw in my hand and forced his face to mine, close. "Cut that out, my young queen: what's going on?" He sobbed more loudly. He was terrified. I let him go. We stood facing one another, panting, calming down. He looked me steadily in the eyes,

"You are not Mister Dove!"

"Correct! Adrian Dove was Arthur's accountant. Died years ago." I grabbed his tunic front, "Who *am* I, Kyla? More's the point, who are you?" He took some seconds to sob, "I cannot tell you."

I laughed with scorn. "You don't understand, do you? I know everything about Arthur. And I think you know about me." He made a sudden move towards the outer door but I grabbed his belt. "No you don't! You're staying, Kyla! You're staying to meet this old friend of mine!" I looked at my watch. "We have three minutes, mate! Three minutes to tell me your life story." I tried to budge him into the salon but he wriggled out of my grasp.

"You do not know Arthur Moreau, Monsieur!"

"Don't come that one, Kyla! They've all been spinning that one! I knew Arthur better than anybody knew him."

He began to stammer, his French submerged in words I could not understand, "Please! I go!" He trembled violently. The fingers of one hand struggled to undo the button of his tunic breast pocket, his eyes were turning up into their sockets. I remembered the tablets they had swallowed at the service station. I wrenched a pack from the tunic, there was one tablet left. I forced it into his mouth and made him swallow it, slipping the empty container into my trouser pocket. He revived in seconds, his eyes enormous with appeal. I felt that he wanted to tell me something. His body, close to mine, shuddered with torment.

I took his waist lightly and eased him gently to the wall, "Go on, Kyla! What do you want to tell me?" I brushed the hair from his forehead with my fingers, as one comforts a child. He cast his face downwards, his ravishing lashes made two ebony crescents below the Olympian line of the brow.

"I cannot, Monsieur."

Suddenly, impulsively, he took me in his arms and kissed my neck. "I will never see you again, Monsieur!" I drew him apart from me. In English I said, "You might."

"It is not possible." He unbuttoned the top of his tunic, unwinding from his perfect neck a fine chain that secured an oblong platinum tag. This, he put into my hand, saying, "Take it! This is me." And he put his mouth to mine and gave me a tiny, chaste kiss. Then he murmured, "Don't drink the wine!", turned and bounded away - a living Hermes.

♠

Don't drink the wine! What did the boy mean? I ran to the dining room sideboard. What wine? There was no wine, only the champagne in the cooler. I had one minute to find some poisoned wine. In the middle of the food heap, supported by a howdah made of spun sugar that was balanced on an elephant of sculptured ice, was a silver-gilt Tiffany salver. On the salver, by a blood-red rose, lay a parchment envelope. The two words on the envelope were done with a fountain pen in beautiful Copper Plate:

LOVER BOY

The hum of an elevator out in the hall whirred to a stop. I was about to cut the envelope open with a steak knife when the click of a latch and the whoosh of a service door alerted me to carpet silenced footsteps two meters from my back. I spun round, sliding the envelope into my shirt pocket and brandishing the knife.

An elderly, grey-skinned butler nipped to the dining table carrying a lacy silver wine holder - the sort I detest. In it, half laid down, was an opened bottle of Bordeaux.

"That looks good, what wine is it?"

He ignored me, placed the holder on the table and wriggled towards the service door.

"Answer me!" He was three-quarters through the gap. I ran to him, put my foot in the door and forced it open. From the hall, a male voice called to the lift attendant, "Merci, Marc".

I held the butler fast by his tails, and put the knife to his neck. "If you don't answer, I'll cut your throat!" The outer penthouse door was shut and locked. . . I heard footsteps cross the vestibule. I let go of the butler's tails.

"Nice meeting you, Sir!", he said, and darted down a steel, spiral service stair.

He was American, his accent was very slightly German.

♠

"And then what happened?" We were four to lunch at my London Club. My brother-in-law had asked the question, sitting in front of a plate of roast beef that he had not touched since I began my story. Frederick was neatly lifting the bone from a sole, while his young American PA, Andrew Park, refilled my glass with Club Claret. It was the day after Arthur's funeral.

"Get on with it, Johnny, for goodness sake!" Frederick gestured with his thumb to members dining near by, "The entire bloody Club is frozen in suspense! We're all waiting to find out who came into that damned penthouse!" I glanced round; people had stopped talking and there was a brittle silence. Andrew, tall, slim, shoulders broad as sails - freshly imported from Michigan - wiped his mouth with a starched napkin, "Let me guess, Johnny. It was ..."

Quick as a flash Peter rounded on him, the fine lips of his sculptural mouth imperceptibly curled with intolerant impatience, "If you don't mind, Andrew!" He signed for me to continue, darting the people at the next table a withering look, so that they turned to talk amongst themselves.

"The person who came into the penthouse was the Assistant Manager who had handed me the pen so that I could sign whatever it was I signed at Reception." Frederick snorted. "How frightfully tedious for you, Johnny! No dinner in that charmingly appointed private dining room with a fellow who thought the world of you! In your position I should have bitterly complained." For all the sardonic humour, Fred's tone was truculent. I suspected he was irritated by my account, as if I wasn't telling him what he wanted to hear. "What did the man say?"

"He was so embarrassed it took him a while to get his words out."

"Faced with a top profile guest who has just attempted to smash a door down with a valuable bronze bust of Louis Quatorze, and who is brandishing a steak knife in an irascible manner, I have a certain sympathy for the chap. *What did he say?*"

"That there had been a terrible mistake." Frederick and Andrew laughed so loudly that everyone went quiet again.

"I should bloody well think there had been a terrible mistake, Johnny! The thing smacks of a French farce!" Fred was serious now, he lowered his voice, "Get on with it! How did you manage to explain your way out? And keep your voice down, Belcher's listening." He gestured in the direction of a table some way off where Sir Bantam Belcher, Fred's formidable rival, was leaning our way. As the pudding trolley came alongside I told them of my exit from the Bradford. "About five minutes after the General Manager had left me, the hotel switchboard received an anonymous telephone call. My so-called guest would not be arriving, the dinner was cancelled and I was to vacate the penthouse at once. The Bradford had arranged for a taxi to take me to the airport, where they had booked a room at The Fleur-de-Lis. The last London flight had gone hours before. I took the first flight this morning."

Fred motioned the trolley away, nobody wanted pudding. "Did you get a sample of the wine?"

"Yes. When the Assistant Manager left me to get my things together I took the bottle to the bathroom, soaked a little wine into a clean face cloth and was pouring the rest down the basin when he re-appeared. I bluffed that the wine was corked."

"What was the wine?"

"Château Beychevelle, '61!"

"A wonder he didn't knock your teeth out, Johnny. You retained the sample?"

"I have it in my bag upstairs."

"Good! We'll take a look at it."

"And that's about it, Gentlemen. As you see, I got myself to London, bought myself a set of fresh clothes, and will return to Aylesford this afternoon."

"The Countess?"

"Corinne knows I'm safe, thanks Peter. She knows nothing else." Fred glanced at his watch with the air of a man who has more important matters waiting in the office. A curious feeling of anti-climax stole round us. Fred said vaguely, "Have we done?" They nodded, and when Peter had gone to the desk to pay, I said, "Would you like coffee? I can't leave the subject in the air! I'm still wound-up." As if he could not have cared less Fred drawled, "Shall we have coffee, Andrew?"

"I think that might be in order, Sir. You have a clear afternoon."

Peter excused himself, he had a meeting in the City. We climbed the luxurious vaulted stairs to the incomparable gallery, mellow with buttery afternoon light flooding from the cut glass lozenges of the Club's superb central dome. We sat on low Edwardian arm chairs upholstered in red leather, Fred and Andrew to one side of a small circular mahogany table, myself facing them. I ordered three ports. Frederick got out his pipe and tobacco pouch. Messing with the pipe, he spoke gloomily.

"I have to tell you, Johnny, that your recent experience - and I am sorry you were put to such risk - has only served to further convince me that Arthur Moreau was a central figure, perhaps *the* central figure, in a murky International crime ring. We suspect a terrorist ring, but there is more to Moreau than pea-shooter politics." Itching to say my piece I began to speak but Fred held up his hand, "No, Johnny! Your thoughts on the matter will be useless to me. I have been almost thirty years fathoming this business. We are not dealing with a *Who Dunnit*! We do not speculate deliciously amongst the compelling fiction of a P. D. James or a Frederick Forsyth. We face the wrangling truth where simplicity is complexity and complexity simplicity. With Moreau there is no neat solution, no Sherlock Holmes in evening dress blithely sorting it all out before a drawing room full of incredulous gentlefolk.

"Wracked by frustration we wend our way in a labyrinth of fantastical reality. The Minotaur hasn't shown up yet, but the seven sacrificial youths and the seven sacrificial maidens represent millions of ordinary people. When the Minotaur does appear, I think millions of ordinary people will be horribly devoured." He lit his pipe, puffing at it, wafting the plum scented aroma of his specially blended tobacco in a cloud of crystal blue smoke. "You see, Johnny, Moreau was out to destroy Humanity." I was riveted. Andrew sat pale, gazing at the meniscus of his port.

"This is why your thoughts are useless, Johnny. I can see much further into the labyrinth than you can. But the more tunnels we explore the more dead ends we find. The more we make sense of one part the less we understand of another." He stopped, sipped his port, and changed tack. "You have the necklace the boy gave you? The youth, Kyla?"

"Of course."

"Give it to Andrew before we leave. The tablets the boy took, any left?"

"Only the sachet."

"Has the laboratory finished with the Moulton Case, Andrew?"

"Yes, Sir."

"Tell them I want the wine analysis by six. If they can do something with the empty sachet, that will be nice." He turned to me, "The Moulton Case is a mere bagatelle, Johnny. Janice Moulton, the renowned supermarket heiress, had her entire Board of Directors reduced to soup in the swimming pool of one of her many residences. Seventy-thousand litres of Prussic Acid were used to advantage. Surprising what can be delivered to your door if you own a grocery business." He puffed at his pipe. "What about the grey-skinned butler?"

"What about him, Fred? I have no idea. He was quite old, easily in his seventies. Portly, but he could move."

Fred blew smoke over the gallery balustrade, "I am not sure, Johnny, if I should involve you further. I don't think you are suited for this game."

"I didn't do too badly."

"You didn't do too well, either! You came away with a platinum chain and tag, a face cloth stained with world class wine, an envelope marked "Lover Boy", an empty packet of tablets that could just as well be aspirins, and the name Dove. I wanted something significant on Moreau and I haven't got it!" I took a mouthful of port, disappointed that I had not lived up to expectations. Andrew lit a cigarette and smiled at me, "Hell, Johnny, you look so dejected. What was inside the *Lover Boy* envelope?"

"A white card with a typed message, the reverse is blank." I paused to recall the text exactly. "It reads, *love me tonight*, then - on a new line - *22 11 marrakech*, and on a third line, *01 05* followed by the letters, *w m d o*. There are no capitals or punctuation marks."

Andrew's cigarette, hardly started, was stubbed out. Frederick took his pipe from his mouth: they both leaned forward towards me.

"*Much* better, Johnny! Andrew, get the driver out of the pub. We leave in ten minutes." As Andrew went to find the chauffeur, Fred knocked tarry tobacco from his pipe bowl into his empty coffee cup. "What are your plans this afternoon, Johnny?"

"It will be nice to get back home."

"You're coming with us."

"Am I to be interrogated, Fred?" His good eye shot me a steely glance as he pulled himself up from the low Club chair and we downed the last of our port. "Because you are a friend, Johnny, no. You are to be questioned. It amounts to the same thing."

♠

In Fred's seventh floor office a single, huge oriel window framed the river scene. Somerset House over the Thames, lit by the pale afternoon sun, seemed like a toy. Andrew took my things, inviting me to sit at a conference table of scented cedar wood. The office made a still, stately setting, its walls hung with purplish brocade, the floor a sheath of Pentelic marble. Near the window stood Frederick's magnificent seventeenth century desk, a gift from the Benedictine monastery of Monte Casino. Sculpture fragments by Tino di Camaino were set about, perfectly lit. Paintings by Raphael, Albertinelli and the French master, Poussin hung in beautifully designed niches. The focal work, Andrea del Sarto's, *Saint John the Baptist,* hung in a marble-lined alcove: the young man's kingly pose made wonderful by his sumptuous, naked torso.

Fred asked Andrew to fetch various files. He dumped a selection of these on the table, then took off his jacket, set his pipe materials in a row by an ashtray that had once been a High Renaissance reliquary, and sat down opposite Andrew and me. He pressed a button. A young woman appeared, seating herself near by. Perfunctorily, she took the cover off a stenograph.

"I favour a stenograph, Johnny. Tape recorders have a mind of their own." He offered me coffee, a brandy - whatever I liked. I chose a *Remy Martin*. A decanter arrived.

"I was despairing, Johnny, over lunch. But you have finally made a fascinating discovery." He turned to the secretary, "Begin, Anita. Every word, please." The quiet clicking of the stenograph followed us into the early evening.

Frederick's voice was clipped, "You have described, Johnny, in Yonroche, an enormous civil disturbance and a funeral the likes of which has not been seen since they buried Caligula. A cardinal of the Roman Catholic Church was present. Three bishops attended him. There was a priest with blue bollocks and scores of teenage acolytes got up like rent boys. The basilica heaved with brawny blokes in high heeled shoes, skirts and silk hats. To cap it all, the principal player, Arthur Moreau, arrived in a giant pickle jar.

"Does His Holiness the Pope know about these *goings-on*, Johnny? I am certain that he does not! If we were to show the Vatican a video of Moreau's funeral - and you can be sure the whole thing was filmed - the Pope would now be chucking excommunications about like custard pies!" Amethyst tobacco smoke puffed from Fred's pipe. He grinned; "Well, the Pope's in luck! He has no worries over Moreau's funeral. . . . Why do I say this, Johnny?"

"I don't know, Fred."

"Because the Roman Catholic Church had nothing to do with the funeral!"

"But how did they manage to . . ."

"You haven't grasped the nettle, have you Johnny? Haven't you understood that there have been no reports from France of anything *remotely* to do with your description of the jamboree in Yonroche? Read any paper, look at any television commentary, listen to any news report, buy any glossy . . . French, British, American, German . . ." He tapped the nail of his left forefinger on the pile of files. "Not a whisper!"

"That's ridiculous! I was there! I saw the crowds, the chaos, the mounted police, the water cannon. I *saw* it! Are you telling me I've made the story up, Fred?" Despite myself, I raised my voice. "If you don't believe me, telephone Jean-Claude Descartes. He's your friend, isn't he? Would he lie to you?"

Frederick stared at me, unmoved. "No he wouldn't lie. It was I who ordered Colonel Descartes to protect you. . . . Don't look like a surprised squirrel, Johnny! We had a sack of Smart Dust emptied over the town the day before your arrival. From the moment you parked your hire car to the moment the Cadillac left Yonroche we trailed you."

"With that level of surveillance at your fingertips, Fred, how come you have wasted thirty years failing to trail Arthur?" I scraped back my chair, stood up, walked towards a statue and turned. "How does the entire population of a town surge into a square, hurl shit and abuse, maim one another, set vehicles on fire - and then go home like school children on a nature walk? How does a town *forget* a riot? How do over a thousand people turn up in scores of black limousines, park all over Yonroche, then go away unnoticed?" I glared at Anita. Expressionless, she watched my mouth, waiting for me to speak again. "How did Yonroche miss Arthur's glass casket? The hearse must have been the size of a truck!" I poured a tumbler of iced water from a Seventeenth Century silver-gilt ewer. "How long did Arthur's funeral take to set-up? I guess at least two weeks to get the basilica prepared, and you insist the Catholic Church knew nothing of what was going on? Are you telling me that curiosity didn't get the better of the townsfolk . . . of reporters on the local paper? . . . Or was this just another day in Yonroche? Something the town takes for granted?"

31

The two men observed me quietly. Breathing heavily, I sat down on an ancient Italian *cassone*. With renewed fervour I dealt my trump card. "Descartes said that the French President had declared a state of emergency in Yonroche that morning: does the French President remember doing so?"

"No!"

"How do you know?"

"I telephoned him as you collected your things at the Club."

"I was less than five minutes doing that!"

"Quite."

"This is mad!"

"You may sit on any chair in this room, Johnny, but do not park your arse on the early Renaissance furniture!" I returned to my seat. Andrew offered me a cigarette, I took it.

"Perhaps you begin to understand what we are up against, Johnny." Fred slid a file towards Andrew. "Arrange the *Isles des Noces* photographs on the table, please."

Aware that a large projection screen had appeared from a sliding panel in the wall I sat glumly watching Andrew lay out twenty-four black and white police photographs in neat rows of six: they showed bodies on autopsy slabs. The light dimmed and a colour photograph of an ornate French château appeared on the screen.

"That is the Château des Noces after Blaisedale had spent five million dollars on the place, not including money lavished on the island itself. We are talking nineteen thirty-five purchasing power. The château was demolished in 1980."

A young assistant appeared with a document. Fred glanced at it, snorted, then murmured to the assistant to go. He passed the paper to Andrew. The image on the screen changed to show a huge room, furnished in fake Louis Quinze. At the end of the room a gigantic chimneypiece of pink and white marble rose like a candyfloss cliff. The focus was an oil painting, a life-size nude youth, splendidly built, with coffee coloured skin.

"This photograph was taken for an American weekly. It shows the main salon of the château where the two hundred victims were poisoned and mutilated. You will be interested, in a moment, to see a close up."

Meekly, I stared at one of the police photographs on the table, of a young man whose skin had been partially flayed and whose bowels had been drawn. I was hardly aware of Andrew's softly intoning voice. "The analysis of the wine shows a substance that defies analysis, as it did at the time of the murders. We guess the secret is bound with genetics. Our research indicates this substance may cause drastic, permanent personality modification. Had you drunk the wine, Johnny, we guess that you would have become a different person from the one sitting by me now. Or dead."

I was not listening. The photographs had turned me sick. "As to the platinum necklace and platinum plate belonging to the youth called Kyla, we know the ore was mined in the USA. A curious combination of letters and digits is etched on the plate." Andrew's educated Michigan accent drawled, "KP2B-C4\i-Ŭ1". He plopped the paper down on the table, patting it smooth with long, soap-clean fingers. He glanced at me with pursed-lipped satisfaction, "What do you say to that, Johnny?"

"Puerile!"

There was a silence. I heard the click of Andrew's disapproving tongue. Frederick, who had been rooting in a drawer of his desk far down the room bawled, "Now, don't spoil the fun, Johnny! Of course it's bloody puerile! That's what fascinates me. It's puerile because the key figure behind all this is a genius. He, I do not think it is a she, has invented a clever game. We have to play that game if we are to crack our nasty nut." He came back to the table, a new pipe in hand. "Somewhere out there, Johnny, is a Circus Master. We are the clowns!" He sat down, knocking out the pipe in a fourteenth century Hungarian goblet of etched gold. "The lad Kyla has a registration number! It means something. If you ask me it's a batch number." He picked up one of the police photographs, "Those young men you're looking at, murdered on the *Isle des Noces* ..." he waved his hand towards the screen, "I think they were a batch. An early batch. A batch that failed."

"You mean test tube babies?"

"Don't use the language of the tabloid press in this office, Johnny! As a matter of fact I do not think they were from test tubes. And before you say it, nor do I think they were from outer, bloody space! Kyla and his friends have been created by a semi-natural process."

"Why did two hundred of them need to be brutally murdered?"

"Because the people responsible for them are criminally insane. Like your old friend Arthur Moreau."

"For God's sake, Fred!"

"Would you say the features of the victims in these photographs are similar to the ones you saw in the basilica of Yonroche?"

"Identical. They could have been in the Cadillac. Only Kyla differed, and the other lad when he had changed his clothes."

"Who cooked up the quotation, *'Women governs America because America is a land of boys who refuse to grow up.'* ?" I shrugged. I was tired.

"Salvador de Madariaga. A Spanish sage. Scholar, diplomat, author of *Democracy versus Liberty.* No fool, Johnny."

"Arthur knew him. We bought a collection of his manuscripts."

"Well, fancy that! Dear old Arthur again, Johnny! Moreau, Moreau and Moreau! [snort] - And who do you think you were supposed to be at the funeral? The lad Kyla blew the gaff, didn't he? Said you were the wrong man."

"Was I meant to be Jo?"

"Your wayward half-brother? I'm not sure. Why should these people want Jo?"

"He took my place as Arthur's business partner; he must know a hell of a lot."

"Good point. So we need to find Jo, see what he's up to." The screen flashed a close-up of the fireplace in the Château des Noces drawing room.

"What do you see above the portrait, Johnny, carved on the blue marble plaque, at the top of the fireplace?"

"W. M. D. O."

"In gilded Roman letters. Now examine the nude's left thigh. What do you see?"

"W. M. D. O."

"Branded. Now look at this photograph. What has been incised into the flesh of the victim's forehead with a chisel?"

"The letters W. M. D. O."

"Good!" He pressed a button on the desk. "Listen to this piece of music, please." Sounds wafted from concealed speakers. I made out the sizzle of an ancient gramophone record; seventy-eight revolutions per minute. From deep within the scratching black bakelite the glissando introduction of a sentimental popular song emerged. The voices of two singers, one male, one female, sang in duet. They sang in a style long forgotten, the hammy, ultra refined sound typical of Nineteen-twenties musical comedies. When the recording swished to a close, Fred held his pipe away from his mouth, "That was a recording of Winnie Melville and Derek Oldham, musical stars of their day. They were singing an enormously popular hit from "The Vagabond King", *Love me Tonight*. Another song from this show, you will find it on the reverse side of the gramophone record in question, was *Only a Rose*."

"That's easy, Fred. The initials of their names spell W. M. D. O."

"Give the man a coconut!"

"The Vagabond King was one of Arthur's favourites. It appealed to his camp taste."

"Bless my Soul! Arthur *again*, Johnny! Your dear old friend turns up everywhere. Now let us turn our attention to the message in the Lover Boy envelope." Andrew placed three copies of the card in front of us.

> **love me tonight**
> **22 11 marrakech**
> **01 05 w m d o**

"What does it mean, Johnny?"

"I couldn't care less, Fred. I'm tired."

"It is a *rendezvous* arranged for the first of May, as in zero-one-zero-five by an organisation styling itself, W.M.D.O."

"Just over two weeks time, Sir."

"Thank you, Andrew. Where is the rendezvous, Andrew?"

"Marrakech, Sir."

"Exactly, Andrew. And what is the password, Johnny?"

"I can't go on with this, Fred! Fatuous passwords and inane riddles. It's all a stupid fantasy. I want to go home. I can catch the eight-o'clock from Marylebone if I'm quick."

"What about your car, Johnny? Do you want me to arrange for them to drive it home for you?"

"Please, Andrew. I've just about had enough."

"*Enough* is not *good* enough, Johnny. What is the password you will use in Marrakesh?"

"Me? Use in Marrakech?"

"You will go to Morocco, Johnny, to be at the rendezvous on May the first, somewhere in Marrakesh."

"Oh, fuck off, Fred! . . . What an absurd idea!"

"And when the person you will identify in Marrakesh says, 'Love me tonight' or some other gambit that we must pick-up between now and May the first, what will you reply, Johnny?"

"Twenty-two, eleven."

"Excellent, my dear friend. You will require a decoy. A young person with no track record, male, good looking. He must be intelligent, in his early twenties: Every Mother's Son. Ideas?"

"Thomas."

"Age?"

"Twenty-one."

"Occupation?"

"My assistant trainee."

"Handsome lad?"

"English good looks."

"Basically heterosexual?"

"Extraordinarily basic. Why should that matter?"

"His ability to be emotionally aloof in a permissive environment is vital. In your estimation can the boy be trusted?"

"Absolutely."

"Any reason why he shouldn't go with his employer on a *jolly* to Marrakesh?"

"I will need to square that with his father."

"Who's he?"

"Sir Robert Paxton-Bright."

"Bobby! Mention my name and the lad's yours."

PART II

Four days after my interview with Frederick a psychic link was forged with an American couple unknown to me.

In Minneapolis, Jeff and Nina Burdet were deciding where to place a piece of contemporary art work in the spacious, open-plan ground floor of their Post-Modern home. They had commissioned a life size statue of a Sioux Indian done in Red Lake stone. Wheeling the abstract figure over a polished beechwood floor on the sculptor's trolley was tiring. At eleven they stopped for coffee: it was a fine, clear morning.

Gazing from a triangular French window, cup in hand, Jeff admired their enviable view of Lake Harriet, then turned to plead with his wife. "We moved it twenty-seven times, Nina. Are you absolutely certain you don't like it by this window?" Jeff quietly waited for Nina's reply; he had been patient this way for years.

"I don't like it there, Jeff!"

"Nina, you gotta have a reason. You can't just say 'I don't like it there.' - not for the twenty-seventh time."

"Why?" She sat down on a leather sling chair, neatly agile for her sixty-five years. She looked at Jeff through huge-lensed, white framed spectacles. Her face assumed an innocent expression, prairie-wide. "I don't like it there, Jeff. Period!" She fingered the fabric of her cream denim blouse. "It has to go outside on the terrace."

"Which terrace Nina?"

"Partner, it's *obvious* which terrace! The one you're standing in front of, with the view of the lake. " She came over and gave him a kiss, hanging her hands on his shoulders that were slightly bowed with age. Nina's Minnesota accent wound brassy round her words, "If we don't move it out there, Jeff, we'll go crazy knowing that we never *did* move it that *last, decisive* time!" She cocked her head cajolingly. "C'mon, Babe. Slide the doors open, get hold of that damned trolley and *pull*!"

Ten minutes later they found the perfect place. "I knew I was right, Jeff. Don't you love him there?"

"Sometimes I wish our house wasn't so relentlessly Cubist, Nina."

"Don't start, Jeff! Modern architecture comes that way. Anyhow, it isn't cubist. It's a cube intersected with *trapezoidal* wedges. That's what Terry told us when he'd drawn the plans and you were the one who signed the deal. We gotta live with those wedges till God decides who's goin' first!"

"Why is that chimney smoking again, Nina?" He had turned to look down the garden, to the opposite side of the glinting, pale green lake.

"Chimney?"

"The chimney from that new block they built round the back of the

37

Blaisedale place. Look for yourself, Nina. Over there. It's the same chimney that we made a protest about two years ago. It's against State Laws in this district for anything like that to happen. C'mon Nina, you made a hell of a fuss at the time."

"Sure, and we won! They agreed to use alternative power." She looked across to the stack. Pale sulphur yellow fumes ribboned from a thin, stainless steel flu. The chimney rose out of a low block visible through trees that bordered a wide apron of lawn connecting the enormous mansion to the lakeside.

"They should be fined. I'm going to discuss this with Jackie Powell before we do anything." Powell had been Jeff's co-partner in a successful law firm. Retired, he was now a member of the City Council. "We won't take this a second time, Nina. But we need City backing." Jeff never lost his temper, Nina was furious.

"Who do they think they are? . . . Who are they *anyway?* That place gives me the creeps. After three years we know nothing about those people, not even their names. Does Mark Roseville know? He sold them the real estate didn't he?"

"Mark knew nothing."

"You stand there and calmly tell me Mark knew nothing about the folks he *sold* that place to? In this city everybody knows everything about everybody! The place went for twenty-five million bucks, Jeff. Surely the people who bought it can't be invisible." She moved with fast, bird-like steps off the terrace onto a paved path and pointed to the park wall of the mansion.

"I'm going in there, Jeff! This afternoon I'm going in there."

"Nina, you shouldn't do that." But she turned, hands on slim hips, legs partially astride, shiny high heels pin-fine.

"Partner, I'm doin' it!"

♠

Getting through the electric gates of the main entrance to the mansion was easy. A truck came up the drive and the gates opened electronically. Nina walked through pausing to look at the name of the place, carved into a giant slab of snow white Italian marble: GRACEWOOD. Below was the date; 1911. She smiled to herself, adjusting her black beret. "You gotta be intrepid here. Cute, that's what you gotta be!"

She was delivering the Catholic magazine. Who could object? "By the time I'm done with 'em, they'll take three of these things just to get rid of me!" She walked down the impeccably maintained drive with springy steps. A tiny figure in neat, pretty lines of black gradually getting nearer the massive, silent façade of Gracewood.

Although Jeff and Nina had lived in Minneapolis all their married life - close on forty years in leafy Edina - they had only had their Lake Harriet retirement house for five years. They had never seen Gracewood close to. What surprised Nina as she approached the mansion was that it was untypical of other big Minneapolis properties. For a start it had been designed by a Frenchman, its lines were based upon the western façade of the Louvre. Coldly imposing, the frontage was also massively lonely. "Aren't those balconies *awful*? Those yawning windows and those horrible urns like in a funeral parlour. Oh boy! Look a that frieze of buffalo skulls. What a *morgue*!"

Nobody was about. No cars were parked. Only this old mansion staring down at Nina with evil eyes. "What a dump! There's no mistaking that!" Pink marble columns supported a grandiose portico. "You drive under it, like those automobile moguls do in Detroit."

Not a leaf stirred. Nina's resolve to have it out with somebody about the smoking chimney waned. "Deliver the magazines and get out of here!" Maybe she was being watched! "That's not funny!" Looking at the marble steps and the bronze front doors with their scrolled gilt fronds and stained glass lights Nina felt eerily disconcerted. Maybe she was being watched by a *murderer*! ... Like in the movies.

"Get a grip on yourself, Nina! This is your friendly neighbour's lovely home, an' you're going to meet your friendly neighbour for the first time and they're real nice folks!" The front doors lay wide open. Somebody's in, she thought. They gotta be. She stepped gingerly over black marble, between bronze and stained glass. She waited a moment.

"Hi-ee!" The tiny sound died a death, fluttering to the floor of the glazed vestibule. She ventured further in, through another set of open, floridly glazed doors.

"Hi-*eee!* ..... Anybody home?"

She walked into an atrium as tall as the house. There was not a sound. Through a painted glass ceiling eighty feet above her head, leather-hued light seeped down to the murky, cobra striped, polished floor. A gallery ran round the first level. Didn't they call it the *piano nobile* in Europe? Richly encased doors, sentinel, gave off from the gallery. White marble busts poked up over the line of the twirling, monstrous marble balustrade.

On the ground floor were massive Chinese lacquered doors, nail varnish red tangled with writhing golden dragons. Oriental vases, two-men tall, sat on ebony plinths at each side of these doors. There were tapestries round the stone walls and two - "My God! *Two*!" - elevators at the side of an ornate, grand stairway. On the landing, daylight leached through a stained glass window big as a cathedral.

There was a peculiar smell. A hospital smell: that strange, particular sweetness Nina knew so well from her nursing days. "Black crystal chandeliers!

. . . They *can't* be! . . . *They are too!* . . . Six black crystal chandeliers big as Greyhound busses. . . . I don't believe this! . . . I must turn one on! I *have* to turn one on! . . . Where's the switch?"

She tip-toed into the cavernous, silent, waiting space.

By one elevator shaft was a bronze bank of switches. It looked antique, but as Nina's index finger went towards the panel a sensor activated. All six chandeliers illuminated. "Not much to write home about. Somebody ought'a have told these people black glass don't light up too well!" She reached her hand towards the plate to turn them off. This time lights shot up through the bases of statues along the walls. Glass statues of male nudes.

"They can't be! Oh my God, they *are*! . . . That's gross!" She tip-toed towards a man-sized statue. It sported a huge, horizontal erection; they all did. "If Jeff could see this! I mean, what in Heaven's name . . . *enormous!* This is enough for me! I'll put the magazines down on that table and get the hell out. She moved quickly to an octagonal, rock crystal table supported by three, gilt-bronze negro-slaves.

One of the pairs of lacquered Chinese doors began to whir apart.

Nina stood in the doorway and gazed at the room beyond. It was the biggest drawing room she had ever seen, not counting London's Buckingham Palace, ("Gee! We paid enough to see that place!"). An *Aubusson* carpet swept to the horizon, on it was strewn a tide of lewd vulgarity. The chairs and sofas were in the shape of naked men, single or erotically entwined. Their pubic hair was . . . Nina went over to a chair and touched some . . . real?

"No wonder they don't invite the neighbours for cocktails!" Engrossed, she failed to hear footsteps in the hall.

She walked over to a massive fireplace, a bulbous quarry of coloured marble. Above the mantle-piece was a big oil painting. "Boy! Was that something! . . . Was he *something!"*

The painting was in a magnificent frame of lapis lazuli set with semi-precious stones, built into the wall. It surrounded a life-size portrait of a naked young man, about twenty, maybe twenty-two. Nina was moved by the boy's unearthly beauty. His flesh was not white, but a delicate dust-cream tan and the artist had made highlights of his perfect physique in golden ochre. He had jet black hair and stood with nothing but the mastery of human loveliness, a loveliness that eclipsed the trashy erotica littering the room behind her.

Somebody coughed in the hall. To her horror Nina saw that the doors were closing. She ran across the room, upsetting an occasional table so that a rampant porcelain faun smashed on the male ankle of a chair. The doors formed a jointless, Dragon-twirling wall. Nina screamed, terrified. She turned and gaped at the portrait, panic making her sight acute. Set above the frame was a plaque: it had something written on it. She read the letters a hundred feet across the room. Then the doors began to open and she turned to face them, valiant now, prepared to talk or to fight her way out of Gracewood.

♠

Facing her in the widening gap, so they looked at one another straight-on, was the butler. His skin was grey like a fish. He stood stock-still, waiting.

"Good afternoon, Madam." He was German-American, his accent unmistakable. She felt better. Three generations ago her family had emigrated to Minnesota from Bremen.

"Hi. I'm Nina Burdet. I'm your neighbour."

"I know, Madam."

"A fine place you got here."

"Perhaps, Madam."

"I came to deliver these." She waved the magazines pointlessly. "St. Margaret of Cortona. Our church . . . opposite your gates." He didn't move a muscle. "Are they church goers here?"

"No, Madam."

"No? . . . Really? That's a shame . . . I thought they might like to join us. We do a clam-bake every second Sunday of the month. . . . It's kind of fun." She glanced at the nearest glass statue, its phallus jutted a foot and a half from the subject's loins, like a mad icicle. "Bring the kids."

"There are no children here, Madam."

"I'll bet there aren't!" He shot her a speaking look, fractionally raising his left eyebrow.

"Please leave, Madam. This a private residence."

"I'll bet it is!" That the people of Minneapolis, she thought, should be sullied by this filthy freak show! "I'll get out right now! But will you take one of these?"

"Show me a copy please, Madam." He put out his hand, she almost recoiled but looking at his eyes that had never stopped looking into her own since their confrontation had begun, she recovered herself.

A door opened on the gallery. A youngish voice called directly overhead; male, impersonal, peremptory. "Who's there, Franz? Who's down there?"

"A neighbour, Sir. A neighbour has called."

"Well, tell the neighbour to fuck off!" A door slammed. Charm obviously did not reign at Gracewood. Interesting all the same: whoever it was had an educated English accent.

Franz glanced through the photocopied pages. Then he looked up at Nina and flickered a smile through his lined, fish-grey face. "Do you see the pathway over there, Madam?" She turned to look out of the splashy, gilded vestibule. She saw a path snaking over the lawns through the trees.

"Yeah. I see it."

"Do you see where it goes?" She peered into the trees for a moment, then turned to face him. "Where does it go?"

"Take the path, please, Madam. You will come to a gate. When you reach the gate, I will open it for you."

"Are you coming with me?"

"No, Madam. I will open the gate from the house." He smiled faintly, "We cannot accept this literature, Madam. Please take it back." He pressed the magazines into Nina's hands, enunciating his words with minute emphasis, as if he was trying to tell her something he could not actually say, "Keep a tight hold on them until you get home." His stare intensified, "Do not do this again, Madam. We do not care to know about our neighbours."

"Looking at what you folks have got in here, Mr Franz, only prompts me to tell you that your neighbours certainly wouldn't care to know about *you*!" She was ushered through the huge entrance doors without another word.

♠

"You don't say, Nina! The place is full of perverted artefacts? Chairs in the form of naked men?"

"Yup."

"Glass nudes with erections?"

"You heard me say it, Babe."

"Nina, do you know how difficult it would be to create a life-size statue in glass? Were these things in one piece?"

"The piece I saw was definitely in one piece!"

"But that's grotesque." Jeff gazed at an abstract canvas: lines of grey on a mottled background. He divided another can of beer diligently into two glasses. They sat on a white sofa in silence, sipping the beer, preoccupied with Gracewood.

"Frieda and Nathaniel Scheffer. How much are those two worth?"

"Nine-point-five billion, give or take. What have they got to do with it?"

"They're *normal* people, Jeff! She shops, he plays golf, their kids grow-up, marry the kids next door, have their own kids. The Scheffers don't sit around on obscene chairs with black chandeliers in the hall, slavering over glass nudes with gigantic erections!" They moved over to the window and stood looking at the Indian, then across at Gracewood. The house glowed serenely in evening light.

"How come nobody knows about that place, Jeff? I can't *believe* they don't know! The postman? Do they have groceries delivered? Who moved that stuff in there in the first place? Sweet Jesus! If I was moving junk like that out of a trailer I'd be *sure* wondering about the folks who owned it!"

"We have to get a witness to back your story."

"What story? I saw nothing bad going on, Jeff. All I saw was a collection of obscene furniture and art works. They have a perfectly respectable butler, I mean he looks unusual but he behaved impeccably. There was somebody upstairs - a guy with an English accent who made it obvious they don't welcome visitors! That's *their* choice. They're wealthy, they keep themselves to themselves - so what?"

"Something's going on in that complex, Nina, and it's not pretty."

"How do you *know*?"

"A smoking chimney, the smell of morphine, the house decked-out like Sodom City Hall. There's something bad happening there and we're sitting right by it. You insisted on going in there, now I feel we have a duty to the community to expose whatever it is they're doing. They could be carving people up."

"You don't *mean* it!"

"Remember Mankato? The neighbours spent years wondering why they ploughed-over the lawns every six months?"

"Jeff, don't!"

"It happens, Nina, and folks stand by and let it happen. We're taking action."

"Like what? We can't keep walking in there with the church magazine."

"I need to see Jack Powell. I wouldn't mind taking a look in there with Jack, myself."

"Not while I'm alive you don't!" She opened another can of beer. Night had fallen. "Do you feel like food?" He waved his hand. "Nor me."

"The butler gave you the magazines back?"

"I told you he did. Only time he acted human."

"Where are they?"

"On the piano." As Jeff sat down by her with the magazines, Nina saw a scrap of paper flutter onto the rug. "Hey! Something fell out of one!" He raised his arms and looked about him. "There, Jeff, . . . *there*! . . . You got it."

"Did this come with the issue?" He turned the paper over.

"No. What is it?"

"It's a pencil written note."

"For heaven's sake, Jeff! What does it say?"

Jeff read the hurriedly scrawled text, *Tonight. 8 o'clock. I will come to your home.*

"Eight o'clock? But that's now!" Then she screamed, he dropped his beer. The glass smashed.

"*Out there!* He's standing out there! . . . Out *there*, Jeff! By the Indian!" She ricocheted off the divan, rigid. "Do something, Jeff!"

"Get on the floor! Roll out of sight!"

"But . . ."

"Do it, Nina!"

♠

Franz von Stotz stood quietly resigned outside the Burdets' window. He remembered, without remorse, a time long ago, waiting like this for Jews to file from of their hiding places in the ghettos of Nazi occupied Poland. The man he watched, it must be the woman's husband, was not going to take any chances. He had a gun and was coming towards the window, towards the interesting sculpture. Franz raised his hands to shoulder height. He had no weapon, only the desire to give these people a hint of the danger that awaited Humanity.

"What do you want?" Jeff's voice came through the double glazing muted but stern. Franz pointed a finger to his lips. He gestured to the sliding doors, signing that it would be best for him to come inside. "Can we trust you?" Franz nodded, they could trust him. Jeff let him into the house. Nina, up off the floor, greeted him cordially enough.

"You gave us a terrible shock. We only found your note a moment ago. Did you slip the note in the magazine when you told me to look at the path?"

"I took a risk. Had you been out this evening I should not have tried to see you again." His German accent ploughed guttural furrows through the phonetics of "risk" and "tried". He was dressed in an expensive black overcoat, he wore a white silk scarf. His face was slate-grey and they both wondered about his health. Jeff noticed that the man was breathing heavily, or was this an act? "You'd better take your coat off and sit down."

Franz preferred the kitchen where nobody could see into the house. He told them he had twenty-five minutes, then he must return to Gracewood.

"My wife was shocked to see the interior of that place, Mr Franz. We are frankly disgusted about what she saw. What's going on over there?"

"I cannot tell you."

"Something's going on, I know by the way you're looking at me. I'm a lawyer, Mr Franz, I know when people conceal the truth."

"The authorities in this city will not believe you if you tell them about Gracewood. They know nothing of what we do. If you make enquiries you will find no person who has the remotest idea of Gracewood and you will be dismissed as fools. That is my job, to make people dream. Do you understand, me? I do not make a joke." This was said in the confident tone of passive finality. Jeff and Nina looked at one another. The man sat like a stone. What was he trying to tell them? That people were being brainwashed? Jeff mentioned the offending chimney. He asked Franz what the new block was for.

"I cannot tell you."

Nina got mad, "Then you can clear right out of here and see if we don't take action first thing tomorrow morning! All of you should be put out on the

..."

"Nina! No unwise statements. Let's hear what Franz has to say. He came here to tell us something, let's hear him." Jeff turned a friendly face to the man. "My wife is upset, she'll get over it. Would you like a drink?"

"I did not take Schnapps for a long time, Sir." Nina got the bottle from the bar and they all had a Schnapps.

"Listen carefully and then you must write down what I have told you. I am Franz von Stotz, of my life story I will divulge nothing. You will not see me again. If you try to make contact you will be unsuccessful." He drained the glass of Schnapps, clearing his throat huskily. "My work is secret but I am deciding to give you a warning. Nobody knows of my decision and . . . they never will."

Jeff poured three more shots into the glasses. Was the man working round to a confession? Maybe he was insane. The trouble was, Jeff thought, expertly eyeing the grey face, that the fellow gave the impression of being all too sane.

"The people at Gracewood have connections all over the world. The strange things they like to live with are nothing to their ambitions. They aim to set up a new order in the world. All you stand for will vanish."

"Is this some sort of Neo-Nazi cult?"

"No Sir! That was long ago. We are not involved with Old Europe! We are right here in the United States of America and we are poisoning you with your own poison, your own death warrant, your own electric chair!" He smiled, showing perfect teeth. Fifty years before he had been devastatingly handsome.

He's a nut, thought Nina, a class-act screwball!

Franz regarded Jeff. "You are known by the CIA and FBI. You are well known in the Pentagon. Please do not try to deny this, Mr Burdet." Jeff gazed quietly across the table. It was true. Franz began to be an intriguing commodity.

"You have worked for these people on many occasions. Even in your retirement they call you. You will carry weight with the people I want you to meet."

"Go on."

"There is a man you must find. He has a code name, Adrian Dove."

"Mr Franz! What do you take us for? For God's sake! Is this a cheap thriller?"

"Cool it, Nina! . . . Is Adrian Dove in the States?"

"He is in Morocco, with a beautiful young assistant called Thomas."

"Is Dove gay? Is your organisation some kind of gay sect? We've dealt with similar organisations, Franz, they're nothing new to us."

"I would rather that the term Homophilia is used in connection with our work. Adrian Dove has to meet a Doctor Tonio Friedemann in Morocco. Friedemann is a scientist."

"Specialising in what?"

"I cannot tell you."

"Why does Dove need to meet Friedemann?"

"He must obtain Doctor Friedemann's final work that is stored on five gold discs."

"You expect us to sit here and swallow this trash?"

"Let him speak, Nina."

"Dove must visit The Villa Friedemann. It is twenty-three kilometres south-east of Marrakech on the Zazahrat road. The village near by is Chousser."

"Give us a description of Dove and his assistant." Jeff took the bottle of Schnapps and poured more shots.

"He is the ideal Englishman, suave, tall, blond. The boy could be a model, he has exquisite deep chestnut hair and a face like the young Apollo. But he is dangerous because, like every English boy, he likes to play games - he is good at riddles."

"Do riddles play a part in your organisation, Franz?"

"They do."

"Like the letters W. M. D. O. over the fireplace at Gracewood?" Nina nudged Jeff's arm, "The letters I told you about Jeff. Carved over the painting of the nude kid."

"What do the letters stand for, Franz?"

"I cannot tell you."

"Shucks, Franz! You told us a hell of a lot already! Why don't you come clean?" Jeff grabbed Nina's hand, "Honey!".

"Jeff, you're too polite! This schmuck's a crook and I ain't afraid to ask him any question I want about his stinking organisation. C'mon, Franz! What do those letters stand for?" There was a long pause, von Stotz scrutinized his glass, rolling it between a powerful thumb and forefinger, meditating, deciding. At last he said, "One aspect of those letters is simple, it involves numbers. The numbers are significant on two levels, one very serious, the other on the level of a code." He then spoke with emphatic gestures, "More information I *cannot* tell you!"

Jeff scrutinized the man with narrowed eyes. The kitchen clock told him there were four minutes to the deadline: he had to decide if Franz was serious or insane.

"Why have you chosen us for this strange task? We are two private people. Even if we were foolish enough to go to Morocco looking for a man code named Adrian Dove - and we might as well go looking for a needle in a haystack - in no way are we trained for this sort of work. My expertise goes as far as probing through documentation, some of it from sources that - just like you, Franz - I cannot reveal. I have zero qualification in field intelligence."

"That is exactly why you have been chosen, Mr Burdet."

"If your organisation is so powerful why don't you see Dove yourself?"

Stotz got up slowly, his mouth a grim line in the grey face. He wrapped

46

the scarf round his neck, put on his coat, and walked into the living area. By the triangular window he sedately turned, regarding them with soulless eyes.

"It is up to you."

He slid open the glazed door and was about to step outside when he stopped and turned again. Feeling in the pocket of his overcoat, he brought out a piece of paper and laid it on a table. He whispered, "A riddle."

"For us?"

"For Mister Dove." Moving onto the terrace with light steps, he delicately touched the stone Indian with the tip of a fish-grey forefinger and murmured, "Exquisite!". Giving them an almost imperceptible nod he vanished into the night.

Nina snatched up the piece of paper and unfolded it. She read aloud, *'At thirteen twenty meters north of the old bridge there are two points to note on the tower. Firstly, left towards the teeth it is shaded before noon. Secondly, the room with three windows has three doors; the correct door is seen through rock. The pass code is a powerhouse across the valley.'*

"Phone the police, Jeff. This whole thing is crazy!"

"Tomorrow morning book a flight to Morocco, Nina."

"Lover, are you mad?"

"Book the Mamounia Hotel in Marrakech. Julie and Kit can look after the house while we're away." He paused, thinking hard. "Book the week commencing April 25th. If there's no sign of Dove in ten days we fly home and get this thing reported to the CIA. I know the contact. I can't believe our news will surprise her."

♠

Thomas and I arrived in Marrakech on April 22nd, eight days after my interview with Frederick and Andrew Park. Thomas loved the idea, for him life was one big adventure. Not for me. During a telephone conversation with Frederick I rammed home my point that professional investigators would stand a better chance of solving the Moreau mystery. Fred bawled, "Get out there, Johnny, and get bloody well stuck in!". Replacing the handset I murmered, "Get stuck in to what?"

"Do you think they have Night Clubs in Marrakech?"

"Lots, Thomas. *You* won't be seeing them!"

"That sounds like my father!"

"Exactly!"

We stayed in a villa in the desirable Mellah quarter of the city. A block away from the Royal Palace the villa sat in the middle of fragrantly scented rose gardens. Our host was an old friend of Fred's - would he have been anything else? Dr Hassan al Khoubbann was a professor at the Marrakech University, a charming Moroccan who spoke French and English with fluent refinement. His delightful teenage family made an immediate fuss of Thomas.

Our brief was as crude as a cardboard cut-out. I was a visiting lecturer, Thomas was one of my students researching Islamic manuscripts. Our relationship had to appear ambivalent; the object was to stand out from the tourist crowd and create gossip. To this end I had been supplied with a generous clothing allowance, plus Fred's clipped directive, "Be an old Queen, Johnny - you will do a marvellous job. The boy has to look like a tart! There's an outfitters in Wardour Street. Give my name to the proprietor, Gervais Dylliss-Tytte. Nice man. One of my people."

We had the use of Hassan's car, a lumbering 1963 Mercedes. Hassan's driver, Khalifa, knew everyone in Marrakech. As we were driven through the crowded streets, or into the suburbs, he would point people out. "They will all come to know who you are, Mr Johnny. Somebody will send a message, you can be certain of it!"

As simple as that! The first of May was less than a week away. Suppose nothing happened? But Khalifa was right, the critical message duly arrived.

It was Friday, the Islamic weekend, aperitif hour. Hassan's family and five dinner guests were sitting by the outdoor swimming pool enjoying the rose-scented air. Submerged floodlights beneath the diamond blue water brilliantly illuminated our white tuxedos and the ladies' elegant evening dresses that sparkled with jewellery. Green coated Moroccan servants flitted amongst the guests handing drinks with white gloved hands. A member of the Royal family was present, conversation was politely superficial. Hassan leaned towards me, "Frederick telephoned today. I told him you have settled-in well but cannot find any clues."

"Sometimes I don't understand Fred. He believes we can sort this business out."

"You know him as well as I do, Johnny. A man who writes his own rules then breaks them. If Fred suspects that a terrorist organisation is at work in Morocco, I have to respect his judgement. But it is impossible that we do not know what happens in our own country. The slightest suspicion of such a presence and the King would soon be told. We run the state like clockwork."

Thomas came over and pulled up an empty chair. The boy had made a great impression, his looks and charm worked wonders. Hassan smiled at him, "So, Thomas! You do not like my beautiful colleague?" He gestured towards the pretty woman Thomas had been talking to, a senior lecturer in his department.

"She's gorgeous. She's invited me to dinner tomorrow night, in a famous restaurant."

"Quick work, Mate. You'll be in bed with her next."

"She's my mother's age, Johnny. I fancy her daughter."

"I knew there had to be a catch!"

"You're old and jealous, Gov'ner." He put his hand on my arm, "Listen, I had an idea. It's about the 22 11 pass code. … Don't roll your eyes!"

"Go on. Make it snappy!"

"Sir Frederick assumed the gambit will be Love me Tonight. Suppose 22 11 is as simple as the letters twenty-two and eleven of the alphabet: V and K. They could stand for Vagabond King, the title of that Musical with the hit song Frederick played on his antique gramophone."

"Love me Tonight. What about it?"

"Maybe if somebody says to you, 'Vagabond King', that is the gambit. The reply is '22 11'."

"Bit puny, isn't it? What about Love Me Tonight, where does that come in?"

"It's all a bit puny, Gov'ner! I have a hunch Love Me Tonight will turn up somewhere."

"Thomas has a point, Johnny. It could be as simple as that. Child's play."

"I suppose, Thomas, that you are now going to tell us that W. M. D. O. are the letters 23, 13, 4 and 15, and that they add up to 55?"

"You're thinking well, Gov'ner! Multiply them together, then multiply the result by 55, and you get 986700."

"And what's so bloody marvellous about nine, eight, six, seven-hundred?"

"It sounds good, Gov'ner. Write it down on your cuff!" My boredom was alleviated by the call to dinner.

♠

We spent the next day wandering about the medina and making ourselves obvious by sitting in cafes drinking coffee or red wine watching a tide of men, women, children, donkeys, old cars and rickety bicycles. Trade was brisk; lamb carcasses dribbled blood, chickens hung in bunches by their necks, perfume stores were crowded with pretty girls with flashing eyes and shimmering blue-black hair. Metal workers sat welding sinks, car panels and beautiful lamps. Fabric sellers gossiped to men older than Genesis. Grocers sold single cigarettes to gangly youths in soiled European trousers. There were box carvers, plasterers, tilers, brass workers and silk merchants.

"You like all this, Thomas?"

"Wonderful!" He pointed to a tall mud wall over the street, "That doorway, Johnny; it's like a mosque." A single front door, dustily dignified, stood tall in the middle of a blank, dun-coloured facade. Immediately to the right of this entrance, wide garage doors began to open automatically. A big American gas guzzler bumped forward, nosing its chromium-plated bumper into the fray. The driver hooted as people scrambled to one side. The car passed close to us. In the front were two identical young men.

"The breed, Thomas. There they are."

A woman sat in the back, elderly, wearing outdated make-up. Over her iron-grey coiffure, she wore a black, netted, pill box hat. When Khalifa arrived to ferry us back to Hassan's villa we described what we had seen.

"The Villa Aubazine, Sir. Famous in Marrakech for the parties they give. It used to belong to a master of French Haut Couture. Then to a Swiss from Lausanne. He was murdered by his boyfriend and the place was sold to a woman from America. She is very rich."

"What's her name?"

"Nobody knows, Sir."

"Strange, don't you think?"

"I am not paid to think, Sir."

That evening Thomas was collected by two young men of his own age and their girl friends. They had provided a spare girl for Thomas and they all went off to enjoy themselves at a traditional restaurant in the centre of the medina. I'd been there often, so it was nice to relax with Hassan discussing Arthur's funeral. Like me, Hassan could not credit that a town forgets a riot and ignores a corpse in a glass casket. By the time we went to bed it was well past midnight. I read and fell asleep. I was woken at three by a gentle knock on my door.

"Come in."

Thomas crept into the room, a little tipsy but none the worse for it.

"Is anything wrong?"

"I have received a message, Johnny." I sat up in bed, turned the light on.

"Where?"

"At the restaurant. They brush you down in the Gents, then spray you with cologne. The bloke said, "Does Love Me Tonight mean anything to you?""

"He fancied you."

"It wasn't like that at all, Johnny. I thought for a moment, then said 'The Hôtel Bradford.', so he slipped this card into my jacket pocket, sprayed me with cologne and buggered off. Exciting, isn't it?"

"Could be. What does the card say?"

"Villa Aubazine, May 1st. 19-30 hrs. Cocktails." I picked up the bedside telephone and dialled Fred on a closed line. He answered immediately. "Bloody good work, Johnny. Give the kiddie a coconut! I want him to get away from the party and scout round the place. See what's going on. You be ready to meet the contact. The woman in the car probably. Sounds just the sort of hard-boiled old cat we're looking for." He rang off. Thomas was wide-eyed.

"Is this the start of it, Johnny?"

"Get some sleep, Mate. It's May the first now. We have to hit centre target this evening. We have one shot each."

♠

We rolled up at the Villa Aubazine looking the part; a typical Marrakech "couple". I wore a lightweight cream suit over a silver-grey silk shirt. The bow tie was a stunner in yellow Shantung brocade. Expensive knick-knacks matter in Ex-patriot circles, so I had slipped on a pair of Swiss handmade shoes that should never have left the box. I selected a Longines watch that had put me back thirty thousand American dollars years before in Zurich. I hesitated (I detest fussy dress) then picked a vermilion silk square, soused it in Vetyver, slopped it into my top pocket, and emerged from my room like a Broadway Queen.

Thomas made a superb 'boyfriend'. He wore pale green slacks, white leather shoes, an oyster cream silk shirt and Wedgwood blue jacket cut fashionably to his card slim waist. His looks made up for the lack of a thirty thousand dollar watch, but hung round his neck was a thin gold chain that lay like a dozing tree-snake on his velvet, richly tanned, flawless flesh. A solitaire diamond graced the chain, it winked in the "V" where his shirt collar - wantonly unbuttoned - gaped alluringly.

"That lot didn't come from Wardour Street!"

"I went shopping with my sister. Girls know how to make boys girls."

"You didn't tell her why, I hope."

"I told her I was going on holiday with you, Gov'ner."

"Christ! What will your parents think!"

"Mother said; 'I've often *wondered* about Johnny!'"

"Thanks a million, Mate!"

"Cool it, Gov'ner! I told my sister I fancied something horny for a party with Penny Carlton. And so what if we're on holiday together? You're monstrously old fashioned!" He blew me a kiss, grinning like a school boy.

The street door to the villa was opened by a liveried servant who lead us through a tile-sated vestibule mazy with geometric Islamic patterns. We were asked to wait in a courtyard open to the night sky: an ink black square set with *diamante* stars. Below, in the centre of a mosaic floor rich as a carpet, lay a circular marble basin veined like an eyeball. The surface of the water in the basin was completely concealed by a floating cape of old fashioned, cream and madder pink roses that gave-off a perfume heady and sensual. The only sound was of water trickling down a single marble column, erect, Arab style, in the centre of the basin.

"Wow! . . . It's like an old movie, Gov'ner."

"Watch out, somebody's coming."

A magnificently muscular Moroccan major domo strode up to us. He was svelte in a dove grey jacket and black trousers of the smartest cut. He wore a muted mauve silk tie. His gold watch shone idly upon the powder-soft, coppery skin of his thick, supple, wrist. Towering above us he courteously introduced himself in English lilted with a Moroccan-French accent.

"I am Daoud, Madame's manager. Would you like to refresh yourselves in private, (he indicated a narrow stone stairway through a Moorish arch) or would you care to join the other guests immediately?"

"We'd be pleased to join the guests." He took us through a huge, fascist drawing room painted indigo and gold. Venetian chandeliers hung like displays of boiled sweets, dimly illuminating black Chinese cabinets and Art Deco furniture. The walls were hung with oil paintings of naked youths.

"Are they *gay* here?"

"You'll be gay if you don't shut up!"

We were shown into a large, floodlit, garden court. Back-lit stained-glass first floor windows illuminated date palms, orgasmic bamboo, cavernous Madonna lilies and gore-red bougainvillea. The place roared with the gossip of two hundred guests. A flurry of over-handsome waiters served pink champagne and Crème de Menthe. I gave our order to a lad with golden epaulettes who returned at magical speed with my gin and Italian and a well-iced Ballantine's for Thomas. Daoud introduced us to two guests, then discretely pulled me to one side, "Madame will approach shortly, Sir. She is wearing a purple evening dress." He vanished into the crowd, trailing a whiff of male virility.

Thomas was not coping well with the two guests, a couple of gay Swiss from Bern crazy to get their hands on the boy. Frankly, one could not blame them, the lad was stunning and I was proud of him. "Been to many of these do's?"

"We come every week, Monsieur, but we never saw anyone so *beautiful* as Thomas!"

"He's hot, boys! Watch your fingers."

"*Monsieur*! Your dry English humour is *sensational*. You *must* come over to our place for drinks tomorrow! We'll be so *cross* if you refuse!" When a gay Swiss lisps you have to hand it to him - there's nothing to beat it.

"Know the crowd here?"

"Nobody knows the social side of Marrakech better than *we* do, Monsieur."

"What about *Madame*?"

"She's a bitch, Monsieur."

"Anything else?"

"Can we take your little boy upstairs?"

"Just a minute, Johnny!"

"You're on your own, Kid!"

The party was roaring. There were dated 'rock-star' banana yellow jackets with mauve velvet collars. There were two-tone shoes in cherry and white. Heavy gold rings gored with bunion sized garnets were rammed onto countless, permanently cocked little fingers. Dazzlingly naked brass zippers fronted lace-trimmed trousers desperately stretched round jelly mould haunches. There were smoke-blue toupees and saucy old mouths soused with rouge in the final attempt to revive vanished Youth. As the Swiss couple lead Thomas away, a crowd of sag-kneed, bag-crotched antique pansies gazed at the boy with stale-egg eyes.

Younger men wore two hundred dollar "T" shirts, their cooking apple biceps honed each morning at the local gym. One glance at the hairline cracks beneath shipyard plates of foundation cream told me there wasn't a man there under forty. The real boys, mostly Moroccans, all fatally good looking, were gathered in a majlis watching a group of transvestites play Blackjack.

"Monsieur Dove?"

A half turn and there she stood. Her French was American, and I replied courteously in English: no point in concealing too much. She smiled socially, extending a limpid hand, her forearms encased in long, Nightshade purple, evening gloves.

"Jayne Blaisedale. Delighted to meet you. Your little friend is quite a star at my party!" She was well over sixty, her face had been lifted at least twice, her voice had that unmistakable rasp of a nicotine and liquor ravaged throat. Fragments of tulip-blue lipstick crumbled from her clam-like mouth falling onto breasts that resembled two rotting mangoes going cheap on a market stall.

"Do follow me, Mister Dove." We glided through the crowd towards a building drenched with bougainvillea. Each guest received a courteous word from his hostess, the few women present - all sumptuously overdressed - were greeted with a five star brand of cracker-dry bitchery. Walking ahead of me in her fluttering purple gown the woman could have been torn from the pages of an Edith Wharton novel.

"I relish the pep of a Marrakech party, don't you?"

"A splendid evening, Madame."

She sashayed to a low Arab doorway and turned, all graciousness and *politesse*, "You're such a gentleman, Mr Dove, and your lover is perfect. Such good taste. I'm a wealthy woman. People in Marrakech come here to take mere advantage of my generosity. They leave without a word of appreciation but your English niceties preserve the heart of High Society. Don't you agree, Mr Dove?"

Was this asinine patter a pass-code gambit?

"I stopped in Paris recently, at the Bradford."

"Springtime in Paris, Mr Dove! I have a house on the Avenue Victor Hugo. I was there last week. I love to walk my little dogs in the Bois de Boulogne."

"How many little dogs do you have?"

"Twelve. A family of Pekingese. *Adorable*! My favourite is Ming-Ming. He's so intelligent he understands every word you say. If he could only talk, what *tales* he could tell!" She gave me a Lincoln Memorial smile and took hold of the door handle, her pendant diamond earrings swirling like jewelled bats in the dusk. "When the dogs get into their basket for the night, I gather Ming-Ming in my arms and take him to my room. I put him on the bed and I say, 'Ming-Ming, you little man! Ming-Ming, I say to him, . . . you're the Vagabond King!'" She stood stock still, regarding my eyes, her face a surgical steel mask of mendacity.

The words took a second to sink in. She'd said it! There was no going back.

"And what Ming-Ming says, Madame, is *twenty-two, eleven.*"

She flung open the door and without looking round grabbed my lapel. She dragged me through the opening with the strength of a karate Black Belt.

"You bet it is, fucker!"

She kicked the door closed so hard it slammed with a crack. To my dismay I heard the softly internal click of an automated lock. She manhandled me into her study, wrenching shut a leather-padded inner door. Edith Wharton was gone with the wind.

"You bet it's twenty-two, eleven, you fucking smooth-arsed Brit! What kept you? We have work to do. Time is short! And who's the bum-boy? I don't want any little vaselined brown-hat nosing round. Get rid of him! If you don't I'll have a Kadet do it for you - they'll rip that kid's fucking sphincter out of his fucking asshole! You were supposed to be here a week ago. Didn't they brief you? What did Stotz say at the Bradford?"

As I had little idea of what she was talking about, I played a modest hand. "Nothing was said to me. I took the envelope, that was all. The first of May was stated, here I am."

"Well you can start by getting over to that drinks cabinet and fixing me a Vodka on the Rocks. Strong! I like cocktails with *bollocks*! Get something for yourself, then get the fuck into this chair and *listen*!" She sat down at a reproduction Louis Seize desk, whipped a cigarette from a silver box, shoved it between the tulip blue lips, struck a match down the belly of a bronze faun, lit-up, and puffed out the match, navvy style.

"Just so you don't feel too much at home, Mister Dove, let's draw up the rules!" She reached down into her brassière and brought out a gold plated, emerald encrusted revolver fitted with a silver-gilt silencer inlaid with Mother of Pearl.

A Lady's piece.

♠

Above Jayne Blaisedale's truck-sized cocktail cabinet hung three framed photographs. Two were interesting. So interesting that I decided to mention them. Pouring a vodka strong enough to kill a normal person, I mixed myself a gin and Italian, marking time diddling with the ice bucket.

"When was this taken of Arthur?"

" 'Forty-two. That's von Stotz with him, the bastard! Then there's Daddy and Arthur in France; I guess the summer of forty-eight. They were celebrating the first batch. The middle frame is Daddy on Christmas Day, 'sixty-nine. The last shot. He died January 'seventy. Good looking to the last wasn't he? A fabulous man, like Arthur. Two of a kind."

"They certainly were." I handed her the vodka, she downed it in one.

"Get me another! . . . Emmanuel Blaisedale the Second, that was Daddy! They said he was gay, well so he was, but he shagged my mother good and hard, and I appeared. I inherited the whole fucking shebang! Did you know Mother? Madeleine Necker-Vandel?"

"Before my time." I handed her the second vodka. "Necker-Vandel?"

"International construction conglomerate; built everything Daddy needed. Places all over the world. Still doing it. Piet Vandel was a Dutch-American, a jerk! That's why mother got herself shagged by Daddy. He shagged her twice. Two girls. My sister's the movie star. Everybody gets us mixed up."

"Can you blame them? . . Another drink?"

"Sure. And, hey! put some *grit* into it this time!"

"Elevators made your family fortune, that much everybody knows."

"Every damned elevator in the world - past, present and future - had, has, and will *always* have, a Blaisedale widget. That was the 1870's when we muscled-in on the Otis empire."

"Your father had other interests."

"You know what went on at St-Christophe as well as I do." St-Christophe? I dared not risk another probing question. We had some names to work on, and the startling evidence of two photographs. Arthur was unmistakable. The man with his arm round Arthur's shoulders was the grey major domo from the Bradford. She'd named him: von Stotz. The shot showed the two men, arm-in-arm, standing in front of the Château des Noces, Stotz in early middle age and extremely good looking. In the other photograph, Arthur and Blaisedale posed in front of a different château. I judged the ugly Gothic Revival style to be around 1908.

Was this *St-Christophe*? Too risky to ask. As for the central frame of "Daddy", this was a typical professional studio portrait, expertly side-lit and touched-up. I fixed two more drinks and sat down. Not surprisingly, my hostess was tight.

"OK, Mister. Take a look at this photograph." She winged a polaroid snap at me. "One of the kadets took it last month. And waddy'a know! The shit was drunk, . . . him, not the fucking Kadet." She swayed in her chair. "Ever seen … him … before?"

"No."

Of course I had! It was my half-brother, Jo. Grossly fat, bald, dressed in a soiled Arab robe, seated on stained floor cushions, surrounded by bottles, glasses and boys. I kept my expression dead-pan. "What do you want me to do?"

"Kill the fucker, grab the disks." Her lips worked grotesquely to form words. In a hoarse whisper, confidentially, she slurred, "Floor safe! They're copies. But . . . we ain't got no time . . . to . . . fff-filch the oh-*ridge*-inals."

"Where are the originals?"

"Don't you quiz *me*! you fucking British faggot . . . you . . . fff . . ."

Her gun fell onto the carpet, forgotten. Reaching into a drawer of the desk she pushed the contents about mesmerically and pulled out a bunch of padlock keys that she tossed at my chest. I caught them, pocketing them at once.

"They'll get you through the bastard's gates." She passed a shaky hand through her hair and the French pleat slopped out of set. She looked ridiculous, hair hanging down in strands, lipstick smarmed up one cheek. She swayed a finger over a button on the desk. Eventually she managed to press it.

"Don't you breathe a *word*, Mister. . . . See! . . . A *word*! . . . When Arthur kicked the bucket, the business got kinda . . . mmm-*essy*! Too many fuck'n chiefs and . . . (she gave out an explosive belch, aiming her hand somewhere near her mouth) Scuze *me*! . . . nod-enough . . . innnj-*uns*!" She swilled the vodka, aimlessly tossing the glass to one side. It smashed on the floor by her desk. "That's the *truth*, Mister! A . . . *mmm*-ess! And I'm goin' to . . . . put the place . . . in . . .(she slumped forward, her eyes half shut) . . . innn-ordah!" She slipped off her chair and - breaking wind with liquid resonance - collapsed, inert, onto a Turkish rug.

Was she drugged? No hardened drinker would have succumbed so drastically, so quickly, to a mere half bottle of Vodka. A door behind the desk opened briskly. In walked one of the breed.

The young man stood over her, handsome, identical to all the rest, wearing the nicely cut suit, white shirt and non-descript tie of a typical PA. He gave Jayne an up-and-down glance, then nodded me a respectful, "Monsieur." Then he turned again, eyes wide, and gazed at me, frozen. Snapping-too, he opened a door of an ornate German Baroque cabinet and reached inside. He brought out a glass pill box: a miniature of Arthur's glass casket.

Staring at me while performing his task, he counted out three, jelloid, oval capsules. They contained a greenish substance that could have been Cod Liver Oil for all I knew. He sat on the desk chair then gently, with trained skill, lifted Jayne Blaisedale across his lap, face up. He opened her mouth and placed one of the capsules on her tongue. As if worming a cat, he stroked her neck ensuring that she swallowed the capsule. He repeated the procedure twice, hardly taking his eyes from mine.

After about twenty seconds the woman began to revive. In less than a minute she appeared to be completely recovered, lucid and composed. Still lying across the young man's lap, looking to the ceiling, she said politely, "The Kadet will show you where Jo lives. Go there immediately, make certain he dies, and bring me the disks. There are five of them. He keeps them in the floor safe of his study. His chauffeur knows the combination." She made a sign with her hand, was lifted up, led to the door behind her desk, and handed through it.

The young man I now knew as a 'Kadet' beckoned me to another door by the cocktail cabinet and we entered an inner study. Here he lead me to a framed map of Morocco that took up the end wall of the beautifully frescoed, vaulted chamber. He pointed to a location on the map, south-east of Marrakech, "This is the estate you must visit, Monsieur."

As I scrutinised the spot, remembering the road numbers, the kadet took my left hand in his own and knelt. He kissed my fingers reverently. I was so astonished I let him do it.

"I know you, Monsieur! Do you remember me?" I withdrew my hand from his, raised the lad to his feet, took him to a chair and sat him down. He was weeping and I dried his eyes with my handkerchief then clasped his shoulders reassuringly.

"Were you at Monsieur Moreau's funeral?"

"I was the woman. My bag was a gun. I changed at the service station. You were angry." I pushed my fingers through his hair, turning his face gently by the jaw.

"My God! So you were. I did not recognise you in the other room." He grasped my hand in his own, pulling it from his face.

"My name is Panno. Kyla is my friend." Sobbing, he blurted, "Save us Monsieur! *Please*! . . . Save us!" Then he drew my face to his, giving my lips a chaste kiss: exactly as Kyla had done at the Hôtel Bradford.

♠

The Swiss lovers took Thomas up to a roof terrace overlooking the Medina where another bar dispensed as much drink as the ones below. They met a couple from Holland, rather old and staid. Thomas tried to be sociable but it was difficult to concentrate while a hand, neatly nestled inside his jacket, caressed the small of his back.

"Why don't we skip the party? Come home with us, Thomas."

"I'm with Adrian."

"An hour under the stars together? Where is the harm in that?"

"Not tonight, Josephine!"

"What?"

"Skip it! Hold my drink, I need the jon." Thomas whipped round and caught a waiter by the arm, "*Les toilettes, Monsieur?*" Down the stairs, to the left. "I won't be a moment, then you can tell me about the mosques of Marrakech." Like hell! He did not mind the indiscretion so much as the assumption that he would let them do anything they wanted with him.

Setting the alarm on his watch, Thomas gave himself twenty-five minutes. A winding stair took guests to tiled lavatories but the passage continued through a glazed door. Thomas slipped through this door and was swiftly round a corner out of sight. He found himself in a sitting room filled with red Moroccan leather sofas and gilt lamps; a large bedroom was visible through swagged drapes of gold-lamé. The bed heaved like a maggot-bloated corpse, the room was loud with bestial panting.

Hearty cheering came through an open door on the other side of the bedroom. Young men's cheering, not too close. Thomas nipped through the bedroom, past the heap of lace-entwined limbs, counting four male heads on the bolster of the bed. One of the quartet asked for some champagne to be brought. "They think I'm a servant. That's lucky."

He stopped on a landing beyond the bedroom and gently shut the revellers in, turning the lock and tossing its key into an aquarium. A marble staircase went down one level: he took it and found himself facing a pair of ornate, off-white double doors fronded with fake *chinoiserie*. Behind these doors he reckoned there were easily ten blokes joking and laughing. Putting his ear to the keyhole he heard them speaking a mixture of French and American English. There was also another language, as Johnny had described of 'the breed'.

"Now or never, Mate!" He went in.

Thomas faced about twenty young men. They were identical, exactly as Johnny had described the young men at Moreau's funeral. They were all Thomas's age, all exceptionally good looking, their features and slender bodies remarkably similar to his. Most of them were resting on two-deck bunk beds in what looked like a barracks. It was as if they were off duty, relaxing, half dressed, lounging about smoking, reading magazines or comics. The room was very ornate but had been stripped of its furnishings, drapes and carpet. A central chandelier still hung from the frescoed ceiling, but it was filthy, smogged with cobwebs. The walls were decorated with stretched, faded rose silk brocade, ripped and stained; Thomas made out dark oblongs where pictures had been hung. The room was stiflingly hot and smelt strongly of young males and nicotine.

By a fireplace, where logs smouldered, four blokes sat round a table. They all wore a white cotton vest, black trousers and no socks. Three were olive skinned, black haired, rapier slim and, like Thomas, superbly muscular.

A bottle of local red wine was open on the table, three empties stood in a line on the hearth. On the mantelpiece soiled glasses crowded a porcelain ash tray gagged with butts. It appeared to Thomas that nobody was bothered by his intrusion, perhaps they assumed he was one of them.

A game of cards was in progress. Perched on his chair back, bare feet on the seat, laconically dealing, eyes half shut against the winding smoke from his cigarette, was the exception. A stunningly handsome version of 'the breed', this boy possessed the same, flawless brand of male beauty as Thomas, but with ice. He also had the same chestnut hair. He turned to Thomas, smiling a generous greeting. Glancing for an instant at the newcomer's slick garb, he spoke in erudite French.

"Please join us. Do have some wine. Would you care for a cigarette?" Thomas took the proffered cigarette. He would be friendly, see what these boys had to say for themselves.

"You at the party?" Thomas realised he must reply carefully.

"Yes. I got bored. What are you all doing?"

"Waiting to change duty rotas." The boy suddenly reached out his hand and ran his fingers gently through Thomas's hair. It was the sort of thing a best friend might do, occasionally, in a brief moment of affection, but not a complete stranger in the first instant of meeting someone. The young man did not seem embarrassed by the gesture. He gently fingered Thomas's hair for a full half minute, as if the bloke had no taboos about touching other men. It was important, Thomas knew, not to bridle.

"You're like me. That's not usual. Did they send you from Lausanne?"

Lausanne? . . . Careful, Thomas!

"No. From England." By now the others were listening, sitting up on their bunks. They were inquisitive, like children.

"England?" The bloke paused, considering. "Then you come from Four. I come from One." He waved his hand in the direction of the bunks, "These are from One and Two, those three by the door are from Fourteen." Four? One, Two, Fourteen? What was he talking about? Thomas smiled: the boy smiled. Thomas glanced round: they all smiled. But they smiled in exactly the same way at exactly the same time, "Like automatons." Thomas's mind began to work, "Automatons!"

Yes! . . . There was something *artificial* about these young men. But it was not easy to explain exactly *what*. Observing them now, Thomas grasped that they were not relaxed and loose-limbed in quite the same way that he would be, lounging with his pals at home, in the sauna, or in a pub. He looked at his watch. How could he get them to open up? Sport? Great idea. Everybody loves sport.

"Do you play rugby?" The chestnut-haired boy bounced from his chair, grasped Thomas by the waist, and ran his hands sensuously up and down

Thomas's flanks.

"They do not play games, but I like football very much, and baseball, but we are not taught those things, we are taught to kill." He spoke of killing as a housewife speaks of going shopping. "We are trained for diplomatic replacement and political misalignment posts. I am senior. I have not much time." Having said these enigmatic things, the youth slid a lissom arm over Thomas's shoulders and began to dawdle him round the room, whispering into Thomas's ear, occasionally giving his new acquaintance a nuzzling kiss on his hair. He was fractionally taller than Thomas, and as he spoke his breath smelt chemically fresh, like a hospital, as if his lungs were made of polythene. "You look so pretty in those clothes! How long have *you* got?"

What did the bloke *mean*? Sure as Hell the answer was not 'Twelve-and-a-half minutes, then I have to get back to Johnny."

"May I have a glass of wine, please?"

"Of course!" He let go of Thomas. "Get another bottle from the fridge! Through the door on the right. Here, take this corkscrew." He brushed a kiss on Thomas's neck. "Be useful, little Kadet!"

Kadet? . . . An American refrigerator stood in a kitchenette, tall as an office block, the sort that makes ice in competition with the South Pole. The interior was groaning with food but he could not see any wine. He flapped down a cover in the door and found about sixty prepared syringes in transparent packs, each filled with greenish serum. They were neatly lined on numbered, dated racks. *Christ!* Were they junkies!

If he did nothing else that evening he had to nick a syringe. Nimbly he pulled one from its grip, bunching the others together so it didn't look as if anything was missing. He pocketed the item, preparing an excuse to get back to the party. He saw the wine and grabbed a bottle. As he came back into the main room a boy close by took off his briefs.

The bloke was naked, reaching for a pair of socks. It took Thomas great strength of mind not to stop and stare like an idiot at the man's loins.

No genitals! There was a tiny, bud-like valve of flesh, enough to urinate, but there was no penis and no testicles, nor was there the faintest smudge of pubic hair.

Not daring to stare, Thomas uncorked the wine bottle, holding it between his knees so that he could use the opportunity to glance surreptitiously about. The bloke with no prick was donning a pressed shirt. If you didn't know what was missing, he looked assertively virile. His well shaped legs, arms and robust chest were sooty with shiny black hairs. Dressed, he looked a true thug. But he didn't have a sign of a beard, none of them did, not even the shadow of stubble! Dawdling with the cork, Thomas saw three other boys whip towels from their waists. Naked, they were identical: they had no genitals.

Time to go. But the handsome host took Thomas's glass, filled it, drank half of it, passed the glass to Thomas and gave him another kiss, "It is nice to meet a kadet that looks just like me. I am Kyla. Who are you?"

"Thomas." . . . So *this* was Kyla!

He was startled by an alarm beeping on the mantelpiece. Kyla straightened up, clipping a command round the room in their strange language, adding in French, "Injections." A kadet went into the kitchen, Thomas heard the fridge door opening. Definitely time to go!

"Do you need an injection, or are you in the other cycle?"

"The other cycle. Look, I have to re-join the party. It's been good meeting everyone." He shook Kyla's hand, "I hope we meet again, you and me." For a full ten seconds Kyla held Thomas's hand, looking deep into his eyes. When he finally spoke, his voice was shaky with emotion.

"So long, little Kadet."

Without knowing how, Thomas felt the bond of youthful love enter them both and a subtle sadness unfolded in his heart, "So long, Kyla. . . . Good luck."

♠

Hassan stood expansively with his back to the fire. "Gentlemen, I congratulate you! A most rewarding evening. I am sure Frederick will be delighted. Tell me the names of the two kadets again."

"Kyla and Panno. They played a key role at Arthur's funeral."

"And they turn up in Marrakech! An odd set-up, Johnny, don't you think? Strange names too. I have packed the syringe in dry ice. First thing tomorrow it will be flown to London."

"We have to find Jo."

"The journey to the foothills of the Atlas Mountains is an hour and a half. The town you are aiming for is Zazahrat. The road is good." Hassan sipped iced orange juice. "Take my tip, Johnny; park the car on the roadside and walk to the villa."

"You knew nothing about Jo?" There was a pause, Hassan dawdled over to the French windows, fingering the tasselled drapes. He turned, his expression troubled.

"Nothing. And this disturbs me. I may add, my friend, that nobody knew there was even a residence where the kadet Panno indicated your half-brother's estate. Officially, the location is … mountain scrub. The home of scorpions."

"An apt description in the case of my half-brother."

"Are you really going to kill Jo, Johnny?"

"*No*, Thomas!"

"But she said . . ."

"Never mind what she said."

"When did you last see him?"

"Years ago. In Switzerland. We quarrelled. Jo, Arthur and me." Thomas was silent for a moment. "Talking of Switzerland, remember that Kyla mentioned Lausanne. Shouldn't we pay Lausanne a visit?"

It was my turn to be silent. "Perhaps, mate." I studied the map Hassan had spread on an occasional table. "What is this big property along the main road?"

"The Villa Friedemann. A German owns the estate. He never leaves the place. Rumour has it he was mixed up with the Nazis. He must be into his nineties."

"Any point in calling on him?"

"Gracious, no! The man is deranged. We have many of them here. Had to get out of Germany at the end of the Second World War."

"Do you know what he does?"

"Listens to ancient recordings of Wagner's Ring Cycle."

♠

The High Atlas have a way with strangers. Nothing so ethereal can be conjured in the mind's eye as their dreaming majesty, a cyclorama of iced indigo extending for a thousand leagues beneath the turquoise proscenium of heaven. Along the mazy peaks a single sunlit skein of gold traces the jagged contour of this unparalleled range: and all Africa lies beyond, mantling the circumference of the World.

We arrived at Zazahrat on schedule. A nice little town, French in character. A good hotel, a couple of restaurants, two mosques and the remains of a Catholic church. There were shops round a passably tidy square shaded by scruffy trees. We parked outside a fly-blown bar and went in. Sure enough, two residents confirmed that an Englishman lived in a villa not far out of the town, past an olive grove.

We had expected the entrance to Jo's villa to be impressively ornate. What we found were weed-choked gates fabricated from crude sections of welded steel wound with barbed wire. "Doesn't look very welcoming, Gov'ner."

"Not your idea of a gentleman's country residence, Thomas?"

"Too right!"

"Get out and see if they're locked." Quickly he returned.

"No locks at all."

"So much for Jayne's keys."

" I can open them if you want. There are tyre tracks."

"How old?"

"This year, they're sharp enough. Should we drive in?"

"No. Do as Hassan advised. We may need to get the hell out of the place."

We took an easy pace down the unkempt track for about a kilometre. Shading his eyes with his hand, Thomas stared into the middle distance.

"I don't think anyone lives here any more."

"You want to take a bet on that?"

"You're always right, Gov'ner. I'll keep my money in my pocket."

Another kilometre and Thomas stopped, "Creepy, this place, Johnny. Don't you feel it? Like it's unreal. Same as the kadets. They're unreal. There's a town less than a mile away. Who would know?"

"You read too many thrillers, Thomas." But the boy was right, a dark wall of malice seemed to have enveloped us, as if we had entered enemy territory.

Round a corner, less than a hundred meters further on, we stepped over a white concrete curb onto shimmering black asphalt. The scrub and rocks were replaced by irrigated parkland; emerald green lawns, groups of glossy Royal Palms. Our route was now lined with brilliantly coloured flowering shrubs - like a paint manufacturer's sample card. We faced a tremendous vista of dramatic mountain scenery, so dramatic that we paused to enjoy it.

A huge, azure blue, *Minerva* convertible limousine - built about 1931 - powered majestically into view and came to a purring halt beside us. A white-uniformed chauffeur, complete with silver peaked cap, jodhpurs, polished leather boots and Italianate looks, skipped nimbly from the running board, smiled radiantly, and saluted.

"Holy shit!"

"Hardly the moment for well chosen sentiment, Thomas!" I looked into the back of the gigantic car. Jo faced me, smiling through tears.

His face was bleared with fat, ravaged by self indulgence. The flesh of his cheeks hung in faded strips like sun-perished silk. He took a handkerchief from his nose and gave me a silly little wave. The chauffeur opened the rear door and the affected, lisping voice of my half-brother screeched theatrically from the gilded, veneered, brocaded, *eau de cologne* scented limousine interior.

It was as if Oscar Wilde had risen from the dead.

"Johnny! ...... *Johnny*! .... *Darling* brother! . . . I thought (he broke into a fresh flood of crocodile tears) . . . Forgive me! . . . Oh, fuck! (he dropped the handkerchief, the chauffeur zipped forward with a fresh one) . . . What a sod-awful welcome! . . . *Johnny*! . . . I thought, dear boy, that I should (he gave two great sobs) *never* see you again! After . . . what I *did to you*, over Arthur!" Inconsequentially, he waved a podgy forefinger at the car door. "I can't get out of the sodding thing, darling: I can't fucking *walk* these days! Bruno has to carry me everywhere, don't you, Sweetie?" He scratched at the Chauffeur's zipper, then blew him a spittle-laden kiss, adding, "You randy little Dago tart!". His fingers lingered round the chauffeur's lapels and tie. Momentarily he

63

seemed to have forgotten we were there. Petulantly, he jabbed the Italian away and looked me in the face. His eyes were sodden with the effect of drink and drugs.

"Bloody old Arthur! . . . I've suffered years of regret, Johnny. How . . . fucking . . . *stupid* we were! . . . *Years* of regret! . . . Like you, my darling, I trusted the horrible old Queen, . . *trusted* him, my darling! . . . (huge sobs) with *my life*! . . . I was his *only* little boy!" Without restraint he blubbered and slobbered so that snot drooled from his dangerously veined nose. Vaguely, he reached towards a walnut wood tray, grabbing, shakily, a heavy crystal tumbler brimmed with scotch. By the tumbler was a glass pill box shaped like Arthur's casket. The chauffeur bent down and took the glass from Jo's hand before it fell. He held the tumbler to his master's mouth. There was a noisy series of sucking sounds interspersed with gurgled pleasure. The travesty of babyhood.

Nothing about Jo had really changed. I remembered the time when he had been expelled from our terribly august public school - that I hated - for raping a young groundsman (who objected) and sleeping with the headmaster's daughter (who did not). I heard again my step-father's powerful voice, "Destiny, Jo, has a nasty corner in store for you!"

It seemed to me that Jo had arrived at his 'nasty corner' at last. This fat little wreck, got up in an oyster coloured tropical suit, the crimson silk waistcoat exquisitely embroidered with white and pink peonies, the natty tartan bow tie, the co-respondent shoes perfectly polished ... here was a man once so captivating, so winning .... always so false.

"The past is forgotten, Jo. I've come to find you, and here you are (I gestured towards the park, at the car, the replenished tumbler), living like Royalty!" I gave him a kiss on each cheek, which started him weeping again, slurring between sniffs and nose blowings, his breath foul.

"Always too good to me, Johnny! . . . Such a *lovely* man!" But his voice had already hardened. Clipped and spiteful, he added, "That was your *big* fault, brother-mine! Too *fucking* lovely all round!" He gazed over my shoulder, for the first time focussing on Thomas.

"Ooooooo! Who's the gorgeous laddie! Not one of ours, I hope?"

"He's English if that's what you mean."

"*Scrumptious!* What's it like with its pants round its ankles?"

"Thomas is my assistant, the job requires his pants to be kept up at all times!"

Jo became excited, like a child on a school outing, "Get into the car both of you! We'll have a slap-up lunch! Johnny, you can sit in the front and admire the scenery." He patted the brocade upholstery next to him. "You can sit by me, you *gorgeous* little tart! I'll show you some scenery! . . . Bruno! Bell cook. We'll be three for lunch!" Patting Thomas's left cheek, he gave out a lewd falsetto cackle, like a drag queen in a cheap night spot.

♠

Lunch never happened. It lay troubled by flies on a long table of rare hardwood that stood like a parked tank in the ivory panelled dining room of Jo's enormous, reinforced concrete mansion.

On arrival, we were shown into his "den", a reception room on the ground floor. A long range of elegant, steel-framed French windows gave onto a terrace that was separated from the park by Art Deco styled chromium railings. The outside temperature had soared into the nineties; in the den knife sharp, ice cold air blasted from a platoon of air conditioning grilles. Unbelievably, we sat round a fireplace piled with blazing logs.

Bruno carried Jo to a sofa, propped him with cushions and put a mink rug over his knees. Six kadets appeared from a service door in their smart, grey uniforms. They poured us drinks, attended to serving snacks, poked the fire and heaped it with more logs. Two of them lowered translucent sun blinds over the French windows, while their comrades wound down external awnings. All six kadets came and stood "at ease" behind our armchairs, three behind Thomas, three behind me. They were just too close for comfort; I could smell their soap.

Twenty minutes later Jo's charred, decapitated corpse had been chucked over the chromium railings, while his head roasted in the fire.

After finishing another full tumbler of whisky, the third we'd seen him sink, sufficient to put most people into a coma, Jo became garrulous, yattering Gay social tittle-tattle. I knew this was an act, I had seen it all before. His darting, black eyes did not deceive me. He must have realised no ice was being cut for he suddenly regained aplomb requesting Bruno to raise the tumbler.

Graciously, Jo proposed a toast, "To Happy Times; to our re-union, Johnny; to a buried hatchet." He turned his eyes to Thomas, smiling affectionately, "And here's to you, my boy; to your future; to your youth and your beauty," then he spoilt it all, ". . . and to your gorgeous little arsehole!"

"What do you do here, Jo?"

"I am the director, Thomas, of Atlas One. The Big *Chief*, my darling boy." I glanced at Thomas: did this cue Kyla's mysterious *'Then you come from Four. I come from One.'*?

"What is Atlas One?"

"Where they make these . . ." he gestured towards the Kadets with a lordly sweep of his hand. "Thousands of them, Johnny. All over the place, aren't you, you handsome hawks?" He belched, uglier in mood, "Hasn't your dirty spy work cottoned-on, Johnny darling? . . . Not doing too well at the game are you, brother?" His face suddenly contorted with thespian rage: "You and your precious fucking bookstall! *Pah*! Don't you fucking try to con me. Nor you, *Tommykins*, you shit-mouthed, fucking hero of some *fucking* stupid Boys

Own *fucking* Paper! . . . Little cunt!" He began to scream obscene abuse. Bruno and the Kadets remained motionless. The tirade lasted for sixty seconds then he calmed down. "Yes, my dear, it was me they invited to Arthur's sodding funeral, not *you*. Me! Only I knew they wanted to kill me, so I (he let out a falsetto snigger) changed the address on the envelope! . . . *Easy*, Luvvy!" He leered at Thomas, "Easy, when you know how, you smooth little cock-sucker!" He screamed at Bruno to fill his glass, agitating both feet on the sofa cushions like a spoilt child.

"Who was coming to the Hôtel Bradford?"

"*Ooooooo*, Johnny!" He waggled a finger archly, "*Nosy*!" Bruno held the glass to his mouth while he sucked at it. He was given two capsules.

"As a treat, I'll tell you." There was a pause, he made a baby noise and his eyes clouded over. He appeared to be paralyzed, propped immobile on the sofa like a stringless puppet. Bruno walked calmly over to us, explaining in broken English, "Two minute. He will be OK in two minute." He touched his lips with a forefinger, murmuring, "No speak. He see everything, he hear everything."

After exactly two minutes Jo recovered completely, and was affable as if nothing had happened. It was time for business, "You have five discs in a floor safe, Jo." The statement appeared to knock him off balance. He began to weep, breaking wind moistly and hugely. I felt Thomas's embarrassment and signed with my hand that he must control himself. Bruno snatched the glass from Jo's shaky grip and began to remove the mink rug but was motioned away. "*Do* overlook my social indiscretions, Johnny darling. A mere technicality of the substance that we are in process of adjusting. I wear a nappy."

"I don't care if you wear a wet suit! I have come for those disks, Jo, and you're bloody lucky I'm not going to act on the first part of my - so-called - orders."

He sniggered, then indicated a framed watercolour above a display cabinet containing a collection of Moroccan swords. "Where's that, Johnny?" We went over to inspect the picture, the Kadets followed, surrounding us in a soap smelling crescent. I recognised the location at once.

"The Salt Mine Director's house."

Thomas eyed me, "What?"

"The scene of our grand squabble, Tommy, dear! Johnny, Arthur and me. *Way* in the past. You are far, *far* too young to know about *that* dark age, my darling boy. Shall we tell Baby the story, Johnny?"

"If you like." Anything to keep his mind alert.

"During one of our continental tours, posing as "Uncle Arthur" and "Nephew Jo", Arthur was so captivated by the Swiss countryside around the town of Aigle that he rented for the Summer a charming house in the mountains that looked across a plunging valley to the ski resort of Leysin. The house had

66

been built as far back as 1755 for the director of the salt mine, below in the mountainside. The bathrooms were about the same period. *Indescribable*! In this love nest I set to work on Arthur. I was determined to oust Johnny from their book business, and take over myself. Not bad for a sprite of seventeen, wouldn't you agree, Tommy my peach?"

"You succeeded, Jo! You turned Arthur against me."

"We had that fatal row on the little mountain train that climbs to Les Diablerets."

"An uncontrolled, drunken brawl, Jo. I am ashamed to remember my part in it."

"Things were said that could never be unsaid, Thomas dear. When we got off the train it was the end of the line for Johnny."

"Next day I resigned my directorship and removed myself from Arthur's circle."

"Did you enjoy that sad little tale, Tommy?"

"You and Arthur were a couple of shits!"

"*Oomph*! . . . What a tongue it has, Johnny!"

I was fed-up now, I could see he was caffling. I rapped, "The disks, Jo. They're in a floor safe. Where is it and what's the combination?" He smiled oddly, shivered, and made an unearthly growl deep in his throat. Looking across the room at him, a cold certainty occurred to me that he was about to commit suicide. I could have walked over to the sofa and prevented him: but I stood still with Thomas by the cabinet.

"Before I let you know, Johnny dear, I'll pour this decanter of brandy over my head and set fire to myself." He took a full decanter from a bottle-laden trolley, held it vertically over his head and emptied the contents onto his head and down his front. The kadets pinned Thomas and myself to the cabinet while Jo let the empty decanter smash on the floor, asking Bruno politely for his lighter. After two attempts he set himself on fire. We saw him, screaming in agony, engulfed in blue flames like a human Christmas pudding. Bruno rushed towards us, flung the kadets out of his way, kicked-in the glazed doors of the display cabinet with a shimmering toe cap, and chose, not without momentary care, a beautiful Moroccan sword. He went over to Jo's blackening shape and waited while the kadets forced us to face the sofa.

Bruno removed his jacket, tie and shirt, laying them over the back of a Charles Eames chair with finicky concern. He stood above Jo's smouldering body, his bared torso a fine-etched cartography of anatomical perfection, the discus-shaped nipples deep lilac set in bronze. He swayed back his arms, the sword out-bound. He posed magnificently for a second then brought the sword round in a sumptuous, whistling arc.

A jet of boiling, brownish gore spewed from Jo's neck towards the ceiling as his head, sliced clean away, bounced over an occasional table idly strewn with recent copies of Vogue.

Bruno cast the sword to one side, came forward, took Jo's head by its retching jaw and slung it into the blazing log fire. Shooting us a defiant stare, legs astride, virile as the star of some ancient silent movie, he pronounced: "*La cosa è fatta!*". Slapping the flat of one hand on his robust chest, he declaimed, "*Io! . . . Sono guadagno la mia **libertà**!*" He beamed us a beautiful smile, "The combination of the safe, Signori, *è il compleanno di Signor Moreau!*".

Thomas fainted.

♠

The melodrama of Jo's demise got me pursed-lipped. Did everything in this weird place have to be done so self-indulgently? I was attending to Thomas when one of the kadets started shouting in their strange language, pointing to the open double doors through which Bruno had vanished seconds before.

Kyla and Panno entered, splendidly in command. They each carried an automatic firearm, American at first glance. A kadet lead them to where Jo's corpse lay. Kyla budged the grotesque lump with the muzzle of his gun, like a loss adjuster inspecting a fire damaged sack. Without giving the body a second glance he rapped out an order, then - extravagantly in my view - blasted out a window lock with a burst of automatic fire. Having demonstrated his authority, he turned gracefully to survey the room, his superb classical features flecked with disdain. It was like having the Apollo Belvedere to tea.

The first thing Kyla saw was Thomas, inert on the floor, white as a sheet. Bellowing outlandishly, the Kadet Commander bounded over and knelt at Thomas's side, cradling the boy's head in his arms, weeping hysterically. As there was no response, Kyla covered Thomas's face with kisses.

"He has only fainted, Kyla!" My terseness produced a paroxysm of tears. Sounding like an exasperated Mathematics master, I added, "He is not dead, Kyla. He will recover in a moment! Why don't you get him a glass of water?" It was no use, it might as well have been Achilles mourning the dead Patroclus. Panno, unconcerned, tapped me on the shoulder. I looked up, "We will go to the safe, Monsieur."

While the junior kadets busied themselves with mops and disinfectant, Panno led me down a dreary marble-lined passage where all the doors were done in a bitter chocolate veneer. Panno opened one of these doors and we entered what must have been Jo's study. The huge, featureless room had a dusty desk, some chairs and, sentinel in each corner, four hideous chromium-plated standard lamps each with five frosted glass globes the colour of boiled cabbage.

Panno grabbed a tarnished silver cigarette box from Jo's desk, flipped open the lid and turned it upside down. Two hundred handmade Turkish cigarettes showered to the floor. They were mummy dry. He took a tiny key from a compartment concealed in the bottom of the box and opened a wall cupboard behind the desk. Here were a dozen empty bottles of whisky, a set of dirty glass tumblers and a lead crystal ice bucket engraved with, "COCK-Tail Time". He placed these items on the desk.

Built into the back of the cupboard was a circular dial exactly like the ones on old telephones. "The combination, please Monsieur."

Arthur's birthday! . . . My mind went blank. I dried.

"I can't remember the bloody date!"

"He was very old Monsieur."

"That's not quite the same thing, Panno." I sat down at the desk, letting my eyes wander over the objects there. "September the eleventh, Nineteen-four!"

Panno turned the dial with painful deliberation as I prompted, "09...11...1904".

We heard a muffled clunk and felt through the floor the substantial vibration of heavy equipment shifting somewhere below us. In front of Jo's desk an extensive section of brown marble separated from the rest and slowly rose. A robust, riveted steel frame emerged and stopped rising when the floor section almost touched the ceiling. In the frame rested an antique safe taller than a man. On the door was imposingly cast, *Sir W. G. Armstrong, Whitworth & Co. Ltd., Elswick, Newcastle-on-Tyne, ENGLAND, 1891*. It had a key operated lock and a brass wheel-turn release. Cautiously, I stepped onto the steel platform. A pencilled note was stuck to the release wheel with a strip of sooty masking tape: *Key in cleaner's room, under sink.*

"Where is the cleaner's room, Panno?" He took me to the end of the corridor, the room was beneath a staircase. I immediately found an ornate brass key in an empty can of floor polish under a salt-glazed Belfast sink.

We opened the safe. Nine out of the ten shelves inside were empty. On the third shelf down was a scruffy plastic bag from a well known chain of liquor stores.

Panno peeped warily over my shoulder, "Shall I take it out, Monsieur?"

"Please, Panno." He edged past me, took the bag and held it open for my inspection. Inside were five, dusty, low quality CDs, carelessly labelled 1 to 5 with a blue marker pen. No titles, no dates: they could have been anything. There was also an unstamped envelope marked, "Jo". In it was a three page, handwritten letter, undated, no address, signed, "Uncle Arthur".

The script was not in Arthur's hand.

"Close the safe, Panno." As soon as he turned the key there was a click and we stepped clear as the device sank back into the floor leaving a barely perceptible brass joint.

Kyla arrived with a rosy faced Thomas. "I'm sorry, Johnny. It was all so horrible. The choice was throwing-up or blacking-out."

"You chose well. You'd better get tough fast, Mate. There's probably worse to come." I pointed to the disks and the envelope, "The booty." He gazed at the five soiled CDs, then picked up the letter with thumb and forefinger. "We've been conned, Johnny. This is junk."

"Leave Frederick to decide on that one. We had better get back to Marrakech and have this lot flown to London." Thomas sat on the edge of the desk, uncorked one of the whisky bottles and sniffed at the top, "We came all this way for nothing, Johnny."

"Did we?" He pouted, glaring resentfully at the whisky bottle. Kyla began to fidget by the door, coughing discretely for attention.

"What is it, Kyla?"

"Come with us."

♠

Outside, the sun's brilliance made us shade our eyes. We jumped into the back of Kyla's open jeep, Panno in front. We roared past the garish carpet gardens lining the pink concrete driveway of Jo's residence and shot through his movie studio gateway. Panno shouted, "We are going up a mountain track, it is not far, but you must hold tight, there are stones!" As he finished this warning, Kyla swerved off the wide road, now lined with powerful arc lamps, and tore down a gravelled track towards a side gate. This opened automatically and we sped up a steep slope, at one point bumpily crossing a single track railroad.

"Does that go to Marrakech?"

Kyla laughed, "No, Thomas. It goes to a food and clothing depot." A microwave mast came into view. We were high up now, way above Jo's villa that showed like a white tile in its colourful park. The track appeared to terminate at a low building next to the mast, but Kyla swerved to the right and shot up a ribbon-thin road hacked into the side of a mountain gorge.

"Jesus, Gov'ner! Does he want to kill us?"

"Shut your eyes!" Suddenly there was a wide platform of smooth rock where the jeep came to a screeching halt. Shakily, we clambered out of the back and followed the kadets towards some sort of observation post.

"How high are we?"

"Above Jo's place? I should say about fifteen hundred feet, possibly more. That's not counting the climb from Marrakech."

"Between five and seven hundred meters?"

"High *enough*, Thomas."

We stepped inside the incongruous structure. It was elegantly robust, an elongated octagon with a flat concrete roof supported on circular columns of hammer dressed granite. The soffit of the roof was covered in gold mosaic. Incised into the polished basalt floor were the letters, W M D O.

A quaint seaside telescope was bolted to a raised step below the central, unglazed observation window. There were basalt benches, and in the centre of the floor stood a beautiful octagonal table, its polished top sparkling with veins of quartz stuffed with amethyst. A cast bronze plate was set into the top of the table indicating compass points, the names of local mountains, and the Worlds capital cities.

By 'London' and 'Paris' two compass lines pointed to 'Yonroche' and 'St-Christophe'. Discretely pulling Thomas to the table by his shirt cuff I indicated these names, then turned to Kyla, "Why is this palatial seaside kiosk accessed by a track a mule would jib at?"

"Monsieur Moreau was afraid of heights. The road was never finished."

"Monsieur Moreau, Kyla, couldn't climb a pair of step ladders without a doctor having to be called. So why, if this place is never used, is it kept in immaculate condition?" The kadets eyed me sheepishly, like little boys caught stealing apples in an orchard. "Well, gentlemen? ... Why? Who is brought here, and to see *what*?"

"Look down, please."

As Kyla bid, we leant on the wide marble balustrade of the central opening and stared like eagles over an amphitheatre of soaring, icy peaks. About seven hundred meters below us was a plateau: and there we saw it.

"For Heaven's sake! ... What on earth is *that*?"

"Atlas One. Where Panno and I were born and have our home."

The size of the complex took our breath away. Roughly estimated, a sixteen hectare area of virgin mountainscape had been levelled, though this word is inadequate; *dead flat* gives the true picture. How and at what cost this had been achieved defied the imagination. On this artificial plateau sat four gigantic, white concrete ziggurats. They were identical and had a Nineteen-Thirties open air swimming pool look.

From ground to apex I assessed each ziggurat to be about a hundred meters high, not less than three hundred feet. From the top superstructure, flues and cooling towers smoked and steamed. Below, level by level, arranged like the decks of a cruise liner, were wide terraces. A band of fenestration ran round these decks while vast sand-coloured courts were grouped round each ziggurat to form a perfect pattern from above.

"The place is swarming with small boys and youths." Thomas turned the telescope, "There are lines of beds on the top deck."

"Beds?"

"Cots, Gov'ner. With babies. Let me focus this thing . . . Yes, they're babies . . . with blokes like Kyla and Panno walking round in white coats."

"As in a soap powder commercial?"

"In one, Gov'ner."

"What are the black-framed windows at ground level, they look like

Japanese screens from here."

"They're curtain walls I think. Easily two floors high. The glass is reflective, I can't see what's going on inside."

Kyla chirped-up, "That is where the older kadets live, Monsieur. *Our* home. There is a school and dormitories and . . . umm . . ." he became vague.

"And what, Kyla?"

"The things we need."

"The courts are massive, Johnny, full of kadets and trucks, like military parade grounds." He beckoned Kyla to his side, pointing, "Are those spaces where you train?" Kyla linked his arm round Thomas's waist. "When we are old enough, Thomas, we go outside. The little kadets are raised on the terraces, on levels one to three."

"Let me tell them." Panno sat on a basalt bench and crossed his arms; he was different from Kyla, a different character, more amenable, less equivocal.

"The top deck, Monsieur …"

"I think it's time you both called me Johnny, as we seem to be teaming-up."

"Johnny … (he smiled like a normal young man pleased to be permitted a privilege) the top deck is always called Level One. This is where the kadets are created, as we grow we progress down the decks to Levels Two, Three, Four and Five. Four and Five, as Kyla told Thomas, are where the grown kadets live, they have the same floor area."

"So the system starts with Birth at the top, then a progression down to ground level, year by year, as the Kadets grow to maturity?" I mused, gazing at the four ziggurats, "Is this a cloning system?"

"No. We are born from slave wombs."

"Women giving natural childbirth?"

"No. It is a cycle."

"That doesn't tell me much, Panno." He looked away, I decided to stop questioning.

"Kyla, what are the square blocks at each side of the courtyards?"

"They contain pools and gymnasia, senior schools, clinics . . . the administration offices . . . and a sanatorium."

"And the same thing goes on in the four buildings?"

"Yes. In each building we are born in a dual cycle that repeats itself every seven years. Every Home Kamp has four dual cycles continuing simultaneously."

"So that was why you asked me if I was in the first cycle, back at the Villa Aubazine."

"Yes, Thomas, when I thought you were a kadet." Kyla nibbled Thomas's ear.

"*Every* Home Kamp? … Are there more?"

72

"All over the world, Johnny."

"What's below ground, Panno?" My question produced another wriggling silence.

"Incinerators . . . I think."

"You *think*, Panno! You are a senior Kadet, surely you know what goes on in a Home Kamp, as you call them." I sat on the basalt bench next to Panno immersed in thought. What the hell was going on? Why should anybody create a surreal complex called Atlas One and fill it with strange children and identical youths? There must be a greater purpose: but what? Kyla and Panno weren't going to tell us. It began to dawn on me that they did not know the answers to my questions. No wonder Jo committed suicide: he knew. As for Jayne Blaisedale, she was a living lie.

"Somebody has designed that lot. Somebody of technical genius."

"Somebody on the wrong side of the line, Gov'ner. Somebody criminal."

"Somebody in Europe or America, Thomas. Somebody whiter-than-white."

Thomas gazed through the telescope, Kyla's arm round his waist. Panno sat dejectedly next to me on the bench. Atlas One shimmered in the Moroccan sun. I decided to try a last shot, "What do you mean, Kyla, when you say that you were *created* in that lot?"

"We were made there. We are "U" Kadets, "Unique". We are made singly, so we are commanders. There are "J" Kadets. This morning you saw them serving Monsieur Jo."

" 'J?'"

"Jumelle. They are made two at a time, they do not command, they are for daily tasks and killing squads, . . . agents of social corruption, . . . and . . ." Panno chipped-in, "Social Demoralization Units."

"Jumelle is French for twins, Gov'ner."

"I'm well aware of that, Thomas!" I fixed Kyla with an eagle eye, "So what is your role as a "U" Kadet, apart from being a commander?" Kyla took his arm from Thomas's waist and reeled-off his lines, itemising each 'role' on his fingers. "We are made for administrative corruption and infiltration into Old Societies at levels of political executive control, management sectors of industry, commerce, and the Establishment." He beamed at me like the swat who has learnt his lines.

"By *Establishment*, Kyla, you mean The Crown, the Ruling Class, the Church and the Army? King, Queen, Knights, Bishops and Rooks?" My irony floored them, both kadets stared at me apprehensively. Standing up, I flung my hand in the direction of the complex. "Can we visit it?"

"No. They will kill you."

"*Who* will kill us, Panno? Come on! You said it. . . . *Who* will kill us?"

"There is a . . ." He paused, his mouth began to tremble.

"*What* is there? Come on, Panno, say it! *What* is there?"

"Nobody knows, Johnny. If you tell people about Atlas One nobody will believe you."

"Balls, Kyla! You lot swarm round Marrakech in full public view. What about Paris and Yonroche?" I took a squint down the telescope, bawling, "Are you telling us nobody knows about *that*? It's the size of ten thousand football pitches! Are you telling us that it just grew? Like a mushroom? And what about the construction? I suppose a bloke with a spade did it, and they asked him not to tell anyone! There must be well over two million cubic meters of poured concrete in those ziggurats alone. That's just the concrete, never mind the windows and doors, the pipes and cables . . . the rest of the junk! Where did it all come from, Kyla? Who put it all together? The local village contractor with a donkey and cart? . . . Look round to where we have just come from. A gigantic microwave mast! Somebody is in regular contact with Atlas One."

"What about satellites, Johnny?"

"Good point, Thomas! Satellites monitor everything on the surface of the Earth, did you know that, gentlemen? Never mind a bloody satellite, you could see that bugger from . . . *Mars* ... without specs on! . . . Well? . . . Where does the buck stop, boys?"

But they only regarded me with confused eyes.

"Arthur Moreau. You were both at his funeral. You tell me that Arthur had to do with *that*? . . . Do you know that I was once an intimate friend of his: *do* you?" Silence, bowed heads, tears began to trickle down Panno's cheeks, dripping pathetically one by one onto the stately marble floor. Kyla sat by him, looking up at me defensively, taking his comrade's hands in his own. Castor and Pollux.

Moved, I spoke to them gently, "Arthur knew nothing about things like Atlas One. He was a second hand book dealer, boys. It is impossible that Arthur was involved with that . . . *nightmare*."

"You're upsetting them, Johnny. If you ask me Kyla and Panno are victims. They blindly follow a set of rules like machines. We have to find the team that cooked Atlas One up; they're the poison. My guess is that they will be masquerading as responsible citizens: probably people with distinguished careers, even titles."

"You mean, 'the great and the good', like your father?"

"Yeah! Above reproach. That's my hunch."

"Keep thinking, you're inspiring me."

"I think we should get back to Marrakech, does that inspire you, Gov'ner?" Thomas laid a comforting hand on Panno's shoulder, "Cheer up, Mate, you're too old to cry."

"I am seven years old."

I looked across at Thomas, "What did he say?"

74

"That he's seven years old. You can't be! You're my age. Twenty or twenty-one."

"We grow quickly." There was a silence. The question of accelerated growth rate, let alone accelerated mental development, was hardly a topic for discussion two thousand meters above sea level in a five star bus shelter.

"Take us back to the gate, please."

They took us to the car. We stood by the Mercedes while the Kadets, French style, gave us a kiss on both cheeks. Kyla made a last appeal, "Take us with you!"

"You need drugs to survive, don't you? Injections and capsules?"

"Yes."

"We don't have those, Kyla. If we take you both with us, you will die, am I right?" They admitted as much, explaining that without drugs, in hours, they would go into a coma and die almost immediately.

"Yours is an impossible request. However, I promise we will try to find a way of keeping you alive."

"It will work, Johnny. We are not like the other kadets, Panno and me."

"Why is that?"

"We are the special creation of Franz Von Stotz."

♠

Thomas was tired, I drove. In just over an hour we were approaching the outskirts of Marrakech. Along the way we had been amicably arguing the million dollar question: why didn't anyone know about Atlas One? Why didn't Frederick know?

"If you can't trust Fred, Thomas, you can't trust anybody!" Thomas was fired-up with a young man's indignation, "But he *must* know, Johnny! They told us these Kamps are everywhere. Everybody must know."

"We don't."

"Then we're stupid!"

"Maybe what we're seeing doesn't exist. Did you think of that?"

"Have you gone crazy, Gov'ner, like your half-brother?"

"Jo wasn't crazy, just dipsomaniac." I laughed, despite myself. "Odd, isn't it? I don't feel sadness or regret watching him burn to death. Maybe later. This business is so crazy, you get used to hideous events going on in front of your eyes."

"What did Fred say about the labyrinth?"

" 'Wracked by frustration we wend our way in a labyrinth of fantastical reality. . . . the more we make sense of one part the less we understand of another.' "

"That dump was no fantasy, Johnny, it was right there below us. Hey,

75

look out! There's a cop ahead, he's waving you down."

"Shit! A speeding fine is not what we need." I opened my window to hear a courteous Moroccan police officer telling us there had been a serious accident. We must take a diversion into Marrakech, entering the city from the north. Saluting, he added that the route was well signed.

"It could be a trap, Gov'ner."

"Organised by Jayne? I shouldn't think so. The police know who owns this car." After ten minutes we arrived in north Marrakech. I turned south off the Route des Remparts into the Quartier des Tanneurs. Almost immediately we drove into a crowd of locals. They blocked the road and I had to pull up.

"What's going on?"

"Some sort of row by the look of it." We were in the Medina, by one of the popular open air restaurant areas. About fifty men had gathered round a table, there was a lot of bellowing and gesticulating. The crowd jostled round the car, their buttocks blocking our view.

"I'll settle this, Thomas. Lock your door." I was forcing open the driver's door, when two hustled tourists, a man and a woman, where pushed across the bonnet.

"Get ready to help the pair into the back if I can get them free." I waded to the bonnet. The couple were American, in their mid-sixties, wiry, prosperous. As I reached them they managed to stand up, angry, shaken. The man faced a big, blazing Moroccan whose Arabic was thick with insults. I gathered the problem was about money. The couple had paid short for their meal, a tattered bank note was being waved in front of the husband's nose.

He remained calm and diplomatic. This was not the case with his wife who lashed out with her hands, telling everybody exactly what she thought of them in a sassy Mid-West accent. I judged it would not be long before the police arrived. That, we had to avoid.

Pinning the young Arab against the car, I looked into his furious eyes and told him in blunt French to calm down. I brandished my wallet and stuffed the equivalent of a fifty dollar bill into the breast pocket of his jallabia, then told him in street Arabic what he could do with himself.

Within twenty seconds there wasn't a local to be seen and I turned courteously to the Americans, "They get excited. They don't mean any harm."

"They cheated my husband over the price of our meal!"

"It's over now, forgotten. You'd be wise not to come here again during your stay."

"We move to Paris tomorrow. To civilization!"

"Can I give you a lift to your hotel?" The husband beamed me a bland smile.

"Gladly. We're kinda shot-up by that crowd. Sir, you sure got us out of one hell of a mess." Thomas came over to us. "Is this your son?"

"My secretary, I deal in rare books." As we got into the car I noticed that the woman would not stop staring at me with a strange, piercing expression, as if she knew me but could not place me. She was small, agile, and smart. Her beautifully cut, expensive, black leather jacket went well with a black and white striped blouse. She re-adjusted a black felt beret to sit on her head at a pert angle. Her silver earrings, like twists of lemon rind, were particularly striking. Unlike many women past middle age who decide to dress with flair, the lady knew exactly what to wear and how to wear it.

"Where to?"

"We're at the Mamounia." It was not far, and we talked politely as I drove.

"Say, Nina, we ought to invite these gentleman to join us for dinner tonight." His wife agreed. "You two fixed-up this evening?"

The invitation, though kind, was embarrassing. We would have to waste an entire evening sticking to bland pleasantries when there were vital decisions to make. I pulled up on the Mamounia forecourt. A uniformed doorman immediately opened the back door to let the couple out. It was a difficult moment. I had to think of a foolproof excuse.

"It's a delightful offer. Unfortunately we have a meeting with a member of the Royal Family, it is bound to go on very late and we cannot leave until he lets us go. I do hope you will both understand."

"Sure. It's a shame." The husband shook hands with me through the car window, "I guess it's goodbye, but thank you so much for assisting us back there." I put the window up and released the hand brake, we moved forward, an attendant cleared the way.

"You're a smoothie, Gov'ner! I couldn't have lied like that." I stopped at a red light by the hotel exit. After a second it changed to green.

"Knowing how to put people off politely comes with age, Thomas." The car turned into the highway. I pressed my foot gently on the accelerator. "I don't know about you, Mate, but I'm ready for a drink. That was one hell of a day."

There was a terrific banging on the trunk, a voice screamed, "Stop! ... Hey, *Stop*!"

"It's the American woman, Johnny."

"Bugger! I hope she's not going to be a bore." I pulled up, cars behind us began hooting. I let the window down, the woman poked her face into the gap, one of her earrings chinked against the frame ...

"You're Mister Dove!"

PART III

A South London suburb, Greenwich High Street close by, half past eight in the morning. In Claridge Avenue shabby houses - once desirable - bulge bulky bay windows encrusted with flaked paint. Front doors have panels fitted with leaded lights of poison-bottle blue. Red brick walls contrast colours of drab cream, pea green and chocolate brown. Lanky Plane trees grow from cracked sidewalks, shifty cats prowl past patchy privet hedges, constipated dogs tremble with the effort to crap orange and vermilion turds.

At spruced-up Number Fifty-Two - "*Balacree*" - Alice Kingston sits in the back parlour by an open patio door. She gazes at the garden, a welcome haven of shrubs and perennials. An ancient pear tree, reminiscent of the Tudor manor that once stood on the site, is in full blossom. Alice takes a sip of Ty-Phoo tea. Her 'Mint Imperial' earrings are bright yellow like the Festival of Britain teacup she holds. Her hairstyle, immaculate, is forty years out of date.

Trained for special combat missions, Alice is an expert with firearms, and a crack shot. She is on the payroll of Sir Frederick Appleby.

Charley Kingston, chain smoking in his shirt sleeves, reads The Daily Mail nearby. "The Government's resigned again, luv. Last night. They was hauled from their seats. Took away in busses. I'll bet His Nibs done it."

"Frederick has been planning the coup for months, dear. No loss to the Nation. They were third-raters, Charley! Not a good apple amongst them. Fred can't understand how they got as far as they did." Despite her refined diction Alice's Catford accent is unmistakable.

"Remember when they was all took off the first time, that Socialist lot? Army trucks it was then. Gor-blimey! I won't forget their faces on the telly when the troops 'auled 'em into two-ton trucks. Ruddy MPs! Smarmy, cheatin' swine. That ruddy Vera Brading, you should have heard the old cow! Thought the sun shone art of 'er ruddy arse, the old bitch! Her *language* when that sergeant give her a shove over the tailgate. . . . *Laugh*? We fell off our chairs down the Legion." A roll of ash dropped from the cigarette lodged in Charley's lips.

"*Charley*! All over my clean cloth!"

"Did you hear the buzzer, luv?" Alice gets to her feet immediately and briskly walks across the room, "I have a feeling it will be connected with Morocco."

"He always contacts you on a lovely day."

"I know, luv; it's a shame when we'd planned to go out, but duty comes first. I'll have to hurry, he'll be ever so impatient if I don't." Transforming herself from a bosomy, blue-rinsed pensioner into a member of Sir Frederick's élite, Alice puts the cup and saucer on a sideboard by the framed photograph of their son killed while serving in Northern Ireland and goes into the hall.

In the cleaning cupboard under the stairs Alice takes a tin of lavender polish from a shelf and touches the underside with the first three fingers of her left hand. A meter thick wall of hardened steel, disguised by shelving stacked with jam jars, scrubbing brushes and household soap, swings open on bomb resistant hinges.

Alice goes down a flight of steel steps into a lead-lined vestibule. An electronic eye understands her presence, an air supply is activated, an elevator door slides open. She descends two hundred meters below Claridge Avenue, steps onto a platform, and into an automatic train. Ninety seconds later she walks into an operations room a kilometre below the River Thames. A smartly uniformed young woman ushers Alice to a seat facing a wall-mounted screen.

"Sir Frederick has been waiting for ten minutes, Alice!"

"He'll be fine, Libby. You know him by now." Alice settles herself cosily in the chair and passes her left palm over a sensor. The screen flickers into play. Frederick is shown glancing impatiently at the dial of the jasper and gilt Napoleonic clock on his desk.

"There you are, Alice! How's life at Number fifty-two, my dear? Pear tree in blossom?"

"A picture this year, Fred. We were thinking of a trip to Rye today, dear, but I've one of my little premonitions that you're going to spoil our fun."

"Absolutely, Alice. I need you to look after two Americans today. Usual routine. They have travelled from Marrakesh into RAF Canterbury, they are resting now at VIP Margate. They have a diplomatic bag containing objects picked up by Debrett and the boy. When you have escorted the couple to me, take the bag to Lab Thirteen."

"Car and driver?"

"Terence Gatcombe is on his way to Claridge Avenue now. Arriving at nine forty-five hours." Alice looks pleased, Terence is her nephew, a fine young man.

"If you are lucky, Alice, he will bring you one of Vera's Dundee cakes."

"We'll have a slice with our tea, Fred. Details of the Americans?"

"Jeff and Nina Burdet, resident at Lake Lodge, Harriet Park, Edina, Minneapolis. She is a trained nurse, born Nina Karl of Duluth, Lake Superior, Minnesota. Fluent in German, good health, no peculiarities. He was raised in Spring Park, Lake Minnetonka, Minnesota. He is a retired corporate lawyer with important FBI, CBI and Pentagon connections. He is aged sixty-five, good health, no peculiarities. Debrett has spoken with me during the night. The Americans were contacted at their Minneapolis home by code name Grey. They were given a riddle and information concerning a Doctor Tonio Friedemann. They were requested to find code name Dove in Marrakech. By a miracle they did. I require you to check that the Burdets are genuine."

"Where do I bring them?"

"My office. No need for extra vigilance. They are a down-to-earth couple, anything too dramatic will put them off."

"You want them to join the team, Fred?"

"Yes, I do. Prepare them, please." Fred grins, adjusting the grey silk square in his jacket breast pocket to sign the meeting has terminated: the screen goes blank.

Back at home with Charley, Alice changes into a smart navy-blue two-piece then brews a pot of tea.

"Rye's off, dear."

"Not to worry, luv. I'll go down the club and have a beer with Harry Soak."

♠

"Mr and Mrs Burdet?" Nina and Jeff got up from a leather sofa. A powerful young man in a chauffeur's uniform opened the door to let a smartly dressed, portly woman into the room. The woman seemed military to Jeff.

"That's us." They smiled sociably, shaking hands politely.

"I'm Alice Kingston and this is Terry who will be your driver during your stay in the United Kingdom. Please call me Alice." She beamed, pointing a white gloved forefinger towards the bullet proof picture windows. "You've brought the sun with you! I hope they gave you a good English breakfast?"

Jeff chose a similarly neutral line of approach, "It was a sumptuous breakfast, Alice. I guess we are both well rested too. They let us sleep when we got to this place. It's as good as the Mamounia hotel. We had quite an adventure in Marrakech, we were aching for sleep."

Nina fixed Alice with a glare, "Where exactly *are* we?"

"You're in Kent, at a seaside resort called Margate, in what we call a Strategic Security Compound." Alice fished about in her crocodile skin handbag for her ID card.

"Some sort'a detention centre?"

"That only happens in America, Mrs Burdet. This is part of a security routine controlled exclusively by Sir Frederick Appleby, the person you will meet today in London." Alice patted Nina's arm reassuringly. "Terry has put your things in the car, including the diplomatic bag you brought from Morocco. Please follow me."

"Suppose we don't want to follow you?"

"You are both as free as air, Mrs. Burdet."

♠

Terry drove towards Canterbury. Nina and Jeff sat in the back of the Jaguar, Alice in the front. Terry was as much a part of the conversation as his superiors.

"Alice, Nina and I aim get an accurate picture of a confusing series of events."

"An understatement, Jeff!"

"We figured from von Stotz that his organisation is some kind of terrorist ring."

"That is how the situation may appear from the outside, Mr Burdet. In reality, the problem is more complex. Moreau was not a terrorist. Sir Frederick will tell you that we are not at war with terrorism. He insists that we cannot wage war on an abstract term."

"You British consider the term 'terrorism' nothing more than abstract terminology? An exercise in semantics?"

"Yes, though your summary would be too intellectual for most British people, Mr Burdet. We British are lead by the gutter press. In Sir Frederick's eyes making war on terrorism is nothing less than political hypocrisy. For Frederick, terrorism does not exist."

"But terrorists exist, surely Sir Frederick must agree with that."

"Genocide exists, Mrs Burdett. Genocide is the fatal flaw of an ideal race. Politicians are the factors of that flaw."

Terry swung the car into Canterbury Cathedral close.

"Hey! Now look at that tower! Is that the cathedral of Canterbury?"

"It is. Everything you see there is the direct result of political hypocrisy."

♠

In Fred's office Jeff came straight to the point.

"Why, Sir Frederick, are we here?"

"You are here because I am certain you can be useful to me. You are not bound to co-operate if you do not wish to do so."

"We have come a long way, Sir Frederick. We are two innocent Americans - citizens of Minneapolis - who appear to have gotten caught in an astonishing mystery. If we can help you, sure, we'll do that. But . . ." Jeff trailed into silence. Nina shrugged her shoulders, "How *can* we help? Espionage is *not* our style. I think you should know that first-off."

"Espionage is nobody's style, Mrs Burdet, as you so succinctly put it. *Style* is reserved for heroes. Where I delve there is no style." Frederick took a report from one of his secretaries, glanced at the cover, placed the item carefully on his desk, then asked a footman to pour everyone present a glass of cognac from a gilt-bronze ewer.

"I am concerned with evil. My people deal with tawdry mediocrity, Mrs Burdet. The biggest fish in the smallest ponds interest my team. Respectable scaffolding of the Establishment. School Governors, local doctors, provincial accountants, small time book keepers, half-baked landscape architects and estate agents, dirty little property developers with their expensive motor cars … bent town councillors. These are my theme: the lowest of the low. Do you know what they all have in common, Mr. Burdet?"

"They all appear to be so darned respectable, Sir Frederick."

"Exactly, my dear fellow! Whitened sepulchres! Nobody would believe you if you even hinted at the murky depths of their affairs."

"Moreau was …"

"Moreau was a master of the game. Franz von Stotz, the man who came to your home that evening and told you his strange tale is what we have termed the 'American with a German accent'. I have known about this person for years, but only by that simple five-word short form. Now, thanks to you, we have a clearer picture."

"What do you suspect Moreau's organisation is planning?"

"Planning? They are three parts there. Observe the political administration of Britain. Corrupt, moribund, mendacious, cunning … second rate. Dizzy with a vision of power that - in reality - does not exist. Did you know I dissolved the British Parliament last night?"

"I told them in the car, Fred."

"Well done, Alice. By the way, have our bright young things cracked those five disks and that syringe the boy got hold off?"

"They've only been at it two hours, Sir!"

"Be a love and pop down to the lab. Kick Declan's arse if you have to. The young man is too bright for his own good. Tell him I want *results*, not a bloody thesis!"

When Alice left the room, Fred lit his pipe and continued, "Something poisonous corrupts these islands, most of Europe, North America and now spreads to the Middle East. For almost forty years this tiny country has been sinking into a state of nebulous languor. Ignorance, vulgarity … the most bestial instincts govern British society. France was the cradle of this poison. Depressingly, if Moreau's tide of dissolution rises at its present rate, the entire globe will be made moribund."

"What is the purpose of making the globe moribund, Sir Frederick?"

"The pleasure of corruption. Pornographers and drug dealers get the same kick."

"Surely corruption is cured by teaching our youth moral standards?"

"Not when our dedicated teachers have been sidelined, Jeff. And a new generation has been manufactured to uphold the dictates of superficiality."

"Is that why you put your parliament into busses last night?"

"I put my parliament into busses, Nina, because they were so far gone with corruption that they will be better off in one of my compounds."

"You don't mean . . .?"

"Good gracious no! I am not Stalin! They have been taken to a luxury hotel complex on the Yorkshire coast. The complex has been designed in the manner of The Alhambra. They live like film stars. Ballroom dancing, champagne, fillet steak … prawn cocktails and Whist Drives. Just the ticket for a pack of show-offs. The public is able to observe them from specially constructed walkways on Thursday and Sunday afternoons. Visitors are asked not to throw food."

"Who is in control of your country, Sir Frederick?"

"I am." He knocked out the pipe and changed the subject. "The Kadet Precinct Johnny and Thomas saw in the Atlas Mountains appears to be invisible to everyone else. Your host there, Professor Hassan, was shattered to hear of the Home Kamp. He immediately telephoned a member of the Moroccan Royal family - Johnny witnessed the call - and that gentleman was equally shattered. They flew a reconnaissance plane over the area."

"And?"

"They think we are mad. Nothing shows up."

"Like a science fiction movie?"

"Not at all. A simple issue of brainwashing. Psychological terrorism, if you prefer. Moreau wanted to brainwash the World. More cognac …?"

"Please, it's good."

"It should be, it was distilled over a century ago."

"What do you want from us?"

"To help me find Moreau's successor."

"Where do we start?"

"France, the town of Yonroche. I have made arrangements for you to stay with the Comptesse de la Breuse. I want you to find the Château of Saint Christophe. It should be near Yonroche. Get inside the place."

"With respect, Sir Frederick - don't you know where this place is? Like, on the map?"

"Nothing Moreau has ever touched is on the map, Nina."

"How many staff do you have working on this case?"

"Including myself, five."

"Five! . . . In the *world*? Are you mad?"

"To grapple with reality, Nina, one is armed with madness as much as with sanity."

"What will Johnny and Thomas do in Marrakech?"

"Pay a visit to the Villa Friedemann." Fred glanced at a Fourteenth Century wall clock, "They should be with Friedemann now."

♠

Thomas and I wasted no time meeting Tonio Friedemann. We were back on the Zazahrat road the morning after our amazing find of Jeff and Nina Burdet. Frederick, over the telephone, had insisted they be flown to London next day. He cautioned me; "Friedemann will be old, intellectual and cunning: a lethal combination, Johnny. Keep your eye on Thomas. He is likely to be lured down a rabbit hole."

Friedemann's villa was more a village than a home. As we turned down his long, dusty drive we soon made out a series of flat, white, single storey walls punctured by windows that were surrounded by wide gold boarders and shaded with Leica orange awnings. We drove past formal arrangements of pools, rose gardens and Royal Palms.

"There's nobody about, Gov'ner." I brought the car to a scrunchy halt on the gravelled court of the principal entrance. "Why should there be, Thomas?"

"Because this is like an old Hollywood movie: there's always somebody about." He wound down his window and sniffed the aromatic air. Sound came from inside one of the pavilions, muffled but distinct, "What's that music, Johnny?"

"Marlene Dietrich . . . *Mein Blondes Baby.*"

"I told you! An old Hollywood movie."

"Cut the romance and ring the bloody door bell."

As Thomas sprinted up a flight of marble steps, gilded bronze doors showing in bas-relief lines of stylised, nude chorus boys - wearing only top hats - slid apart.

Tonio Friedemann was well into his nineties. He was diminutive, bowed a little, the well preserved flesh of his gentlemanly face mildly tanned. A Swiss valet of indeterminate age held his master's arm, gold-topped cane, and straw Boater.

Friedemann smiled questioningly as I joined Thomas by the massive bronze doors. For fifteen frozen seconds the old man stared at us, then he turned to his valet, murmuring in the impeccable German of a past generation, "The boy is exquisite. I have been waiting for this child to arrive, Heinrich, for half a century."

"Be careful, Dr Friedemann. I understand you. My father's family are from noble Prussian descent." He replied in exquisitely pronounced German.

"You do me an honour, Sir, visiting my home. Though I am not at all sure if you are welcome, Mister Dove."

"Franz von Stotz has asked me to meet you, Doctor. He tells me you are in possession of vitally important information."

"And the beautiful boy?"

"Will be the witness to everything we are to be shown today."

Friedemann turned to the valet, "Drinks, Heinrich. Lunch in forty-five minutes. What is the boy's name."

"Thomas."

"Come, my young arch-angel! Come and meet Bettina, my Great Grand daughter."

♠

Bettina was a ravishing bombshell blond with breasts served on a punch-hole bra like pears poached in red wine. Thomas did not know what to do with himself.

Lunch was spent idly at opposite ends of a shimmering, twenty-four seater Maplewood and ivory dining table supported by crouching, life-size, bronze, naked steel workers. As we finished, the footman attending to Friedemann helped him stand. He raised a frail Venetian glass goblet, a confetti of gold dust caught for ever in Sixteenth Century webs of archly manipulated crystal.

"Gentlemen! Bettina! … To a New World! To a New Creed!"

We heard his heels click.

"You will take coffee and liqueurs on the terrace, Gentlemen?"

"It would be a pleasure, Doctor."

"Bettina, dear child, ensure that everyone is content."

During coffee, Friedemann suggested that Bettina took Thomas for a swim. The boy was half out of his chair when I pinioned a mean hand on his arm.

"Thomas has no bathing gear!"

"I'm sure somebody can lend me . . ."

"No they *can't*!" I raised a warning finger.

"I can't understand what you are saying, Johnny. I don't speak German."

"You speak fluent body language, Thomas, and that is not what we are speaking at the moment." I thrust a scalpel-sharp glance at Friedemann, "My young friend needs to hear the rest of our conversation in English, Doctor. Is this condition acceptable to you?"

"English it is, Mister Dove." He dismissed Bettina with a waft of one hand. Prettily, in passing his chair, she flashed Thomas a medium close-up of her ample bosom. I could hear the testosterone flooding his arteries.

Friedemann removed his sunglasses and laid them down on a rosewood occasional table. He looked me in the face with hard boiled eyes.

"You are lucky to be alive, Johnny Debrett."

"I didn't suppose for a moment you were deceived, Doctor Friedemann."

"Call me Tonio. We are - in our different ways - on the same side. Ideological allies you might say … when you begin to understand me better." He deliberated. "I knew Arthur Moreau and your half-brother Joseph intimately; were you ever aware of this?"

"Never."

"I had always assumed that was the case. Arthur was a master of deception. I know Franz von Stotz intimately too, but I will not admit him here, nor will I speak to him. Franz was my lover. I was also married five times though women have never held a lasting fascination for me. My love for Franz is a dried bloom. I do not know what he is doing and I do not care."

"He seems to care about you."

"Yes, they want my final work. They have already tried to steal it."

"The five disks?"

"You will find the copies useless. The job was bungled."

"How did you get to know Arthur?"

"He became interested in my work years ago. September 1942, if I am to be precise. We were guests of Emmanuel Blaisedale at the Isles des Noces. I had become hopelessly infatuated with Franz by this time, we wanted to be away from the war, to make love, to power our minds."

"What where you working on?"

"Research on a monumental scale, Johnny. For the Führer - for Germany! Franz and I worked together in a secret installation not far from Ravensburg. Accessible to Switzerland over Lake Constance. I was the director of a programme . . ."

". . . controlled by an enigmatic formula?"

"If you like, yes. Superficially, it was a programme dedicated to the genetic reconstruction of a German Master Race." Sighing, he passed the back of an old-skinned hand slowly across his eyes. "A long story. Too long to tell."

"We are good listeners."

"You are following Arthur's trail, aren't you?" I nodded. "Then I judge you need to hear only one chapter of the story. The last chapter. Won't you come into my study? They have made a fire in there. During May, even in Morocco, I nowadays feel the cold."

♠

Doors opened as Friedemann spoke, though he had not commanded any servant, or touched a control.

"My study is my single susceptibility, Johnny."

The double height interior was modelled on the hall of a Bavarian Schloss. Over the open grate, where ornate wrought iron fire dogs supported brightly burning logs, the stone canopy was painted with gaudy heraldic devices. The walls were hung with pelts and shields. Huge oil paintings hung proud of richly coloured tapestries. There was a stone flagged floor, there were rusticated beams and a circular timber chandelier that would have crushed ten people had it fallen on them. The furniture groaned with its own weight. On huge sideboards polished pewter chargers were arranged, alternating with massive beer steins of gold, silver and horn. The room was a fest of fake Teutonic regalia.

Thomas heaved a young, bored sigh. "Can I go swimming, Johnny?"

"*No!* Get a load of what's in those bookcases on the end wall."

We wandered to a stainless steel bank of glass-fronted book cases seven meters high. The upper cases were accessed via a steel spiral stair leading to gunmetal galleries. It looked like the engine room of a battleship.

"The collection is priceless, Thomas."

"The spines are bound in red leather ... each with an embossed swastika!"

"How many books do you reckon he has, Thomas? Make an assessment, don't guess. I haven't trained you for nothing."

"Twenty thousand?"

"Good. More like twenty-three thousand. He has a huge number of tiny volumes half way up." Friedemann's voice scratched through the stifling air, "Twenty-three thousand, one hundred and thirty-four, Gentlemen. Arranged in fifteen sections covering fifty-five subjects that are all related to my research. Genetics, Engineering, Chemical Warfare, Model Farming, Soap Manufacturing, Diamonds, False Teeth and . . ."

Thomas murmured, ". . . gas chambers." I gripped his arm.

"Don't say a word, Mate. Listen hard. He is so conceited he might just give their game away." We were crouched low behind a sofa, trying to slide open the glass front of one of the bottom cabinets. Friedemann could not see us. I put my mouth close to Thomas's ear, "Stay by the shelves, witness everything, remember all we say. I'll sit by the fire and get him talking. Be ready to get the fuck out of here if I make a move for the terrace, OK?" He smiled and made a thumbs-up sign. As I got up I flicked the back of his head affectionately.

Sitting down by the fire, having removed my jacket, I met Friedemann's arrogant gaze. Standing with his back to the massive chimneypiece, staring at nothing in particular, he began his story.

"I was trained as a geneticist in Berlin just after the Great War. I was too young to fight. This was before the science of Genetics came to be prominent. The nineteen-twenties were pioneering days. The subject had not advanced from its Nineteenth Century roots.

"I became well known for my work, notorious you might say. I was outspoken. My papers and books were eagerly awaited by an international following.

"In 1935 I made something of a break through. This is complicated so I will explain what I discovered in the simplest way." He poured, generously, three brandies, smiling the benevolent smile of a kindly old man. Behind him the flames of the fire flared magenta.

"I discovered how to change the fundamental nature of Mankind by the simple application of a tablet, swallowed with something as innocuous as a cup of tea or a glass of water. The formula can also be injected directly into the blood stream as you might inject an infant against Polio. Quite simple - as they say - *'Once you know how!'*." He took a noisy slurp of brandy, licking round his flaccid, mauve lips with a little strawberry tongue. "The recipe is; Vanadium, Aluminium, Beryllium and Phosphorous blended with a pinch of Caesium. Water and sugar to taste . . . the secret ingredient is a substance extracted from human spinal fluid. In the Germany of 1935 - if you may understand me, Johnny - we had no shortage of donors."

"I understand you only too well, Tonio."

"Now when I say the 'fundamental nature of Mankind', I mean the very characteristic of our Race; to its heart; to its soul: to its eternal core! The core that only God knows. God and *me*." He coughed, pausing to wipe his mouth with a silk square. "As all scientists know, Johnny, God is merely a picture we comfort ourselves with. God is in fact a mathematical equation. I set out to solve that equation and at the instant of my success, I became God." He turned to warm his worm-pink hands for a moment. "I have the equation on the shelves at the opposite end of this room, in a volume just behind Thomas's left shoulder. Also on disk number two of the set of five you so earnestly wish to obtain, Johnny."

"You tell us that you can change the way we are?"

"I can manipulate the controls that govern our particular Universe. Note I use the word *particular* - there are an infinite number of Universes. I can create life, I can destroy life. I can destroy the World. I can terminate Existence . . . as we know it."

". . . 'as we know it' ... I don't follow."

"Please, *please* do not bore me with your childish scepticism. Science! . . . *Ha!* . . . The constant, drivelling need to *prove*! Science is the bauble of infantile minds. Einstein! *Pah!* . . . I knew him well. A little fake too clever for his own good."

Tonio walked with purpose to a bulbous Bavarian dresser. "Allow me to demonstrate my powers." He darted over to the fireplace with the agility of a twenty-one year old and pulled at a bell cord. Entering the room by a door concealed in the panelling surround of the fireplace, a ravishingly beautiful youth appeared. He was dressed in the garb of a servant, white jacket and black trousers. He was a kadet, but more perfect than even Kyla and Panno. Friedemann spoke to him in the guttural Kadet language we had come to know, turning the boy to face us.

"This is Tayno. He was created as the result of my latest work. From insemination to birth, three months instead of the original accelerated seven. He has a physical and mental age of nineteen after only three years."

"What do you mean, *accelerated seven*?"

"Accelerated growth and developed intelligence rate, you fool! AGADIR for short."

"Can you be a little more …"

"Never interrupt, please! Have a good look at Tayno. I am going to slaughter him in front of you and bring him to life."

Thomas was at my side, gripping my elbow, "That's impossible, and I don't want to see it happen. Let's get out of here, Johnny."

"*Doubting Thomas*! You handsome pest." Tonio pranced to the fireplace and touched a fire dog with the toe of his elegant, handmade shoe.

"Shall we inspect my laboratory?" he said, archly.

♠

Twenty-three thousand books immaculate in their steel bookcases, along with the spiral stairway and gunmetal gallery - all five hundred deadweight tonnes of it - droned smoothly upwards through the fake Gothic ceiling. Within twenty seconds the library had vanished. A huge room lay beyond the opening, floodlit with silver light. A laboratory floored with lime grey linoleum, walled with black steel, the ceiling a sheet of illuminated frosted glass. Everything was arranged with military precision.

"What's that smell, Johnny?"

"Ether. You are too young to remember old fashioned hospitals."

Seated at a bench, staring at a computer screen, was a blond young man; Western, white, fit and sleek. He wore a pair of light blue denims and a garish Hawaiian shirt. His forearms were strong, the fingers of his square, male hands, fine. He looked up from his work and waved.

"Hi! I'm Martin. Tonio's senior assistant. Great to meet you guys." He was American, I guessed by his accent from Florida, an agent of Friedemann's horrible mind.

"I know what you are thinking, Johnny. My team of scientists are American. Who else could understand destruction so immaculately, so callously, as they? Come! We have work to do. Martin, if you please, I will destroy the kadet. Prepare a syringe."

"Right now, Chief?"

"Of course, damn you! We are putting on one of our little party tricks for our guests." The American clicked-on a grin, "You'll be amazed, guys. Not many people see this kinda thing every day."

"I don't know if I want to see anything, Tonio. It was enough to witness Jo's decapitation yesterday."

"I can't stand another murder, Gov'ner."

"As you appreciate, Thomas feels the same way as I do."

"Don't be ridiculous! A wonderful sight!" He snapped a command to

Tayno who immediately removed his clothes and stood naked before us while Martin delved in a deep freeze, fishing out a smoking phial.

"Tell him to stuff it, Johnny. I'll be sick."

"Try to control it. We won't be able to stop him." Friedemann turned Tayno's shoulders to face us. "Regard the physique, my friends. Perfection! As splendid as Nature could achieve and it is I who have created this boy."

"He has no genitals, Tonio."

"Pah! There is no need for reproductive organs in a dead world! Unfortunately the first Kadet Cycles were not so well adjusted in this respect. They often display quasi-erotic tendencies that they are only able to satisfy upon themselves. I think you will have noted this little failing in Kyla and Panno, two *dreary* mistakes of poor Franz! Like Pygmalion, he falls in love with his own work. It is his fatal flaw!"

Taking Thomas and me by the elbows he walked us forward, cajoling, avuncular, as if leading us towards a birthday cake to blow out its fluttering candles. "Come closer to the fire, please gentlemen. Sit down and relax. . . . . Martin! The syringe exactly forty-four seconds after the death!"

"Sure thing, Chief."

Friedemann spoke to Tayno in Precinct language. The Kadet trotted obediently to a section of wall sheeted with purplish marble. He stood waiting quietly with his back to us.

With fussily elegant steps the old man returned to the vulgar Bavarian dresser. He took a gun from a drawer, an old fashioned Luger, heavy and brutal.

"Oh, God! I'm going to faint, Johnny."

"Put your head between your knees." Gently massaging the back of Thomas's neck, I was on the point of asking Friedemann if he would let the Kadet go back to the kitchen when Tonio turned to me with cool assurance. "The floor and wall can be quickly cleaned of blood afterwards. Now, I appreciate Johnny, that this is difficult to stomach when you are unused to such demonstrations. I also warn you that as Tayno is revived you may *both* pass-out because the intellect refuses to accept that the impossible is actually taking place. The brain, in self-defence, closes the sensory system down." He gave Thomas a doubtful, withering glance. "I earnestly advise the young man to remove his belt and loosen his collar. And *please*! if you are going to vomit, dear boy, do so outside!" Testily he commanded, "Ring for a jug of iced water, Martin!"

"Sure thing, Chief."

"Sit quietly, Johnny, compose yourself, breathe normally. Most importantly, do not attempt to stop me as I aim and fire. I am not the shot I used to be and we cannot have the boy suffer prolonged agony if I miss the mark." Deftly, he checked the gun's magazine, adding absent-mindedly, "It is necessary to shatter the spine between the shoulder blades and burst the chambers of the heart, do you follow me?"

"Do we have to go through with . . . ?"

"Good! . . . Now watch carefully." I felt Thomas making himself straighten up. His face was ashen, but he wasn't going to be beaten. "I'm watching, Gov'ner. We may need to make people believe this."

Placing himself by the dresser, Friedemann put one foot forward, the toecap of his left shoe digging into the thick pile of a Moroccan carpet. Holding the pistol in his left hand, he raised it to be horizontal with the slow deliberation of a trained marksman. His left arm was entirely outstretched, the palm of his right hand clamped firmly into the crook of the other arm as a brace. He began to aim with meticulous care. He had a stylish manner and assessed the final aim to a deliberate degree. His old forefinger gently, irrevocably, brought the trigger to its hairline of no return.

The gun fired with a huge noise. Outside, hundreds of birds flew up from the bushes and palm trees like a cloud of burning oil smoke.

Tayno's body was hurled into the marble wall so hard that we heard the bones of his nose and jaw shatter. Where his matchless back had been there was a riven, black-red gash of gore, the ribs partially exposed as if he hung flayed in a butcher's window. Simultaneously with the shot he had shrieked, but the desperate appeal was terminated as blood welled into his throat to cascade from his mouth, nostrils and eye sockets. The body recoiled from the wall to crumple, jittering and swerving, onto the bluish, polished floor. A catastrophic death agony made the corpse angle crabwise three meters towards us. With a wrenching squelch, front up, it came to rest. Nothing human remained of the chest; in a hideous imitation of *spaghetti al ragu*, the bowels were slopped over the thorax that stood vertically like a can lid. The lovely face had been ripped from the skull and the tongue - messed with fragmented teeth - lay like a skinned mole a meter from the head. A lake of dark blood treacled towards the hearth, blending with the water from a fallen vase of scented roses.

And there was a white rose by Tayno's lifeless hand.

It was with some effort that Thomas and I took command of ourselves. We went over to the body as the laboratory assistant fetched his prepared syringe. Friedemann, suave as if he had purchased a silk tie in the rue de la Paix, looked down on the wreckage of Tayno.

"You will agree, gentlemen, that the kadet is quite dead. Now Johnny, you are going to tell me that my formula cannot work its powers on dead flesh. Ah yes! Do not shake your head like that. They *all* tell me the same thing, and they all shake their heads in exactly the same way. What will occur comes from the action of the governor of Existence. That governor - believe it or not - is acting on Tayno still, even though he seems to our limited intelligence nothing more than a hound's supper."

"We are in your hands, Tonio. Do what you must, but do it quickly!"

With a manicured fingernail he tapped the seconds on the glass of a gold fob watch. "Forty, forty-one, forty-two, ..." Martin expelled an air bubble from the syringe - God knows why - and positioned the needle over a place on Tayno's empty groin. Thomas knelt at the head, I crouched by Martin's cologne scented flank.

"*Now!*"

The needle sank into the flesh of Tayno's almost undamaged groin, flesh already blackening with the shock of death. The plunge was depressed and about ten millilitres of whatever Friedemann had cooked-up entered the corpse. How it was supposed to circulate in the blood stream left me guessing.

"Suppose you left the corpse for a week, Tonio?"

"Silence! . . . *Watch*, damn you!"

I fixed my gaze on the chest, the part so destroyed that it was impossible to imagine that a surgeon could even begin considering re-construction.

Six seconds passed.

What we beheld cannot be fully described because, as Friedemann had advised, we could not mentally comprehend the images passing through our eyes to our brains. All I can say is that the process of Tayno's re-creation was undertaken in a language that we are not equipped to comprehend, and never can be.

When I was a child my Mother occasionally read me Bible stories. Later, as a teenager, I read the Gospels for myself. I often wondered (first with boyish curiosity, later with the typical scepticism of a confused adolescent) what Christ's disciples actually saw when, for example, he took a few loaves and fish from a basket and divided them up to feed five thousand people. Did the disciples see the extra bread and fish forming from the existing material, like a dividing amoeba? Or was the bread and the fish suddenly *there*, in Christ's hands, inexplicably created from nowhere?

Kneeling by Tayno, my trouser knees soaked in his blood, I had my answer: the bread and the fish were suddenly *there*, in Christ's hands, inexplicably created from nowhere.

"Bloody hell, Gov'ner, he's coming back!"

"Can you see how?"

"No, it's like they blur criminals' faces on television ... Look! His chest is whole."

"It's very emotional. Try not to break down."

"Weep! . . . *Weep*! Damned you! Everybody else weeps!"

"We're not everybody, Tonio."

Tayno's body did not begin to heal, then go through a process of knitting itself together - as if a film of his murder had been run in reverse: he was, at a stroke, whole. As we looked, the Kadet was perfect. He breathed, sat up, smiled and spoke to Friedemann. Then his hands slipped in the pool of blood behind him and he wiped his palms on the sensual skin of his gorgeous, yielding thighs.

"There you are, Gentlemen! Wasn't that a treat? Not a bruise, don't you know." Martin raised Tayno to his feet while Tonio proudly ran lascivious fingers up and down the Kadet's chest and back. "Better than new! . . . Isn't he?" He became swollen with conceit, unable to resist speaking to us arrogantly in German, "Satisfied, you idiots? A Master Race! All my own work! A race that will destroy Humanity and the Earth!"

"Marvellous, Tonio." I murmured to Thomas, "Anything to shut him up."

"Now you understand my work. You are the only people outside Arthur Moreau's select inner circle to witness the power of life over death. But as you knew Arthur so very well, Johnny, I am - to coin that delightful English phrase - only 'keeping it in the family'."

Standing up, I turned to Thomas, murmuring, "Bring the car round to the terrace, I'll pay my respects. Be ready to move-off fast as soon as I jump in." Thomas went outside. Friedemann was so full of himself he didn't notice.

"I have ordered afternoon tea to be served in the Summer House, Johnny. It is a five minute walk through the park. The pavilion gives exquisite views of the High Atlas mountains. Some of my wealthier neighbours have already arrived. They long to be introduced to you." Without giving Tayno another thought, he linked my arm in his and lead me out onto the terrace that was now tranquil with pale azure light.

"My trousers, Tonio! How can I meet people when they are steeped in blood?"

"Look down, Johnny." I looked down. My trousers showed no sign of blood.

"You see, nothing to worry about." Again, he became arch, "We are having special cakes, Johnny. The kitchen staff have been most excited preparing them. The pastry chef is *excellent*, the sperm that created him came from Bremen. I love German fancy cakes ... with a little glass of Apricot liqueur." He lead me past a black marble urn, lush with clouding, creamy roses, adding roguishly, like a great-uncle, "What do you say to that, dear boy?"

"Most appropriate, Tonio."

♠

Thomas sat down on the hot, wide steps in front of the main court. He was exhausted, the heat battered his skull. Five meters away, its engine running, the Mercedes baked in the sun. He had hardly touched the steering wheel when he had to get out, feeling as if he might be sick.

Resting his head in his hands he let out a long, unhappy sigh.

"Shit, this is horrible!" He raised his head and looked round at the vast, empty courtyard, at the pseudo Moroccan architecture, at the flaming flowerbeds, the dazzling gravel. For the first time since his arrival, he wanted to go home. "Why aren't I in the White Hart with Lewis?" But handsome, sporty Lewis, with his Mini Cooper and his bevy of girl friends, was a thousand miles away. "I can't bring the car round ... I've had it. Johnny, why don't you come to the front door?" He started to get up, he would have to go back inside the dump. There was now an eerie silence about the place. "Where are you, Johnny?" Shit! Fifteen minutes had passed. Were they still in the old loony's study? Friedemann was so disgusting anything could have happened. Thomas blew breath from his lips, exasperated. "Do I have to go back and find you?" . . .

He tousled his hair with one hand, once more glancing up at the silent courtyard.

"Something's gone wrong! . . . Please God, don't let something go wrong." The bronze doors behind him slid apart and he heard the prissy sound of a smart woman's high heeled shoes tip-tapping over the marble pavement. He turned round to see Bettina floating down the steps towards him in a gauzy, unfastened bathing wrap. She wore a bikini ... a tiny cerise bikini! Was this a dream? She came right up to him ... her voice seemed distant and strange. Hang on! . . . She didn't look like a girl any more. . . . Shit! She wasn't a girl, she was a sharp-jawed business woman, predatory in red lipstick. Her evil smile slashed a canyon through her face.

"You look all-in, honey! Did you get a shock back there?" Thomas regarded her quizzically in silence, his mouth half open, head cocked on one side. Bettina leant forward, searching the boy's face with a concerned frown, like a nurse. "You OK, honey? I think you'd better come inside where it's cool. C'mon! Take my hand an' I'll help you in. You need to lie down, Sweetie."

"You're not German!"

"You got it, babe. I'm not German."

"And you're not nineteen."

"Never try to guess a woman's age, honey. Didn't your Mom tell you that?"

She lead him through two brown marble halls, then down a long, glazed, shaded corridor by the side of another garden court. Like a hospital. He became confused. . . . A Hospital. Was this place a hospital?

"No, honey. It's Tonio's home alright. He likes everything to look dandy, so it's a bit sparse in places. But it ain't sparse in here, honey!" She buzzed him through a pair of double doors into a luxurious crimson and gold suite. A lake of red plush drapes enveloped his mind, a hanging forest of chandeliers, a sea of pollen-orange satin. He remembered an ancient Hollywood movie . . . a tart's parlour. *Gone with the Wind* - that was the movie! Bettina was exactly like the tart in the parlour. Only Bettina didn't have a heart of gold . . . she was ...

He froze. Bettina was evil!

A trap! Fuck! He had to pull himself together. "I need to get back to the car."

"Nonsense, Sweetie! Lie down on this couch and I'll fix you a drink."

He seemed to be lying on the couch anyway. She was taking his shoes off, loosening his belt, fingering round his fly. . . . Now she was stroking his hair and brow. Mmm! He felt himself getting horny.

"Now drink this like a good boy!" She held a glass to his lips. Her grip was steel hard, forcing him to sip the stuff.

"*No!* I must spit this out!" But he drank it. . . . "Why did I do that?"

"You take a rain check, honey! Johnny's with Tonio. They're having a tea party down the bottom of the garden with a crowd of Tonio's geriatric friends. Johnny's quite safe."

"What do you mean?" His voice had already misted over with an irresistible desire to sleep. At the same time he felt incredibly randy, he wanted to slide his tongue inside the woman's vagina. God, she was sexy. She was . . . forty if she was a day! He wanted to have sex with her, but he couldn't move.

"What I mean, honey, is that Tonio's old friends ain't in the know, see? So Tonio has to act normal, understand? So Johnny's quite safe. Now go to sleep, baby. I'll come for you when it's time to go home." She stroked his flank, he snuggled close to her, reaching his hand between her legs.

"Why are you American?"

"Now what did someone in London tell you, you flirty boy? Huh? They told you never to ask questions because it's the surest way of discovering the answers." She took his hand from inside her bikini and gently placed it on a plush cushion by his sleeping head. She watched him coldly, listening for the deepening rhythm of his breathing.

"Bastard!" She got up and went into the adjoining bedroom, closing the doors behind her. Martin lay naked on a gilded, lace-frothed bed.

"Is he sleeping?"

"He'll be out cold for three hours, Martin."

"Wow, that boy's a white hot fetch! I could have screwed his ass off in there!"

"Do we have instructions?"

"Kill them both. Came through from London twenty minutes since. Shame about the kid, he's cute!"

"They're all cute at that age, Martin, but that ain't our problem. We serve three masters and right now these three masters all want their hands on Uncle Tonio's cookie box! That is one hell of a problem, Martin."

"Give me a good reason why."

"The decoy disks have failed to impress, Mister Craig Vandyke!"

"Don't use that name! It gets me mad. We are no longer American."

"That's what our papers say, babe. So what's paper? We are Americans, born under the Stars and Stripes, and we're going to fuck America, like I'm goin' to fuck you." Animalish, she scratched at his bare chest; she had a yearning to dig her teeth into its fuzzy mat of earthy blond hair. He parted his thighs, grasping her arse.

"Does Appleby say anything?"

"Not as far as I know."

"Good!" He pulled her over the sheets by his naked side, "That gives us three hours worth of steamy sex! Kneel on me, suck my cock!" She removed her wrap and inched the bikini bottom over her toes. Martin was already hugely erect; she smelt the musky scent of his pubis. Already well aroused by Thomas she straddled him. Feeling his tongue lapping her cunt she greedily slipped her mouth over the tangerine sized end of his hammer length phallus and went to work.

"Stop! Don't make me come. I want you behind like a whore!"

"The boy will hear me wailing, you know it turns me insane."

"He can join us. I fancy murdering him when he comes into your mouth!"

"You're so dirty, Martin! You're a freak!"

"Bitch! You love it! Now get over to the mirror while I put the collar on."

"And one of those . . . glass jobs?"

"Yeah!" She began to moan, "No, Martin. No!" Clearing a dozen perfume bottles to one side of her dressing table with a sweep of her arm, she bent to face a mirror framed with lights. She watched Martin's reflection push a spiked steel circlet down the bottle thick shaft of his penis. With a crooked smile of sadistic want, he slipped an industrial glass dildo deep into her vagina.

"Aaahhh! That is *so* painful! *So* good!" . . . He scratched his fingernails deeply down her back, drawing blood: she screamed in ecstasy. "You fuck'n slut! I'll rip your fuck'n - uuurrgh!" The bushy hillside of his gut muscles contracted as he gripped her buttocks with square, hairy hands, and began to gyrate his squirming, bullockish hips, easing himself luxuriously into the woman's stretching sphincter.

"*Mart'n!* . . . The knuckle dusters! . . . Use the knuckle dusters! . . . Break my face!"

"In a minute, honey! . . . Look at us! . . . Oooagh! . . . Look at us in the mirror!"

They looked into the mirror, at their disgraceful tableau, and as they looked, over their heads, they saw the reflection of Kyla's head. Kyla, in full uniform, standing behind them.

And that was the last thing they ever saw.

♠

Sheathing his bloodied serrated knife with Olympian disdain, Kyla glanced professionally at the details of his act, nodding with satisfaction. He then rushed into the adjacent sitting room and knelt down by Thomas's rousing form. He took Thomas in his arms, slightly raising the young man from the cushions, burying his face in the crook of his friend's neck and shoulder.

"I love you!" This was a difficult thing to say when he did not know what love meant. One thing he did know, that he wanted to possess Thomas: to become part of him.

Thomas opened his eyes to find Kyla's eyes staring deep into his pupils. "Kyla?" He felt so drowsy that he did not know if this was a dream or if he was actually awake.

"I heard screaming. A man and a woman screaming."

"They were fighting. I stopped them." Kyla. So close! So warm! . . . Thomas gazed hazily into Kyla's Sistine Chapel eyes. Wow! He looks just like Lewis when we . . . "Shit, my head! Hell, Kyla! My head! What did she do to me?" Kyla stroked Thomas's cheek and sat up beside him. Lying back amongst the velvet cushions, Thomas saw how majestic the kadet was, how easy in his statuesque grace.

"It doesn't matter what she did. She's gone away."

"Where's Johnny?"

"He's gone away." It was as if a brick had smashed the window of Thomas's apathy.

"Gone *away*! . . . That's impossible! *Where*?" He tried to get off the couch but Kyla's rock hard arm held him fast round the waist and tightened, like a boa constrictor. With his other arm, effortlessly, the Kadet brought Thomas round in front of his chest, pushing his head down amongst the plush, locking the young man's stomach over Laocoön-like thighs. Winded, Thomas couldn't make a sound. "He went away." Kyla curled the palm of one hand expertly over the nape of Thomas's neck and took from his tunic pocket a moulded mask of impregnated felt. Gently (normally he would crush the victim's nose back into the skull) he fitted the mask over Thomas's face. In seconds the body was limp. Kyla turned his friend over and brought the lolling head to his, kissing closed the sightless amber eyes, feeling the long lashes sensually brush his murmuring lips.

"Little Kadet!"

Panno came into the room. In a few moments the two Centurion Kadets had placed Thomas's limp body into the back of their waiting jeep.

♠

Nina woke, instantly forgetting her weird, waking dream. She sat up in the strange bed. Where was she?

The Château de la Breuse. . . . "Oh my Gosh!". She gazed at the high windows of the fabulous room. Fairy wing shafts of gold morning light danced through the gap between two gigantic, silvery silk brocade drapes. "They must have opened the shutters when we were asleep." Nina climbed down off the Napoléonic bed realising that the huge feather mattress had given her back ache. She limped over to one of the windows and manhandled a drape, "*So* beautiful! ... Boy! An *avalanche* of minute embroidered roses." She managed to haul an armful of brocade to her nose. "You can almost *smell* them!" She looked round at the bed.

"Jeff? ... Hey! I'll bet this place is ice cold in winter."

"Alaska couldn't beat it, my dear."

"You're *awake*!"

"I'm awake."

"The Countess is darling. No wonder Johnny fell in love with her."

"Do they bring breakfast to the room, or do we go downstairs?"

"Boy! Could I use a cup of American coffee! French coffee doesn't hold a candle to what we have at home. You seen the garden out here?"

"I would need to join you on the balcony to do that, Nina."

"Well, come-on! It's amazing."

"I think they call them parks, Nina."

"OK ... the *park* is amazing! Now get your ass off that bed and *look* at this place!"

He stretched, folding his dressing gown carefully to fit his sparse frame. He put his arm round her, and they leant gently on the pale cream stone balustrade of a wide balcony, looking, not without romance, at the long, manmade lake imprinted in a sea of emerald grass. Greening woodland edged the lawns, laced with cold, gorgeous statues, like the painted pearls on a Renaissance portrait.

"Did you sleep, Nina?"

"Not too much. You gotta stop that clock chiming."

"There are two clocks. They both chime."

"The one with three naked dames hanging round the dial making eyes at the guy with an apple chimes every *quarter*!"

"The Judgement of Paris. He's handing the apple ..."

"I don't care if he's handing a subpoena! Stop that clock or I *quit!*"

"It's too valuable to mess with, dear. It's almost three hundred years old."

"Like everything else in this joint."

"Why don't we shower, get dressed and join our hostess. I'm dying for a cup of her wonderful French coffee. I'm going to dip that delicious bread in my coffee like a Frenchman."

"When we get into town, Jeff, I'm going to find a Starbucks!"

♠

"Of course you can have the clocks silenced. I employ a clock winder. Charles will see to them this morning. There are over a hundred time-pieces in the château. I'm so used to them I never hear them." Nina and Jeff loved the way Corinne pronounced English like a movie queen. There she was, elegant, pouring their coffee herself with aristocratic hands. Her hair done so neatly, . . . and her perfume! That misty hint of French perfume *said it all.*

"I have ordered the car for eleven, we will drive to Saint Christophe but I am afraid you will both be very disappointed. The château has been derelict for years. I do not think it is possible to get close to it. I will ask my chauffeur, Maurice. He was born in the village … he knows all about our region. I am sure he will tell me that the main gates are padlocked. Even if we could get in, I am almost certain the château is bordered-up."

"Won't there be other entrances to such a big place?"

"Yes, Jeff, there are. But it is a long time since I visited Saint Christophe, I don't even know if they'll be usable. Driveways cost a lot of money to maintain, leave them for a couple of years and they turn back to woodland, I should know, we have twelve kilometres of driveway here. More coffee, Nina?"

"Thanks, Corinne. It's delicious. You say you visited the château?"

"Before I was married. It belonged to my Great Uncle, the Duc du Brezolles." She snapped open a silver box and took out a slim cigarette, "Do you mind?"

"Not at all." They watched her walk to the window, a young footman darted forward with a lighter. She inhaled nervously, it seemed to Jeff almost irritably. "That was my mother's side, the Duke died mysteriously. Our family history on both sides can be traced to the time of Clovis."

"Died mysteriously?"

"He sold the château to an American just after the Second World War. He had no choice, they were penniless. It was hideous anyway, it had been rebuilt in a terrible imitation gothic in the early Nineteen Hundreds. The cost ruined them. My mother's family have a history of extravagance that, thankfully, I have not inherited. My Great Uncle sold on one condition, that he stayed in residence, in one wing, for the rest of his life."

"The American took care of that?"

"It was never proved, but we suspect the Duke was poisoned."

"Was the American called Blaisedale?" Corinne fiddled with a Meissen vase of roses, re-arranging the blooms, turning the display to the left then turning it back to where it was. The young footman discretely cleared the breakfast things. He did not look at Jeff or Nina.

"I have no idea. But he was on social terms with Arthur Moreau."

"Did Moreau visit you here?"

"Out of the question. My husband was a very arrogant man, until his death we mixed exclusively with our own rank. Does that sound terribly snobbish?"

"It goes on in America just the same."

♠

Corinne's chauffeur brought the shimmering, black Citroen DS to a smooth stop outside the ivy infested main gates of Le Château de Saint Christophe.

"Those gates are thick with rust, Nina." Jeff got out of the car, closely followed by the Chauffeur who he considered a mite too clingy, as if the man were checking on their every move, maybe to make a report. He inspected the three enormous padlocks that fastened rusted chains that held the gates closed.

"Nobody has touched those locks in years, Nina."

"The lodges are bricked-up, and what are these concrete cubes?"

"Anti-tank devices. That's the only wrong note: why on earth go to those lengths?"

"Because you don't want the army or the police to get through?"

Jeff lowered his voice, speaking to Nina only when he noted that the chauffeur was talking to Corinne by the car. "Don't discuss any of this. Act like we're disappointed, like she said we would be. Don't look at anything else. I suspect we may be watched."

"The place has the same creepy feel as Gracewood, Jeff."

"Exactly. Get into the car. We'll ask Corinne to drive us round the perimeter of the estate, than we go back."

"She's taking us to lunch at a local restaurant, then for a ride on the coast."

"Fine, let her do it."

They found every access point identically blocked, they saw no gaps in the walls that were a relentless brick barrier over five meters high topped with spiked steel and rusted coils of barbed wire. It was impossible to see the château, but through one of the gateways they could see the roof of a large building way over the inky, scrubby woodlands of the estate.

"What's that?"

"If I remember, those are the original Eighteenth Century stable blocks and muse. They were not demolished." Corinne got out to have a cigarette, the chauffeur lit it for her. Nina prodded Jeff's elbow. "There are crops growing in those fields, Jeff, see, beyond the line of trees to the left. Somebody gets in."

"Not us, Nina. The place is dangerous. If Sir Frederick wants to get in there, he can use his own people."

♠

They arrived back at La Breuse just after six in the evening. The lunch had been memorable, the trip along the French coast very beautiful, but Nina and Jeff were tired and somehow depressed by Saint Christophe. The young footman brought them drinks then bent low to speak to the Countess who sat with faultless elegance on a superb, silk embroidered, Louis Quinze *fauteuil.*

"S'il vous plait, Madame, the clock winder, Charles Barra, pays his respects and asks if he may have a word with you."

"Still here? How long has he been waiting?"

"For some hours, Madame, but - he much regrets - it is important."

"It can't be that important, Pierre!"

For the first time since Jeff and Nina had met her, Corinne showed visible irritation. "Can't it wait until tomorrow? We are only talking about clocks." Jeff went back to the console to pour more soda into his rye: a pretext. He had an instinctive feeling that the message was not concerned with clocks. "Have him in, Corinne. We don't mind. I'd like to meet the man who winds your clocks, he must be an interesting guy."

Charles Barra was ushered into the room. Personable, dark, tall, well dressed in a smart jacket and slacks, he was about thirty, eyes glistening with intelligence. Jeff got the distinct impression that Barra was more than a factotum. For a start he spoke in cultivated French. "There is a serious problem with the central alarm system, Madame la Comptesse. I regret to say that it requires immediate attention. May I advise you that the engineers are brought from Paris as a matter of urgency. My opinion is that the problem may take a week to rectify." Turning to Nina he smiled charmingly, explaining in English salted with a gentle French accent, that as well as winding the clocks he was also responsible for the day-to-day checking of the security system at La Breuse. He was explaining that this installation cost half a million francs a year to maintain when Corinne cut him short,

"For goodness sake! I paid for the service a month since!" She was furious, hardly attempting to conceal her mood. "What is the matter with it?"

"The computer, Madame."

"*Damn* the computer! You are the matter! *You* are incompetent! The people in Paris are *fools!*" She snapped at the young footman to replenish her glass. The servant, apprehensive, mistook the brand of Scotch. "This is filth, Pierre! *Get out!*"

"But Madame . . ."

"*Out!*"

Corinne switched to sweet, sociable charm so fast that Jeff became suspicious.

"Delight our guests, Charles. Make the carillon clock work for us. Look at it! One of the finest examples of automaton clocks to survive the French Revolution. Have it play something, Charles!"

While Corinne and Nina sat on gilt chairs that were upholstered in rose pink damask listening to a tinkling minuet by Mozart, played with gusto by the enormous, marqueterie festooned automaton, Charles deftly signalled Pierre to his side. Glancing round to ensure the ladies had not noticed this move, he lightly took hold of Jeff's elbow, whispering, "Follow us."

Unobserved, the three men went down a long passage to one of the later extensions of the château where they came to a coldly classical vestibule, stern with austere Doric columns. Charles whispered, "Put the lights on, Pierre." His comrade frowned, "If I put them all on we can be seen from the park."

"Are we being watched?"

"You are being watched constantly, Mister Burdet. Everything you say is recorded."

"Who are you?" Charles smiled, by his side young Pierre, just twenty, smiled too. "Friends. Is that enigmatic enough?"

"Friends of Sir Frederick?"

Charles pursed his lips, "Never ask any questions, Mister Burdet ..."

"... it is the surest way of getting to know the answers."

"So now you know who we work for." The lights above a huge mural flashed on. Jeff looked over the painting with amazement. It showed three great houses set in a formal tableau of gardens and flowering trees. Jeff turned to the knowingly smiling young men, "The place in the middle is Gracewood!"

"That's right. And the building on the right is Blaisedale's summer place on the Isle des Noces, and this one on the left is Saint Christophe."

"How on earth ...?"

"Her husband was part of Moreau's empire. He was Blaisedale's French lawyer."

"Does the Countess know?"

"We can't say. But many people meet here. That is why the château is wired. This vestibule has been neutralised by Pierre for an hour."

"This gets more tacky by the minute. How do you come to be involved?"

"Monsieur, my father was made an imbecile by Arthur Moreau. My father knows so much but can tell us nothing. He worked at the design studios Moreau created at Saint Christophe. He was discovered trying to smuggle vital information out of the place in order to send it to London." Tears of emotion swelled on the lower lashes of Charles's eyes. "They injected him with a drug that destroyed his mind."

Pierre whispered, "We must get back to the ladies. The clock is coming to the end of its copper disk."

♠

Jeff and Nina finally got to their room past midnight. They were exhausted. Friends had arrived soon after Charles Barra had taken his leave and

Corinne's idea of a 'light supper for three' swelled to an five course dinner for eight.

"Nobody spoke English to us, Jeff! They could at least have . . . what's the matter? Honey, what's all this hand signalling?" Jeff quietly closed the door of their suite, then carefully locked it. Turning to Nina he held a finger to his lips.

"What gives, Honey? What's with this hush-hush stuff?" He took her onto the moonlit balcony, they stood by the glimmering balustrade. "The place is bugged, Nina. I think Charles Barra is something to do with Sir Frederick, but I can't be sure."

"If he is, then why did Sir Frederick ask us to come out here?"

"I don't know. The whole thing is so . . . disconnected."

"Don't you mean crazy, Jeff? Like our political situation back home? Why don't we clear out?"

"Because we're part of it now, Nina. So listen to me, please. The entire château is under surveillance, even the car we drove in today is bugged."

"Are you telling me the Countess is . . ."

"I don't know. But when she got mad earlier, I was kinda surprised."

"I was disgusted."

"She's French, Nina. Highly strung."

"No wonder they had that revolution. It figures."

"Forget it, honey. Keep to small talk and don't act suspicious. Cameras are watching and recording. Probably in here in this room."

"Jeff, I wanna go home! Call a taxi!"

"It's almost one in the morning, honey. And who do you think might be driving the taxi?" They folded the shutters and sat on the edge of the bed.

"Did you hear that rasping sound?"

"It came from the clock, Nina."

"Which clock?"

"The one with the three dames." He peered through the glass dome of the larger clock. "There's a piece of paper in there."

"Read it."

"I have to take the glass dome off first."

"Suppose somebody's watching?"

"What can they do, Nina; come in and shoot us?" Jeff carefully lifted the glass dome from the exquisite gilt-bronze clock and placed it noiselessly on the marble top of the console. Nina nipped the folded piece of paper from between two figurines. Jeff replaced the dome.

"So what do we do now, Jeff?"

"Stand in the jon and read it."

"Maybe they bugged the jon."

"We flush the damn thing!"

By the lavatory, using Jeff's key-ring torch, they read;

Tomorrow the Countess will be called away on urgent family business. You will be left to amuse yourselves. Do not accept Maurice's offer to take you shopping in Yonroche; you will be murdered. At 11-30hrs go inside the winter pavilion - the circular building with a green copper roof at the end of the lake - wait for me there. When you read this, you will have met me so you know what I look like.

Charles Barra.

Over breakfast, a maid handed Jeff a crested envelope.

"Corinne apologises, honey. She's had to leave for Paris on urgent family business."

"That's too bad! . . . . When will the Countess be back, Mirabelle?"

"Tonight, Madame. La Comptesse flew in her private jet. But Maurice says he will take you out in the car today. In Yonroche there is a well known restaurant, *The Bonaparte*. It is owned by my aunt, Madame. She has heard all about you. After lunch Madame can look round the shops."

"Sounds like a neat idea, Mirabelle, but please tell Maurice that we are tired after last night, so we'll stick around the château. We will eat at your Aunt's place another time."

"Of course, Madame. Coffee?"

"Strong n' black!" The girl went out.

"Call a taxi, Jeff!"

"Pass the juice, honey."

♠

Charles and Pierre waited inside the Winter Pavilion. Jeff and Nina approached slowly along the "Grand Canal". They made play of pointing to the magnificent flower beds, gazing at fountains, behaving as if they had nothing better to do. As soon as they entered the pavilion, Charles wasted no time.

"Follow us, please." They walked to a clearing in a Chestnut wood. A car waited.

"Please get in. We are taking you to Saint Christophe." Settled in the car, Jeff asked a burning question, "Is the Countess part of Moreau's empire?"

"We cannot answer. Her late husband was in Moreau's pay. The Count was responsible for bribing police, ensuring that Departmental officials turned blind eyes, that Government Ministers kept silent. Amenable politicians were given vast expense accounts to keep them happy. Most significantly, her husband ensured that every French President was never told anything."

"That's impossible!"

"Monsieur, you are well acquainted with these matters. Think about it. If the Head of State is clueless you can do what you like. It happens in America all the time." Pierre drove them along a farm track to an ordinary gate. In half an hour they reached Saint Christophe. The gaunt, ruined entrance loomed gloomy.

"You can't get through it, Charles, we checked the gate yesterday!" Charles smiled as they swept past. "You did not check well enough." Three hundred meters along the road Pierre turned the car down the driveway of a private villa .

"You will notice the garaging of this house projects from a hillside."

"Sure."

"Observe that the garaging is extensive."

"Five bays. They must be crazy about automobiles."

"Look closely."

"C'mon, Charles! What are you telling us?"

"That the entire frontage is a wall of painted steel." Pierre pressed a button on the shift. Jeff and Nina watched as the garage elevation folded to one side. Pierre moved forward into a steel-lined chamber. The wall behind them closed. The wall in front of them sank into a smooth concrete floor.

An illuminated, air-conditioned tunnel appeared. They sped through this tunnel and within forty seconds emerged through another set of controlled doors into the park of Saint Christophe. A thick band of trees blocked the view of the main road they had turned-off only two minutes before.

"This is the estate where Moreau, Stotz and Tonio Friedemann created what we know to be the Progenic Cycle: a bio-physical ability to produce artificial human beings. It is also, we believe, where Friedemann perfected his serum, a genocidal poison intended for mass distribution by the Kadets."

Pierre brought the car to a standstill by the creeper crawling facade of the eerie, ugly château.

"Welcome to Saint Christophe! Laboratory, Sex Palace and Death Camp."

"Is anyone in there?"

"Thousands, Madame."

"What do you mean?"

"Of the dead. Otherwise the place is deserted. The most important buildings are the stable blocks you see in the distance, through that archway."

"We saw them from another gate yesterday."

"They are all that remains of the original complex. The château was completed around 1777. They were all guillotined in the French Revolution."

"What can we see?"

"Some of the underground chambers that stretch as far as the monument down that avenue of trees."

"That *obelisk*?"

"Yes, Madame."

"Boys, that thing is over a *mile* away!"

Pierre turned from the driver's seat and stared at Nina. He spoke in perfect American English with a Boston accent. "It is a city below ground, Nina. A complex of laboratories, accommodation for over a thousand staff and research workers, cell blocks for the victims, incineration bays, offices and vehicle loading bays. There is a helicopter port like they have on aircraft carriers. The place is as large as an army camp. We shall see a fraction of the installation this morning and I have to warn you, it is a disturbing experience. There are five million bodies down there ..."

"Five *million*!" Pierre's eyes were calm.

"Would you like to count them?"

"But ..."

"With people like Arthur Moreau *nothing* is impossible. It is only with the leaders of our limited World that the impossible becomes a vibrant force." Charles opened the front door of Saint Christophe and bade them enter the château. "My family has this key. You need not be perplexed. My father used to work here." He turned away for a moment.

"This is a terrible place. Maybe we should go without seeing all that horror."

Pierre raised his hand, "No. Like Johnny and Thomas, you must see everything."

"What's with this swell Boston accent, Pierre?"

"I am American. I majored in Psychology and Political Science at Harvard. I am acting a twenty year old footman. Incidentally, my Dad owns Burfordine Stores."

"Burfordine *Stores*! My *God*! Do we get a discount now we've met you?"

"Not if I know my Dad you don't! But enough of me. We shouldn't waste time. Occasionally kadets patrol the park. It doesn't take long for Maurice to find out what everybody's up to."

"How come the Countess doesn't suspect Maurice?"

"You ask another key question, Jeff. The relationship between the Countess and her domestic staff is a mystery we cannot fathom. I should know, I'm with them in the Servants' Hall every day."

"You sleep in the place, Pierre?"

He grinned, "I sleep in the village with my girlfriend."

As they walked round the perimeter of the château, Charles and Pierre pointed out various features, "Please take a careful look at the tennis courts on your left. Notice that they have settled in the middle."

"Mass graves have a tendency to sag."

"You know a lot, Jeff." They climbed a timber staircase in one of the

106

empty, converted stable blocks.

"So how did your father get involved, Charles?"

"Papa was a structural engineer trained at the École Polytechnique. He was brilliant. In the 'thirties, just after marrying my mother, he emigrated to America and was employed by Blaisedale, innocently I must add. Father and Mother had a comfortable life in Minneapolis but after the war, at Blaisedale's personal request, they returned to France and settled in Yonroche. My twin sister and I were born in Yonroche - we were late arrivals - so I saw what was going on from being a little boy. Papa was set-up all along. He was on the design team for Friedemann's Kadet Precincts, but he *thought* he was creating a system of combined factories and offices for Third World redevelopment projects."

"Where did he work?"

"Where we're standing now. His drawing board was over by that window."

"And he never knew what was happening?"

"Not a hint. We suspect they began to alter his mind as soon as he started work in America in 1934. He would come home and tell my Mother what he was doing, but she became concerned when he kept repeating himself, going on for hours about a colleague's sore thumb, or the way a secretary had her hair tied."

"But he completed the plans."

"To the last detail. One day he took me to see his office, right here in this loft. I met Arthur Moreau. I was sixteen, old enough to know an old queen when I saw one. But he was devastatingly charming, you could not help liking him. Yet there was something rotten about him, like one of those plants that eats flies.

"I had a young eye. I noticed all kinds of weird things going on here. Later I said to Papa, 'Don't you think Moreau's place is crazy?' He didn't reply. Then he became ill and before we knew it he had dementia."

"He went mad?"

"Nothing specific. It's like he crumpled. A superbly fit, highly intelligent professional - for no reason - became a cabbage."

They were shown some of the tawdry interiors of the château. The bedrooms were decorated in a revolting wall paper of blue roses.

"My God, Jeff! It's like that TV show they have in England."

"The show where they have their homes gobbed-up like brothels? ..."

In one of the garages built for Blaisedale's fleet of limousines, they were shown something that might have been on exhibit in a gallery of Modern Art. A hospital trolley gone mad. Glass wreathes made from fluorescent tubing hung from the sides and the top was a substantial sheet of semi-opaque glass.

"See how that glass is scored all over." Jeff looked across at Pierre, "Did this thing support Arthur Moreau's casket?"

"Yes, but nobody remembers the funeral in Yonroche." They walked back to the car and quickly returned to the main road.

"Would you all like to have lunch with my wife and I?"

"That's a swell idea, Charles. Will it be any trouble?"

"Not at all. My wife is always expecting people … even Pierre." He pinched Pierre's cheek. "I feel we need to talk; there is so much to tell you about that place, and the local gossip about Moreau could fill volumes."

Towards the end of the simple French meal Nina put her spoon down on her plate and said, "So why doesn't Sir Frederick know what you both know?" Charles held his glass of *Moulin á Vent* to the window, took a mouthful, and paused - trying to put his words into a form that would make immediate sense.

"Sir Frederick is a Theocrat, Nina: his level of operation is beyond average comprehension. He understands matters we cannot guess at. He leaves the business of ordinary vision to ordinary mortals. Moreau's people are perfecting a system that confuses the wave-lengths of ordinary vision. Once you know what they are doing, it is easy to fathom their system. But to do that, you need to understand the truth."

"So what's difficult about understanding truth?"

"Moreau's people have made us believe in a lie, we see the true picture, but we no longer recognise it as the truth. Like snow-covered ice, we trust the surface, but we slide to our deaths as soon as we walk there."

"Aren't we just the fools of decadence?"

"We are as wise as we can be. But Moreau's system relies on a form of insidious corruption, psychological terrorism. Moreau has made us forget that Truth is ice-hard, lying beneath all Human purpose. Frederick is not concerned with ice, but with fire."

"Fire?"

"The Fire of God."

"And what is that?

"Truth!"

"Don't confuse us, Charles. Pierre, what's he talking about …"

"Never ask any questions, it is the surest way of getting to know the answers."

"You have a halo, Pierre." But the young man was not joking as Nina joked. "Sir Frederick knows all the answers, but he allows us to sink or swim. It is the privilege he gives us. That is why you are both sitting round this table, today."

♠

It was late when Pierre drove Jeff and Nina back to La Breuse. The

Countess had not returned from Paris so they decided to wait for her in a vast drawing room, the Salon de Talleyrand where there was a welcoming fire. Pierre brought them cognac. Back in his footman's role, Pierre spoke broken English with a heavy French accent. Filling their glasses with soda, putting by a bowl of tiny, salted biscuits, Pierre took his leave.

"This is spooky, Jeff. What's with that boy?"

"He's no boy, Nina."

"Well he sure looks like one."

"He doesn't act like one, Nina!"

They talked of the day's experiences. After twenty minutes, Pierre returned to the salon, "Madame la Comptesse is on the telephone, Monsieur. She would like to speak to you. A telephone is on the grand piano."

Jeff picked up the receiver, "Hallo! . . . Corinne?. . . yes, . . . *Now*? (She wants us in Paris right now!)"

"It's late, Jeff."

"Your jet is waiting? . . . OK . . . Maurice will . . . (Our cases are already in the car!)"

"That's crazy! Ask her if something is wrong."

"Are you OK, Corinne? . . . (I don't think she's right at all.) . . . Where are you? . . . I'm sorry, I didn't catch . . . (She can't say where she is.)"

"You mean she doesn't know, or she's not allowed to say?"

"Is somebody with you Corinne? Answer only *Yes* or *No*. (Somebody's with her.)"

"Is she in danger?"

"Are you in trouble, Corinne? . . . (She's in trouble, honey. She's close to tears.)"

"Tell her we're on our way!"

"We'll be right with you. When I put the 'phone down, we're moving. . . . OK . . . Yes, I will . . . as soon as we can. . . sure . . . Bye." He handed his glass to Pierre, "One more shot, please, and make it good. Same for *Madame*." He sat down then got up immediately. He walked over the polished parquet to the console. Taking the replenished glasses from Pierre's hand he murmured, "Do you know what's going on? . . .Speak English."

"Yes. Don't worry about the jet, we'll fly you. We have a plane near by."

"But our things?" Pierre reached into his tunic and brought out a wallet, "Give me two minutes, I'll fix Maurice." He darted from the room.

"Now what?"

"Paris by night, Nina."

PART IV

I left the Villa Friedemann driven at speed by a kadet to Atlas One. We entered the complex through a gateway as prominent in the surrounding countryside as a war memorial. I found myself back in Jo's concrete palazzo under house arrest.

Where Thomas was - alive or dead - I did not know and I was not going to be told.

In luxury, with five kadets to wait on me, I lived alone in Jo's para-paradise.

I discovered his library, a room lined with sycamore wood bookcases. His collection was uniformly bound in gold-tooled olive leather. Every binding was stamped with Arthur's cipher, the ubiquitous adolescent cherub. The entire collection was of pornography. Trashy American magazines of the Nineteen-fifties, tawdry French paperbacks of the Nineteen-thirties; all exquisitely bound. There were rare editions. Three volumes printed in Florence were dated 1695.

My professional interest got the better of me. I set about cataloguing the collection. I trained Panno - who visited me every day - how to clean the books without damaging them and give each a 'shelf mark'.

"You don't seem impressed by the illustrations, Panno."

"What are they doing?"

"Have you no idea?"

"No, Monsieur".

On the eleventh day of my captivity I made a significant discovery.

"A Miscellany of Pleasures, or, The Wanton's Directory" was edited in London and published in Paris in 1899. The book was illustrated with lewd steel engravings, some finished in an early colour process that gave naked flesh the tint of sugar mice.

Late Victorian libertines, browsing through the two hundred and sixty-five pages of the volume, discovered how up to twelve people might make the best use of their time during long winter evenings. Everybody had plenty to do and the engraver had made sure there were no slackers. It was a weird old manual with sections well thumbed. I was about to hand the volume to Panno when I noticed that the last five folios, blank in the original, were covered with hand written notes done in pencil.

"Just a moment, Panno."

Arthur's handwriting was unmistakable. Panno poked his finely shaped head over my shoulder, gleefully exclaiming, "That is Monsieur Moreau's writing!"

"How do you know, Panno?"

"He wrote things everywhere."

"If you know so much, tell me where they are keeping Thomas."

injunction produced a moody silence and lots of dusting. I adjusted my chair, placed the book carefully on Jo's library table, and began to read Arthur's neat screed;

"Marrakech, 197...,

A marvellous success! After years of trial and error Franz and Tonio have finally made our children live. I feel like God.

Eocracy for ever!

Friedemann's poisons show remarkable results. These idiot local mayors let us through their gates like a Trojan Horse! I'll bet they squeal when my darlings pump their backsides with molten lead.

Atlas One almost finished! Franz says in twenty years, maybe less, we won't have to rely on slave wombs. Filthy bitches!

Patience Arthur - one step at a time!

If only Tonio will give me access to his final work 'J' and 'U' kadets will spend a fraction of the time in the womb. They'll mature faster and live longer. My pretty Kadets! Why the fuck doesn't Tonio tell me what he's up to?

Stotz is a funny bastard. I can never make him out. I could never make him out in bed. New York 1955! What a Summer of Sodom it was! Franz had a superb arse. Generous. There'll never be another decade like the Filthy Fifties!

I need to watch Franz. He's too clever. Not half as clever as Friedemann, but we can't all be top Nazis. Kraut cunt! Thank Christ I never knew Hitler personally like old Tonio did.

I'll make Hitler look like a saint when my show's on the road. A world of men! The New Way. Arthur's Eocracy. Every woman slit down the belly and burnt.

Women! Nauseating bitches! Their unspeakable cunts!

French brie.

I'll see them hacked to bits and paraffin rubbed in the lumps.

I'll throw a cocktail party when we get back to France. I fancy a firework display. Something pretty at midnight.

If only Tonio will tell Franz about his latest formula. Evil old bugger.

God, how I'm going to mess with the World! Kids slitting their Mums and Dads open. People exploding in shopping plazas. Every sodding rotten local council corrupt as bottled shit! Governments heaving with saucy little faggots. Science and Art the Byword for corruption. School Governors dog turds in aspic! Youth, cunts in gold leaf. Arch Bishops with arseholes like the Barrier Reef!

They'll all die in sperm-sluiced shit!

Delicious thought!

And all because of my pretty Kadets and their naughty tricks.

I don't believe half of what Franz is telling me about Friedemann's

112

formula. He's lying. Franz is a power seeker. I'll have to watch Franz.

I'll poison Franz's people at my cocktail party. Die in agony during the fancy firework display. Skin the cunts.

Wonderful week here. Sunny. Scores of Moroccan lads to fuck. Restful.

Lovely Roses.

1000 Progens created this month in Atlas One.

100% mature in five years. That isn't counting the work of dear ... [two words erased here].

Don't give it away, Artie, you old Sprite!

Lunch with the PM last week. Not the first clue. Surrounded by them. Two hours of flattery and a barrel of laundered lolly up her clouts and the grisly old cow was mine.

Politicians were ever thus!

I'm fed up to the back teeth with Joey, that sore on his prick isn't healing. Fucking tart. Tired of his old Dad, is he! I'll gut the bugger.

Can I trust my darling Joey much longer?

I wonder.

As soon as he puts the screws on Friedemann I'll bin the cunt.

Hope the new carpets are down when we get back. Not sure about the blue roses on the wallpaper. Not St Christophe at all! More like Lillie bloody Langtry.

Joey made me buy the wall paper. I told him it was horrible. I knew he'd have one of his nine day sulks. Bought three miles of the stuff. Tasteless bitch!

Johnny always lets me have what I want. Mind you, Johnny's a poker-faced cunt. Ignorant as stale piss; not the first clue.

Shit-soft twat!

Peaceful out here. Exquisite fountains. Marble filigree.

Gorgeous!

Here comes Mahmoud with the drinks trolley. I'll buy pretty Mahmoud a car tomorrow. My dusky lollypop in his fancy white suit on cherry red leather.

Cock like a zeppelin.

I'll take him to London.

Tea at the Ritz.

My stomach turned like summer-soured cream. The avalanche of Arthur's criminal insanity was almost too disgusting to contemplate. I made myself read the piece again then walked to the line of high French windows and took deep breaths of the aromatic air, admiring the silver-gilt sunlight of Morocco.

With finicky attention, using a box wood ruler from Jo's desk, I disengaged the final five folios, folding them precisely in half and slipping them into a clean envelope.

"Put the book back, Panno. The shelf mark is L32." Panno's scent; soapy, boyish, drifted to my nostrils as he climbed the library steps close by my chair.

"My pretty kadets . . . !"

There he was, a pretty kadet, his actions made perfect by a perfect physique, sliding a valuable book to its place.

Panno! apparently so charming and so guileless, born of some unspeakable artificial process: half god, half monster.

My hands trembled with indignation. The confirmation of Frederick's view that I knew nothing of Moreau was hard to take. All the while I had known Arthur, since our first introduction at that Oxford college dinner, I had been his unwitting stooge. Frederick was right: Arthur had been the organ grinder, I the monkey.

"Eocracy" - the "New Way"

A madman's crazed dream was coming true and nobody on Earth had the faintest idea. Panno stood beside me, smiling sweetly. "You seem serious, Monsieur. Did you not find the Master's words funny? He always made us laugh. He bought us presents in Paris and London. Silk ties and gold cigarette lighters. He was funny."

I took the boy's exquisite face between the palms of my hands. I drew him gently to me, as a father draws a wayward son.

"Funny is certainly the word, Panno." I disengaged him, and lead him to a chair. His eyes looked into mine, faithful, cascaded with tears.

"Please, sit down. Now that we have time, explain in detail the 'U' and 'J' Kadet system. Tell me how you were born."

♠

Before he could reply, a section of shelving swung open and a clear American voice piped up, "Kadets come in two classes, 'U' and 'J' - these are the initials of the French words, *unique* and *jumelle*. They mean a single birth, literally *unique*; that's one kadet from one womb, and *jumelle* - meaning twins - that's two cloned kadets from one womb. 'U' Kadets are born in batches of five hundred from five hundred 'Progen slave wombs', as the Progenic System terms them. 'U' kadets are genetically structured to be intelligent managers. 'J' Kadets are born in batches of one thousand, that is two each from five hundred Progens. They are worker kadets, brawny, non intelligent, and structured to be subservient." The man walked further into the room, he was fair, late thirties, with a genial expression. He was dressed in grey slacks and a short sleeved,

114

white cotton shirt. I recognised him immediately.

"Panno is a 'U' Kadet, so is Kyla. However, just to confuse you, Johnny, Panno and Kyla are special, a single, separate experiment by Franz von Stotz. They are very nearly, but not *quite* - please note - real human beings. They have cocks and balls for a start, none of the others do, or ever will." The man extended his hand, smiling, "Hi! I'm Stanley Casper. You're Johnny Debrett. Would it we too corny to say that I've heard so much about you?"

"Stanley Casper! The famous news photographer! You died in a plane crash in the Sahara two years ago. The tragedy made international news: *"Stanley Casper meets untimely death!"* The BBC ran a three-part documentary on your career. Your New York funeral was attended by two thousand people."

"I 'died', Johnny, right here in Atlas One. They brought me in a helicopter and it sure didn't crash. That crate dumped me on Jo's lawn below this window!"

"Let me guess. You attempted to investigate Arthur Moreau."

"Yep! For NBC. We planned a gilt-edged scoop."

"You used a pretext."

"Right-on, Johnny! A Summer Special on French cuisine for Frobisher Magazine."

"Your first stop was Yonroche."

"You got it! Where I managed to interview Arthur Moreau. Boy! Was that old man *smooth*! He took me to St-Christophe were I met - can you *credit* this, Johnny? - Anthony Brash and President Zipper swimming round an oval pool!"

"What were they talking about?"

"Blowing the Arabs off the face of the earth, and what they did for sex. Wonder-boy Kyla was there, serving champagne cocktails to some big-shot French guys in the bar."

"I know Kyla very well."

"*Do* you, Johnny? I took a good look at that kid. And I *looked* at him! And I thought to myself, 'This ain't no ordinary Romeo. Something's *weird* with this kid!' And I looked round at the decor of that place, with all those grisly blue roses down the walls, and I said to myself, 'Stanley, there's somethin' *spooky* goin' on in this heap. And they ain't lettin' on! So I crept round that sleazy old château with all those folks in black rubber doing mischief to themselves and I took as many shots as my tiny camera could shoot! And I stood on the steps of that place waiting for Moreau's car to take me back to my hotel and I tell you, friend, I smelt that old, old stink of *evil*!"

"I know the smell."

"I know you do, Johnny. You get that stink in your nostrils once and you know it anywhere!" He suddenly gave Panno a friendly squeeze round the shoulders, "You OK, boy?"

"Yes, Stanley."

"They're starved of affection, Johnny. I tell you, it's cruel how these man-made kids are treated. Anyhow, let me invite you down to my cell and offer you a drink. We'll compare notes. Lead the way, Panno!"

Stanley's 'cell' was an air conditioned, three room apartment with sliding glass doors off the generous living area giving onto a huge indoor pool constructed below the lawn.

"I swim fifty lengths every morning, Johnny; never been so fit. There's some sort of tunnel beyond the pool but they don't let me in there."

"I expect the place is riddled with tunnels."

"Crazy! And not a soul outside knows the first thing about Atlas One! It's the scoop of a lifetime. What will you drink? I got everything here but freedom."

"Gin and Italian."

"Real English tipple! I prefer Bourbon and Canada Dry."

"How do they get hold of all this, and nobody knows?"

Stanley added ice to my drink from a silver pail, "Private supply direct from France and the USA. Flown into their own airstrip, there's a railroad line to the complex. Jo lived like an Emperor. Nothing - but *nothing* - but the best, Johnny. Panno, fix yourself a beer and sit down quiet like a good boy. I taught 'em how to pour beer from a can."

"You treat him like a like a teenage son."

"Delinquent, serial killer, first rate at espionage ... some teenager. Sit down, Johnny." He indicated an expensive, suede covered armchair.

"Well, who's going to start?"

I waved my hand, 'You start, Stanley'.

"OK, I'll try to be brief. With The Arthur Moreau Story ... brevity is not easy."

"What put you onto Arthur?"

"Second hand books. Don't laugh! I know your business is second hand books. I'm *nuts* about them, our New York apartment is walled with them. My wife threatens to leave me if I buy one more! There I go, still not used to the fact that I'm dead. I sure as hell hope Daisy hasn't re-married. I don't blame her if she has, she's a lovely woman, but it's going to be a rough ride if I ever get out of this place and she finds herself doin' time for bigamy!"

His humour was infectious. At thirty-nine Stan was well knit, tough, good looking in a manly way, careful about his weight. He had blue-grey eyes and his hair was the dusky side of blond. His voice was knife-edged with enthusiasm. A cub reporter in Oregon, his home town, Stanley worked his way to The New York Times, and into television. His weekly "Heart of the Matter" news show took top ratings for five years.

He told me about Daisy, admitting to being blissfully married. "We had triplets, I tell you, Johnny, those girls are the three most *gorgeous*, blond, All-American women you ever saw. Twenty years each, and I can't tell them apart! Birthdays cost a fortune. I need a bank loan just for the goddam *cake*!"

He poured more drinks. "Now listen good, Johnny. My favourite second hand book store is on East 95th Street. I was in there one morning - I guess about five years since - and I got hold of this amazing first edition of Oscar Wilde's 'De Profundis'.

"One of only sixteen volumes printed by the New York publisher, Paul Reynolds?"

"That's the one, Johnny. Fifteen were privately distributed but the sixteenth was put in Reynolds's window and nobody recorded the name of the person who bought it."

"It's worth millions."

"It's worth more to us, Johnny. It was from Arthur's collection. He'd written stuff in the back."

"In pencil? Notes like these?" I handed him the envelope. He took a moment to scan the five folios.

"Exactly, Johnny. Grim. Anyhow, my journalist's mind went wild. Who was this dude? What was he doing? - You notice that nothing he writes about is ever quite explained."

"What gave you the break?"

"Your half-brother, Jo. We had a lot of material on Jo."

"His natural father owned an Australian diamond mine."

"His great aunt, on his father's *mother's* side, was Sir Frederick Appleby's great-grandmother."

"Lady Annabel Trune."

"That's the dame! Johnny, I got this irrepressible hunch I had to meet Appleby."

"Difficult."

"*Impossible*! Then it turns out the guy who does my research is from Michigan."

"The brother of Sir Frederick's PA?"

"First cousin. Billy Park. So Billy calls Andy and Andy speaks to Sir Frederick and he gives us the OK to investigate Moreau. I knew Moreau's business was in France, so I made an appointment to see him in Yonroche."

"Did he mention me?"

"No Sir. But he showed me an awesome selection of rare books, mostly decent, not like in the room upstairs."

"Did Fred brief you?"

"I only spoke to Andy Park. He was kinda taciturn. Warned us to be careful, told us that Moreau was mixed up with some sort of crazy sect, secret society, ... terrorist movement? Fascinating, but nothing to dine out on."

"You felt that Frederick knew much more than he was prepared to reveal?"

"Absolutely. I also checked with a contact in the CBI, a good friend. No dice. It seemed like a gigantic lead lid had been slammed-down on Moreau."

"So you only got as far as St-Christophe?"

"Yep. That car they told me was bound for my hotel took me to an airstrip, God knows where. I was escorted aboard one of the most luxurious 707s in the world; fitted-up like Versailles palace. There was a false marble fireplace and a cabaret with a line of twenty chorus boys! I met Stotz and Jayne Blaisedale. We talked, and I was about to tape an interview with them when I blacked-out. I woke up in a helicopter, landing out there on that lawn. Exit Stanley Casper!" He laughed, then looked round. "We got empty glasses again, Johnny. Hey! Where's the kid?"

"Asleep on the couch."

"Let him crash. They had two hours baseball and an hour of English cricket today."

"You teach them sport? Kyla told Thomas they don't do sport."

"They do with Uncle Stan! You see, Johnny, I'm getting a few of these boys a fraction human. They're mad about baseball and they adore cricket! Fuck Eocracy! Get 'em to love us and trust us and they'll lead us to the centre of Moreau's evil maze. Tomorrow they got net practice. Kyla's coming over. The kid's burning with envy because Panno's a better bowler. By the way, Thomas is with them, he makes a damn convincing Kadet."

"Will they bring him tomorrow?"

"If I give Panno another beer, maybe they will."

"Let's drink to that."

♠

Stanley and I sat on the terrace of Jo's villa watching kadets muddle through an improvised game of cricket. The sun was hot but the players were so keen they didn't appear to notice. A "U" kadet called Rolt sat with us in his flannels and pads waiting to bat. Nearby was Jo's huge wicker cricket basket loaded with two teams worth of kit; whites, stumps, bats, balls - nothing but the best. Occasionally Stanley or myself would go over to the players and give them instruction. Panno, more natural in his movements than the others, was shaping excellently. We had been discussing our next move, Stanley summarised: "Two priorities: get into Atlas One and get out of here."

"There's a third, to pay Friedemann a visit - unannounced. We must get hold of those five gold disks, who will believe our story without them?"

"Who will believe our story anyway, Johnny? That is the biggest problem of all." A jeep sped round the corner and scrunched to a skidding halt on the raked gravel. About a dozen kadets scrambled out of the back and raced to the cricket basket. Kyla bounded from the driving seat and to my relief, dressed in a grey para-military Kadet uniform, looking healthy and happy, Thomas bounded after him.

Looking at Thomas I sensed he had matured. Leaving Kyla in charge, he lead Stanley and me to a walled rose garden. Here, unobserved, we could talk.

"I'm sorry, Johnny, that I didn't communicate with you. I judged it more important to merge with the Atlas One routine as a kadet. I would have blown my cover contacting you."

"Did they do anything to you?"

"Nothing. The worst that happened was when they drugged me at Friedemann's place. They were going to kill us both. Kyla and Panno got me away then organised for you to follow. Kyla liquidated Friedemann's assistant, the one called Martin, and the fake granddaughter, Bettina. Kyla says they were professional infiltrators using a string of code names. They could have belonged to any number of international terrorist groups."

"Pity Kyla was so thorough; we might have learnt something from the duo. How's your accommodation?"

"I am staying with Kyla in his quarters, with a hundred other senior "U" kadets, that's ten Centurion Kadets and ninety Wolf Kadets."

"Christ!"

"Wait until you see what goes on in the ziggurats."

"Is anyone in charge?"

"An American called Hoover. He has no idea that I'm an impostor but I need to be careful, the "J" kadets are trained to inform. I am certain there are regular visits from people outside but we are never around when these take place. Hoover sees to that."

"Surely he knows about me and Johnny?"

"If he does he never mentions it."

"How often do you see Hoover?"

"A lot. Me and Kyla run his office, so I know all about the day to day management and supply of the precinct. Fred will be pleased. It's a massive operation. During a period of maximum occupancy - the Progenic Birth Cycle is complex - there are over twenty-one thousand kadets and Progens in Atlas One alone. The supply logistics are incredible. Twenty tonnes of food is flown-in from France every month!"

"Who supplies all that?"

"An In-house agency. The stuff is shipped from Marseilles to Agadir, then loaded onto planes and flown here."

"And nobody knows?"

"Nobody. The Moroccan officials, the French … nobody. Supplies reach a central service zone that supplies those four Precincts we saw from the mountain."

"The ziggurats."

"They are A, B, C and D." He laughed at my incredulity, his manner somehow more graceful; his boyishness had a manly edge. "I'll take you round Precinct A this afternoon."

"We must also pay Friedemann a call."

"Kyla says that the real disks containing Friedemann's latest work are kept in a vault under the floor of the laboratory. You have to *think* the code to raise the vault out of the floor."

"Oh God!"

"We still haven't solved Stotz's 'Old Stone Bridge' riddle."

"Shove it up Stotz's old stone arse!" As we walked back to join the others I said quietly, "You and Kyla seem to be close. Be careful, he might slit your throat."

"He won't; he loves me."

I faced Thomas in vicarage mode, "I hope there's been no hanky-panky!"

"He loves me like a brother!" He rolled his eyes but added keenly, "I've had to tell him all about sex, and *girls*! What we really need here is my sister and her two best friends."

"I'm sure their Mothers would veto that merry idea! . . . Did Kyla tell you any more about Friedemann's code we have to *think*?"

"No, it was late, we'd been whispering for hours. He went to sleep."

"Whispering! . . . He went to *sleep*!" My lips pursed like a dowager's reticule, "What do you mean, 'He went to *sleep*.'? . . . Was this *pillow* talk?"

"You're monstrously old fashioned, Gov'ner!"

♠

Later that day Panno drove us from Jo's villa to collect Kyla and Thomas from the Senior Kadet House, a residence planned on the lines of campus student accommodation.

The precinct ziggurats loomed above a rocky mountain shoulder as we drove through the arch of the Kadet House into a paved courtyard. The place was severe. A two storey stone building with rooms accessed from open galleries round the square court.

Kyla's compact apartment was on the first level and had his Kadet registration number painted over the entrance, *KP2B - C4\i - Ŭ1*. The elusive combination on the necklace he had given me in Paris.

Kyla was all on. Dressed in full ceremonial uniform, he wore a superb sash over the immaculate battledress top, a broad band of ice blue watered silk. On his chest was a diamond-set platinum star. He carried a gilt embellished ebony baton, like a Roman commander. He smelt strongly of expensive scent.

As we entered the scrupulously clean living room, Thomas came out of another room, in equally smart kit though without sash or star. As Thomas greeted us, Kyla gave him a kiss on the nape of his neck.

"You look very impressive both of you. What is the sash and star, Kyla?"

"I am the Ulysses Kadet, the first of all Kadets."

We took a quick look round. The quarters were spartan; no drapes, no rugs, no pictures. The living room had a stone floor and plain wood furniture. There were no cushions on the seats and there was nothing like a television or radio, certainly no bookshelf. Off this room was a room containing Kyla's kit. Here was a pressed metal rack from which hung, in gleaming order, two serrated commando knives (one over a foot long), a cutter sharp as a scalpel with a rubberised grip handle, a strangling wire, and an instrument I guessed was a flayer. Finally, there was a branding iron. Without touching it, I made out the letters, W.M.D.O.

"This is charming, Thomas! Remember what I told you this morning?"

"He won't, Gov'ner."

"Too busy kissing you, is he?"

In the bedroom there was nothing that usually adorns an young man's den. No silly cards from lovers, no pin-ups, no posters showing football teams or rock stars. There were no cuttings from magazines illustrating Ferraris or motorbikes, no expensive audio equipment with a collection of compact disks chucked about, no classical or electric guitar. Only cigarette butts heaped in scorched plastic ashtrays and dirty wine glasses.

"That's Kyla's bed, Gov'ner. My bed is in the next room."

"And what does that prove, Thomas?"

"We'll be late if we don't move, Johnny." Stanley was anxious to get the visit over with. He had the feeling that we might be harmed if they thought we had seen too much.

We drove at rattling speed while Stanley and I rehearsed the questions we planned to put to Doctor Hoover. The jeep took a bend in the track, rounding the rock outcrop to join a ceremonial avenue, straight as a die, three lanes wide. Dead ahead, unbelievably enormous, stood Kadet Precinct Atlas One. Boldly sunlit, crisply outlined against the azure sky, backed by awesome mountain slopes, the complex glimmered in sinister detail.

Larger than the pyramids of Gizeh, each of the four identical Home Kamps stood like a monument to Terror. From countless pinnacles and rock ledges came the cries of thousands of ravens that scored the diamond-keen air like a black plague. The ziggurats were surrounded by smooth, white-sanded parade grounds. They reduced us to the scale of snails as we sped towards the central archway of the entrance to Home Kamp "A".

This structure looked like a Nazi version of the Arc de Triomphe. Around a hundred and twenty feet high by sixty wide, the single arch through it was about twenty feet across. The corners were edged with rough-hewn keystones of cream marble as big as trucks. Aloft its summit, on a basalt plinth, was a gigantic white marble sculpture group of three naked kadets. Their arms were entwined round their waists like a male equivalent of The Three Graces. Stanley was not impressed, "No cocks, no balls, Johnny!"

Crowned with laurels, their bland, chiselled faces were set in classical frowns, their sightless eyes scanned the mountain scenery with god-like *angst*.

"I was the model for those."

"You don't say, Panno!"

"Read what is says underneath." He pulled at Kyla's shoulder, saying something in precinct language. The jeep came to a halt. Beneath the sculpture group, set proud of the wall, was a laurel-framed travertine marble plaque. In Roman capitals three men high that shimmered with gold leaf, we read;

ATLAS ONE

AND WHO HATH BROUGHT UP THESE?
BEHOLD, I WAS LEFT ALONE:
THESE,
WHERE HAD THEY BEEN?

Below the panel, set into the central keystone of the arch in bronze, were the initials A.M.

Panno chirped, "Monsieur Moreau wrote that!" Stanley, furious, gripped Panno's arm so tightly that the Kadet squealed with pain.

"Now you hear me good, Panno! That ain't nothing to do with Moreau! That's the Holy Bible up there, boy, the Prophet Isaiah: that's God speaking! The real McCoy, little kadet! Monsieur Moreau was an evil lunatic. Right now, son, he's roasting in Hell because the fool tried to kick God in the Teeth." He gave Panno's arm a final tweak, then let it go.

"They don't know about God, Stanley."

"Then they better be learning fast or they're in for a rough time. Get this crate moving, Kyla! Let's see what kind'a hole Atlas One is."

"Why so ill at ease?"

"I don't like any of this, Johnny. It's crazy, it's dangerous, it stinks. I think they're into some sort of psychological spinology here, we're being brainwashed by crooks and slobs."

"Sounds like home, to me."

"Nobody can see it going on, nobody has …"

"Nobody has any idea, Stanley."

"They're out to corrupt the World … and there's damn-all you and I can do about it."

122

"We can! We *are!*"

"Thomas, you're an adorable kid, but you're young and *stupid.*"

"Here's the entrance, I'll take you to Hoover's office."

The principal entrance of the ziggurat was set into a smaller arch topped with a heavily swagged, monumental urn - I should say about five meters in diameter, nearly sixteen feet. The urn was of pinkish concrete and contained Madonna lilies carved in white marble. From these blooms rose a thin trail of sulphur yellow smoke.

Kyla said, "That's from the cremation ovens in the basement." I shot him an old-fashioned look, "Who gets cremated?"

"We do."

♠

"You're welcome!" Hoover beamed us a plastic, quasi-smile. We weren't welcome at all. Suspicion shadowed Doctor Hoover's clean shaven, putty-jawed face. He was around thirty-five, pouchy round the neck and not too sure of his ground with strangers. Wearing a pair of rimless spectacles that had a black ribbon attached to the left frame looping down to a button hole, he looked the archetypal boffin-in-a-white-coat. Interesting that the lenses were flat glass, like specs movie actors wear before camera.

His office had floated through Time from pre-war Berlin. The man was wondering if he should throw us out when Kyla, radiant with superb authority, his diamond star sparkling in the fluorescent glare, the silk sash tracing the stunning sheath of his torso, opened a cabinet and whipped out a bottle of fine Russian vodka, removing the cork from its neck with perfect, Polar-white teeth.

"Drink, Doctor?"

"Why, I don't mind if I do, Kyla . . . Why don't we all have drink?" Hoover stood up, reeled a little, changed his mind about something, and sat down again. Stanley glanced at me, we realised that the man was sodden with booze, like Jayne Blaisedale.

"Gentlemen! ... Sit down 'n tell me . . . *frankly*, . . . what the hell you're doing in my office." He took from Kyla a tumbler full of vodka and tonic, dashed by Thomas with bitters. Stanley and I held our glasses diplomatically close to our chests.

"We've come to see the kadets. Tonio tells us that they are developing much faster now. A success story wouldn't you say? We'd like to have a look at them."

Panno and Kyla, now menacingly physical, stepped forward and placed their hands on the corners of Hoover's enamelled steel desk. Hoover waved a rubbery hand at us; "A wonderful story! . . . Wonderful! We are one huge happy family. 'Happy, Healthy and Hopeful.' is the Precinct motto."

"Hopeful of what, Doctor?"

"Of greater things to come. *My* responsibility in the four Home Kamps that make up this Precinct, Atlas One, the very first - is to raise these boys from birth to adulthood in the best way possible. It is our mission to make perfect gentlemen of them. A mission we check-out each day, to ensure they enjoy a life that is exactly what the motto of the Precinct says; 'Happy, Healthy and Hopeful'. Responsibility rests heavily upon my shoulders." He drained the glass, pushing it towards Panno for more. Without a word, Kyla and Thomas left the room.

"Why do you call the Kadets 'boys', Doctor?"

Hoover made play of dipping two fingers into his replenished drink, fishing out the half slice of lemon and sucking at it noisily. It seemed that he had not heard my question. "This is the generation of a Perfect Society: harmless, svelte, conformist, clean and neat."

"Without individuality; amoral, lying, callous, characterless hoodlums. Is my description better than yours, Doctor?"

"Who the fuck are you?"

"Stanley Casper."

"The television star ... in my office! ... Wow ... Panno, be a cutie 'n get the fucker out of here!" He gazed at his desk lamp with wet-fish eyes.

"You didn't answer my question, Doctor."

"It's not my job to give interviews to jerks. My job is to see to the welfare of an army of young men. I have a great deal of work to do this morning!" He tried to get up but he was too drunk. He slurred, "We must bring this happy social occasion to a close. I have a lot of …. The Ulysses Kadet will take you back to Marrakech." He darted a cunning look through the fake specs like a lizard, "Panno, go find Kyla."

Panno stood still by Hoover's chair.

"I said, go find Kyla!"

Panno didn't move. "You clockwork shit! Fucking *move!*"

Panno picked up Hoover's steel desk lamp. Swinging the heavy base back, he grasped Hoover's fleshy neck. In a second the man's brains spattered over the grey tiled floor. The top of his skull lay bloody by the silent telephone.

"For the sake of Sweet Jesus, Panno! Did you have to do *that*?"

"He insulted me."

"He was important to us alive, Panno!"

The doors burst apart. Thomas appeared, smiling, followed by Kyla who waltzed into the office with six tiny, identical infant kadets who grasped his fingers and wrists with minute, gorgeous hands. They were very cute, dressed in little white cotton robes and wearing diminutive sandals. They were also exquisitely beautiful, their big, round eyes agog with curiosity. Seeing the office, then us - they took no notice of Hoover's corpse - they went silly with shyness and hid behind Kyla's and Thomas's legs, holding on to their guardians' thighs and peeping round them while Kyla, fatherly, shone us a broad, happy grin and bent down to gather two of them in his arms, giving each a smacking kiss on the top of their beautiful, raven-haired heads.

"If you want to see fourteen hundred and ninety eight more, follow me!" Panno and Thomas gathered the little ones into a flock, cooing at them like young mothers.

"Don't look at the desk, Thomas. There's no time for fainting today."

♠

Friedemann's Progenic Cycle is easy to grasp in simplified principle. Beginning at the top of each, identical, Home Kamp ziggurat, called Level One, the system provided a birth floor, then worked down, year by year, level by level, through infancy, childhood, adolescence and early adulthood in sixty months - to Wolf Kadet status. Therefore, the ziggurats had Five Levels above ground, Level Five at ground level. There was also a basement, vast and deep.

The last two years of the cycle, spent on Levels Four and Five, were concerned with basic education and preparatory training. Wolf Kadets were then sent to Switzerland where, near Lausanne, "J" kadets spent some time in a military style training camp, while "U" kadets received management schooling at the Moreau Eocratic University. This University was staffed by third rate academics from Britain and the United States, at the time, a breed in plentiful supply.

I have not mentioned the kadets' "mothers", the Progens, or living wombs. These profoundly mutilated creatures were supplied in batches of five hundred per cycle. As well as bearing six kadets in sixty months (four "J" and two "U") a Progen reproduced itself in duplicate *twice*, creating two thousand more Progens before being incinerated. These supplied other Precincts, transported in plastic crates like beer bottles. The most rudimentary mathematical calculation quickly demonstrates that the Progen and Kadet birth rate followed a soaring parabolic curve. This curve is ideal if you wish to create a new generation of millions of beings in a matter of decades, *if* your Precinct system can keep up.

The Progens we saw had been inseminated by sperm donated from normal men who were captive in Moreau's *Stallion-Zones*: converted holiday camps, caravan parks and Country House hotels. Friedemann had created artificial sperm but his formula was locked in the five gold disks.

The development of the primary batch of Progens, the five hundred that began the first cycle, was mainly Stotz's work, Friedemann being wholly concerned with designing the two kadet body types and engineering "J" and "U" kadet standard personalities. Progens were Stotz's major contribution to the

Eocratic Strategy, after which he and Friedemann began to disagree on points of ethical significance and Stotz distanced himself from his lover. Finally, he abandoned Europe taking charge of the superb laboratories at Gracewood where he created his own masterwork, Kyla and Panno.

♠

Embellished with ostentatious vulgarity on the exterior, the Home Kamps were plain and utilitarian within. Each level presented an endless grid of tall, slender, octagonal reinforced concrete columns, painted gloss white, as in a factory.

Grasping the hands of the tiny Kadets, we ascended to Level One in a slow, grinding, plank-lined freight elevator, arriving with a judder.

We walked through a lobby that contained lavatories and washrooms. It smelt of carbolic with a dash of urine and excrement.

"As I see it, Johnny, this building could easily be shipped in pre-fabricated parts from France. The larger units could be cast on site. You could get one of these ziggurats up and running in six months with the appropriate manpower."

"That's the point, Stanley, what is the appropriate manpower? To construct this in six months would require thousands of men." I turned to Kyla, "Did Kadets construct Atlas One?" His reply was ducal. "Certainly not! It is for lesser beings to do manual work!"

The place had a lonely atmosphere, crude, clinical and inhumane. Acres of cream ceramic floors, the walls coated with industrial grade white paint, timber and steel painted black, the glass - everywhere - Georgian Wired safety plate. Basic economy strip lighting without diffusers glared down in never-ceasing lines. All services were housed in surface-mounted, unfinished galvanised steel conduits.

"How can you stand this place, Kyla?"

"It is our home."

As we approached a series of hospital type rubber doors the stink of excrement and urine far exceeded the not unpleasant odour of carbolic. Four kadets appeared, swarthy and brawny. They made low bows to Kyla, who - I presumed - ordered them in Precinct language to take the infants away.

"You will see them again on the level below. Shall we proceed?"

"What's that horrible smell, Johnny?"

Panno had opened a set of rubber doors. Immediately we were bathed in a pervasive, cloying, animal stench. I looked at Thomas doubtfully, "Smells like a woman's menstruation to me; a bad one."

"It's disgusting, Gov'ner!"

"Get married! You'll find out what women have to put up with."

126

Panno opened a second set of doors and the full force of the stench hit us like a stone wall. I had to prevent myself from retching but Thomas, finicky at the best of times, went green. "Can you take this?"

"I'll try."

We were shown into a space lit dull orange, like a photographer's developing lab. There was a constant gurgle of running water accompanied by faint whistling sounds, like a giant lavatory cistern. Three "U" kadets in white overalls came over and greeted us. They gave Kyla, Panno and Thomas the usual kiss on the lips which caused Stanley to tut-tut. "What this place needs, Johnny, is dames!"

By a bank of stainless steel cabinets about twenty kadets were attending long, open drawers, as in a mortuary. We could see water dribbling from hoppers above each drawer and saw it draining away in steel channels below. We entered a large cubicle enclosed by stainless steel partitions. Here a team of white clad kadets were pouring greyish liquid from stainless steel buckets into a large tank that had a mixer laboriously revolving in its centre and various temperature gauges round its rim. The equipment looked old fashioned and what they were doing wasn't very precise. The mixer slopped liquid over the side of the tank onto the tiled floor that was constantly sluiced with water that drained away through steel floor grilles.

Kyla lead the way. As he approached, the team of assistants immediately formed a line and reverently bowed their heads. He waved his baton, touching the shoulder of a kadet.

"This is Philo. He will show you the Progens, but now he will explain the batch system." The kadet took from his neck an identical platinum tag and chain that Kyla had given me in Paris. He showed us the combination of letters and numbers stamped on the platinum dye. Stanley read out, "*KP1D-C3\iU078*. OK, Philo, so what does it mean?"

"I am created here in Kadet Precinct One, that is KP1, in Home Kamp D, from Progen Cycle three, phase one - that is C3\i. I am a U Kadet of Birth Batch Number seventy-eight of five hundred, that is U078. On the main frame computer you can find the Progen that bore me, the date I was created, the donor of the sperm that inseminated the Progen, and the technical data for my batch. The Progen has been destroyed long ago. They keep a history."

"Who keeps a history, Philo?"

"I do not know."

"If I recall, Kyla, your stamp gives KP2."

"Where me and Panno were invented is unimportant, Johnny. KP2 is in the United States. Its full address is Minnesota Two."

"And you have an unusual Latin letter, an accented capital Ǔ ... with simply the figure one after it."

"Panno has the same code as me but he is Ǔ2. Now, *please* listen to Philo.

He is an important key for you."

Philo spoke in finely pronounced American English, "Progens are not women. They are living wombs. They have neither personality nor intellect, they do not need such facilities. They have been developed from the female of the Human Race by a humane and painless method devised by Doctor Franz von Stotz. The batch of Progens you are going to see now were born on the first of April last. They are Batch "R4". Please come with me. Be careful not to slip on the wet floor and do not touch the Progens."

"If I want to be sick what do I do?"

"Are you planning on being sick, Thomas?"

"It depends."

"There's a door over there. Be sick outside on the terrace."

"Suppose it won't open."

"*Improvise!*"

Along an aisle of stainless steel cabinets we got accustomed to the dim orange light and a more abominable stench. We walked past cabinet after cabinet. Beneath a paddle fan that was revolving so slowly it made no draft, Philo drew open three drawers in the faceless steel wall. "Batch R4 is fifty-four days old, not fully mature."

In each drawer, lying on a specially moulded stainless steel tray, naked and obscene, was a pear-shaped lump of flesh about five feet long - a meter and a half. Each lump was dominated by a bread knife length vagina curtained with huge, lolling labial veils, as are the rubber skirts of a freight carrying Hover Craft. From these slits poked protuberantly, as richly hued as a turkey cock's crop, a gorged, stinking, slimed clitoris: so deformed that I can only compare it with a joint of glazed, roast ham.

The Progenic flesh was the colour of cheap processed cheese, the pudenda a mop-sized triangle of jet black hair that reminded me of the sweepings on a barber's floor. Each Progen had a tiny, eyeless head. Their noses were unrecognisable but for two snotty holes in the pastry-like ball. There was a lipless mouth that sometimes opened to reveal a pinkish, jelloid void that was tongueless and toothless. They could make no sound for the larynx had been done away with. There was no hair on the skull and no sign of ears. Almost without necks, the heads twitched continuously. There were foetal arms and legs but no sign of hands or feet; the putty coloured stumps writhed spasmodically. Philo turned a Progen on its front, the anus had been reduced to a liver brown, crinkled sphinctoral valve. Out of this stinking aperture oozed a sloppy excrement the colour and consistency of *crème caramel.*

The dull grey fluid we had watched being mixed a few moments before slopped about with the excrement in the moulded recesses of each drawer. Philo explained that the grey liquid was the Progens' last feed and would soon be sluiced away.

"I have fed my twenty Progens. Now I rinse them down with a warm solution that prevents ulceration of the skin. To feed them we put a tube into the mouth void and pump liquid food through an adaptor. They can't taste but their digestions are exceptional so they do not defecate solid matter, simply the slime you see and this is easily drained. Urination is not a problem as they have no bladders."

"Why no limbs, Philo?"

"Progens do not need to walk, they lie like this for the span of their lives. That is for one hundred and eight months. These Progens will be ready at fifty-one months to be prepared for the first insemination. The pregnancy period is reduced to seven months. The stubs you see on the shoulder areas will soon begin to develop into bearing pads. These are attached to each side of the birth pen during labour allowing the Progen to bear down correctly as birth takes place. The birth pens are presently closed for maintenance. They are on the other side of Level One, beyond the central partition you can see over there.

"In these cabinets we have Progens of the advanced batch." Philo lead us to another cabinet and suavely opened a drawer as though he were displaying quality lingerie in a department store. The body within had swollen to form a huge pelvic region, like an Earth Goddess of early civilizations. Breasts were evident but no nipples. The vagina was now two feet long, around sixty centimetres, and mountainous, like a trifle. It had wide, sleek, liver coloured lips. It was gushing a sticky, pale green secretion, the Friedemann version of vaginal fluid that appears when a normal woman is sexually aroused. Suddenly the Progen went into a spasm, the fluid bubbled then spurted a rope-thick jet of stinking slime over our heads.

"It is having an orgasm, please stand away, the fluid can stain your clothes."

Thomas turned leek green. "Get out onto the terrace!"

"I'll be alright."

"You've been here for nearly three weeks, Mate. Haven't you seen this?"

"I only know the levels below, with the little ones." He managed a wan smile. "It's the shock. I feel more angry than sick."

"Too *right* you do!" Stanley's voice shook with emotion, "This is horrible! What I ain't seen round this globe ain't worth talking about, but I ain't seen nothin' like this!" He glared at the kadets. "What do *you* think: Philo? .... Well? .... Kyla? Panno? Do *you* think this is horrible?"

"We do not think anything, Stanley. We do not know what a woman's body looks like."

"Well, it sure as Hell don't look like *that,* Kyla! That is *satanic.* Evil!"

I was sharply insistent, "Show us the basement, please. Just the important areas, we don't want to see kitchens and food stores."

"But you haven't seen . . ."

"I guess we've seen more than enough, Panno. The sight of … that terrible abnormality makes me feel ashamed."

"It is the glorious creation of …"

"Get us *out* of here, Kyla!"

♠

An elevator car as junky as the first juddered to a halt about thirty meters below ground level. As Panno and Philo manhandled the clattering gates we had to raise our voices to be heard above the noise of gigantic ceiling-mounted extract fans.

We stepped into a cavernous concrete hall as long as a cathedral nave. Way above, freight station sodium lamps beamed surreal chrome yellow light. Flush with the steel plated floor, rails like tram rails snaked. A train of steel wagons slowly moved past us. Each wagon was piled with dead kadets in full dress, their flesh turning to black slime as we looked. The electric locomotive pulled this cargo towards a steel-framed opening in a concrete wall. The last wagon of the train was a simple platform equipped with a control console manned by two kadets. Kyla ordered them to stand down, then beckoned us, "Please, climb on board."

The train passed through the opening and took three minutes to reach an enormous cliff of incinerators where it stopped in a siding. Beyond cast iron railings, the sort they have on seaside promenades, about forty kadets were busy raking ash out of fifteen ovens. These were similar in design, but much larger, to those photographed in the captured extermination camps of Nazi Germany. They had an old fashioned, riveted appearance; the ghoulish doors speaking of death in every sinister curve. Kyla hopped over the railings and pushed a control lever on a metal box with the end of his baton.

The wagon sides let down automatically. "Come! We will watch the kadets load the ovens." Six 'J' kadets began to drag bodies from wagon nearest to us and fork them onto a moving griddle that slowly advanced towards the door of an oven. As they laboured, despite the din, Kyla spoke to us with professional dispassion as if he were giving a lecture to medical students in front of a corpse.

"These were 'J' kadets, from many different precincts, who reached the end to their life span. This one has only just been put down, he is still fresh." A dead kadet was hooked from the pile. We saw the semblance of a normal, fit, seventeen year old. He lay with eyes open, the expression betraying neither pain nor fear. "We have a life span of one hundred and forty months, then we are exterminated by fatal injection. The full span is in fact one hundred and forty-four months, but if we were permitted to live out the last sixteen weeks of our span, great suffering occurs resulting from a catastrophic degeneration of biological cell structures."

Belts were removed from every corpse. Panno explained that this was to save brass. Friedemann, he told us quietly, had developed a formula that would permit kadets to live up to thirty years before extermination.

"Is the formula set-out on Tonio's golden disks?"

"Yes."

I watched while a pile of over a hundred corpses slid into the oven and the doors automatically closed. "Are 'U' Kadets treated in the same way, Kyla?"

"Of course! When our term is through, we are nothing more than slime."

"You don't fear death?" He turned his head, avoiding my eyes, saying, "The re-cycled ash is used to mix concrete for new Home Camps." I was too angry to care about concrete mixing. I sensed Stanley was past fury. I was also mad because we had no camera: who would believe this? The situation was simplified when Thomas sank to the floor and was violently sick.

"Take him upstairs, Philo. We'll join you soon." Thomas had given me the excuse to separate Philo from Panno and Kyla. Somehow, the kadet seemed to spark them with male jealousy, they were becoming arrogantly threatening, perhaps dangerous, like tigers.

I stepped over to another moving griddle and made Panno reach inside a dead kadet's tunic and take out his identification necklace.

"This one says KP9A. Where is Kadet Precinct Nine?"

"India."

I took Kyla by the sleeve and pulled him to one side. I shouted into his ear, "Do you know where the golden disks are?"

"They are in a floor safe, in Doctor Friedemann's laboratory." I shouted over to Stanley, beckoning him to join us, bawling, "Kyla knows where the disks are."

"Does he know the code?"

"It is a picture."

"What picture?"

"In the laboratory, of an man in a costume." I glanced at Stanley, "Do you agree that we take these two with us?"

"Fine by me, Johnny. But they need drugs to live."

"Doctor Stotz can make us live, Johnny. He is our creator."

I decided to take the risk, "If you introduce us to Franz von Stotz, will you keep faith with us?" In answer Kyla bent and kissed my hand. When he faced us, his expression was lit with a beautiful, radiant smile.

♠

We got out of Atlas One in Kyla's jeep as easily as tourists driving away from a hotel. In the back Stanley, Panno and Thomas straddled boxes of drugs and syringes necessary to keep them alive for six months. Round their feet were bulk cartons of Moroccan cigarettes.

We turned off the main Marrakech road and took the disconcerting track to Friedemann's villa. Just before the ornamental gateway to the main complex Kyla took a spur leading to the servants' quarters, a fake Neo-Classic building with a pretty frontage. We pulled-up outside the ground floor garaging, twelve double doors set in stone arches. These were all shut and no lights showed in the upper floor windows of the servants' quarters. Stanley whispered, "It's eight in the evening, Johnny. This place should be buzzing."

We walked silently along a paved path. Following Kyla, we stole over the lawns to the principle entrance court. Two burnt-out Bentley convertibles smouldered by the marble steps, the chauffeurs' bodies lay nearby. The men had been shot in the head. It seemed as if the bronze entrance doors had been blown open by an explosive charge. The hall was wrecked.

"Somebody got here before us?" Stanley grabbed Kyla by the lapels, "Do you know about this? Are you playing a game with us?"

"We know nothing!"

"We have to trust them. Better to find out what's going on." We planned that Stanley searched the ground floor with Panno and Thomas, while Kyla and I searched upstairs."

"In ten minutes meet in Friedemann's study."

Kyla and I stole up the wide, Japanese onyx staircase. Friedemann's taste betrayed the luxurious neutrality typical of the best International hotels. A landing furnished with sofas upholstered in sapphire blue satin lead to a generous corridor. Here, doorways were regularly spaced between pairs of Tang Dynasty, black and gold Chinese vases. We walked stealthily in the snow-thick, carpeted silence.

We came to a dead end, an oval lobby lined with mirrors framed in coral and silver. A pair of closed, red lacquered, Regency doors faced us like the entrance to a Pharaoh's tomb.

Kyla carefully turned the gilt-bronze handle of one of the doors and we faced a heavy curtain of flamingo-hued brocade bordered with black Burano lace. There was an almost overwhelming scent of jasmine blossom.

"Dead silence. Nobody. You can always tell." I drew aside one of the drapes, holding Kyla back until I had made sure.

Friedemann's bedroom was an opulent fantasy of solid silver and rock crystal furniture, the gold-leaf drenched, boat shaped bed was canopied with marble and ivory youths entwined in sexual frenzy. A lumpen mahogany standard lamp with a pom-pom shade showing views of Windsor Castle and Westminster Abbey on scorched, fake vellum struck the single, somewhat unfortunate, note of anticlimax.

By this lamp, on a polished, ornately patterned parquet floor, was a delicate, gilt framed, Louis Quinze *fauteuil* upholstered in white silk embroidered with violets. Placed on the chair, fully dressed in a three-piece suite of Austrian cut, the trousers *Plus-Fours*, the orange silk shirt and chocolate brown bow tie immaculate, his hand-made brogue shoes of light cream hide, was Tonio Friedemann's corpse.

Friedemann had been shot cleanly through the cranium by a professional: the back of his skull remained intact. The small, neat weapon had been placed on a rock crystal occasional table just out of Friedemann's reach. In his manicured right hand was a flat, clean sheet of blue, Venetian writing paper - a handwritten suicide note. It was a most suspicious arrangement, clearly a 'set-up'.

"Who was here, Johnny?"

"Anybody's guess. Let's look round. See if there are other items of interest besides this note." I slid the paper from the waxen hand. The handwriting was identical to that on the fake letter in Jo's safe.

Stanley bawled from the top of the stairs, "You OK? There's nobody alive down here."

"We're fine. Friedemann's been murdered."

"There's been a raid, Johnny. The old boy's lab has been wrecked."

"We'll be with you in two minutes." I wrapped the gun in a silk square from a drawer, and folded the note. Before pulling the drapes to we took a last look at the hideous decor.

"A dirty weekend in Blackpool."

"I don't understand, Johnny."

"It would be a miracle if you did, Kyla."

♠

Downstairs, we sat about in Friedemann's library considering the next move. "So what do we find? The library wall has been raised, the laboratory has been turned upside-down, some peripheral damage to the main entrance, two limousines burnt out, the chauffeurs murdered. Other bodies? Any servants about?"

"Nobody, Johnny. There's a mess in one of the apartments over the other side where Kyla sliced-up two of Friedemann's people. They're high as kites."

"Boys, you really shouldn't kill people like you were peeling bananas, they *were* evidence!"

"Sorry, Johnny."

"Anyone else?"

"The place is deserted, Johnny. As if Friedemann was planning to get out. Looks like the staff were fired in advance. The kitchens are mothballed, the rooms are dusted, ashtrays empty. Entire place like a museum. His luggage was about to be loaded into the cars; the stuff's in a porter's lodge by the hall. Nothing in the cases but clothes."

"Somebody surprised him on the point of departure."

"Looks like it."

"But they had to leave in a hurry. Maybe the sound of our jeep."

"They were after the disks. Take a look at this, Johnny. Found it on the terrace out there. A sheet ripped out of a file binder. Typed paragraphs from some sort of assessment report. The last line is significant; *We require the disks by the end of May.*"

"Nine days time. Interesting that the handwritten notes in the margins are by the same person that faked Tonio's suicide note. It matches the letter I found in Jo's safe."

"You didn't send that to London?"

"No. I want to hand these items to Frederick personally."

"Any reason?"

"It's difficult to say, Stanley. I have an instinct about this spiders web of tiny clues."

"Open the volume on the sideboard, Johnny. Friedemann's original plans for the precincts, all bound in leather. Each plan is signed by him, some dated between 1934 and 1936 - dedicated to Adolph Hitler. There's a final section of plans dated from 1949 to 1951. Those are dedicated to Blaisedale."

Expertly, I leafed through the sensational tome; the architectural drawings were brilliantly executed. "At last, something to go on. I turned sample folios to the light, sure enough they were watermarked Watman, the years of manufacture matched Friedemann's dated drawings."

"All beautifully bound in tooled leather."

"Why put a Swastika on the spine in 1951?"

"Because, Thomas, there were then Germans, Friedemann is a good example, who believed that the Nazi movement had not been destroyed." I asked Thomas to put the items in the jeep lock-up. Getting up from my chair I strolled towards the wall where kadet Tayno had been slaughtered. Running my fingers down the polished marble, it was awesome to think that the event had actually taken place. Kyla was examining the debris in the laboratory, he called out, "They didn't find the disks. The location of the cabinet is untouched."

"Get thinking, gentlemen. Another loony code to dream-up."

In the lab, though stuff from drawers and cupboards had been chucked about, little was seriously damaged. A wall safe had been jemmied, but the contents - a bottle of Marie Brizard and six pink aperitif glasses - remained untouched. The safe was normally concealed by a large, metal framed, sepia photograph. The frame was hinged to the wall. The photograph, under glass, was of a famous Victorian actor-manager dressed in the role of a king, Sir

Francis Benson. It had been personally autographed: *To Tonio, with fond respect, F. R. Benson.* On the lower side of the frame was an engraved inscription in German that I read aloud: *"Nun ward der Winter unsers Missvergnügens".*

"Hey! You're fluent."

"My father was German, Count Otto von Heilbronn. He hated the Nazis and was forced to get out in 1938. He met my Mother in Switzerland, settled with her in England and died when I was seven, killed in a mountaineering accident in the English Lake District."

"I'm sorry. But how come your name is …?"

"Stanley! … It would take a novel to explain. The immediate problem is to raise Tonio's cabinet from the floor we're standing on."

"I have a hunch that what you just read is a clue. What does it mean?"

"It is Shakespeare. Part of the first line of Richard III. The photograph is a still from an ancient movie of the play, made as far back as 1911. Benson, who directed the production, is Richard III and the quote is Gloucester's famous opening phrase, *Now is the winter of our discontent …"*

That's only half, Johnny. The full line goes, *Now is the winter of our discontent …"*

"… Made glorious summer by the sun of York;. . ."

Noiselessly, a large, polished bronze cabinet rose from the floor to the height of our chests. Its sides were of plate glass. Screwed to the solid top was a silver plaque.

Thomas ran into the room.

"Bloody hell! It's empty!"

♠

"We can see that, clever-bugger! What does it say on the plaque?" Thomas, Kyla's arm round his waist, squinted at the top of the cabinet, "Electro Plated Nickel Silver. Fattorini and Sons. Bradford" I shoved them both aside, "For God's *sake*, man! That's where the plate came from. What does it say in the centre of the blasted thing?"

"Oh! I didn't see that."

"Well, bloody *look*!"

"Johnny, I'm parched for a cup of coffee. Kyla, Panno, go to the kitchen and fix us some coffee please. Maybe Johnny would like tea?"

"Coffee will be fine, Stanley. *Black* for Thomas. Wake the bugger up."

The two kadets happily sped-off to the kitchens, leaving the three of us perplexed at Friedemann's cunning, fatuous riddle, a jingle in English;

W and M and D and O.
Number them!
And What do you Know?

"Right, Thomas! You're going to sit down on that stool and remember the crap your puerile little mind cooked-up when we first arrived in Marrakech."
"Crap?"
"That's right, Mate! The balls you told me and Hassan. The 22-11 rubbish. The Vagabond King crap. It worked with that old bitch at the Villa Aubazine, now get your arse into gear and recall your wizardry for W.M.D.O!"
He sat down and gave out a sigh.
"Well, Brains? Have you remembered?"
"I reasoned that if *22-11* stood for *V.* and *K.* in the alphabet - because the twenty-second letter is V and the eleventh letter is K - and that was the cue for *Vagabond King*, then it might follow, using the same method, that W. M. D. O. stands for 23, 13, 4 and 15."
"It gets less plausible if I recall."
"I added the four figures together, I don't know why, it just seemed the thing to do."
"Fifty-five."
"And if you multiply them together you get seventeen thousand, nine hundred and forty. And if you multiply that by fifty-five . . ."
"You get nine hundred and eighty-six thousand, seven hundred. Are you keeping up with this parlour game, Stanley?"
"What's so fucking brilliant about nine, eight, six, seven, zero, zero?"
Within the cabinet a golden plinth arose. On its top, fixed by diamond encrusted platinum clasps, were five golden discs. The glass sides of the cabinet retracted. Etched in three languages on the gold plinth, we read the following statement:

THE MATHEMATICAL FORMULA CONTROLLING THE
GOVERNOR OF THE UNIVERSE WE KNOW
IS WRITTEN UPON THESE DISKS.
THE FORMULA IS BEYOND THE REALM OF TIME AND WILL
DESTROY IRREDEEMABLY ALL WE CAN KNOW AND ALL THAT WE
ARE.

THIS IS THE MIND OF GOD

The room shuddered: the whine of a siren began, getting louder, to the point when it passed the threshold of pain and we could hardly think. I made out

Stanley shouting, lip reading his cry, "The disks!". I felt Thomas grip my waist, his hot breath in my eyes as he screamed "*Kerosene!*" Something wet was falling, like dew, like a shower bath . . . the smell. Then I knew, we had seconds before the place went up.

The lights went out, but a single searing cone of silver light from a powerful mercury lamp illuminated the cabinet in unearthly focus. The beam strobed. I saw Thomas on his knees by the disks, his image in ribbons, the nimble fingers darting at the disks. I knelt by him, "The discs are loose. Here's two. Grab them!" Stanley waded into the beam of light, contorted, mouth speaking, eyes wild. Thomas pushed two disks into his hands.

"Get *out*!" With spiders' legs, faint with the stench of kerosene, we raced through the study, given insane courage by the fear of burning to death. Stanley smashed a French window and we got through as parachuters jump from a plane.

I ran like a beast. Fresh night air reviving me, rose thorns ripping the backs of my hands. I ran over a lawn. Palm trees in silhouette. The lip of a marble fountain basin almost broke my shins. The water was bath deep, warm. On my back, like some madman, eyes tight shut, nose snorkelling, squirmy gold fish nibbled stupidly at my hair, I held the two disks well under the water.

Friedemann's villa exploded with a thunderclap. In a terrible roar the complex dissolved into a gigantic fireball that shot upwards and outwards, scorching towards us at the rate of a hundred meters a second before it suddenly gave out . . . had we been thirty meters closer we should have been boiled alive.

I sat up. The column of flame was half a mile high: a quality cremation. After three minutes, which seemed years, there was silence. I stood up to find Stanley and Thomas had shared the same basin. We were drenched, sluiced with waterlilly roots, but unharmed.

"Shame! I planned-on loading some of the books and tapestries."

"How many disks you got, Tommy?"

"One."

"Johnny?"

"Two."

"And I've gotten two - that makes five. Winner takes all, boys. Let's get of out here."

Thomas cried, "Kyla! . . .Panno! . . . I'm going to find them!" Stanley grabbed him by his belt, "Don't be a fool! They're dead! Nobody could survive that."

We looked once more at the pall of smoke, eerily illuminated from below as the shell of each concrete pavilion burnt dull red. Two stone eagles on the main archway remained intact, their calcinated wings spreading majestically over the ashes. Four palms stood in tattered silhouette against this ruby cyclorama. Where Friedemann's study and laboratory had been a billion sparks danced like fireflies.

Illuminated by stars, we walked along the dark estate track to the undamaged servants' quarters where the jeep waited in good order. In two hours we were sitting in Hassan's comfortable majlis, showered, changed: thankful to be alive.

♠

"I did not for one instant suspect that you were dead, Gentlemen." Hassan had left a neighbour's dinner party when he was informed of our return. He stood by the fire of his study in a white tuxedo of faultless, dated, cut. "It is a pity about the two kadets. They would have been ample evidence that your experience is true. However (he proffered a box of cigarettes) in this country - indeed, throughout the Islamic world - death is soon disposed of."

"Who will believe us?"

"Two people on Earth believe you, Johnny. Myself and Sir Frederick Appleby. That reminds me; I have a letter from him. It arrived yesterday." Hassan leafed through a neat stack of papers on his desk while Stanley warmed his hands over the flaming logs,

"How can anybody *not* know about Atlas One, Hassan?"

"They don't, Stanley."

"They must be crazy!"

"I am sure, Stanley, that our King is not crazy."

Thomas had been silent since leaving the wreck of Friedemann's villa. I knew how much he had cared for the two kadets, Kyla in particular. He got up from his arm chair. "I'm very tired. I'm going to bed." He rushed out of the room before I could remonstrate.

"Hey, Johnny, the kid's upset. Shall we go comfort him?"

"Leave him. We'll go to his room later."

"Fallen in love with Kyla?"

"Something like that."

"Young men! They don't know how romantic they are at that age; fall in love with anybody . . . mostly with themselves!"

Hassan handed me an envelope, "Addressed to you, Johnny. From Sir Frederick. Shall we leave …?"

"Not at all, gentleman. I will read the letter aloud."

Pierre Rouge Hotel
Paignton
Devon

May 15th 19....

My dear Johnny,

Vera and I are spending a week at this marvellous hotel enjoying sea views and wholesome English food. Denton's Dance Band as good as ever; brushed up my Fox Trot. Vera has won twice on the Bingo. Ghastly vases! Will be given to White Elephant stall in Barnet on our return. Your sister joined us for lunch today. Charming as always but remarkably coy about her figure. I asked point blank if she were pregnant. Vera did the usual hush-hush routine.

Closed down five cathedrals last week. They are to be converted into factories; Durham shoes, Salisbury shirts, Winchester chocolates. Canterbury and Wells seats for electric trams. I have told Deans and Bishops now is their chance to show that they can be as successful in the rough as they have been complacent in the smooth. Workers tell me how nice it is to run an assembly line in the midst of beautiful architecture.

Archbishop of Canterbury awkward about the whole business, (York loves it, They make tools for Africa in the Minster). I had to threaten Canterbury with a job driving a delivery van if he didn't change his attitude. His wife (that toque!) viperish.

Hassan tells me that you have discovered the Atlas One Kadet Precinct. Mum's the word. Why? Because nobody will believe you except yours truly and dear Hassan.

I am so pleased to know that Stanley Casper is alive. Vera and I adored his marvellous Middle America series. However, Stanley must immediately return to the United States and wait my instructions. It will be all he can do to stave-off the media ... it's not often a man returns from the dead! I have arranged for one of our people to fly him to his Summer home in Ohio. Stanley's family eagerly await his return. Please tell him - a matter of no small importance - that his charming wife has not re-married.

Stanley will be interviewed in Washington by the CIA. I advise extreme caution; Phelps tells me that they will not believe his story and will attempt to have him certified as insane.

Stanley has to convince President Faulkner. She is an old flame of his. Phelps became hideously winsome on the subject at The Club the other day, I told him he resembled a nun from The Sound of Music!

Johnny and Thomas:

I would like you to drive to Casablanca where you will be met by Colonel Jean-Claude Descartes, Hassan will arrange the rendezvous. The Colonel will supply fresh documents and replace your clothes and luggage. The Coniston Queen - a coal-fired cargo ship (somewhat arthritic) will take you to Almeria on the Spanish coast; she sails on June 7th. The Captain, Alphonse du Fleur, is a trusted associate. I may warn you, he is also a seasoned whisky tippler.

My people will meet you in Almeria and fly you to a town in the Jura region of Switzerland, the name of which I shall not divulge. Take the local train to Lausanne and check into the Léman Imperial Hotel on June 9th. The manager, Paul Crissier, is a good friend - don't be deceived by the eye-patch.

At the hotel, I have arranged for the Hollywood film star Ramona Delano to meet you - Miss Delano's real name is Lana Blaisedale.

Find out what she knows. She has agreed to meet you in the cocktail bar of the Léman Imperial on the evening of June 9th.

Thomas must be prepared to meet a Count Malvin. The boy will need to be sharp; Malvin is no Scout Master! Thomas must find, and - most importantly - visit, the Moreau Eocratic University. Not an easy task; nobody in Switzerland has the remotest idea that the location exists.

You, Johnny, having met Delano, should immediately make your way to Geneva. I leave you to decide where you will stay. You should change hotels at least once before June 15th when I will meet you inside Geneva Cathedral at 14-00hrs. 4th row from the back, right hand block of chairs. Bring what you have obtained in Morocco in an unassuming brief case.

Must dash; the post goes in three minutes. Vera and I are to have dinner with a delightful couple from Morecambe, Lancashire. She is internationally renowned for her work on the Notebooks of Leonardo da Vinci, he publishes Dirty Postcards for the seaside trade. We are fellow members of The Pekingese Fanciers' Club. What could be better?

Please give my best wishes to Hassan, Stanley Casper and The Boy,

As always, Johnny, Your devoted Protector,

Fred.

"How does he do it, Johnny?"

"God knows!"

"I mean, he seems to know everything."

"I've already been through that one, Stanley. He turns his blind eye to you and snorts with contempt."

We took a bottle of champagne to Thomas's room. It did the trick. He dried his eyes and put a brave face on the death of Kyla and Panno, saying dolefully, "They could have got away, you know. There was time."

"Believe it, Kid, and maybe it's true."

"Was Ramona Delano in a movie called, *The Embers of Lust*?"

"About forty years before you were thought-of, Thomas, yes she was."

He sat up in bed, interested, bushy-tailed.

"They showed the movie on television. She dances on the edge of the Grand Canyon in fish net stockings and a dash of tulle."

"Correct, Thomas."

"And we're going to meet her?"

"You bet you are, Boy!"

♠

We checked-in at the Lausanne Léman Imperial on June 9th. Stanley was flown to the States on the same day.

The Léman Imperial is a mad-house of luxury. Our five-room penthouse was furnished and decorated in Rudolph Valentino mode: sort of molten Neapolitan ice cream.

Refreshed from the bar, having admired the stupendous panorama of the Alps above Evian over Lac Léman, we showered and changed.

I stood in front of a mirror making a hash of my bow tie, listening with mild irritation to Thomas singing in his bathroom. He appeared in a towelling dressing gown dewy from the shower and settled, lush, on the arm of a gigantic sofa. Tiny, glittery, coal black hairs curled round the base of his opalescent neck. He sensed that I was pre-occupied.

Munching olives, lager in hand, he pulled at my shirt cuff, "Sit down, Gov'ner! Tell me about it." How could I ignore his boyish charm?

"What is in focus, Thomas? - Don't drip in my drink! - There is no *hub*, no anchorage. Nothing connects." I glanced at his lovely, dripping hair. His Vermeer eyes were luminous with the tolerant impatience of Youth.

"Insidious corruption is the link, Johnny. I thought about it. Moreau was a master at the game. A world delicately decayed by vice. Light-fingered corruption in every corner. All over you, me, everyone."

"Where does it stop?"

Snicking open another can, he poured himself more lager, sucking at the rim of his glass. Spumey froth stayed white on his gorgeous upper lip.

"Moreau's world is poison, Johnny. We drink it, we eat it, we breathe it. We accept it as the norm. That is their game, Johnny. Dragging us painlessly into their mire of corruption."

He placed his glass by mine on a ridiculously ornate occasional table and slid down to kneel beside me on the cushions of the sofa. Bending forward, he gently adjusted and tied - beautifully - my bow tie. As a wife might do.

"Come on, Gov'ner! You're the one with the nerve when they start shooting."

"Get dressed, Mate. She'll be waiting for us if we're not careful. That would never do."

♠

Ramona Delano entered the Hôtel cocktail bar swathed in glamour and seduction. She glided towards us like a Manta Ray. The wife of a couple from Nebraska nudged her husband's elbow so hard he almost shot his drink over his shoulder,

"*Harald*!"

"My love?"

"Ramona Delano just walked in!"

"You're kidding!"

"Ramona Delano just walked in!"

"You're *kidding*!"

No she wasn't. Ramona Delano had just walked in and all the world knew - and the world *still* took photographs, and *still* wanted her autograph. Never was a woman so revered since Anthony fell in love with Cleopatra.

Smiling simply at no one in particular, the Star directed her gaze towards Thomas. With sizzling aplomb, as a waiter removed her white mink wrap, she blew Thomas a kiss from a long, white gloved hand. The handsome young waiter turned to face her, standing close. Removing her gloves, Ramona traced a crystalline fingernail down the front of his aproned chest, setting luxurious pressure at the point where, they both knew, his tightly muscled navel lay beneath. "Good Evening, Anatole." All he could whisper was, "I want you!"

"Later, my darling, . . . you will have me." As she walked towards our table, I saw the boy nuzzle his lips in the scented mink of the wrap.

"For Pete's sake don't get up, gents! . . . Mr Debrett, a pleasure … And this is Thomas! Isn't he *darling*?" She pulled out a chair and sat down on it as easily as if she was in a location trailer.

"Let's skip formality, Mister Debrett. I'm Ramona, you're Johnny, and the kid's gorgeous. You must let Thomas stay long enough for me to get to know what he looks like without a tie!" She gave out a peal of laughter, just as she had done in her films.

"Listen, Boys! We got a lot of talking to do and right now this place is picking up every word. Why don't we go to one of my favourite restaurants. It's a cute little place down the lake, at Coppet. The owner's a good friend, what's more he's - I guess this is the word you're looking for, Johnny - *discrete*."

"Sounds perfect."

"Great!" She beckoned the favourite waiter, "Anatole, darling. Tell the chauffeur to bring the car to the garden entrance. By the way, my dears, this is Anatole, he's a pal of mine. He knows Lausanne and this perfect little region *intimately*."

"Like he knows you?"

"Johnny! That is so un-*English* of you!" She squeezed my hand, "I can

142

see we're going to get on famously, darling."

♠

"Daddy could buy me a slice of Hollywood, but his money couldn't make me a star. That's one hell of a mission, boys. You have to know you got it because, sure as Hell, nobody else is going to tell you. Celluloid is one of the toughest materials in the Universe. "

"You didn't live at Gracewood?"

She gave out her crystalline laugh, "No way, Johnny. I left home at sixteen. Apart from Daddy's funeral in 'Seventy, I never saw Gracewood again."

"Your mother, Madeleine Necker-Vandel?"

"We sisters never knew Mother. ... Are you happy with one helping of the Perche? They'll give you another plateful if you want. OK, fine. ... Mother bore us, nursemaids looked after us, she got killed in an automobile smash: period. Jayne was eleven, I was three."

"That's sad."

"A lot's sad, Johnny, when you're born rich." Ramona produced a powder compact and perfunctorily dusted her nose . . . "Mother's death terminated the Necker-Vandel connection. Daddy hated Piet Vandel, Piet hated us girls and we hated Daddy."

"Why?"

"Daddy was the most unlovable man on Earth. Piet was a slick little drunk. That's why. Mother got hold of Daddy in self defence. She was beautiful in a kinda butch way, so I guess he could pass her off as a boy between the sheets."

"What took you to Hollywood?"

"I was bedded by a studio boss at some wild teenage party and he arranged a screen test. The studio loved me and showed the test to Daddy. He wrote me a cheque for twenty thousand dollars, had the butler hand it me on a salver, then stood by the fire with his arm round some little faggot he'd been reaming and drawled, "You got one hour to get the fuck out of here!" She laughed, feeling Thomas's left biceps with a murmur of approval. "I guess the movies became my life. Not much else I can do."

"Did you ever meet Arthur?"

"*Uncle* Arthur! God! Was he *weird*! Didn't you find Arthur weird, Johnny?" I inhaled the bouquet of superb wine, replying that I had never found Arthur weird.

"That's strange. I guess he must have had a dual personality. He was often around, usually with this snaky old Kraut, von Stotz. Stotz was one of Daddy's mummified faggot friends. Every goddam corner you turned in

Gracewood there were these antique queens shafting each other's collapsed butts.

"Anyway, at twenty-six I co-starred with Neston Charles in a movie they shot at Cine-Cittá in Rome and I discovered Europe. I never really went back to the US."

"Your sister?"

"Jayney! My *big* sister. Can you believe the witch you saw in Marrakech started life as a Harvard blue stocking? She wasn't bad looking in those days; a leggy blond with Chevrolet sized tits. She was hot for a young Senator, his family were in steel. I fancied she might get herself to be first woman president of the USA. But somewhere along the line Jayne fucked-up. Now we know why, she got-in with Moreau."

"Did you ever go to Saint Christophe or Marriage Island?"

"Never. Daddy's holiday haunts had no appeal. In reality, Johnny, they were sleazy clubs. Celebrities, politicians, sports gods, prostitutes. All fucking and boozing."

"What happened to Necker Vandel's construction empire?"

"Way back, Johnny, when California was still an Oak forest, old man Necker got in with my Grandfather. Necker was a civil engineer. Elevators were hot property, the highest downtown blocks were up to eight floors. Necker designed a elevator shaft and all the junk they put into those things using my Grandfather's invention - Holy of Holies - the Blaisedale Widget. Together they patented the combination. My Father expanded the empire by taking-on a construction boss, Piet Vandel. This meant we could built the goddam buildings with the elevators in them all over world as a *package*. Result? Dollars pouring through every fucking ceiling in sight!"

Thomas was fiddling with his *Crêpe Suzette*. "The Kadet Precinct we saw in Morocco is unbelievably big. Could Necker-Vandel be constructing those things?"

"Thomas, you're cute!" She bent over and kissed Thomas's ear. "The answer to that is 'I don't have a clue.' I have no contact with the family, or the business. I'm independent, living off my money that I made in Hollywood. And I guess the royalties of my movies. I have managers and a secretary to organise every moment of my day. If I could help, I'd be in there with you. Finish your pudding like a good boy."

"I don't like it!" At once she rang for attention. The door opened immediately. The owner's mile-wide shoulders blocked the gap. Ramona rested a dazzling forefinger on Thomas's wrist, "What do you prefer, Cheri?"

"Chocolate ice cream." A nod from *Madame*; a nod from the owner.

"Aren't you being rather a baby, Thomas?"

But he sat back with his thighs stretched wide, scratching his tummy button, mooning at me like a little boy of eight.

"Don't be a party-pooper, Johnny! I never had a kid of my own, so when they're cute they get anything they want because Mama likes to pamper her *babies*, doesn't she darling?" She swished her right palm along Thomas's left thigh, snapping, "Johnny, Sweetie, clam-up and have some Nineteen-thirty-nine cognac!"

♠

Ramona and I sipped the formidable cognac while Thomas washed down his ice cream with a pint glass of champagne. "Boys, did you know that there's some kind of plague in Switzerland?"

Thomas belched, pushed his plate away, kissed Ramona's shoulder then glanced at me like the cat that's had the cream. "Can you help us with a riddle?"

"I adore riddles, Cheri. Shoot!"

"Stotz gave a piece of paper to the Burdets when he visited them in Minneapolis. This was on it." He frowned, "I'll try to get it right first time;

'At thirteen twenty meters north of the old bridge there are two points to note on the tower. Firstly, left towards the teeth it is shaded before noon. Secondly, the room with three windows has three doors; the correct door is seen through rock. The pass code is a powerhouse across the valley.'

"Sweetie, you're so beautiful when you concentrate. Just a moment, (she shoved around in a tiny pocket book for a propelling pencil and a minute engagement diary) . . . Isn't this pixie? I paid a dime for it in Montreux." She shoved the diary and pencil in front of Thomas. "Write it down, Darling. Sounds like a map reference to me. Bound to be a place in Switzerland. Don't you agree, Johnny?"

"How can you be so sure?"

" *the powerhouse across the valley* is an atomic power station above the Rhône valley along from Villeneuve, a little town at the east end of Lac Léman."

"The power station is at Chavalon. Four reactors and an enormous chimney. Shows up white on the mountainside."

"That's the pass code sorted: CHAVALON. Next!"

"What is *across the valley* from Chavalon?"

"The town of Aigle, Sweetie. Over the Rhône. You pronounce it 'Eggla'."

"The old stone bridge in Aigle!"

"Hard by the mountain railroad station."

"The scene of my final quarrel with Arthur and Jo. . . *At thirteen twenty meters north of the old bridge*." Ramona rang for attention as I spoke. The owner appeared, concerned."

145

"Is everything to your absolute satisfaction, Madame?"

"That would be asking too much, Philippe! Be a darling and tell the chauffeur to bring some maps up here. I need 1:25000 Monthey, number 262, and 272, and . . . better be on the safe side, St-Maurice and Lausanne . . . wait! And the *Dents du Midi*."

Thomas lit up, "Dents du Midi? That's French for *teeth in the middle*."

"A beautiful chunk of the Alps, Baby. Almost as beautiful as you." You see them down the Rhône valley from above Aigle. A magical sight." The chauffeur appeared with an armful of folded maps. He wore a dazzling white uniform like movie Stars' chauffeurs should wear. "Lay 'em out on the table, Albert! They gave you food downstairs?"

"Yes Madame."

"What did they give you?"

"Baked beans on toast, Madame."

"I haven't eaten baked beans on toast in fifty years! . . . *That's* the map we want! . . . I love maps, Boys! Thomas, be a perfect Darling and spread map 272 across the table, the one with the title *St-Maurice*. Find Aigle and take the town as datum for our riddle."

"How can you be so certain?"

"Cos I was raised in Hollywood, Kid! In Hollywood you gotta see what's round the corner before you've seen the goddam corner! . . . Find the old bridge over the Grand Eau in Aigle, by the mountain railroad station."

"Got it."

"Draw a line up North from the bridge . . . here, use this thing to rule." She passed him a silver bon-bon dish, tipping the chocolates from it onto the table cloth. Make it neat, Babe!" Thomas applied himself, drawing a pencil line with a sure hand.

"The line goes off the edge of the map."

"Put map 262 alongside - keep drawing."

"Where does it lead?"

"The *Dent de Jaman*, Johnny."

"Another tooth, is that part of the riddle?"

"I don't feel no vibes, Honey. It's a plug of Alpine rock visible for miles, but I guess it isn't the plug we need." Ramona was well into the chase. "We want a tower and something in the plural; *'there are two points to note on the tower; firstly, left towards the teeth it is shaded before noon'* - the teeth are the Dents du Midi. We're correctly orientated above Aigle."

"*the correct door is seen through rock . . .* the rock is transparent. Arthur's casket. Hewn from rock crystal."

"Johnny, you're magic! . . . *What*? That slob was buried in a rock crystal casket?"

"He liked extravagant gestures."

146

"Who did he think he was? Maker of Heaven and Earth!" Thomas rubbed his forehead with the back of his hand. "Do you think *thirteen twenty meters north of the old bridge* refers to height rather than distance? The height above the old bridge?"

"Isn't he so cute when he's rubbing his hot little head like that? (another kiss). Find the first 1320 meter contour along the line you drew." She glanced at me softly, "Shoot the kid a pool-sized shot of cognac, Johnny."

"Shows three peaks, *Tour d'Ai, Tour de Mayen, Tour de Famelon.*"

"Tour! Tower in French. Three towers. The *Tour d'Ai* is the most celebrated."

"Let's assume it's the tower we need. We can expand the first part of the riddle like this, 'At contour line thirteen twenty meters to the north of the old bridge at Aigle there are two points to note on the Tower of Ai; firstly, when viewed from the left, as one looks towards the Dents du Midi, it is shaded before noon.' Is it?"

"Every day. Hey! Does *tower* have a double meaning; is *tower* the catch? A mountainous plug of rock and a tower *building*? This is so exiting I gotta go to the jon."

"A tower building with a room in it that has three windows?"

"Thomas, *darling*! I'm crossing my legs, Babe!" She flung an arm round Thomas's shoulders. Thomas gabbled, "Listen! When you look at the Dents du Midi if you stand *here*, this place marked *Luan* …"

"It's a neat little hamlet, Babe. Has a cute restaurant."

"… the *Tour d'Ai* is to your left.

"Pokes up like a sore thumb, Johnny." Thomas marked a pencil dot on the map.

"That is where the tower with the three windows has to be."

"The Moreau University?"

"Yep! The place Fred wants me to visit. I go to Luan, get into the University, find the tower that has a room with three windows . . ."

"Are you trying to tell me that Arthur's casket is in that room?"

"For Pete's sake, Johnny! We've been through enough fantastic situations. Why not have the casket in the tower? There's a door in the room, it will open when I say, think, or tap out on a keyboard, the word *Chavalon*."

"Boys, maybe we've had too much to drink! You see, there's nothing in Luan but a few farms, this neat restaurant, then fields, Swiss cows, mountains . . . and fir trees!"

That evening, I took a taxi to Geneva and checked-in at The Rhône Excelsior. Next morning I checked out and took a local train to Lyons where I spent an agreeable five days. I bought clothes and a set of luggage. I ate marvellous food at memorable restaurants. I returned to Geneva on June 14th and checked into a suite in a comfortable hotel on the Quai Wilson that I'd never stayed at before. To the staff of the *Grande Étoile Noir* I was just another well-heeled tourist.

♠

On his day-off, Anatole suggested that he showed Thomas round Lausanne, and took him on his motorbike round the wine producing villages down the lake. They had good time, met Anatole's friends, and became close. Anatole dropped Thomas back at the hotel just after six in the evening. The young woman at reception whispered, "There is a gentleman to see you, Monsieur. He is waiting in the Cocktail Bar."

Count Malvin stood at the bar, chatting in cultivated tones to the barman. Malvin was tall, rake thin, gaunt faced and impeccably dressed in an English three-piece suit. Thomas paused at the entrance sensing that he was on treacherous ground. Nothing of the man before him rang true, despite the suit, the perfectly parted thinning hair, the handmade shoes.

"Monsieur Thomas! How pleased I am to meet you." Thomas shook a long, bony hand and flooded Malvin with a cathedral smile. "They telephoned to tell me you had arrived in Lausanne. We must get together as soon as possible, luncheon or dinner as you like. I think you will agree, my dear fellow, that we have much to talk about." The English accent was actorish, the words clipped and mannered in a way that was both effete and menacing. What did the old snake mean, 'so much to talk about'? . . . Who had telephoned him?

"That is very nice of you, Monsieur ... I'm sorry, I don't know your name."

"How remiss of me! I should have introduced myself." He handed Thomas a card. "Gustave Malvin. Do not think of addressing me by my title; we are - after all - men of the world. I live down the lake towards Montreux, St-Saphorin, not far from Vevey. Won't you come and have dinner tomorrow evening?" Malvin gave Thomas a hooded cobra glance, the dead-pan stare of one who has seen people die under torture. "Perhaps I can send my car to pick you up from the hotel." He waited, infuriated by the young fool's silence. Petulantly he snapped, "Take a taxi if you prefer, they all know where I am. Seven-fifteen for eight. I have invited some friends, they would enjoy meeting you." He downed a tiny green glass of apricot liqueur but he did not offer Thomas a drink.

Instinct told Thomas not to be messed-about, "I'm afraid it will not be possible for me to dine with you tomorrow evening, I have already accepted a previous invitation."

"How most inconvenient!" Intolerantly, Malvin banged the flat of his hand on the bar, his heavy signet ring clacked into the mahogany. "I suppose you'd like a drink!" The barman regarded Malvin with a blend of professional obsequiousness and insolence. "Give our young friend a glass of lager! . . . That's about your level, isn't it? Lager. . . . I will take a Crème de Menthe!" He was handed a tiny apricot coloured glass of Crème de Menthe. "Be reasonable, my dear fellow! I have invited a selection of *highly* distinguished people to meet you. Important people who cannot *chop* and *change* their arrangements like a pack of students!"

"With respect, how was I to know? With further respect, how did you know I was in Lausanne? How do you know about me at all?"

"How dare you ask me such questions!"

"As a man of the world, Count Malvin, I'll ask you what questions I like."

"Do you realise to whom you are speaking?"

"No. But I could have a good guess! I'll come to dinner on the thirteenth, in three days time. I will make my own way, thank you. I shall arrive at seven-fifteen precisely!"

"Perfect!" Hissing with rage the Count tinked his tiny glass back onto the bar and swept off, moving among the lobby sofas like a swerving python. The barman mixed Thomas a Vodka Alexander, "My word, young man! That was a performance I'll not forget in a hurry. Wait till Miss Delano hears about it. She'll double-up. Well done, Mate! It's time the old bugger got kneed in the bollocks . . . that is, if there's any bollocks to knee." Grinning, he leaned across the bar and shook Thomas by the hand.

"You're a Londoner!"

"Too blinkin' right I'm a Londoner, Mate! … Me and Miss Delano go back a long way. We teamed-up at Elstree Studios when she was making, *They Named Her Jezebel!* She starred with Glenn Crush. Gawd! 'ee was 'andsome! What a duo. Well before your time, lad!"

"I haven't anything decent to wear for Malvin's dinner! We arrived with very little luggage."

"There's a boutique in town, I'll telephone them tomorrow morning. Arrive, mention my name, and they'll fit you out. Swiss lads are spoilt. You have to look what the French call *beau*. That will impress Malvin."

"What are you suggesting?"

The barman leant forward, looked round the bar before he murmured, "I'm suggesting you take bloody good care of yourself, Mate. Malvin is not a nice man."

Two evenings later, Thomas paid the taxi and climbed the flight of granite steps at the base of Malvin's gaunt, mediaeval lakeside keep. At the top he grasped a wrought-iron bell pull of an ancient, iron-bound front door. It was seven-fifteen.

He was shown into Malvin's extensive, mid-fifteenth century drawing room with its five pointed windows overlooking the lake towards the forested mountain sides rising above St-Gingolph five kilometres away on the opposite bank. Thomas's appearance aroused in the male guests standing about holding drinks a sexual excitement they could hardly contain. The three female guests, standing silently by a chamber organ, were too ill to notice.

His jacket was of white camel hair. It's ashen shades set-off the Greek vase quality of his looks. The trousers were fine, gunmetal grey, and perfectly cut to reveal his compactly profiled thighs. The bump of his neat crotch was sensuously apparent. Around his luxurious neck a broad necklace of white gold glimmered from a silk shirt of peach-blossom pink. The division between his feminine-masculine beauty was impossible to accurately define.

Two guests, high in the ranks of Swiss commerce, quietly laid bets on who would bed the boy first. "Gustave never fails in the excellence of his choice." The two men were in the final stages of psychological readjustment induced by Friedemann's serum. Their cinder-charred bodies would be found by shoppers besides petrol cans and matches on a supermarket parking lot the following afternoon.

During the meal one of the women left the table, lay down on the lavatory floor, and died. She had been something to do with Arts and Leisure in the Canton of the Vaud. Close circuit cameras recorded the instant of her death and her body was immediately wrapped in plastic sheeting by three kadets, taken out through the service entrance via the kitchen, to be driven away in a refuse cart and chucked down a ravine.

The day before Thomas came to dinner, Malvin had received a batch of Second Phase Serum from Friedemann's laboratories located thirty kilometres from the centre of Zurich. For the first time the serum was to be pumped into the City water supply. This was excellent work! Gustave was pleased with his success. Tonight, he had awarded himself a succulent treat! A pretty English boy. The meddlesome little pig who had very nearly spoilt their plans in Marrakech.

Not surprisingly, the staff who served at dinner were kadets. For a moment Thomas was not sure if one of them might be Panno but it was impossible at a smart dinner table to turn round and stare. Surely Panno would have given him a sign of recognition.

He talked in French about his interest in books and sport: jolly topics for old men.

Coffee was served at the table and soon after they had drunk it Malvin's guests departed. They seemed to rise in unison, paying profuse compliments to their host and bowing in courtly Swiss style to Thomas whom they sincerely hoped would visit their homes during his stay in Lausanne.

Thomas made conventional noises about leaving and began to rise from off his chair. Malvin objected. Thomas must stay and talk a little longer. Would he have a cognac - rare and old? This was poured. Would he care for a cigar? A cigarette? But of course, why not! A gold box was placed on the table. Opened, it contained two hundred dark purple cigarettes with silver tips like bullets, the sort of cigarettes, Thomas mused, a bishop might smoke. Malvin's tone was friendly and lightly encouraging. "That's better," he murmured, "far more comfortable!" Yes indeed, Thomas must stay and talk; one of the chauffeurs would drive him back. Thomas heard cars starting in the courtyard, the sound of their engines droned into the night. Silence fell amongst the debris of the dinner table. No staff were to be seen.

Malvin now turned a pair of softly amused eyes on his deliciously nervous ward. How like an old fashioned rose was a blushing English boy!

"Shall we go upstairs." It was not a question.

♠

On the floor above they entered, to Thomas's relief, a small drawing room lined with oak panels hung with the works of Duccio and Fra Angelico. Two large, stained glass windows were wide open. Thomas placed his hands on the stone sill and leaned out, peering down into the darkness. Far below he heard the glutinous lapping of the lake against the castle walls.

"I'm afraid you won't be able to dive from there. The rocks, Monsieur Thomas, will make rather a mess of your sculptural skull." Thomas stood rigid, facing Malvin. Neither of them smiled. "Sit down. We cannot delay our conversation a moment longer, can we . . . my young friend?"

The gothic interior of the room, genuine, the low level of diffused lighting, and Malvin's tall, elegantly cadaverous figure attired in evening dress standing sentinel before the roaring fire as he said, '... *my young friend.*', could have been a scene from one of Thomas's father's boyhood adventure stories where the enemy was invariably a highly cultivated German spy while the hero was English, twenty-eight, excellent at fencing and always wore white, torso-hugging polo-neck sweaters.

Dryly, Malvin continued, "Before I take you to bed. . . . Oh yes, boy! you'll go to bed with me! (This was a major departure from the boyhood adventure stories), before that delicious sin is perpetrated, I want you to know that your presence in this country, indeed your presence in *any* country, is unwelcome. And that, my dear young man, is an understatement!" Malvin slid from the mantelpiece a miniature glass casket, placing it carefully on a low, wrought iron coffee table before him. Watching, Thomas failed to hear two kadets creep up behind him. They took him by the arms in a power-vice grip. Startled, he struggled, breathing hard, but they were too strong. One arm was brutally wrenched upwards as they walked him towards the coffee table. Malvin lifted the lid from the glass casket and set it gently down on the cover of a dog-eared copy of *The Field*.

"This is what your particularly *stupid* compatriot saw in Marrakech, wasn't it? One of these?" Malvin motioned towards the glass box with nicotine stained fingers. "Did you know that we have followed every move of ... that stinking little squirt, Debrett? . . . *Well?*"

"You bastard!"

"See what your meddlesome amateur bungling has lead to, *mon camarade!* Poking about where you shouldn't have - weren't you, my *handsome* young eagle!" The kadets tightened their grip.

"Leave me be!"

"Oh, pooh-pooh! What a sulky boy it is! You weren't so difficult earlier were you, chirping on about your fatuous rugby balls! - *Sit him down!*" Thomas was forced down onto a low chair, the kadets stood beside him, pressing strong hands on both his shoulders while twisting his arms behind his back. He was immobile, watching Malvin become knife-thin with hatred. "You and your associates! Johnny, idiot Debrett and kind Uncle Frederick! Pah! What a farce! As if any of us were deceived by that geriatric old fool in London. You have been followed from the moment you bordered the jet at Heathrow and took off for Marrakech. Do you *understand* what I'm telling you?" He took a silver-gilt jug from a drinks tray close at hand and poured some fresh orange juice from it into a tumbler.

"We know all about your *mission* - and we don't like it." He placed the jug down by the lid of the miniature casket where it immediately began to make a ring on the cover of *The Field*. "Tonight, it is *my* turn to be avuncular. Merciful Uncle Gustave. I am not going to kill you. You are too - how shall I put it? - too valuable a treasure to smash. I'm going to warn you once . . . .," he picked up the tumbler, almost imperceptibly sniffed the orange juice, and replaced it on the table. Then he took a silver spoon from the tray and dipped it amongst the capsules in the casket, balancing two capsules in the spoon and leaving it poised on the rim of the tray, ". . . and once only. Then I'm going to have you carried to my bedroom, stripped and raped unconscious. . . . The treat will involve a *very* nasty dildo. . . . One of my collection of rare mechanical toys."

Malvin lifted the spoon with the delicacy of a chemist and carefully dropped the two capsules into the orange juice. Gazing with disinterested languor at Thomas he began slowly, without watching what he was doing, to stir the capsules into the juice. Thomas could see them beginning to dissolve. He was almost paralysed with pain but an influx of adrenalin prepared him to fight to the death.

"Tomorrow a car will arrive at your hotel at nine in the morning. You will be ready to leave, . . ." Malvin gave a short, dry laugh, ". . .*if,* and I place a certain *experienced* emphasis upon the word, you can walk! - Don't fret, boy! My people will help you to the car. - You will be taken to the Aeroport de

Genève and escorted onto a jet bound for . . ." vaguely, he wafted pterodactyl fingers about the rim of the tumbler, ". . . I wonder *where*?" He motioned to one of the kadets. "*You! Make him drink!*" The kadet leaned over and took the glass in his hand while still keeping a tight grip on the victim's shoulder.

"If you dare to return to Switzerland, or continue with your fruitless investigation elsewhere, you will be murdered. So will your *ridiculously* snobbish mother, your *hideously* pompous father and your silly little *tart* of a sister! All your friends will die - with their families - including the irredeemable Debrett." Malvin lit one of his long, purple cigarettes and, inhaling deeply from its silver tip, slowly drew down the lids of his eyes like sated boa constrictor.

"What are you waiting for? Make him drink!" The kadet concerned pressed the glass to Thomas's lips and, releasing his hand from the young man's shoulder, grasped his victim's chin while his mate expertly applied pressure to two nerve points at each side of Thomas's neck as Panno had done with Jayne Blaisedale.

Horrified, Thomas realised that he could not prevent himself from opening his mouth. But he had one shoulder momentarily free: the instant for action had arrived. His mouth agape Thomas gave a roar and kicked-out with both legs, sending the jug, the juice, the casket and low table hurtling into Malvin's shins. The kadets jolted back and lost their hold. Finding his balance, Thomas sprang round, flailing about him with wild arms in time to see his adversaries draw serrated knives from their belts.

Too late! They had lost the advantage. Thomas booted one in the face, then slammed the other's head into the side of a stone pillar. He sprinted through the room, out onto the gallery and leapt down the heraldic oak staircase roaring at raucous volume. Ripping through the hall he overturned a wrought iron standard lamp that successfully tripped Malvin's butler who had emerged from Below Stairs. Thomas slammed into the great front door, shot back its bolts, tore it open and hurled himself down the flight of granite steps to land on well-sprung thighs, upright and unscathed at the feet of . . . Ramona Delano!

For a second he did not know where he was.

Ramona stood camera-still: molten in moonlit chinchilla.

♠

"*Baby*! You sure are looking suave tonight!" She caught the boy by his lapels and whispered, "*Get into the car! Over there. Back seat - and fast!*" Then she gave him a kiss on the lips, quicksilver sweet, before continuing up the steps to greet Malvin (who the butler was wiping down) in a peal of conventional gladness generously spangled with social *diamanté*.

In the back of her tank-sized Rolls Royce Ramona leaned all over him, awash with scent and motherly emotion. "You're all-in, darling!" She breathed over his neck and chin, then cheerily snapped a command up front, "Step on it, Albert! The kid needs to lie down!" She laid a cerise gloved hand to his cheek and he felt warm, perfumed satin sliding to the base of his neck. He turned deep amber eyes on her, large with wonder and fatigue.

"They tried to kill me."

"Sweetie, you were damned lucky they didn't. Malvin is *not* a nice guy!"

"How did you know I was there?" New energy began to strengthen his limp frame, he settled into the damask upholstery gazing at the roof of the car. His neck, head thrown back, was exquisite. The gold necklace ran in rivulets over his softly nestled collar bones. Ramona breathed close, desirous to touch the boy's relaxing, potent body.

"My good friend, the barman at your hotel, telephoned Albert, who got me out of a boring cocktail party," she fingered his wrist watch, whispering seductively. ". . . I had one of my six-sense things, darling!" She played with his necklace. "Too damn right I did! . . ." She nuzzled her lips to his shoulder. The car stopped. Without pause, Ramona belted out, "Albert! What the fuck are you doing?"

"The lights, Madame."

"Drive *through* for fuck's sake! Any fool that hits this tub'll know about it; and how!"

"Albert?" In French, pronounced without the 't', the name was magically exotic.

"My chauffeur, darling. You know Albert! He's right there in front." She raised her voice, "Albert! Give Thomas a wave! . . . That's nice. . . .Albert's been driving this crate for ten years since Twickenham died. The car is my trademark!" She laughed gaily. "I can never dump it. My public would lynch me! It cost seven million bucks forty-years ago. They don't make 'em like this now." She placed her hand on his thigh. "What did Malvin try to do, Baby? Something unspeakable?"

Thomas smiled and his teeth shone in a matchless row, dabs of reflected light in the Vandyke brown shade of the great limousine. She stroked her hand up and down his leg soothingly, gently caressing the taught bow of well developed muscle. It felt so good! His insides went liquid as desire pulled him closer to her. Animal heat curled between them.

"He knows all about us! He was going to . . . oh, it doesn't matter . . . he didn't . . ." Recovering now, inquisitive, he asked; "Why does the car have paintings on the roof?"

"Picasso did them, Sweetie. I asked him during lunch and he did them after. He was old by then, but *great* company. He said it was his Sistine Chapel. Can you believe that! I had these art experts from New York drooling round the car for months. They wanted the roof in the Guggenheim - only the roof, mind you. I told'em, 'What the fuck am I going to do when it rains on the goddam

154

expressway? Put up a *parasol*?'"

Thomas looked out of the window in time to see the car sweeping through enormous gates that were closing electronically behind them. It stopped by the formidable silhouette of a lakeside palazzino. Albert opened Ramona's door, a young man from the house opened Thomas's. In the moonlight the marble lakeside mansion had no perspective, appearing to him as if from the depths of an enchanted dream.

They walked towards a long Ionic portico, scrunching on gravel, then climbed pinkish marble steps. In a cream stone hall forested with pearly Corinthian columns staff attended to Ramona while Thomas was shown into an enormous restroom lined with antique Persian tiles. He washed in lilac scented water, was handed a perfumed towel by a steward sent to attend him, and selected a fragrant cologne.

He was shown into a drawing room filled, it seemed, with low, clubby, square-cut arm chairs upholstered in white. Nothing was horror-gothic here, nothing fake *Louis-Quinze*. Everything was smart, simple, pale gold and white. Colour was provided by the biggest potted azaleas Thomas had ever seen.

Ramona dismissed the staff and mixed drinks herself ("I guess we could both use some!"). Gently accepting the glass she handed to him, he stood gazing through an arched window that looked over a brilliant acre of silver moonlit lawn towards the lake and the unearthly magnificence of the Alps beyond. The expanse of water seemed to be slivered with a billion reflected shards of the moon's ivory orb.

She murmured his name. The room was quiet: unlit by lamplight.

"Thomas."

Moved, he turned to face her, his eyes brimmed with tears of emotion. They put their drinks down and slowly, irrevocably, they came so close that touch was but the splendid notion of desire. Wantonly, they kissed.

♠

In the oyster satin bower of her bedroom they dallied for two hours. He lay amongst Brussels lace, his slender, muscular, naked form iridescent and sensual. Ramona toyed with the boy, not herself completely yet undressed but astonishingly *déshabillée*. Sitting at his side on the edge of the bed, alternately kissing his lips, his nipples, his eyes, his boy-scented hair, she never quite, never ever quite, reached down to his loins.

Open windows made a proscenium that revealed the panorama of resplendent mountains. Scored by stars, the *Dents du Midi* spun from their snowy spires a drifting skein of frozen breeze that wound to the land below. Warmed on the summer waters of the lake it licked cloudily, in fronds, round the marble palace where the couple lay.

155

She took off her diamond necklace, tiered and priceless. Adroitly she placed it round his neck, fastening the clip slowly while he gazed at her, sifting the fingers of one hand between her breasts. Two hundred diamonds reflected blue-pink light from the bedside lamp. The stones spat light - like lust, setting the brilliant match of his broad shoulders.

They heard a distant thrum of a motor bike. Ramona had been listening for it. Eventually, the sound was heard to stop at the front of the villa. Seconds later, down below, a door shut. There was a pause. The private elevator hummed.

"Anatole."

That is all she said. Thomas smiled, the breath releasing from his nostrils in animal pleasure. There was a soft knock on the bedroom door and immediately the dark-haired young man entered. Out of his working clothes he appeared sinuously compact.

He walked to her side, looking at them both, smiling, making no comment. He bent down, gave his mistress a long kiss on the mouth, fondling for some seconds Thomas's hair.

"Close the drapes, darling, it's chill."

He walked over to one side of the vast windows, felt for a control and pressed it. Then he came back and stood at the other side of the bed, looking across at Ramona and Thomas entwined. As he stretched, his shirt came adrift at the waist to show curling, dark, thick pubic hair in a winding string up the centre of his underbelly. The image of his new friend cut into his consciousness as the scintillating diamonds sprayed spurting light over Thomas's chest and beautiful, darkly pigmented nipples that - with force - Anatole badly wanted to lick.

The steady, rhythmic hum of closing shutters, the slithering scrape of hide-thick silk, stopped. The click of the released buckle of Anatole's belt, the sight of his taught, satisfyingly thick erection, profoundly aroused them all.

Ramona raised an arm towards her lover, beckoning. Casting aside his clothes, he knelt on the bed to join his face with the fingertips of Ramona's hand, tucking himself along the length of Thomas's flank. As he entwined with the other man, his head amongst lace, diamonds and scented flesh, he murmured in broken English, his voice husky with lust:

"Three is company - two is a crowd."

♠

The following morning was gentian blue. Anatole drove Thomas towards Aigle in one of Ramona's *"liddler"* cars. They did not wish to analyse their affection: sharing Ramona in the night, and each other, had been wonderful - that was sufficient.

Ramona had said during breakfast, sitting in bed, flounced in a pink merino shawl, "You two go off and do the sights. Take the Packard, it's *liddler* than the others. You gotta see the cute chalets, the beautiful flowers they have in the fields. In winter you can't see nothin' but snow and ice!"

"Where do you go in Winter?"

"To my old movie pals in the Caribbean . . . or my place in Morocco."

"Morocco?"

She tapped Thomas's buttocks with a butter knife, "Sure, Honey! Marrakesh. There are more things to Marrakech, Sweetie, than *kadets*!". . . . Anatole, Baby, come off the balcony, it's like a berg in here!"

She mapped them a route that ended up in Luan where Thomas would investigate Moreau's University.

"You said it doesn't exist."

"The way you and Johnny talk, it may exist for *you*!" Bored with maps, randy, Thomas and Anatole started fooling with each other. *Quit that*! . . . Get dressed and get out before I get mad!"

In Aigle they found the old stone bridge, had a beer, then continued towards the Col des Mosses, up into the sunshine. The Packard hood was down and the young men brimmed with seeping elation, like warmed oil.

"Those are the three rock towers: Aï, Mayen and Famelon." A lake sparkled below, imprisoned by Wagnerian slopes. They wound through aromatic pine forests. They stopped for cigarettes, gazing at a flower-embroidered meadow where truculent cows swung their kling-klang bells. They kissed until a passing car broke their mood.

Anatole parked outside the restaurant at Luan. Close-too, The *Tour d'Aï* needed no introduction; a plug of brutal rock like the fortress of a primeval god. The natural amphitheatre below, where Luan nestled, was impressive, half covered by a pine forest.

Stotz's tower rose above the pines in the location where it should have been: exactly where Thomas had made his pencil dot on Ramona's map. About half way up the tower's grey granite walls were the three windows.

"The riddle has come true."

"Like a fairy story."

"We're a couple of fairies!" They couldn't stop laughing, even at the bar of the restaurant where a pretty girl served them two beers. "Wait for me here. I'll see if I can get into the place. I shan't be long."

"Why do this, Thomas? It is a dangerous, creepy place. Can't you tell them that you have seen the tower. Isn't that enough?" He clasped Thomas's hands in his, oblivious that the girl was mildly disgusted.

"This is the part I have to play, I can't let Johnny down." Anatole wrenched his hands free. Turning abruptly on the bar stool he stared at the bottle of beer in front of him. "Go! But for God's sake be careful!" In bad

157

English he said, "This place give to me the feeling of fear."

The gates of the College were open and unattended. As far as Thomas could make out, peering amongst the trees, there was no security at all. He walked past a deserted lodge onto the campus.

Dressed by Ramona's maid from a selection of five husbands' clothes ("Spouse Number Three was exactly your size, darling!") - Thomas matched the Kadets walking to and from class through the trees. "Beverly Hills casuals, darling. Pass you off as a Kadet in mufti." Her judgement was spot-on, he had that smart, neutral look of the kadet students, as if he were peddling Bibles for an Evangelical sect.

Soon kadets were thronging the driveway. Getting-by with Precinct vocabulary that he had learnt from Kyla, Thomas arrived unnoticed at the main complex. This block might have been designed by one of Stalin's favoured architects. The massive scale of the gaunt, central tower gave the structure a gloomy, occult feel. Phallic gargoyles jutted from the corners in hideous parody of a church. At the base, the arched entrance reminded him of the Sagrada Familia in Barcelona.

A shrill electric bell rang and the entrance was opened by two "J" kadets. The students swarmed into a hall. Thomas joined them. As the crowd filed into a lecture theatre, Thomas saw a staircase. No longer apprehensive, he nipped up the stairs before anyone had time to notice. In an instant he was on a spacious landing out of sight. A secondary staircase was accessed through a pair of pewter-sheathed doors. He took these stairs two at a time as far as they went, about a hundred and seventy feet, around fifty meters. Now well up into the height of the tower, Thomas arrived at a second, generous landing.

He rested, getting his breath back, looking at the deep brown wall panels, the thick plum-red carpet, listening to the sound of his panting. Feeling dizzy he bent forward like a runner, legs apart, and took deep breaths. Recovered, he straightened up, to see more detail. Along the walls, lit by reproduction Etruscan lamps, were paintings of naked youths.

He walked towards the only doorway. It was a double door, huge and important. The architraves were enriched with porphyry and lapis lazuli. The leaves of the door were solid, beaten gold. The handles were phalli carved in petrified oak, set with rubies and black pearls.

"Witch craft! … Black, bloody magic!" Suddenly he was frightened. A forceful instinct made him want to dive back down those stairs, rush through the arched door, hare down the drive - to Anatole, and away!

"Open the door or bugger off? Which?" He glanced at his watch, adjusted its alarm to three minutes, took a deep breath, and took hold of one of the phallic handles.

As soon as his fingers grasped the lewd shaft, the doors swung inwards on electronically assisted hinges. The vaulted chamber beyond was awash with the light from two thousand electric candles. The ornamentation was so profuse that the young man could make nothing of it but a spangled vision of gold mosaic, alabaster and shot silk. The place stank of sickly incense, like hyacinths past their best.

Thomas stared at Moreau's glass casket. Enormous, vulgar . . . and empty.

Thomas crept round the casket, warily keeping his distance. Looking through it, he saw the three windows in exact accord with Stotz's riddle, as was the view when he looked out of them. He turned his attention to the casket. "How did they get the bloody thing up here?" He examined the marble podium upon which the casket rested. In the polished granite floor round the perimeter was a fine, brass-edged joint. Of course! The thing was on an elevator platform. It had been raised up a shaft.

His watch alarm sounded. He darted to the entrance and poked his head out of the golden doorway. Nothing. "Here goes!"

He returned to the three windows and sat down on a seat fitted to the sill. This gave slightly with his weight. He stood up and felt under a projecting edge. The seat was hinged and lifted. In the box below was an enamelled metal panel like a typewriter keyboard.

"Easy!" He typed-out *Chavalon* with two fingers.

A white marble panel behind the casket separated from its frame, moved forward like an aircraft door, and glided up through a slot in the ceiling.

"*Very* easy!" Pleased with himself, without pausing to think, he slipped through the new opening into the well lit operations room beyond.

It was a treasure trove. Everywhere there were maps of Kadet Precincts worldwide, their exact locations marked, explanatory photographs, plans, construction details. Racks were stuffed with files detailing public figures and famous personalities next in line for liquidation, files of people who were accomplices, of VIPs targeted for the next phase of Serum induced 'corruption conversion'. Lying open on a desk was a file listing Heads of State and their deputies already under the influence of Friedemann's serum. Thomas noted that the British parliament had been rubber stamped "ACTIONED", the American Senate "PENDING". Along the walls maps and charts showed serum production plants, sperm banks, and an amazingly detailed Five Year Plan.

In this one room, Thomas reckoned, was enough information to blow Moreau's Eocratic dream apart.

Full ashtrays littered two long tables. They had been placed carelessly on maps and reports along with thirty or so plastic cups, some half full of - Thomas sniffed - of brandy. On a sideboard was a Cona jug of coffee. He was too elated to notice that the coffee was still steaming. He had to select one key item that he could stuff under his shirt. Which? He began to riffle through the bank of files, now oblivious of his precarious situation.

With scarcely a hum the marble entrance door slid down into place, engaging, sealing, almost becoming one with the wall surface it had merged with. Thomas leapt over to the spot where seconds before an opening had been. He traced his finger down the joint: the thread of a silk worm! Panicky, breathing hard, he saw no handle, no button, no lever. "Oh God! . . . Get me out of here!"

He stuffed the selected report down his pants, trembling with fear.

"*Oh, fuck!*"

The lights went out. The place was darker than night.

♠

Dressing on the morning of June 15th, I gazed out of my Geneva hotel window at Lac Léman, permitting myself - for once - the luxury of complacency.

Since leaving Thomas in the capable hands of Ramona, I had taken the train to Lyon where I had bought a cheap leather brief case and five CDs featuring dud rock groups nobody had heard of since their first hit dived off the charts. I dropped the disks into the River Saône from the Pont Bonaparte. Now, on my hotel dressing table, Friedemann's five golden discs were concealed by the tacky covers of the plastic CD cases.

I put these into the brief case, along with a file containing Arthur's lurid memo from Jo's library, Friedemann's faked suicide note, Arthur's supposed love letter to Jo, and the sheet ripped out of a file with its hand written margin notes that Stanley had picked up from Friedemann's terrace before the fire. Friedemann's volume of plans went into a plastic bag. Cheaply and simply, I was prepared for the *rendezvous* with Frederick.

I entered the Cathédrale Saint-Pièrre at 12-00hrs and saw Fred at once. I sat quietly down beside him. He looked tired and vexed, dabbing his blind eye with a cream silk square. "Let us visit the Art Gallery, Johnny. I'm sure you like pictures as much as I do."

Outside, a car waited. "Get in." He said nothing as we were chauffeured the short distance to the Musée d'art et d'histoire where we did not stop at the swaggering main entrance but turned down a long, gently sloping ramp into a cavernous basement service bay. Here we were welcomed by the Museum Director who assured Frederick that the public had been cleared from the building until 16-00hrs. He offered us a drink in his office but Frederick said, in marvellously correct French, "Later, when we are through. Have you placed the *Rousseau* as I requested?"

"But of course, Sir Frederick!"

"Thank you, we shall be delighted to see the work. Johnny, please follow me!" When we were out of earshot, climbing the resplendent limestone staircase, Fred drawled, "I particularly value a first class art gallery for secrecy. You would not credit, Johnny, that most of my best people are hidden behind the scenes in art galleries and museums all over the world." We arrived at the principle floor where the hall leading to the galleries was smothered in *fin-de-siècle* frescos. "You see, when you think about it," - he spoke with the self-absorption of an enthusiast, wagging a demonstrative finger, "the work of a museum curator is parallel to the work of an agent: meticulous attention to minute detail, security, the constant vigil of preserving intact subtle, fragile signals from the other side - in the curator's case, from the Past - the ability to interpret what is in the minds of those beyond reach."

We entered a gallery hung with enormous paintings in juggernaut frames. Alpine landslides crashed with splendour, a posse of garishly costumed bandits attacked a coach full of fainting ladies, Greek gods posed on Olympus with superior smiles. We sat down on a long, leather upholstered bench.

"Who is it, Johnny? Who is stirring the cauldron? A single human being eludes us. Who is it?"

I stared at a group of handsome, clear skinned barbarians with neatly plaited hair, each manacled to his fellow tribesman. Swarthy Roman soldiers, the captors of this noble group, seemed to reek of garlic.

"I don't know, Fred. I thought it might be Friedemann but he was too philosophical to be a ringleader. I don't think it can be Stotz, whose loyalty seems to be ambivalent. Arthur is dead and we know nothing about the figure at Gracewood, the voice with an English accent that Nina Burdet heard."

"She never saw him. A pity. I believe that person is holding the Burdets hostage. Your lover told us."

"Corinne! Is she involved?"

"The Countess? No. She was driven back to her château as the Burdets left. The story goes that she had telephoned them from Paris in some distress. The truth is that she had not telephoned them at all. The Countess is presently under our protection. She is quite safe. Please do not attempt to contact her."

"You tracked us, Fred!"

"Think nothing of it, my dear! A waggon load of junk shunting about in Space. I always take advantage of the stuff. Protecting you is my concern. When you waded into Atlas One we might have had to fish you out. What have you got in the case?"

"Friedemann's disks. The proper job this time." He opened the brief case, taking from it one of the CD cases.

"*Larry Bollocks Gets It Up!* . . . Good heavens, Johnny! I thought you were a Mozart fan! . . . Ah! That's better . . ." He examined a gold disk through a Jeweller's eyeglass. "Mmm! . . . very good." He lined the four other cases on the bench, opening them one by one.

"Excellent, Johnny! ... There they are. Fancy! I could not have obtained them, but you, a bungling amateur, and the kiddy, an innocent abroad: you have gone where angels fear to tread." He took a pair of white gloves from a pocket of his jacket, put them on and gently disengaged a disk from its plastic grip. Lifting it to the light he examined the sheen.

"I've a good mind to melt them down."

"Thanks, Fred! If I'd known, I'd have stayed at home selling *books*!"

"You know nothing, Johnny! Keep it that way. The copies you got hold of were good enough to get the drift of Friedemann's achievement. The Mind of God, simultaneously wonderful and terrible, visible and invisible." He collected the cases together, placing them in the brief case, "What does it say in every Christian church, in every Islamic Mosque. What do the Buddhists say, the Taoists? What, even, do the Humanists say?"

"In one form or another, Fred, 'Do not take the Name of The Lord God in vain."

"Precisely! . . . Friedemann had genius beyond genius, there *will* be written there, as he warned on the inscription you read in his villa, the mathematical formula controlling the governor of our particular Universe. I am not at all certain that we should delve. Perhaps it would be better for the sake of Humanity to destroy these five originals un-tried."

"It can't be as bad as that, Fred. Friedemann was some sort of warlock. I'll bet the disks contain a lot of nonsense." His single eye fixed me with a glare that froze my words.

"Moreau thought he was God, Johnny. Friedemann thought he would play with God's Will. These *dreadful* people involved with Moreau's mission think they are on a par with God. *Fools*! God has no concern with politicians and tyrants, yet beware! It is possible - still - that Moreau's crass *bunkum* may bring us to destruction. My dear friend, if you know what is good for you, listen to my words and be silent." He sat regal as a prince. I knew then his power.

"Who do we seek next?"

"The English Voice on the gallery at Gracewood?"

"I suspect that the 'English Voice' is one of two possible successors. I have the feeling that the other possible successor murdered Friedemann. He wanted to get his hands on these (he tapped the briefcase) and rule over a form of Nihilism."

"It is already happening . . . there is plague in Switzerland."

"Officially the malady is a form of flu. From swine, they tell me. The swine are those in charge! Flue does not cause the inexplicable deaths - on a global scale - of seventeen million people in three months."

"We are going to have to coerce Stotz to join us."

"Agreed. He is probably the only person alive who understands Friedemann's work."

We had by now moved to a smaller gallery where an easel had been specially set up by one of the windows. It displayed an exquisite pastel portrait, by Quentin de Latour, of Jean-Jacques Rousseau as a young man. Had the real Rousseau walked into the room and stood by the portrait, we should not have been so impressed by him as with his likeness in pastels. Fred peered closely at the artist's matchless technique. "Where is the answer? *Think*, Johnny! Be certain that the answer exists like this portrait. It is before of your eyes!"

"In the briefcase are four key documents. One is genuine, by Arthur, two are faked and the third is from an office file. The handwriting on the three documents is identical."

Frederick opened the case, removed the wallet and examined Arthur's supposed letter to Jo. I began to explain but he cut me short. "Oscar Wilde's *De Profundis!* Lifted word for word. Listen; *'Only what is fine, and finely conceived, can feed love. But anything will feed hate. There was not a glass of champagne that you drank, not a rich dish that you ate of in all those years, that did not feed your hate and make it fat. So to gratify it you gambled with my life, as you gambled with my money, carelessly, recklessly, indifferent to the consequence.'* Oscar Wilde at his daunting best, Johnny."

"The person that made the copy was also required to create two fake letters and has written the notes in the margin of the typewritten file document."

Fred put the papers back into the case and handed it to me. "Keep them! I have no use for them. Burn them! Get hold of Stotz. He is our only hope."

I do not know if I was more shocked than surprised by Fred's dismissal of the file. It seemed to me that the documents were vital pieces of evidence, yet he wanted them destroyed. I was about to say something when the director arrived, nervously hesitating in the doorway. "Gentlemen, it is nearly four. I regret, but we cannot keep the public out of the galleries beyond the agreed time limit." He was afraid of Frederick, the poor man's hands were trembling.

"Good gracious, Klaus! We quite forgot the time. We'll have that drink you offered." Fred waved airily at the Rousseau portrait, "Crate it! My people will fly it to London in the morning. It will do nicely in my office. We'll send you a copy, the public won't know."

Over a glass of Swiss wine we talked of the many fine art collections that grace Switzerland. As Frederick was describing the museum of St. Gallen, the thought struck me that we had not spoken of Thomas. For an instant, Fred frowned. "We've lost the randy little blighter. He's out of tracking. Must have changed his clothes. Sensors were sewn into the garments provided at Casablanca."

"Taken them off, more like."

"Bed with Ramona Delano?" Frederick turned to the director who was glancing at us quizzically through a pair of rimless pince-nez, "Don't you wish *you* were in bed with Ramona Delano, Klaus? I'm damned certain I do!"

"The bronze you are standing beside, Sir Frederick, is by Rodin. A little known study of Voltaire. It attempts to capture (he coughed in that pernickety way of the thoroughbred academic) Voltaire's elevated *intellect*."

"I was talking, Klaus, of Ramona Delano in bed!"

♠

A quiet dinner to oneself in the neutral ambience of a first rate hotel acts as a tonic. The sound that well placed cutlery makes, the polite voices, the tinge of hothouse blooms, the smart garb of a really good *Maître d'hôtel*: impressions such as these lend solitude potent charm. Could I fail to be soothed by the attentive staff, or pleased by their youthful smiles? Could I fail to be gently delighted by the *sommelier's* deft handling of a bottle of Château Ausone '79? Would I have relished more the perfection of my meal had a companion been at my side? There are times when life crowds too close, leaving no space in which to enjoy the exquisitely lingering, sumptuously indulgent, instant of the Present . . . *alone.*

It was not late. I dawdled with a liqueur, smoked two Turkish cigarettes, then drifted from the dining room. I wandered into the hotel gardens, lit with concealed floods that made lavish viridian crinolines of the cedar trees and illuminated groups of chattering guests seated idly on frondy, white, cast iron chairs. I took a contemplative stroll by the lake, walking some way along the Quai du Mont Blanc, enjoying like a lover the rapturous conference of water, night and luxury: the beating heart of Geneva.

In pleasurable quandary, I called-in at another famous hotel for a nightcap in the resplendent bar they have there. The Italian-Swiss lad who served me had worked in Aylesford. We talked of the cosy English town for half an hour before I bade him 'Adieu' and stepped out again into the lovely night, to return to my hotel.

The carpet was thicker than I remembered as I arrived at the door of my suite feeling for my key. On the glass-topped table in the vestibule fresh flowers drowsed before a delightfully framed mirror. I went into the main room and turned on the light:

"You keep remarkably well-preserved for your age, Johnny!"

Shock forced from me a barking cry! I spun round, wild-eyed, an iron bar in every muscle with the instinctive, rigid urge to defend myself. I looked forward, at the diminutive figure sitting in a chair surrounded by six huge, standing kadets. The image gradually came into focus as it spoke again,

"Aren't you going to offer an old friend your hand, Johnny?" Gagged by the shattering realisation of what I saw, I could only whisper,

"Arthur!"

There was a shivering silence before I found the nerve to exclaim,
" . . . . . *alive!*"

"And kicking, Johnny. Oh yes! And kicking, my dear." He rose up out of the chair unaided, a tiny old man wearing a ginger wig, his powdered face showing two hideous polka-dot patches of rouge. He wore a battle dress like Mao Zedong, and a pair of tiny, clip-on, diamond earrings.

"We have your deliciously pretty boyfriend tied up in a net ready to be flayed alive, Johnny." He took a glass from one of the kadets with a gracious nod. Then he took a bottle of gin from another, this time blowing a dainty kiss, pouting his shrivelled, purplish lips at the kadet's melting eyes. He poured gin into the glass while a third kadet added Italian Vermouth and a fourth, ice and a wafer of lime. He held the glass out for me to come forward and take. His hand shook ever so slightly.

"I think the time has come for us to have one of our little talks, Johnny. Like we always used to have . . ." he raised, typically, an ironic eyebrow, ". . . in the hazy, golden days of yore."

PART V

"I'm into this life of luxury, Jeff. Up to my armpits!" Nina grabbed a chocolate from an ivory salver. "Pass me the other magazine, this one's last weeks."

"Call the kadet, he'll bring some more."

"Do you see how they're polishing those floors out there? These boys know how to clean a place down! That parquet shines up real good."

"I don't give a damn! I'll go mad if something doesn't happen soon. Sixty-one days, Nina! Eight weeks and five days since we came to this place ostensibly to rescue Corinne and fell into their trap!"

"Press the bell, Honey."

"I just did, Babe!"

"Do it again, he's late!"

"*Nina!*"

"We should never have believed those guys."

"You mean Pierre and Charles? Hell, Nina, that's unfair. We dissected every detail of our stay with Corinne a thousand times. They *killed* Pierre!"

"That's too bad! What was he doing mixed up with that crowd? Was he the American he said he was? He told us his Dad owns Burfordine stores. A kid who's Dad owns Burfordine stores doesn't stooge around France as a waiter! Those two guys were double crossing rats like everybody else round here." She got up off a silver silk, cushioned canapé and walked over to the bell push, "Why's he taking so long? . . . Honey, those guys saw us coming the moment we left London. Charles Barra told you the Countess's place was littered with bugs and video cameras. He controlled that junk! Those folks knew what we were doin' every second we were doin' it." She dumped herself down on a pink pouf, "Barra has to be in league with . . . *somebody*!"

"Somebody! . . . That's good, Nina. Like who? . . . C'mon, Nina! *Who*?" Jeff motioned with his hand round the 'twenties deco interior, "Who's running this place we're in now? Who are Corinne's friends she was so worried about? She told us she was in Paris: I don't think we're in Paris!"

"We must be. Pierre's pilot flew us to Paris!"

"Oh yeah? How do you know where he flew us? It was night!" He shut one of the tall windows, latching it impatiently. "What's with this place? The air stinks of burning corpses!"

"Don't go overboard, Jeff! Keep hold of what we can see. A courtyard, four neat walls with big, shuttered windows, a gutter all round, three chimneys."

"And the top of a church dome, Our Lady messed by sea gulls."

"Do they have sea gulls in Paris?"

"They have everything in Paris!"

"Why worry! We're treated like a President and First Lady! All those sweet boys giving us anything we want, well most of what we want; and the food! . . . the wine! We ain't been troubled by no hoods. Cool down, Lover!"

"Look across at those windows. Nobody! No sign of life in those rooms for eight weeks! The only thing we hear close-by is a helicopter. The hum of city life? You'd think they were all dead out there. As for your 'sweet boys' Nina, they could come into this room and slaughter us. You want magazines? You get decapitated!"

"No way, Jeff! We're valuable. We have something they don't . . . maybe they want us to do them a favour, that's why they're being good to us. And we're *alive*, Jeff. So is Corinne . . . she telephones every day."

"Are you sure it's Corinne? Her voice sounds very odd." He dumped himself dejectedly on a silver and grey chair, "Doesn't it concern you, Nina? All this complicated secrecy that Sir Frederick wove round us and we're no secret at all?" He began pacing up and down the high, silver and mauve *salon* of the suite allotted to them in the converted hotel constructed in 1925 by Piet Vandel for Blaisedale Europe.

Jeff and Nina felt they were grasping at straws: in fact, they were on the rim of truth. Corinne had not made a telephone call from Paris eight weeks before. Her voice had been simulated. They had been flown to Marseilles. As Pierre drove them from La Breuse, Corinne's Rolls Royce was approaching the château by another road. They were thirty seconds apart. The pilot of Pierre's plane was a freebooter hired in Minneapolis. Pierre's throat had been cut by a kadet as he stepped out of the fuselage while Jeff and Nina were speeding away in a chauffeur-driven car. Nina turned to look through the rear window and saw Pierre's body plummet to the floodlit runway. Her cry of alarm went unheeded.

The Burdets were driven to Moreau's European Headquarters overlooking the Old Port of Marseilles where they became prisoners. The dome topped by a statue of the Madonna belonged to the *Cathedral de la Major*.

The acrid smoke the couple could smell was indeed from burning corpses. Piles of semi-cremated bodies littered the streets and squares of Marseilles. The great French seaport was the first wholesale victim of Friedemann's serum: mains water, milk, brands of French beer, cigarettes, a famous Cassis - all carried the fatal substance capable of warping the minds of millions to accept acts of untold brutality as a way of life.

The latest atrocity was the mass murder by axe at a bus depot of over five hundred people. Thirty-two high school students had wielded the axes before splitting each other to bone-chunked gore in an orgiastic finale. Lumps of flesh rotted where they were. Passengers were inconvenienced by flies, stench, and ravening rats. Surprisingly, their complaints were about the re-arranged bus parking bays that made it confusing to know where to queue.

What Jeff and Nina did not know was that in another part of the building two hundred people enjoyed a life of sumptuous privilege on towering expense accounts. These were the higher ranks of Moreau's European executive: a band of elevated spivs, failed intellectuals and shady aristocrats. An army of kadets waited on them day and night: no luxury was spared, sex included.

Nina grabbed another chocolate, changed her mind and put it back on the salver. She went over to Jeff and wound her arms round his waist affectionately, "Pity I got in there, Jeff."

"Got in where, Nina?"

"Gracewood, Honey."

"You insisted, Nina."

"Now that's not fair! *You* insisted on listening to that creep Stotz! If we hadn't swept off to Marrakech we'd be enjoying the grandchildren in Minneapolis."

"Grandchildren can be noisy."

One of the locked double doors of the salon was opened with an efficient swish. Listlessly, for they were used to sudden interruptions, Jeff and Nina turned to see what was going on. A 'J' kadet stood to attention at one side of the silver-plated doors. They heard the sound of determined, booted feet marching over a gleaming parquet floor.

A magnificent kadet appeared, acknowledging the 'J' Kadet with a nod like a prince. He strode to the prisoners and stood towering before them, handsome as a god. He wore an impeccable white jacket with a high military collar and shimmering gold epaulettes. The jacket was embellished by a superb, ice blue, watered silk sash. A diamond-encrusted star was pinned over his heart. In one hand he carried a golden baton. His long, perfect legs were sheathed in black trousers creased like cut-throat razors and made impressive by two cerise bands down the outer sides. His profoundly intelligent eyes were agate brown, like his slicked, thick hair. He gave off a natural, sweet fragrance and his bronzy, broad neck supported a head that surpassed in majesty and beauty that of Michelangelo's *David*.

It was Kyla.

Nina goggled; "Oh *my*! You look like you walked out of a Norman Rockwell!"

"I do not understand you, Madam!" He spoke - Jeff noted - in beautiful English, not arrogantly, but with the cultivated dignity he had learnt from Stanley and myself.

"Norman Rockwell was an American illustrator, Sweetie!" Motherly, Nina took hold of Kyla's free hand, "Don't you worry about it. Tell us the news."

"Somebody wishes to see you. Please follow me."

♠

He took them down a corridor to a bank of onyx faced elevators. They went up eight floors and stepped out of the pink mirrored car into a hall where ranks of kadet secretaries worked robotically at computer keyboards. As he passed them Kyla's presence caused each kadet to stand and bow low from the waist. The air was thick with respect.

The hall was an impressive three floors high, top lit by a stained glass ceiling big as an inverted swimming bath. The walls were lined with black marble zigzagged with rose quartz. At one end, Jeff and Nina were shown through a pair of twenty foot high, stainless steel doors. Kyla turned to them, indicating a group of low club chairs upholstered in murky chocolate brown leather.

"Please sit down!"

The two Americans found themselves in a huge office. Polished brown marble gave the general effect, veined yellow like liver. To one side, dusty lace curtains concealed seven tall windows. By a vast, dull, gravy brown desk, stood an ugly brass standard lamp with a mushroom beige, pom-pom fringed shade.

"Adolph Hitler!"

"Nina, keep your voice down!"

"This room is *exactly* like those pictures of Hitler's place we saw on TV."

"The room could be bugged, Honey."

"That *awful* desk! Why, that thing could hold up the Empire State Building." She nudged the back of Jeff's hand with her fingertips, murmuring, "Above the desk, on the wall. Those gold letters."

"W.M.D.O."

"You got it, Jeff"

A door behind the desk slid to one side. The couple gazed without interest at the opening. Kyla whispered, "Please stand."

"Now look here, son! . . ."

"Do what he asks, Nina. Let'em think we're hooked."

An ordinary looking man appeared, wearing a grey business suit and a parrot green tie. He was a well preserved forty-five. His thinning, mouse brown hair needed combing.

"The room is indeed bugged, Mr. Burdet. I have heard every word of your interesting conversation." It was a light, supercilious, middle class English voice. The words were enunciated with irritating emphasis. He came forward to greet them, extending a too friendly hand too frankly. The lacquered smile wavered between conceit and impatience.

"Rick Stackton. Pleased to meet you. Come over to the desk and take a seat. I have something important to say, then I must leave." Sitting down himself, Kyla attentive behind his chair, Stackton adopted a pose of charitable concern veneered with menace.

"I do hope everything is alright for you here, that you are comfortable." It was clear that the man couldn't have cared care less about them. In his own estimation he was a clever fellow, but he wasn't clever enough to disguise from Jeff and Nina his callousness, grasping selfishness, and monomanic lust for limitless power. Jeff regarded Stackton's eyes, now tooled with Good Will. In the man's inky pupils he recognised the unmistakable signs of a congenital liar.

Briskly, Stackton continued, "I won't tell you what I do, that need not concern you. However, I *shall* tell you that . . ."

"I know you!" Nina sat still in her chair. Immediately Stackton rounded on her, his face prim with displeasure. "I'm sorry? . . . Did you say something?"

"You're the guy on the balcony at Gracewood. The dude who shouted at the butler to get me out of the place!"

Jeff cautioned her.

"I don't care, Jeff! This is the guy on the balcony. I'd know the voice anywhere." She turned to Stackton. "Ain't that right, Mister? When I was giving your creepy butler those church magazines? . . . Old *Franz*? Don't tell us you ain't heard the name! You came out of an upstairs room in that dump and you stood on the balcony above those obscene statues, and you told Franz to turn me out." She stood up, leaning forward, her hands on the thick rim of the desk, "You don't impress me, Mister, because you're nothing but some kind of jumped-up jerk!" She waved her arm round, "This place stinks, you stink, an' I'm not afraid to say what I want to say because I'm an American, an' we *all* ought'a have spoken-out a long time ago about freaks like *you*! . . ."

"*Insolence* in your position is a silly idea, Mrs Burdet! A very silly idea *indeed*!"

Nina wasn't bothered. "You got us here to ask a favour, isn't that so, Rick?"

"*Nina*! For Christ's sake don't do this!"

"It's OK, Jeff, Rick and me have an understanding, isn't that so?" A Dog Daisy smile crowned Stackton's expression with white petals of accord. "I may have underestimated you, Mrs Burdet."

"Call me Nina."

"What I have to tell you both may come as something of a surprise."

"Tell us."

"Arthur Moreau is alive."

"Who the hell cares!"

"Mrs Burdet, I am tired of your wayward behaviour. This is a sociable audience. If you continue to be aggressive I will separate you from your husband in alternative, less salubrious accommodation." Stackton nursed a sulky mouth.

"What do you want us to do, Rick?"

"American common sense at last, Nina. Please come to the windows." Stackton stood up, went to the windows and was about to draw a net curtain

171

when Kyla did it for him. At that instant the kadet stood behind Stackton looking intently at Nina. As she studied the godly face, Kyla gave her a tiny grin. Pointing to Stackton's back, he frowned and drew his hand across the base of his neck. Nina understood, giving the kadet an almost imperceptible wink. As if relieved that he had communicated his innermost feelings, Kyla radiantly smiled.

"Look out of this window, both of you. Do you see the ship moored over there?"

"It would be difficult not to, Mr Stackton, she's just over the road. Looks like an old time liner to me."

"In one, Jeff! She is Moreau's floating Headquarters. 'The Eocratic'." Stackton returned to his desk leaving Jeff and Nina eyeing the enormous, white-hulled liner.

"That's a dumb name for a ship."

"Arthur's idea, Nina. A combination of two Greek words; Eo, meaning *dawn*, and Kratos - meaning *rule*. The dawn of a new rule, thus an Eocracy rather than a Democracy. Do you follow me?"

"Perfectly."

"Why does Arthur Moreau need to call his ship such a stupid word?"

"Because ... because, frankly, he's mad!"

Jeff had been looking at Stackton, quietly observing the man's slippery expression, the nervous mouth, the uncertain eyes. "You want us to kill Moreau, Mr Stackton, don't you?"

"Jeff! I am delighted by your common sense! I certainly *do* want you to render him permanently inoperative. On board the Eocratic, if you will. Far out at sea. Choose your moment and do the deed with gusto. It might be said that Arthur was lost at sea. You have three days to meet my deadline. If you fail your entire family will be liquidated. They are already under observation."

"Rick, you can make burgers out of me and Jeff, but you don't touch our kids or our grandchildren. Any more cheap threats and . . . " Jeff grasped Nina's hand, "Honey, do as he asks." He squeezed the hand hard, smiling at Stackton whose expression flashed-up like a lighthouse beam. "Be sure we'll meet your deadline, Mr Stackton, won't we, my dear?"

"Too right we will, Jeff!"

"Kyla will take you on board the ship immediately. You have a State Room on "A" Deck, The Novello Suite. Now I must go." Without giving them another glance, Stackton slithered through the door behind his desk like a lizard in a rockery. The door slid closed immediately, leaving no trace of a joint.

Nina walked over to Kyla and hugged him. "I guess we could use a drink, my dear. And I guess you're dying to dish the dirt."

"I don't understand you, Madame."

"Tell us your story."

Nina went to the window and looked apprehensively at the liner.
"Jeff, this is all so *awful*! What are we going to *do*?"
"One step at a time, Nina. One step at a time."

♠

"One step at a time, Johnny dear. One step at a time." Arthur's affected, lisping voice had been droning all night. Dawn was almost done, the light of early morning glowed through the generously pleated drapes of the Geneva hotel suite. I was fuddled with lack of sleep and too much gin, though cold sober. As I was offered glass after glass I drank the stuff, anything to keep him talking, explaining, revealing his lurid nightmare plans.

I listened in amazement. Occasionally I asked a question when he would immediately rebuke me. I was carefully, constantly watched by the cohort of six standing kadets; they did not shift a limb but merely breathed. I saw the gentle rise and fall of their immaculate chests while the master's voice rasped and croaked, his tongue sometimes protruding suggestively, or slavering revoltingly as his ancient, manicured fingers jittered across the loins or the thighs of one kadet or another. The room became stuffy after an hour or so and I began to smell Arthur's breath, unhealthy, reeking of the bowel. I realised that beneath the pungent female scent he was soaked-in there was the taint of malady and stale urine. The smell of a geriatric wing in a home for the elderly.

Arthur alone controlled every corner of his empire. There were no deputies, but an individual had been named as his successor: the First Eocrat. Who this person was and where he operated Arthur cunningly did not reveal. I guessed Gracewood to be the Imperial hub but Arthur waggled a python yellow finger to rouged lips whilst his frosted eyes twinkled with malicious humour, "Don't be a nuisance, Johnny, darling! Asking naughty questions will get your pretty boy's gorgeous bottom smacked!"

I was worried sick about Thomas. What had the lad been doing? What scrape had he got himself into? Clearly, Arthur knew all about it and it seemed from what he said that a word from 'The Master' would activate Thomas's instant execution.

"I so enjoy having victims murdered on the spot, Johnny dear."

My strategy had to be 'off-the-cuff' and Frederick's image of the Minotaur's Labyrinth proved inspirational. Somewhere in that mad body, that hideously deformed mind, a fragment of the original Arthur still lived, the Arthur I had known so well, who responded best to a combination of gentle flattery and genteel menace. All I required to do was up the tempo.

"Can I be of service to you, Arthur? Your plans are so immensely impressive that I don't think Appleby has ever understood how powerful you actually are."

"Johnny, dear! I knew you wouldn't take much persuading."

Breakfast arrived, wheeled-in on two trolleys by kadets. We sat over jellied eel, cockles and stout planning my new role, he gabbling, me nodding approval making him believe I was hanging on his every word. The act took some skill.

"Isn't it all so exciting, Johnny!" He tapped my knee, "How *superb* to see you looking so fit, Johnny. Quite a fetch, and well over forty! I'm going to award you a *pretty* prize! - I won't hear of you refusing because I know you'll be missing your wickedly lovely boyfriend *horribly*." He sucked his breath lasciviously, winking at me with coquettish coyness. "I have decided to give you one of these." He grasped the tallest, most sabre-shouldered kadet by the crease of a trouser leg and pulled him forward, slurping saliva as he pawed the curve of the kadet's statuesque buttocks. "It's called Aaron. Can you guess why?" Wiring a smile I said, "We have discovered that they don't have genitals, Arthur. We discovered that particular ... how should I put it? ... quirk of Friedemann's Super Race in the first week."

He became furious and began to choke. Ordering a spittoon to be placed under his chin he fetched-up a gobbet of grey-brown bile. "I don't want Aaron near me, Arthur."

"Good gracious, Johnny, what a *roughneck* you are!" Glancing at me doubtfully, he dabbed at his lipstick and became peevishly dignified.

"You have known me for years, Arthur. You knew from the beginning that I am not 'that way' inclined."

"You were such a good influence on me, Johnny." Arch were his anchovy-hued eyelids. "I've missed you so! It was such a blow when you left me in the hands of *horrid* half-brother, Jo!" He produced a burst of crocodile tears, taking the head of a kadet onto his lap, gently stroking the shimmering, lacquer-black hair as if he stroked a cat. "My little ones, my Angel Army. All-pervading power is a lonely business." I took up the cue, ingratiatingly, "You have indeed achieved all-pervading power, Arthur. The power to destroy the fabric of Western Society. Do you actually intend to carry out your plan?"

"Oh yes." This was said with absolute indifference, as if I had asked, "Do you actually enjoy wearing a ginger wig?"

"Who was in the glass casket?"

"Piet Vandel, dear, why?"

"The body resembled you - exactly."

"Plastic surgery, luvvy. We cloned. He was a marvel! Funded everything. Never had to ask. Cash on the table every time. Died in sixty-eight. Put him in a freezer. From Minneapolis, you know."

"Yes, we know." He gave me a saucy glance and pulled the kadet's statuesque head from his lap to give its minutely parted lips a fruit-moist kiss. "You're a *terrible* Sherlock Holmes, Johnny! I was *livid* when they told me that you and that *grisly* little American reporter were hanging around Atlas One like a couple of tarts round a sailor's cock!"

"Where is Thomas? If you don't tell me I'll break your neck here in this room. Don't think these kadets will stop me!" He became the spluttering coward whining for mercy. "Well Arthur! Your choice. Tell me what you've done with Thomas or I'll smash your brains out before you can say 'Tonio Friedemann'."

"And what if I do tell you, deary?"

"My people could help your plan succeed."

The old game: promises and threats.

"Thomas! . . . . You're such a baby snatcher, Johnny!"

"I last heard that line at Jayne Blaisedale's party. Have you harmed him?"

"How *uncivilised* of you to think so. He's been given a shot to keep him quiet. Such a *brawny* boy! Fought like a young lion. We had to fend-off one of his little pals as well, a French waiter my dear!" He shivered theatrically, "And a very *nasty* woman. She appeared in a scarlet Rolls flapping about in some Dior number like a bat from a fucking belfry! . . . Vulgar old bitch! . . . *Frightful!*" He shuddered, caressing the Kadet behind one ear, "Some *dreadful*, moth-eaten movie star, darling! Do you remember 'They Kissed The Stone.'?"

"No!"

"She starred in it. Looked like a fucking dog's breakfast *then*, my dear! A gorgeous co-star, Tristan Mentone. Married Eva Snellard, the Girl in the Golden Gown. They hired an entire floor of the Prince Klaus Hotel for years until he decided to become a woman. Retired to Los Angeles as Mabel Farroosh. I expect . . ."

"Ramona Delano happens to be one of Emanuel Blaisedale's daughters, Arthur. Her real name is Lana Blaisedale. . . . As you well know! So don't give me any more crap. . . . Where's Thomas?"

"Waiting in transit, dear. With the casket. We have a luncheon engagement tomorrow, near Lausanne, then we pack. We sail from Marseilles on *The Eocratic* in three days time. You're coming with us."

♠

We were chauffeured to a marvellous villa overlooking Lac Léman surrounded by vineyards. Early next morning I tiptoed from my bedroom, fortunately located on the ground floor of a discrete wing. A winding footpath lead down through vineyards to the hamlet of Villette where a private bridge took me over the lakeside railroad tracks to the quay of a tiny port where an old fashioned paddle steamer was about to depart for Evian. I took it, buying my ticket on board from the delightful Swiss conductor, "Do you know the lake, Monsieur?"

"I know it well. My father owned a house at Epesses."

"There's an emergency going on. Some type of virus is killing people by the score. Disastrous for the holiday trade. We are the last steamer on the lake, most of my colleagues are ill."

Ashore at Evian I looked up a café I'd not been to for over twenty years. It was still there, along the main street, past the Spa.

Would I be remembered? They had changed the traditional painted frontage for garish plastic but in the window a graveyard of bluebottles by the cake stand reassured me that Camille was still in charge.

"Bonjour, Monsieur .... *Johnny!* I don't bloody believe it. You gorgeous boy!" She rushed from the other side of the counter and folded me in an embrace. "Darling! I thought you was dead!" I squeezed her to me, remembering the scent of her dried-out, peroxide blond hair. Camille Bayswater! The oldest flame of my earliest youth. "Who's in, darling? Any English?"

"Is this important, Johnny?"

"Do you think I'd be squeezing your arse like this for damn-all after twenty years if it weren't? I'm sure you know what's happening on the other side of the lake."

"They're dying like my bluebottles round the cake stand. Same as in France."

"Well, I know why. I need to get some information back to London." I took out of my coat a manilla envelope containing the papers Frederick had refused to countenance.

"There's an English couple down the far end having breakfast. They wanted bacon and eggs . . ."

Danny and Evelyn Briscoe were in their fifties, from Weston-Super-Mare, prosperous, and worried sick. They told me that the British Consul in Geneva had issued a warning concerning a fatal disease sweeping through Switzerland. All UK passport holders should arrange to return home at once. "We've spent a fortune coming out here! My husband has a heart condition they can put right in Montreux. We're staying at the . . ."

"I'm sure that Johnny doesn't want to hear about our troubles, dear!"

"I am asking you if you will take this envelope back to England. I want you to deliver it - in confidence - to the person named on the address. You must hand the envelope to the person herself. She will understand." I read out the address, "*Alice Kingston, fifty-two Claridge Avenue, London SE10*. That's Greenwich." I watched them deciding. "Well? Will you do it?"

"Are you . . . Interpol?"

"Please! Don't ask any questions." There was a tense silence, then Evelyn grabbed the envelope, "We'll take it to Alice the moment we've landed in Dover." She looked at her husband, "Won't we, Luv?"

"The second we set foot on English soil, Sir! . . . Like true Brits." I thanked them, made sure that Evelyn tucked the envelope safely in her bag, gave Danny my card, and re joined Camille at the bar.

"Gin and It, Johnny, my love?"

"I don't mind if I do."

"And what's my reward?"

I looked at my watch, "Forty-two minutes of bliss?"

"*Gaspard*! . . . Take over the bar!" She pushed open a connecting door to the upstairs flat, "You'd better make it good, my boy!" ....

♠

I returned just in time to change for lunch, choosing carefully from a pansy's wardrobe. There was a sensational gasp as I entered the fabulously furnished drawing room.

"How simply *ravishing* you look in that gorgeous satin shirt, darling!"

"Thanks for the splendid new clothes, Arthur." I glanced at the crowd of guests standing by the open French windows in pools of brilliant midday sunshine.

"I thought we'd start you off on a gay note, so I chose pastel shades, they go so *beautifully* with your blond complexion. You were always something of an Adonis, Johnny!" He was extremely breathless, he had to be supported by two kadets. Grotesquely, he had been dressed in a crimson brocade robe with an upright, fan shaped, lace collar. The ginger wig had grey pearls wound into it, and a farcical ostrich feather. Sapphires and topaz dangled from his long-lobed ears.

"You're not well, Arthur."

"*Shhht*! Not a word, darling! The old bitches will be *green* with envy!" Lewdly, he poked his tongue into the corner of his mouth. "An all night session, luvvy! Knocks me for six at my age. Couldn't resist him. Fairground boy. *So* athletic, dear! . . . Like being fucked by the Eiffel Tower!" I knew he was lying; his breath stank of corruption and his skin, for all the face powder and rouge, was jaundiced, as were his eyes. I was certain he had a cancer, bowel or liver. A stunningly pretty lad of about fifteen trotted up to him, "You will take Coco into lunch, Johnny." Arthur's vermilion varnished finger nails caressed the boy's chin. "He's been promoted recently, he was the cabin boy on the Eocratic, but he's grown *far* too big for that."

We were now surrounded by a troupe of weird old queens gabbling in French and English, all of them in the most extravagant drag of bustles, lace, velvet chokers and lorgnettes. Their bomb-sized falsies heaved with strings of pearls, their ridiculously piled wigs were set *en fin de siècle*. I gazed ruefully out of the open windows at the tranquil little path winding down through the vineyards towards Villette and freedom.

"Come and meet one of my most important people in Switzerland, Count Gustave Malvin. *Charming* man. Can't think why you never met him years

177

ago." Malvin, having made the customary polite noises, wasted no time coming to the point.

"Look here, old boy, as two gentlemen amongst this crowd of queers I thought we might have an understanding, do you follow me?" He nervously fiddled with a gold cigarette case, taking out of it an exotic Egyptian brand that I had not seen for years, *El Muqattam*, purple with silver tips. "Will you smoke?"

"No thank you."

"Do you mind if I do?" I made the usual demure gesture and he lit the pungent, opium tainted tobacco with a diamond encrusted lighter. "Now look here, old boy. This young fellow of yours, this . . . Thomas. You realise that he has been the cause of some serious inconvenience to us."

"Arthur told me all about it."

"He has some information that we really would rather he hadn't. Do you follow me?" I edged away from the narcotic fumes of the *El Muqattam*, "What do you want me to do?"

"Get hold of the stolen file, murder the boy, and return to me as quickly as you can."

"Where is he?"

"In a hold on the Eocratic. Below the water line - deck K." He held out the diamond encrusted lighter, "This is the key." I was wondering what he meant when he murmured in German, "They are watching us. Come outside on the terrace." Here he explained that the lighter was faked, that its body was an electronic key. "It will open any door, bulkhead, trap on the ship. For God's sake don't lose the bloody thing! I have gone to a great deal of trouble getting this copy made secretly, I don't need any blunders from you! When you've retrieved the file and made sure the little beast's dead, get off the boat before it sails and go immediately to Moreau's Headquarters. I'll meet you there. You know where I mean, old boy?"

"Of course." I didn't know what he was talking about but preserved an impeccable front, "Is that all?"

"No! They plan to murder me during lunch. You see, I made rather a hash of dealing with your boy the other night. Let him go, if you see what I mean, old chap? They don't like mistakes. Nor do I. A bit of a botch-up, old boy. The Brown Hat's not too pleased with me."

"Can I help you?"

"Would you be so good as to create some sort of a scene? Argue with the little tart they've given you, insult Moreau's boyfriend, anything you like in order to cause a fracas - it doesn't take them long to fly into the air like a flock of parakeets. I can slip off the hook, if you get my drift, old man."

I thought, *Just about sums you up!*, but I said, "Why did you accept the invitation if you knew they intended to murder you?" He never had time to

178

answer, a gong sounded and I felt a sweaty hand clasp mine, and the tickle of lips nibbling kisses along my finger tips. It was Coco. *"Get* off!" I gave him a brutal cuff round the left ear and he bit me. "You little wretch!" The pantomime dames all turned to stare in a cackling flurry of shimmering satin. It wasn't going to be easy *not* to make a scene over lunch. . . . The last thing I had in mind.

Malvin was horribly murdered as he swallowed a mouthful of food. Pathetically the mouthful spurted all over the table cloth in front of his place as three kadets cut his face open, splitting the skull from chin to forehead up through the nose with an instrument that would have done justice to an abattoir. They stood him up facing the table. His jacket, tie and shirt were ripped apart down the front, his belly slit, and they drew him, winding the entrails into a silver-gilt basin placed on his chair. Alive long enough to see his guts poured onto the carpet and greedily attacked by three Borzoi hounds, Malvin collapsed over the Eighteenth Century table centrepiece and his head was raggedly taken off with a bush saw by one of the old drag queens who screeched, "There you are, Arthur! A job well done for you, deary." He hurled the head out of an open French window, then took up one of the eight wine glasses arrayed by each place and bawled, "Here's to the immortal memory of a Swiss-Kraut cunt!" and we all stood - except Arthur - and repeated this erudite toast: at least, I worked my lips. I sat down and stared at the blood soaked table cloth, at the corpse sluiced in gore and excrement.

Arthur had watched the procedure with a child-like smile, sipping champagne from a wide Venetian glass while a kadet attired in a pale pink jacket, white trousers and shoes played a harpsichord with accomplished technique. I recognized a pavan by Giles Farnaby.

♠

The drive from Arthur's Swiss residence to Marseilles took a day. A convoy of fifteen, replica grey Lancia Lambda VIIIs contained the Court and our luggage.

Arthur went on ahead with his doctor, secretary and male nurse, travelling in a magnificent cream and black Hispano Suiza 68, the genuine 1936 limousine. Fortunately for me it had been decided that Coco would not do. My travelling companion was the Second Officer of the Eocratic, Didier Gabriel, who joined the cortège at Valence, a city smouldering with funeral pyres. Didier was personable and, I judged, straight. We got on well, though my questions about the sea voyage we were about to make were very carefully phrased.

He told me that the officers and crew of the ship were hired, "I do not know who the owners are, but the crew is changed regularly, so you never get to know anybody."

"How long have you been with the ship?"

"Eight months, a long stretch, most officers leave after three trips."

"Where do you go?"

"All over the world. We deliver revolting lumps of flesh called Progens, and good looking lads with black hair. Their quarters are in sealed areas of the ship."

"Kadets is what you mean."

"I couldn't care less, but the Progens stink like shit." He lit two cigarettes at once, placing one between my lips with gracious bonhomie. "The Captain is Italian, Bruno Zanetti, the other officers are French like me, most of the crew are Chinese or Dutch. A few Norwegians. There's a Scottish old timer."

"Old timer?"

"Jock. A steward." he laughed, "He's a wily bastard. Knows a thing or two about the sea. Good company. Better than the passengers. They're a right load of queers!"

"Have you met Arthur Moreau?"

He dabbed his ash out of the car window, "God no! They say he's dying. Has a glass coffin in the hold, on an elevator. It can be raised into the main lounge. Can you believe that?"

"Yes. Planning to have his funeral on board, is he?"

"Nobody knows. Crackers, if you ask me, . . . the lot of them! There's another old boy hanging around as well. He keeps to his quarters, never see him in the public rooms, not even on deck. Has his own galley, chef, staff. Occupies half of E deck. Completely sealed off. One of the lads who serves him says it's like a palace down there. Full of old china and dirty pictures, nude women doing it with swans."

"What's his name?"

"Franz von Stotz. Wears a black cassock with a huge gold collar round his neck, has a big circle of jade dangling on his chest. He's like a wizard!"

"You don't say! . . . How do you mean, Didier, 'Completely sealed off'?"

"The ship's an old tub, fifty years or more, she really ought to have been scrapped, she's well below minimum regulations. They had her completely refitted for Moreau, spent a fortune. But the decks are sealed in four horizontal compartments, two above the water line and two below. From the Bridge we can get down to the engine room and we can get into the holds and the bilges. We can get into certain public rooms, but not all. Moreau's suite is sealed, even the Captain is never invited there."

"So about half the volume of the hull is sealed-off from the officers and crew?"

"That's about right, yes."

"Isn't that rather ridiculous? Suppose something goes wrong? You're a professional, Didier, why have you agreed to work in such an unsatisfactory arrangement?"

"Money. We're all paid a fortune. I'm paid more than a French Admiral and I'm only the Second Officer. We sign a disclaimer, the owners are very good about that."

"Disclaimer?"

"If anything goes wrong they won't hold us responsible. Leave the buggers to sink! Do you think it's mad?"

I smiled, gazing out at the Roman triumphal arch as we passed Orange, letting Didier's question hang in the air. Shortly afterwards, the line pulled up in three ranks alongside a roadside restaurant where Didier and I made for the bar, grabbing two ham rolls and bottle of pastis. We stood listening to the queens complaining that there wasn't enough time for a full lunch.

For the rest of the trip to Marseilles we talked about football and Didier's girlfriend in Tunis who was pregnant. He didn't know if the child was his. He didn't seem to notice that every town we went through was silent, the streets littered with fly-blown corpses.

♠

As the motorcade sped along Marseilles docks I observed a typically Moreau style phenomenon. A gigantic neon sign rigged to a scaffold frame on the roof of a huge warehouse was visible for miles, "NECKER-VANDEL CONSTRUCTION". I asked Didier what Necker Vandel was, fascinated to hear his answer. "They make big concrete buildings in pieces, then ship the pieces all over the world. The plant covers an area of five hectares. It's impressive! The ships are loaded directly at special quays."

"What sort of buildings?"

"Hospitals. For the Third World. You know, all those starving blacks on the telly." He took out two more cigarettes, putting them between his lips while I felt for Malvin's lighter, snapping its flame to the dark tobacco, "How long have they been in Marseilles?" He took the cigarettes from his mouth, handing me mine, blowing smoke in my face, "Years! Everybody knows about Necker Vandel! . . . Bloody Hell, Johnny! Your lighter's covered in diamonds!"

"Really? I hadn't noticed." I took a pull at the strong, French cigarette, exhaling with pleasure, "I don't know about Necker Vandel, Didier."

"You're a close one. A real James Bond. Will you come up to the bridge and have a drink with the lads when we're at sea? We have good fun when it's calm."

"Sure I will. Is that the ship?"

"That's The Eocratic all right." Two squat, broad, ovaloid funnels rose above a line of warehouses. We turned a corner and there she was, floodlit.

Arthur's floating headquarters was a twenty-seven-thousand ton ocean liner measuring two hundred and nine meters - around seven hundred feet - down the quayside. Her funnels were unusual, like giant base drums. The old fashioned riveted hull towered above us, peppered with portholes. Her stern decks had been modified to accommodate a helicopter landing pad upon which was parked a bullish 60B Seahawk. The ship's livery was pink and Prussian blue, the hull was painted dazzling white.

"Magnificent! I haven't seen a properly designed ship for years."

"We completed the upgrade of the diesel engines last month."

"Diesel! So she makes about eighteen knots at full speed." I wound the car window down and craned my neck to stare at the ship's superstructure. The squat funnels and the square-cut decking struck a chord in my memory. "If you ask me, Didier, I think this is the old *Pagan Star*. I went to New York on this ship with my Great Uncle when I was a little boy. We sailed from Liverpool. She was a comfortable old tub."

"When was that?"

"A million years before you were born." We got out of the car and walked with the fluttering rabble towards a covered gangway. Three kadets followed with our luggage. "I don't even know where we're going!"

"To Bermuda. Moreau took the island over ten years ago. He will recover from an operation they are going to perform on board, then fly to Minneapolis with von Stotz while we deliver a batch of Progens and Kadets to Rio."

"And the passengers?"

"Depends on Moreau. He'll probably put you all ashore." He grinned, playfully shadow boxing me on the cheek. "To keep you out of trouble, Johnny."

"The Duke and Duchess of Windsor were kept out of trouble on Bermuda, Didier."

"Who?"

My lightly ironical reply was drowned by the boom of the ship's horn.

♠

Didier left me in the entrance foyer crowded round by Arthur's excited courtiers. "Don't forget that drink with the lads!" he called, opening a door marked *Private*.

"I won't".

The superb Art Deco interiors of The Pagan Star had been stripped-out. Mock "Queen Anne" ruled. Limed oak, oyster cream panelled walls, black and white floor tiles, potted palms and bronze athletes: naked - naturally. Eyeing the sugar pink globe of a gilt wall sconce, I resigned myself to the weltering tat, wondering how I could find Thomas.

"Mr Debrett, Sir?" I looked round to see a white jacketed steward with an immaculately parted haircut slicked with Brylcreem. He was a well preserved sixty: Glaswegian.

"Yes?"

"I'm Jock, Sir. Your personal steward during the voyage, Sir."

"Why aren't you a kadet, Jock!"

"Keep your voice low, Sir; there's ruddy microphones in every ruddy potted palm. They'd have them up their arseholes, Sir, if their arseholes were free. If you get my drift, Sir."

"Crystal clear, Jock. Where do we go?"

"This way, Sir. They've *you* taped, sure enough, Sir. You're away down, and you cannie move unless the old man signs a chit, Sir!"

We took an elevator - the doors showing Zeus tearing into Ganymede - down three decks. Along a maze of panelled corridors, Jock opened a steel bulkhead using a nugget of metal like Malvin's sham lighter, but without diamonds. As I followed him, Jock twittered sociably, as stewards do. With his dour humour and wiry, straight-backed demeanour, I felt it might be possible to trust this experienced servant. I needed to be certain. Double talk is a tricky art. "Here we are, Sir, *The Tristan Mentone Suite* ... all the State Rooms on this deck are called after Hollywood Stars of yester-year, Sir."

It was spacious accommodation for all the deck was only five meters above the water line. The walls were done in bland, olive wood veneer and the deck was covered by a stodgy green carpet. The double bed had an oyster satin counterpane decorated by a machine quilted figure of a Wolf Kadet. I could have checked-into a stuffy London hotel, except for a single wrong note: behind the bed, wider than the bed, was a fitted, full height mirror, its frame integral with the low, 'Chippendale' headboard. I fingered the frame thoughtfully.

"The mirror requires an imaginative mind, Sir!"

"How do you mean, Jock?"

"There's two ways of looking at it, Sir."

"There are two ways of looking at most things, Jock."

"Aboard this ship ye can say that again, Sir."

The lounge-dining room was separated from my bedroom by a wide, elegantly chamfered opening that could be closed-off with a folding partition veneered to match the walls. The room had three portholes that were masked at night by full length, wall-to-wall drapes patterned with claret and cream Regency Stripe. A sideboard topped with malachite was the bar. Above was a floridly gilt-framed oil painting of Tonio Friedemann in his fifties. In a gap amongst the swirling fronds of the frame I noted the glinting lens of a camera.

"Shall I unpack, Sir?"

"Yes, Jock. Is the bathroom through there?"

"Aye, Sir."

A black Vitreolite bathroom was accessed along a corridor by the hull.

The distance between the bathroom and bedroom was near-on six meters, not far short of twenty feet. This link ran parallel with the lobby to the State Room. The lobby and link were separated by a gap the width of the mirror behind my bed, a gap easily three meters wide - over ten feet.

I considered this arrangement as I poured myself a gin and Italian, watching Jock put my shirts into drawers. There had to be a rectangular void between the bedroom, the bathroom, the vestibule and the bathroom link: a void with an area of approximately eighteen square meters, nearly two hundred square feet. If this was a ventilation shaft, it was a big one. And too near the side of the hull.

"What is going on behind the bed, Jock?"

"Did you find the ice, Sir?"

"Everything I need, thanks. Just keep supplying it."

"I shall, Sir." He came over to me, took my drink and put it on an occasional table by one of the bedroom portholes. "This is the best place for a cocktail, Sir. A sort of dead area, Sir. Where ye can relax and … say what you need to say." I got his drift and sat down in an armchair by the occasional table, "The mirror behind my bed."

"If I guess correctly, Sir, ye've nay a taste for hanky-panky. Two-way mirrors and lassies with whips and crimson suspender belts wi' folks leering at ye through the glass, Sir."

"In that department, Jock, I like things simple and I like them sweet." I took from of my jacket pocket Malvin's fake lighter, "What's this, Jock, when it's not a cigarette lighter?"

"It's exactly the same as this, Sir (he fished in his pocket and took out the metal nugget he had used to unlock various doors in the ship). Only a few of us have them, Sir. Yours is a trifle Ritzier than mine. If I might be so bold as ter say, Sir, it's tarty!"

"The man who gave it to me was no tart, Jock."

"If it was one of Moreau's people, Sir, he was a genocidal murderer."

The ship bumped gently to the quay side, I looked out of a porthole to see a warehouse slip by, "We're on our way." I went to the side board, poured Jock a stiff malt whisky and handed him the glass.

"It's against Company Regulations, Sir, but thank-you all the same."

"Was this ship the old *Pagan Star*?"

He clinked his glass to mine, then took a swig of whisky that would have burnt a normal stomach raw. "You're a sharp one, Sir. She certainly was. I was Chief Steward on her fer thirty year, Sir. Proud to be so. I know every inch of the ship, (he indicated the wall behind the bed with his thumb) they cann'ie fool me with hidden companion ways, Sir."

"Leading to the sealed decks?"

"You have it, Sir."

"There's a lad on board, Jock. Thomas. He's somewhere below, probably in a bad way. Do you know about him?"

"There's been no word of the wee laddie, though there are passengers aboard that we didn'a have on the original list. There's a film star, Ramona Delano. Takes you back a bit, doesn't it, Sir? There are two Americans from Minneapolis. They all have staterooms way up on "A" Deck, Sir." He drew aside one of the porthole drapes, "The mirror over the bed, Sir, can be opened by keying your wee widget to this plate." He pressed a Wedgwood plaque set into the veneered panel, it sprang open to reveal a brass plate. "Pop the end into the slot, Sir, and the mirror will rise. The stairs are immediately behind." He carefully clicked the plaque closed. "Down the stairway is Stotz's suite and Moreau's coffin. May God save us, Sir! It is a terrible sight. Up the stairs, there's a short passage, then up two decks and ye'll come to one of the funnels, Sir. It is false, housing two messes, one fer the officers, one fer the crew."

"Can't I just take the normal route?"

"You cannie leave this State Room, Sir! You're a prisoner. All your food will be brought to you here, and I'll see to your every need. But the way we came here, Sir, is barred with solid steel."

"And if we founder?"

"You're in a fix, Sir."

"If I am meant to be a prisoner, Jock, why give me a cabin with an escape route?"

"That is the sort of question Sir Frederick never asks, Sir."

"You . . ?" He put a finger to his lips, replenished my glass, and went to the State Room door, formally stating, "A steward will be through in one hour with the dinner menu, Sir. If you have no further needs, Sir, I will attend to my duties above."

Alone, drink in hand, I gazed out of a porthole as *The Eocratic* sounded a majestic farewell to Europe. Three long, low blasts of her horn echoed over the inky, oil-streaked waters of the port and the silent city of Marseilles. Feeling the ship gathering speed, I watched her pass through the dock entrance into the dark turquoise Mediterranean.

♠

Stanley Casper sat with his lawyer, Bernard Cook, in the East Room of the White House. They waited for a private audience with President Faulkner. In the ceiling an air conditioning unit rattled intermittently.

"This used to be a ball room. She had the place transformed."

"She didn't transform the cooling system, Stanley. This is the room where they put Kennedy's casket, remember?"

"Who doesn't?" Stanley sighed. He was depressed, angry and indignant.

A kadet swished into the room and stood to attention by the door.

"Who's that kid?"

"A kadet, Bernard. The place is swarming with them. The President doesn't know."

The white and gold doors opened on the dot of the appointment and the two men were introduced to the President by a "U" kadet. Stanley was shocked to see his one time High School date looking so much older than kindly television screens revealed. Her hair was almost white, though beautifully tinted. Even the Chanel suit and restrained jet jewellery failed to disguise a personality under stress. Turning to the Kadet she said, "Thank you Philip. I'll ring for you." She turned to Stanley and for the first time smiled in the way he remembered. Charm, drive, with a dash of sweetness. He couldn't help softening a little, there were some tough things he had to say, but he would spare Leonora his resentment.

"It's a long time since we talked through those nights of our youth, Stan!"

"Sure is. And look at you now! President of the United States of America . . ." he waved his hand round the famous interior, ". . . and all this! Remember how you were dead-against democracy? See where all that campus bolshevism got you."

"We don't have long, Stanley. I have two appointments after yours, and a private funeral to attend. We should get together when I'm out of politics and catch up. Daisy and the girls OK?"

"Worried sick. Can you blame them? For eight weeks I'm kept under house arrest in my own country! The story of my return from the dead is blocked to the media. I'm forbidden to make contact with my old associates. Forbidden to *work*! And if that ain't bad enough, a score of Pentagon psychologists put me through tests they do on nutcases. I suppose, my dear, that you're going to sit in this beautiful room and calmly tell me that my experience in Morocco is a dream!"

"You should address me as Madam President. I have permitted you a rare privilege, Stanley; a private audience. I'm sorry that you thought it necessary to bring Mr Cook along. We might have done better dealing with your problem on a person-to-person basis."

"Problem? I have no problem. Unless *truth* is a problem in the White House! After what I've been through I think the presence of my lawyer is necessary. If I have to address you as Madam President, then please address me as Mister Casper! . . . Hell, Leonora, if I say *my dear* it's because - to me - you are dear!"

"You really should do what the President asks, Stanley. Play a straight bat."

"This is *not* a baseball game, Bernard!" Stanley stood up, walking to the fireplace he stood with his back to it, "Leonora, you have received no less than six, twenty-thousand word reports from me, each written by me. You have read scores of reports by others about me. You have already been advised by a host of experts. You have already decided on a course of action. So why don't we come straight to the point, Madam President . . . person-to-person? Why won't the administration of the United States accept my witness to a terrible - a lethal - secret sect run by a set of psychopaths, who maintain their inner sanctum in the midst of our nation, in *Minneapolis*? I am a witness to this terror, I have seen these people, I have seen their awesome constructions, their horrific system, their unspeakable progeny.

"If you call Philip back into the room, I will show you that this young man has been *manufactured*. It is a monster, Madam President, not a human being. He has no genitals for a start! Would you like me to demonstrate, Madam President?" Stanley sighed, adding quietly, "I am one of three witnesses. Three in the entire world!"

"You sound like a crank, Stanley. And you behave like one. Your reports read like the ravings of a man off his head! Didn't they explain that, the psychologists we sent over? . . . The only reason why you are here with me today, is that I felt I had to judge for myself. Because we are old friends, I could not bring myself to accept my advisors' conclusions without giving you a chance to . . . to re-habilitate yourself."

"What are you telling me, Leonora? That I've been signed-off as a madman?"

"Maybe we should have coffee, maybe it might help . . ."

"Damn coffee! What are you trying to say?"

"You saw nothing, Stanley."

"I saw what I saw! *Nobody* can tell me I didn't!"

"As President of the United States of America I am ordering you to erase from your mind the grotesque fantasies that you have been so troubled with in Morocco."

"Leo! What are you ..."

"I am *ordering* you to erase from your mind the grotesque fantasies that you have been so troubled with in Morocco!"

"*Stalinism!*"

"If you persist, we will commit you to an asylum. A compound reserved for malign individuals. You will be taken there immediately - from this room. I have signed the forms. They wait on my desk in the Oval Office."

"Signed ..."

"You will be incarcerated for the rest of your life, Stanley. Do I make myself clear?"

"Madam President is warning you for the last time, Stanley. You have no option."

"You're in this, Bernard, aren't you? ... Deep as your ass?"

Cook shifted in his chair. "Yes I am, Stanley. . . . I'm sorry."

"I'm more sorry, Bernard. You just killed a friendship of twenty-five years."

"I was only ..."

"Go! ... As for you, Leo, if that's what power does to a soul, may God help you!"

"Shall we take a walk in the Rose Garden? I will cancel the next appointment - it was a briefing. We need a little more time together. Mr Cook, you may go. Thank you for your assistance, I will deal with this matter alone. Stanley, please come this way." In the Rose Garden, her security team held at a discrete distance, he took her hand, "How can ... ?"

"Stanley! ... don't ask. You know that I'm ..." She took both his hands in hers, close to tears. "My love, I cannot break-down. They're watching ..."

"I don't care, Leo!" He kissed her, consummating a past that neither could forgive.

"I'm sorry I behaved so badly back there. It seems as if we are caught up in a nightmare. Frankly, I'm lost for an answer."

"That makes two of us."

"Do you know about Moreau?"

"Of course. Officially, it isn't happening." She sighed. "It's so difficult to explain. I made myself listen to advisors, an army of stuffed-shirts with hyper-Establishment minds. Stanley, dear, I have to listen to their warped logic night and day. Generals, diplomats, Senators ... an endless troupe sharpening their careers like carving knives! What *is* Moreau?"

"The enemy."

"There is no enemy, Stanley. Moreau is a nebulous element we cannot define. Since we buried The Marriage Island case . . . oh yes! we buried the incident under a thousand feet of poured concrete. We Americans did it! We hid behind drapes pretending nothing happened. Sir Frederick never forgave us, nor did the French. In politics you don't face up to trouble like normal people. You use trouble to keep the show on the road!"

"Terrorism is keeping the show on the road?"

"In a nutshell, Stanley, terrorism is good for business."

"Denying the truth is *shit*, Leo!"

"I know you saw what you saw in Morocco, but I am not permitted to say that."

"Did you speak to Sir Frederick?"

"The Senate considers Sir Frederick 'Old Europe'. To be ignored."

"He's a wonderful man, Leo."

"Wonderful men are dangerous commodities. Look at Christ. Frederick never asks questions, he knows all the answers. We'd all be out of a job if we listened to Fred Appleby."

"What are you going to do?"

"Nothing."

"You can do anything you like, Leo! You're the President of the Untied States."

"George Washington would have disagreed with you, Stanley. A President who does what he or she likes is a tyrant."

"But ..."

"I mouth what I'm told to mouth."

"But what are you going to *do*?"

"Stanley! . . . Right now what I want to do is have your love and you. I can't have either." He put his arm round her shoulders - "*Don't!* They're looking! I can't even weep in your arms, Stanley. Please, go home and stay home till this thing blows over. I will give the order that you are driven to Marble Hill. Stay with Daisy, safe in Ohio, care for her, care for your girls. And ..." She turned abruptly, pushing her gloved hand to her face, wiping tears away. "I must go. I have a funeral to attend."

"Senator Mac-Larne?"

"The son of Al and Denise Burfordine. Great friends. Their boy was murdered in France. Marseilles. Gotten himself involved with a quasi-religious organisation. There's been a harrowing inquest. Awful for the parents. He was twenty. Good looking kid. Great future."

♠

Stanley was set-down in the early hours at the gates of Marble Hill, his wife's family home near Galion, Ohio. One of his three triplet daughters, Nissa, rushed over the lawn to embrace him.

"Daddy! We've been petrified with worry. Why didn't you call?"

"Too complicated to explain, my dear. Where's your Mother?"

"In the living room, she's catatonic. Grandmother went to bed hours ago." Nissa took his case, "Was it amazing? I can't wait to hear about the White House!"

"It was amazing alright." They walked through the panelled hallway into the wide living room. Daisy Casper was angry with worry.

"Stanley, for the sake of Sweet Jesus, what have you been doin'? .... Don't say a word! Fix us all a drink, give me a kiss, and tell."

"In that order, Daisy?"

"Right-on! . . . and the story better be damned good." Two hours later Stanley yawned wide, "God, what a mess! We don't budge, Daisy, till I get the call from Washington."

"From the President? You sure she's goin'to pick up the 'phone just like that? Chat to her old pal Stanley? She has enough on her plate. We have this plague bug, a war looming in the Middle East, the economy on the rocks. Be realistic, Stanley. You went to Morocco, period. So *what* if you met the guy who cooked-up some lousy serum! Who cares about a bunch of twisted old men?"

"It's not as simple as that, Daisy. You know what I've been through." He looked at the windows. "Let's go to bed. The birds are screaming from every tree."

The telephone rang in the hall. The three of them froze.

"At *four* in the morning?"

"Stanley, answer it!" He walked towards the telephone with a cold presentiment that the caller would be somebody to do with Moreau.

"... *Who*? ... Panno! .... Where are you?"

♠

"I *have* to meet Stotz, Daisy. Damn my promise to Leonora. This is too important a chance to miss!"

"I won't hear of it, Stanley! A million times, *no!* I have suffered the agony of widowhood once in my life, I can't do an encore."

"It's five o'clock. We've been up all night. The kadet is arriving here at ten this morning. Let's sleep for a couple of hours. I am going with him to Toledo, and I'm going to meet - like it or not, Daisy! - Franz von Stotz."

Daisy burst into tears. Her mother came downstairs in a dressing gown with her hair in rollers. Nissa grasped Stanley's hands, "I'm going with you, Daddy!"

"Nissa! I forbid it!"

"Mom, I'm twenty years old and I'm going with Dad." Her grandmother poured black coffee, her rasping Tennessee accent shrilled through an acid silence, "Right-on, Nissa. You go with your Dad and hang that mean old bastard by the balls! Daisy, stop that snivellin'! You two get upstairs and sleep, you're white with fatigue. When this jerk arrives, if he gives one hint of trouble I'll blow his brains over the gate. I already got the six-shooter from the clock case and gave it a dusting down. Where did we put the bullets?"

"Under the parrot's cage, Grandma."

"Good! I'll be aiming from the billiard room window. That two-bit dork'll never know what hit him!"

♠

Panno stood waiting at the entrance of Marble Hill a little after ten. He was dressed in glove-fit, sky-blue denims and a short-sleeved, open necked white shirt. His platinum Kadet registration necklace shone clean at the base of his Olympian neck. Darkly tanned, hair groomed smooth, he could have been a wealthy neighbour's grown-up son.

"He's so *handsome*, Daddy!"

"Nissa, for God's sake! Damn well and stick fast with Larry Smart!"

"Larry'n me split up last month. It's final. You were too busy on those reports so I didn't tell you. Shall I open the door?"

"Definitely *not!*" Stanley pushed past her. "Panno! Well waddya know?"

Sat down on a sofa in the living room Panno was shy and refused the cup of coffee Nissa proffered with a maidenly blush.

"Franz is ill. He is at his residence at Westmoreland, Toledo. He has vital news . . ." Panno faltered. His ravishing face flushed with embarrassment, fluttering Nissa's heart.

"Well, Panno?. . . You know me now, you can say anything you want here."

Panno took from the breast pocket of his shirt a slip of paper from which he falteringly read, "Franz von Stotz is an old, sick man who wishes to tell Mister Casper the truth." There was an awkward pause while Panno stared down at the slip of paper. Stanley grasped the notion that a formal response was required. Enunciating clearly, he said,

"Mister Casper will be pleased to visit Franz von Stotz at his home in Toledo."

"He wants to see you today."

"They'll murder you, Stanley!"

"Cool it, Daisy. I don't think Stotz would be inviting me to a classy location everybody in this State knows if he wanted to murder me."

Daisy's mother snapped, "Daughter, stop hollerin' and listen to your husband. This boy's telling the truth, ain't you, Son?" She sat down by Panno and gave his hand an affectionate squeeze. "What this fine young man needs is a plateful of Marble Hill steak. He's as lean as a poet! I've a mind to have Cook do him a grand-slam Ohio breakfast right now!"

"You've changed your tune, Ruby."

"Darned right I have, Stanley! An if you 'n Nissa don't get along to see this old fool, Stotz, I'll have Penley drive me over to Westmoreland *myself*!"

♠

"We go to Fostoria, Stanley. Near by there is a Kadet Precinct at Arcadia, then we take a helicopter."

"Anything you feel comfortable with, Panno."

They drove away, soon reaching the sign, *Arcadia 5 miles*. The looming ziggurats of Kadet Precinct Arcadia Three shone in morning sunlight.

"Holy Smoke, Daddy! What is *that*?"

"What Johnny, Thomas and myself saw in Morocco, Nissa. They're standard issue."

"It is called Arcadia Three. It is the third precinct to be constructed. The first is Atlas One, then Minnesota Two, Arcadia Three, then Outfall Four in England, then Hollywood Five, and so on."

"We have *three* of these things in the US?"

"Completed, yes. There are six more in construction."

"And nobody believes you saw *that* in Morocco, Daddy?"

"It seems so, Nissa."

"But those things are as big as *mountains*! And nobody can *see* them? I mean, what about the folk who live round here? Any *idiot* could see that heap over the other side of Lake Erie!"

"You're beginning to get the picture."

"Is the President stupid, or something? It's insulting, Daddy. It's … disgusting!"

"It's politics, Nissa."

"For Christ's sake, Panno, where the fuck does it all *come* from?"

"Nissa, calm down! You're making Panno nervous. They're not used to women."

"With looks like that they damned well ought to be!"

They drew up in Parade Ground C of the Precinct where a pink and blue helicopter waited for them. One side of the craft had been damaged.

"Is this thing OK to fly, Panno? It's badly dented."

"It is safe. It took off from a sinking ship. Everybody drowned but me and Franz."

"That sounds like fun, Panno. Who drowned?"

"Johnny and Thomas."

♠

Stotz reclined on a stainless steel *chaise longue* in the middle of a room frozen in time by Modernism. Daylight drenched the drawing room of this glass-walled home: 1055, Oxenford Drive, Westmoreland, Toledo.

Stanley had met Stotz briefly, once. Now his impression impression was of a refined European intellectual, old but well preserved, a man of supremely good taste; eccentric but no crank.

It quickly became apparent to Stanley and Nissa that their host had endured a trauma, and was suffering from mild, delayed shock. The left side of the old man's face was badly bruised with a bad graze down the grey-skinned cheek. He could not raise himself up from the couch to greet them properly and wore a pair of rimless dark glasses and - strangely - white gloves. He wore a long robe of night blue brocade and round his neck was a huge golden chain from which was suspended, resting on his breast, a five inch diameter disk of smoke-grey Kunzite.

Stotz's voice trembled as he spoke. It was a kind voice, the softly guttural German accent soothing. "You will take something to drink? Some coffee perhaps, or something a little stronger?" He waved a gloved hand slowly towards Panno, "Bring them brandy, my dear, old Bavarian brandy. Make fresh coffee, my dear. Strong. Serve it with the rich, yellow cream from my own farms." When Panno had gone from the room, Stotz turned his head with difficulty, addressing Stanley with a smile of pleasure, "Witness his loveliness, Mr Casper. My own creation, my own boy!"

"Twinned with Kyla?" Stotz slowly removed the dark glasses.

"Ah, Kyla! The beautiful one! . . . Oh, yes." He paused, gazing towards a seventy foot length plate glass window that showed a groomed lawn banked with blue roses and edged with stainless steel mastabae. "I made the beauty of Kyla. . . *incomparable!*" He dropped his hands to his lap and after a further melodramatic pause raised his dimming eyes to the light with timed deliberation, intoning, like the sound track of an ancient movie, "I am afraid that my beautiful boy . . . is *dead!*"

"Why do you say that?"

"He never made it off the Eocratic. She went down so very fast. They were all drowned. A tragedy! I myself would not have sunk her, but . . . the *fools*! They have messed with our dream!" he took a glass of brandy proffered by Panno, "Thank you, my dear . . .", he drained the glass, Panno refilled it as Stotz stared gravely into Nissa's fascinated eyes. "That is why I am asking you to help me, Mr Casper." He took Panno by the wrist, telling the kadet in Precinct language to stand by a gauntly elegant Venetian mirror. "*Look* at him! There is our dream! An *angel*! His brother an *Archangel*! . . . They have crushed all we have created with crude fingers, the filthy fingers of politicians . . . the fingers of *guttersnipes!*"

"I'm not yet sure what you're getting-at, Doctor Stotz. But I know one thing about these kadets - and I've handled a bunch of them at Atlas One, so I know what I'm talking about - sure they look like angels but you sewed evil into their souls. You created an army of beautiful psychopaths."

"That can be rectified. But only with Panno and Kyla. With Panno and Kyla I am able to make adjustments. But if Kyla is dead, I can do nothing."

"Adjustments to only two! Out of how many?"

"Around three million. The total multiplies hourly. The rest must be destroyed. The crux of our problem is simple to understand. I told Arthur twenty years ago. I argued with Tonio until I could argue no longer. Our disagreement destroyed even our love."

"What did you tell them?"

"The precinct construction programme can never keep up with the five year Progenic birth cycle. In their greed for power the fools understand nothing!"

"So you intend to destroy three million beings?"

"Do not worry your pretty head, young lady. They will melt painlessly to a harmless liquor when a signal is sent into the atmosphere. Kyla and Panno will be fine, they do not have the same genetic structure."

"So how do you adjust Kyla and Panno?"

"I require a natural born donor, then I can make from Kyla and Panno a new race." Stotz poured more brandy into their glasses with a trembling hand then asked Panno to serve some sweet cakes. When the Kadet had left the room he leaned towards Stanley, whispering, "I need Tonio Friedemann's final disk, the fifth of five you yourself took from his villa. On this disk is Tonio's discovery of a genetic key that - for some reason known only to Himself, even Almighty God put back into a file *unused*. One phrase on that final disk will solve everything for me."

"What's on the first four disks?"

"Information concerned with converting attributes of another Universe to improve our own. The construction of Time. The conversion of Time into another medium. The formula that terminates our particular Universe. ... A few other things of less importance ... pre-fabricated plastic Funeral Parlours ... and so on."

"Are you telling me, Franz, that you want out?"

"I want only to complete my own cycle of research and then I can die at peace with my Maker. Without the fifth disk, without my precious Kyla, I am able to complete nothing."

"I don't see why Kyla should let himself go down with a sinking ship. Even so, Doctor, I can't get hold of those disks. Sir Frederick Appleby has them."

"Sir Frederick will destroy them! I know him only too well." Stotz became agitated, breathing heavily.

"Hey, cool-it, Franz. I don't think Appleby will do anything in a hurry."

"Frederick is an altruist! He is not concerned with the creation of a Master Race, with an Olympian vision." He raised himself up on one arm, shouting, "A vision far from the vulgarity of stupid men. Men who are to be enslaved! Men who. . ."

"Sounds like a re-run of *Mein Kampf*, Doctor. You'll be screaming about the Jews next. There's only one Master Race on this planet, Franz, and it's called Humanity."

"Panno, my dear . . . fetch our little contraption. We will show Stanley Casper and the fragrant Nissa our magic lamp. Like the pantomime, Aladdin. I used to adore English pantomime. Ha! Cinderella! What a joy it was in those days to see the Ugly Sisters!"

"You and Friedemann are the Ugly Sisters, Franz!"

"*Panno*! . . . My dear, what are you doing?" But Panno didn't move, he was staring at Nissa who had caught him staring at her - and she was not displeased.

♠

A steel box on a white trolley was wheeled to Stotz's side. He wafted a gloved hand in the air and a cinema screen hummed down over the window. A white and gold Wurlitzer cinema organ rose through the floor and a kadet in white tails and a white Irish tweed cap played a medley from "*Rose Marie*". The drawing room lights dimmed as gauze curtains drew noisily and shakily across the screen. From a projection room a conical beam shone. The curtains immediately parted. On the screen a white marble Ionic portico stood fine before a blue sky: *Pearl & Dean*.

"No, no, *no*! Panno. We don't want an old movie?" He waved his hand at the box, the curtains and neon lights folded out of sight, the Wurlitzer sank below the floor.

"Watch carefully. The images on the screen will be live. Wait for the signal … it comes from a kadet …. wait, you see the blurr clearing now, you see the beautiful office, and the wonderful desk … who is sitting at this desk?"

"It has to be Sir Frederick Appleby."

"Correct, first time! In his office at this instant. And there, Stanley, by his side, on that beautiful desk, what do you see?"

"The five goddam golden disks. Are you sure this isn't faked, Franz? How do you get a camera into Sir Frederick's inner sanctum?"

"There is no camera. The box is linked with the kadet's mind, you will see the kadet hand Sir Frederick some papers soon."

"Are you telling us that Sir Frederick is …?"

"He has no idea."

"For Pete's sake! How do you *know* he doesn't?"

"I cannot tell you." Stotz waved his hand and the picture flashed-off. Another person appeared.

"That's President Faulkner in the Oval Office! That's Leonora …"

"Ah! Mister Casper, you are in love with her. … And this is the Prime Minister of Germany, and this is the President of France, and this is the Chairman of the Chinese People's Republic and this is the Russian Head of State, and this is the Finance Minister of the Sudan, and these are some English Members of Parliament shaking vinegar over their French Fries in their sordid restaurant at the Palace of Westminster."

"Can you show us Buckingham Palace? That would be fascinating."

"Impossible, Miss Nissa, there is no kadet presence near the British Monarch. Arthur and Tonio considered the idea vulgar."

195

"Snobs as well as maniacs!"

"Correct, Miss Nissa. It is a symptom characteristic amongst the psychologically deranged. Who else would you like to see? . . . Name who you would like to see!"

"His Holiness the Pope."

"Miss Nissa, you *cannot* see the Pope!"

"Why can't I see the Pope? He doesn't have a kadet presence?"

"The kadets refuse to wear the uniform of a Swiss Guard."

"This is real spooky, Doctor. You tune-in to your kadets?"

"The registration number they are created with is the access key, then . . . Hey Presto! How do you say it? . . . Bob is the Uncle and Fanny is the Aunt."

"Why don't you tap out Kyla's number? You may get to know where he is."

"I dare not! He is dead."

Nissa pointed to the plate, "Is that what you use, Dr. Stotz, to tap these numbers out?" She moved round and sat next to the old man, affectionately cajoling him with her tone of voice, "Come on, I'm sure he's not dead. I'll tap Kyla's number if you tell me what it is. Don't be nervous. I'll bet we see Kyla flash up there on the screen just as good as gold! If you say he's even better looking than Panno, I can't wait!" She gave Stotz a seductive smile, "C'mon Doctor, tell me Kyla's number and I'll key it in for you."

Panno got up from his chair and sat himself next to Nissa, leaning over her, his chest hot against her side, whispering, "I will tell you his number." He put his hand over hers, guiding her index finger on the keys. The scent of her hair, her warm body, turned him faint. "There!" He sat back, mysteriously overcome with a strange, incomprehensible emotion.

They waited, watching the giant screen flutter and sizzle.

A modern domestic interior flashed-up, coloured white, lemon and grey. There were oddly shaped windows and a statue of an American Indian in red stone. They saw a group of people sitting round a glass-topped table. Stotz, spellbound, was the first to speak, "Ah! It is the house belonging to the Burdets in Minneapolis! They are all *alive*!"

"There's Johnny. He looks OK. Never met the Burdets, is that them on the right?"

"Nice couple."

"I don't believe it! . . . The glamorous woman drinking coffee? Why, that's Ramona Delano!"

"Ramona *who*, Daddy?"

"An old-time movie star, Nissa. Superbly preserved by the look of her. . . . Hey! There he is, coming in the door. There's Kyla!" Stotz gave out a gasp. Nissa turned to him, "Are you alright, Doctor?" He was weeping, "My beautiful boy alive!"

Nissa squealed girlishly, "Oh gosh! . . . He's *stunning*! . . Out of this *world*! . . . And who's the other boy? .... He's so *cute*! Wait till I tell my two sisters! Look at his gorgeous buns!"

"That is Thomas, Nissa."

"If Gilda and Zona were here they'd go crazy." She put her hand on Panno's iron hard biceps, "What a hunk! . . . And look at Kyla! . . . He's devastatingly beautiful! Like a god! . . . And Thomas is so *dreamy*!"

"Nissa, calm down. You sound like a page from a teenage weekly."

Stanley shook Stotz's shoulder, "What's going-on, Franz? Is something happening at Gracewood? Why are they all at the Burdet's place? You know. I know you do. So tell me the truth."

"I know everything. But most of all, I know who is Arthur's successor."

"At Gracewood? Decision time, Franz. Are you going to help us? Maybe you get the fifth gold disk as a reward." The silence that followed took Stanley all his patience to endure. Stotz breathed heavily, his hand held over his eyes, his mind ranging back over the decades, his lips set in an iron line. He sighed, resigning himself to failure. When he spoke his voice was thick with emotion.

"We will go to Gracewood immediately, Mr Casper. Panno, dear, tell them to prepare the helicopter, and . . . be sure to load the *white* box." He looked Stanley straight in the eyes, slowly turning on his couch, "We have little time. The opposition is poised for victory." He closed his eyes, joining his fingers over the Kunzite disk as if in death, "I will finish the work begun so long ago."

♠

Alice Kingston walked Danny and Evelyn Briscoe to their car and waved them off, watching to see the car turn out of Claridge Avenue. She returned slowly to the house, pausing at the front door to take a look at her roses and the tiny, faultless front lawn. Going through to the back patio, Alice sat at a garden table. Instinctively, she had been expecting a communication from me.

Making sure that her husband was asleep in the parlour, Alice put the manilla envelope the Briscoes had delivered on the table and regarded it grimly. She fished in her handbag for a small pen-knife. Gently, accurately, she slid the blade along the top of the envelope and pulled out the inner packet I had secretly prepared in the Geneva hotel before leaving with Arthur's entourage. I had folded each document from Morocco in tissue paper from new shirts. I had purchased the envelope, with the cheap brief case, in Lyon.

I just had enough time to write an explanatory note. This is what Alice read;

Geneva, June 16th, 19...

THE ARTHUR MOREAU STORY

Alice, Please find enclosed 4 Items of evidence. Sir Frederick took a fifth item (a book from Friedemann's library) with Friedemann's five golden disks, from me personally, as arranged yesterday, in Geneva.

[Item 1] Arthur Moreau's handwritten "thoughts" (removed by me from a book in Jo Debrett's library at his villa on the Atlas One complex, Morocco)

[Item 2] a letter supposedly from Arthur Moreau to Jo Debrett (in its original envelope, found in the same villa)

[Item 3] Tonio Friedemann's 'suicide note', (found by Friedemann's body in his villa at Chousser - shortly before the villa burnt down)

[Item 4] A typewritten memo, on a single A4 sheet, from a file (whereabouts of file unknown) with handwritten notes in the margins, found by Stanley Casper at Friedemann's villa before it burnt down.

MY CONSIDERATIONS ARE AS FOLLOWS:

Item 1] Genuine. I know Arthur's hand. The content swings between monomania, obscene fixation, sadistic fantasy and genocidal tendency.

Pending the opinion of a psychologist specialising in this field the document would seem to demonstrate that Arthur Moreau - though at the time appearing to be plausible, reasonable and urbane to those who knew him (myself being no exception) - was criminally insane by the mid 1970s.

Item 2] - Moreau's love letter to Jo Debrett - Fake. The writer has not attempted to counterfeit Moreau's hand but has copied a passage from Oscar Wilde's, De Profundis. I would judge that this item - found in Jo's safe with the five 'dud' disks - is intended as a piece of subterfuge.

Item 3] - Friedemann's suicide note - Fake. I am certain, from the way his smartly dressed body was neatly seated on a chair, with a single bullet lodged in the brain leaving the rear of the skull intact, that Friedemann was executed by a contract killer - an expert, who was instructed to place the fake suicide note nearby but did not make a convincing job of it.

Item 4] appears to be genuine, from a typewritten office memo listing internal civil airline flights from various US airports to New York and Washington. The marginal notes on this item are in an identical hand to that on Items 2 and 3.

I believe that we must identify the writer of the manuscript on items 2, 3 and 4. I have the feeling that this person is close to the centre of Moreau's operation. Fred behaved oddly when I showed him these items at our meeting yesterday. He agreed with me that Item 2] is a fake, identifying the passage from Oscar Wilde. When I handed him the file I had prepared containing the items you have now, he refused to take them, advising me to destroy the items.

I leave the matter to you, adding that the situation is not good here. Amazingly, Arthur Moreau is alive. He turned up in my hotel suite last night with a bodyguard of kadets. Thomas, he says, is held hostage somewhere. I have not heard from Stanley Casper since his departure from Marrakech.

Arthur is convinced that I have changed sides. I have no option but to 'tag along' and see where the trail takes me.

Regards, J.D.

PS - Will find a reliable tourist to smuggle this package to you; best I can do in the circumstances.

Alice slowly straightened-up. Expertly, she unwrapped the four items, examined them over and again, reading and memorizing the text. Intently, she studied the handwriting. Moreau's she knew, Frederick's team had analysed it often. The other hand was difficult. Stubby, with no style . . . except for the capitals B and E. These letters were done with an unnecessary flourish, as if the writer were trying to imitate a more august hand.

She gasped, feeling in her handbag for a bottle of cologne and a hanky. *'Trying to imitate a more august hand'*. . . . She turned the type-written sheet this way and that, her eyes fixed on the hand written notes …. *'Trying to imitate …"*

The person's face came to her with visual force, in ice cold focus. Despite herself, Alice let out an exclamation of horror - half gasp, half scream. Her husband called, "You alright, girl? Wasp stung you, has it?"

"No Charlie, dear. Nothing's stung me, leastways not a wasp." She got up, dabbed her forehead with the cologne soaked hanky, got a grip on herself and went into the back parlour, "Shall I make a pot of tea? I could do with a cup."

"You're pale, Alice! Not like you. Something's up, ain't it? I can always tell. Sir Frederick getting at you, girl? Our British heroes! Never a moment's peace."

"Calm down, Charlie, there's a love. I'll put these papers away and we'll have a good, strong brew."

While Charlie slurped his copper coloured tea, Alice gazed at him with sad, deep affection. "Charlie!"

"Yes, my love."

"I'm going out later. I may not be back for a while. You'll be alright won't you, dear?"

He paused, raised his wrinkled lips from the rim of the canary yellow china cup, and looked across at her quietly. His head trembled very slightly with the first visible manifestation of dementia. He placed the cup down on its saucer and stiffly leant over towards her armchair, putting his hand on hers like he always did when something serious came between them. "Is this a duty call, my love?"

"Yes, dear. A very important one."

"You sure you can manage, girl?" His quavery Cockney accent bolstered her courage. She locked her fingers with his, squeezing his knuckles affectionately.

"I'll have to manage, dear. There's only me that can do it. I'll take Terry. He'll be the driver. I'll telephone him now."

"I've never argued with you over duty, Alice, and I'm not starting now." He got up, went over to the stained oak bookshelf and fished behind a set of encyclopaedias. He took out a small tin that had a picture of Brixham harbour on the lid. Sitting by Alice, he fumbled the lid open, trying not to show his tears. He took out a tiny, Victorian gold locket.

"You never knew about this, girl."

"No, dear, I didn't. You know I never touch your encyclopaedias."

"Open it." She clicked a minute latch and the painted lid sprang open to reveal, in tiny Copper Plate script, "I'll Love You To The End."

"Oh, Charlie! You were always a bit of a poet!"

"You're my poem, Alice." He brought her hand to his lips, tears spilling onto her wrist.

"I'll wear it tonight, my love. Never lose hope, Charlie. God's in this if I'm not mistaken. God don't clown around, my love. Not His Style."

♠

It took Alice until seven that evening to set the trap. Many contacts were alerted, all had to drop what they were doing and move fast. At eight-thirty Terry scored out of central London in an unmarked car, Alice in the passenger seat beside him. No handbag, twin set and pearls this time: she wore combat dress, and was equipped to kill.

Eventually, taking a number of planned detours, ensuring they were not trailed, Terry parked half way along a Regency crescent in the East Anglian town of Wisbech. The nearby church clock chimed half past midnight. "Bang-on, Alice."

They sat in the car scrutinizing the local museum housed in the end building of the crescent. Alice got out and walked to the entrance. As planned, the door was open and she went in. She walked through the hall into a room that looked like a museum piece itself. She tried the glass panelled door of a mahogany exhibition case. All was exactly as she had instructed. She returned to the car.

"Contact Colonel Descartes. Tell him Barra has done his work well. Add that it's a fine night here, perfect for the job. We shall require full surveillance. I'll go to the high street and see that they've put the lights to green." She wasn't five minutes, saying a few words to a Special Branch police officer on her return to the car.

"Colonel Descartes is standing by, Alice. He speaks dead posh English for a Frenchie, I could understand every word!"

"He was educated at Harrow, dear." There was a pause, tense, the night outside unbearably still. Not a window of the crescent showed light. Terry shifted in the driving seat of the powerful, low-slung car. Alice heard the young man swallowing with nerves. He fiddled with the steering wheel, drumming his strong fingers round its ivory circle, wanting to say something that troubled him. At last he blurted,

"It's not Sir Frederick, is it?"

"Terry! That is a question you *do not* ask! You know I will not say."

"Sorry, Alice. You see, you never told Sir Frederick about what we're up to …"

"*Terry*! Sit quiet and gather your strength. You're going to need it."

"Do you think anybody will turn up?"

"I don't have to think, Terry, I know. Now stop asking questions. Keep your eyes peeled on that museum."

They waited in silence. The church clock chimed two when they heard a car engine thrumming. A vehicle was parked round the corner of the Museum, out of sight. The engine stopped and soon a figure walked into view and stood still at the steps to the museum entrance. Alice activated an infra-red movie camera while Terry watched through night-sight binoculars and described the action into a microphone. The figure waited on the pavement. Four others appeared and stood in a group. The figure and two of the group went up the Museum steps. Before going the door, the figure turned and spoke to the two men on the pavement. He faced the car and was better illuminated by the moon.

"For fuck's sake, Alice! . . . I don't believe it!"

"We'll need to edit that bit from the recording, dear. Do watch your language."

"It can't be true, Alice!"

"Nothing stranger than truth, dear. Now watch them. They've gone inside. They should be about ten minutes, they have to clear the china and replace it exactly."

"China?"

"Friedemann's five disks are placed in a gun metal container behind the velvet lining of a cabinet in that museum that displays pieces of the Emperor Napoleon's travelling breakfast set captured by the British Army at the Battle of Waterloo. The pieces are of Sevres china, and when they have the disks, they must put Napoleon's cereal bowl and all the other things back in the case exactly as they found them. Those extra minutes give our people time to set Zero Fix. . . . Understood?"

"You're a crafty one, Alice. How did you know about Napoleon's breakfast set?"

"Common knowledge, dear."

"We haven't seen their vehicle, I hope it's not too powerful."

"It's a Jaguar X-300. You know that as well as I do. We've twice their power."

"How far do you think they'll go?"

"A location on The Wash is my guess. Fifteen miles on bumpy fen roads at top speed. Be ready for some exhibition driving."

"I'm shocked, Alice. I've got goose pimples. Tell me it's all a bad dream."

"Young men! Worse than girls." Alice put her hand to Charlie's locket. She gave Terry's arm a squeeze, "Courage, love! If we get this right, in two hours we'll bring their nightmare to an end."

♠

The Eocratic sliced through a smooth sea, making through the Straits of Gibraltar at thirteen knots. The Atlantic was enjoying a July calm and the ship surged to its full speed of a stately 18knots making almost due west. It was July 11th. Jock was serving my breakfast, "We should dock at Bermuda in a week's time, Sir, unless they decide to put the old man under the knife first."

"Bowel cancer at a guess."

"Right enough, Sir. And heaven knows what else. There's a team of surgeons round him all the time, Sir. They've an operating theatre on board that makes the Glasgow Royal Infirmary look like the place Florence Nightingale forgot."

"You told me that if Arthur comes through OK there'll be a party in the Eolian Saloon."

"Fancy dress, Sir. The theme is Sodom and Gomorrah, Sir."

"That should be jolly."

In the early hours of July 16th, unable to sleep, I was standing at one of the state room portholes gazing at the reflected crescent moon on the surface of the sea, when the engines slowed. After a while we were not making much more than eleven or twelve knots, ambling over the ocean at the speed of a bicycle. I guessed that Arthur had been taken into theatre. I poured myself a brandy and raised my glass to the moon, "Well, Arthur, I wonder if you're going to save us all the bother of doing you in."

♠

"How long to Bermuda at this speed, Jock?"

"A day and a half, Sir, unless the Captain orders full ahead."

"I'm going through the mirror to find Thomas. Coming with me?"

"No, Sir."

"Why?"

"Ye'll be needing me here, Sir, when ye return."

"Why will I be needing you, Jock?"

"If you find the boy, Sir, and if I guess right, he'll need me ter look after him, Sir." He gave me a knowing look, "I'll make sure there's medical attention at hand."

The mirror behind my bed rose into a slot within fifteen seconds of my fiddling Malvin's diamond-studded lighter into the brass key port. A landing appeared carpeted in boarding house Axminster. Like so much of Moreau's empire, the "secret shaft" was nothing to write home about. I climbed into the space and went down a steel spiral stair as far as it would go. The air smelt of diesel oil and kadet precincts.

The engine room was near by and the deck vibrated badly. A battleship grey corridor was dimly lit by steel-caged ceiling lights. There was now a smell of gravy, cabbage and corned beef hash. I nipped along the corridor to a bulkhead, using the lighter to open it.

Here was a short flight of carpeted stairs flanked by potted palms in ornate brass containers. From speakers, soft organ music played Nineteen Thirties Dance Band hits. A pair of mahogany doors with Gothic stained glass windows had a polished oak stand by them. On a brass plate I read, FUNERAL CHAPEL.

The chapel was carpeted in solemn midnight blue, the steel walls were surfaced with gold leaf, the ceiling presented a mass of crystal droplets pinkly illuminated from above. In the centre of the space, set on a vulgar bronze bier, was Arthur's glass casket. It had been secured against bad weather with thin steel cables tensioned to eye-hooks bolted round the walls. Beyond the casket a pair of silver candelabra stood at each side of a small altar with a brass grille in the front of it, giving me the impression of a radiator housing.

Stepping back to examine the altar in better light I tripped on one of the steel cables. Cursing, I grabbed hold of the altar to prevent myself falling but found to my consternation that it began to topple towards me. I managed to back into the end of the casket and hold the altar firm, hurting my spine on a gilt crucifix. In the steel wall behind the altar was a small, square hole. I presumed that this opening was the termination of a ventilation duct.

As I heaved the altar back into place I heard a faint moan coming from the hole. At once, I wrenched the altar aside and put my head through the opening. There was a strong smell of sewage.

"Who's there?"

"Johnny . . ." He was very weak, and I could not see him.

"Thomas. I'm right here. I'll get you out." I heard sobbing in the dark. I whipped out Malvin's lighter and with its faint flame saw him on the floor of a cell no bigger than a packing case. His naked back and buttocks faced me as he lay in his own excrement. Above him was a grating gobbed with scraps of rotting food. I spoke clearly and gently, loud enough for him to register my words, "You're going to be alright. I'll be back with help. Do you understand?" He moaned, then broke down. I scrambled clear, got to my feet, and turned round.

By the casket stood a single figure, grave, silent, arms crossed. The figure wore a dark blue damask robe enhanced by a magnificent gold chain held in an arc over the man's chest. Resting at the level of his thorax, was a single, flawless, seventeen centimetre diameter disc of polished, glimmering Kunzite.

"Franz von Stotz."

"Johnny Debrett! . . . So!" - He pronounced it *Zo!* - "The time has arrived to meet you." He smiled benignly, his manner calm and regal. One would not have dreamt that five meters from this stately being a young man was lying in a pool of his own shit.

"You will take a glass of Schnapps with me?"

"That would be a pleasure."

"Please," - he pronounced it *Pliz* - "follow me. We will go to my study, it is just round the corner. I am so glad you have called-in. I have important items to discuss with you."

"Does Arthur know of these items?"

"You are a wise man, Mr. Debrett. Your question has pin-point relevance. I have admired from afar your courage and your perception." He clicked his fingers at a place in the Chapel vestibule wall and a section sprang open. "Do come in." Sweeping before me, we entered a vast area, unusually high for a deck so deep in a ship's hull. The Kunzite disk glimmered splendidly as Stotz said, "My floating home. Do you like it?"

I might have stepped into a Bond Street antique dealers showroom. Aubusson carpets, Napoleonic furniture, walls lined with glass-fronted cabinets containing thousands of priceless pieces of historic porcelain. "My little den! And here, on a sofa asleep like a baby, one of my little boys." He stroked the head of a superb kadet who groaned luxuriously, stretched and turned over, opening gorgeous eyes to observe, sleepily, his Master's guest.

"Panno!"

"Yes, it is Panno. Home from home, Herr Johnny, no?" Stotz's laugh was Winter white, low, guttural and long, as if he were enjoying a private joke as he gently stroked Panno's tousled hair watching the kadet recognise me and, with a shout of joy, spring up on the cushions of the sofa to launch his arms round my waist and bury his head in my chest.

"Run and fetch our guest some fine Schnapps, the finest we have, my dear. Bring Venetian glass from the Palazzo Cavalli. Our guest enjoys so much the precious things of life." He motioned me to sit on the sofa that Panno had vacated, the cushions were warm and scented. He cleared his throat discretely, "You never leave well alone, Herr Johnny."

"Interfering has become my specialty, Doctor."

Panno handed me a frail fifteenth century Venetian glass goblet filled to the rim with antique Schnapps. Stotz eyed me from his desk, thoughtfully fingering the Kunzite disc. There was no time to waste, I dived straight in.

"Something has gone seriously wrong, hasn't it? Whoever murdered Tonio Friedemann has ruined your plans, not to mention the fact that Sir Frederick Appleby has Friedemann's five "Mind of God" disks safely hidden from you. You chose to reveal yourself to the Burdets in Minneapolis when it seemed to us that you might have had your doubts about Arthur Moreau. I know for certain that you would never have considered revealing yourself to me now unless you were in need of my help. Why are you plying me with old Schnapps, Franz? Is it because you need me?"

Slowly, Stotz rose from his chair and went over to one of the cabinets that contained a vast, sumptuously decorated dinner service. He took out a plate and handed it to me. It was Royal Berlin, a single item of a seven hundred and sixty piece service originally commissioned by Frederick the Great.

"There are many treasures aboard this ship, Johnny, but no treasure to compare with Tonio's final work."

"The Eocratic is a last refuge, isn't it?" I handed the plate back to Stotz, "Arthur Moreau is dying, Friedemann is dead, you are too old to be the leader of your so-called Eocracy, and now there are others. Younger. They're rats, aren't they, Franz? The sort of rats that come out from the sewers when a healthy Society is run onto the rocks by people like you? Your Eocracy is a mediocre regime in the hands of shams, mountebanks and half-bakes. That is the state of our Nation, isn't it? That is the state of America and Europe. And now, even you are sickened by the slime that intends to take power."

"I have ideals, Johnny. My philosophy is like that of Frederick the Great."

"Frederick the Great, Franz, was no half-bake! He never lost sight of Reason, Justice, or Culture. His heart was reserved for his people. How can you talk of Reason and Justice? How can you talk of Culture when you work to destroy each finer aspect of the Human character? You poison and pervert, you deal in ridiculous codes and fatuous riddles; the mumbo-jumbo of a tin-pot, gimcrack political regime. You deal in mendacity, you pull the wool, you piss in our soup and we drink it.

"Your Eocracy is a sick fantasy and *you* are sick, Franz! Your trumped-up ideals are mediocrity personified. That is the sum total of Friedemann's work. Mediocrity! You can only bring Society to a state of diseased nihilism, you are a form of political leprosy where the hands and feet of the People become stumps, and where the flesh of Democracy falls away to reveal the stinking sores of vulgarity, ignorance and the gutter-level viewpoint of the Second Rate."

"I intend to cure the leper."

"Miracles again, Franz? Please don't tell me you are God, I have heard enough of that from Moreau and Friedemann. Even Panno thought that Arthur was God until we gave him a good belting."

"I need you to get for me the last disk of the set of five, without it I am powerless, I do not have the genius of Tonio. I must have his work if I am to destroy Moreau's influence."

"Surely, all you need to do is get hold of the chief rat and put the bastard behind bars? It should be easy enough to shut down the Kadet programme, just don't produce any more. The poor things will die and the precincts will end up as tourist attractions."

"Get me the disk I need and I will help you."

"I'm not at all sure that Fred will buy that one."

"If you are not quick, somebody else plans to have them."

"Who, Franz? Who is the chief rat, Franz?"

"I cannot tell you."

"Then you remain the enemy. You cannot be trusted, can't you understand?"

"Do you want the boy back?"

"How can you ask such a question?"

"You can have Thomas back if you promise to obtain the last disk and to keep Kyla and Panno in safety and comfort after my death."

"Kyla and Panno?"

"My children. Kyla is on board with Arthur." I went over to a cabinet stuffed with Meissen figurines worth millions of dollars. My laugh was sardonic, "I want Thomas brought to this room immediately. There is no guarantee we'll let you have the final disk, and we might decide to put Kyla and Panno to death. They may look like Greek statues but they are nothing less than serial killers. If you wish to help us, Franz, your actions will be the only guarantee that we *might* grant what you wish."

"You are an English gentleman, who could doubt your honourable word?"

"That sounds like the line from a novel."

He beckoned me to a cabinet that began to swing out from the wall. Again the smell of excrement wafted towards me as Thomas came into view. Stotz touched the Kunzite disk and the shackles round the boy's wrists and ankles clicked open, the chains that held him fell to the steel deck. I crouched down and pulled him to his feet, he was shaky but not as bad as I feared. I drew him to me and, for all he was slimed with filth, embraced him.

"Like the Bible, Gov'ner! Saint Paul released from prison."

"Do you feel like Saint Paul?"

"I feel like a shower, a beer, and a bloody good steak. I'll have the beer first." He turned back to the cell, crouched down and felt behind some pipes. He handed me a red file.

"The cause of all my troubles, Johnny. From Moreau's operations room above Luan. It gives you the locations of the kadet precincts world wide and has a section on Moreau's Social Disintegration Programme." Panno draped Thomas in a towelling dressing gown, Stotz brought him a stein of Bavarian beer. As he took a shower I read through the file, handing it to Stotz when I had finished, "Is this all true?"

"I suppose so. I do not involve myself with mundane matters of daily administration."

♠

Panno insisted on returning to my State Room with Thomas. Jock advised that the Ship's Doctor must examine Thomas, "Ye cannie be sure, Sir, that the laddie hasn't been tampered with! Fed some of the dope they boil-up, Sir!"

"How do I call the doctor?"

"Ye'll find them all at the top of the spiral stair, Sir." He glanced dubiously at the stains on my shirt and trousers, "Ye'd better wash and change afore ye go. And may we have wee Panno sent back to Mister Stotz, Sir, if it's all the same to you."

I took two minutes to access the Officers' Mess.

"*Johnny!* . . . You're on board! Hey, everybody, it's Johnny! ... Capt'n! Come and meet the man who got us all into this mess. . . . Did you hear me, Jeff? Put your booze down and show the man a big welcome."

"I don't understand, Nina. How on earth did you all ...?"

"We booked a cruise on the Moreau Line, and here we are! "

Everybody left-off standing round the bar and crowded round me. Didier Gabriel introduced me to the Captain while the Ship's Doctor hurried away to examine Thomas. Ramona got me in a Hollywood clinch, "Wow, Johnny! What a *kisser*! Reminds me of *Sun Child* - I was Anne of Austria doing this hot love scene with Fulton Du-Frey. He kissed me so good I damned near bust my stays!"

The group was parted by a superb figure, his eyes orbs of emotion. Attired like a duke, Kyla stood before me, his hands on my shoulders, "You have come at last, to end this nightmare."

Captain Zanetti was a lugubrious Italian with a dry sense of humour. He told a steward to mix me a gin and Italian and sat me down on a sofa. He clapped his hands for attention. Everyone grouped round to listen.

"I must go on the bridge soon, but now we have welcomed Johnny aboard - and I confess that I was unaware this passenger *was* aboard - but then, I am unaware of most things happening on my ship - I think we should consider what is, in reality - ignoring the fribble Arthur Moreau has round him - a grave situation. Moreau came out of theatre nine hours ago after a difficult operation to remove an obstruction from his bowel. There will be a fancy dress party at three this afternoon in the Eolian Saloon. Moreau will attend in his hospital bed. The other passengers have been preparing for days. Their costumes - I leave you to imagine the details - are bulky.

"The Burdets are supposed to assassinate Moreau during this voyage - ordered to do so by one of the leaders of Moreau's . . . how would you define the organisation, Johnny?"

"Psychological terrorism."

"Let's call them murderers. Anyhow, Rick Stackton is the individual who has ordered Moreau to be assassinated, and I consider a fancy dress party the ideal time for this *indiscretion* to take place. But now we have Johnny with us, perhaps he has an alternative idea that will present, for Jeff and Nina at least, a more agreeable option."

"Are we far from Bermuda?"

"We're due to dock at Front Street, Hamilton in the early hours tomorrow morning. Didier, go check our position."

"Must we reach Bermuda, Captain?"

"Are you suggesting I scupper this vessel on the ocean?"

"I suspect you have considered the possibility, considering the cargo and the character of the passengers you have to carry."

"A perceptive man, Johnny. I have not only considered the possibility, but have arranged for explosive charges to be concealed along the hull below the water line. They have been calculated to fatally damage the vessel, but leave time, as she founders, for two boats to be lowered for the crew and ..."

"... the nice people."

"Thank you, Ramona. You see, Johnny, despite being paid three million American dollars a month to captain The Eocratic, I privately consider my masters, and those they choose to have aboard, to be traitors to Humanity worthy of execution." He pointed to Kyla, "This one, and the one they call Panno, are excused - for not only are they are very nearly human but they strive to be. Has anyone here an objection to my point of view?" There was a silence until Nina said, "Get 'em slaughtered! They'd do the same to us any time you like."

Didier returned from the bridge and handed Zanetti a slip of paper. "Good. We are making twelve knots through a calm sea. We are four hundred nautical miles to the south east of the Bermudas, over the Nares Deep."

"The deepest part of the Atlantic?"

"That is the Puerto Rico Trench. The Nares Deep isn't far behind. Three thousand, eight hundred fathoms. Let me see ... that makes just over six thousand, nine hundred meters. For the Americans round this table we're talking a little less than four and a half miles ... to a sailor like me, three point seven-five Nautical Miles."

"Deep enough for Arthur, don't you think?"

"Nothing is deep enough for Arthur, but it will do. Didier, go up on the bridge. Tell them to reduce our speed to eight knots and circle the ship round this same position unless I order otherwise. Call Bermuda and have Langley send out the *Adele Astaire* to pick us up. We shall be sixty-two people in two boats. I want the life boats made ready with extra clothing, food and drink, and a supply of drugs for the two kadets.

"When I give the order, sound the ship's horn three times. All crew members are to assemble on the Promenade Deck. Those who linger may go down with the ship. Should any member of Moreau's entourage wish to join us, they must be given a place in one of the boats, that is my single concession to mercy. Ask the Chief Engineer to join me on the bridge in half an hour." Didier nipped out of his chair and vanished through a glazed door.

"The *Adele Astaire*, for your information, is another of Moreau's converted liners. You may not believe this but she was once the *Versailles*, sister ship of the *France*. She is enormous and fast."

"How do we reach Minneapolis?"

"From Bermuda in one of Moreau's aircraft. Around six hours."

All this while Jeff had been noticeably silent. He now spoke with quiet deliberation, "Why Minneapolis, Johnny?"

"I am fairly certain that is where Stackton is now. At Gracewood."

"Aren't we being kinda hasty? Sort'a nasty? Must we sink this ship? Do we have to murder Moreau and our fellow passengers? Moreau's a sick man. Stackton's sick in the head, but from what me and Nina saw of him, he's a dork. If we corner Moreau, Stackton will fall apart. Can't we take over, sail to New York and deliver Moreau into the hands of Justice?"

"Lover, Moreau didn't give a damn when he handed out genocide like it was the best thing since motion pictures! As for Justice, *what* Justice? There ain't no judges left alive to judge! We have to agree with Captain Zanetti and Johnny, they know the game, and we have to do what they say." Zanetti glanced in my direction, then at Nina. It was difficult to argue with a lawyer and a friend.

"I respect your viewpoint, Jeff. It would have been mine three months since. Not now. With Thomas and Stanley I have witnessed more of Moreau's evil than all of you here, apart from Kyla who is created from it. Sir Frederick would tell you, as I tell you now: we have to rid ourselves of Moreau and all his empire. We have to ensure there can never be an encore. Having said that, I believe we should attempt to persuade Franz von Stotz to come with us. He has the will to help us, I talked with him less than two hours ago. He has the vital knowledge of Arthur's people and Tonio Friedemann's work."

Kyla tapped his baton on the table for attention, we turned to him, "I will speak to Stotz, Johnny. He will come with you." I was about to thank Kyla when, looking more like a Greek god than ever, he silenced me with a graceful wave of the baton. He stood up and modestly glanced round the table.

"I will kill Moreau. Leave the responsibility to me. I will need Didier and Thomas, also Hans and Conrad, crew members who are strong. I need to know, Captain, when you will blow out the hull." Zanetti considered for a moment, "Seventeen-thirty hours. That will give us half an hour to evacuate the ship, the *Adele* will be with us by twenty-hundred hours at the most . . . hmm . . . a maximum of two hours in the boats with daylight and a calm sea. Perfect! Seventeen-thirty hours it is. Arthur's party should be roaring."

"I need your key, Johnny, the one Malvin gave to you."

"Surely you have a key of your own, Kyla?" His smile was radiant, "I am just a passenger this time, Johnny. Isn't it lovely to be a passenger like everybody else?"

Arthur's Recovery Ball was themed Sodom City Hall. The fun was at full-pelt when the Captain lead Ramona and our party into the Eolian Saloon mid-way through the afternoon of July 18th. Our fancy dress consisted of warm clothes ready to abandon ship.

We pitched into a throng of ninety drunken queens who wore, with few exceptions, the most lewd costumes imaginable. It was difficult, amongst these frothing revellers, to see where they had put Arthur's bed.

The Eolian Saloon was a staggering one-hundred-and-twenty feet long - thirty-six meters. It was three decks high and had a huge, glass-vaulted ceiling, a sort of Art Nouveau spaghetti of young men kissing on a bed of yellow irises. The ends of the Saloon, fore and aft, were caves of treacly wood panelling, brass fire fenders, Persian tiles and stained glass lights depicting raunchy shepherd lads. The centre of the saloon was in fine Louis Quinze style - gold, white and grey. The effect, blazing with crystal lights from above, was sensational, although the atmosphere smelt strongly of old ladies:- camphor oil and lavender water.

Mountains of food, fountains of booze were being consumed, swine style, by the outrageous revellers, many of whom were as drugged as they were drunk. I felt a moist hand clap hard on my shoulder.

"Johnny! ... It's Jack Tubbs!" I stared at the man. "Surely you remember your old school chum, 'Tubby' Tubbs?" The bloke put his stinking mouth to my ear, his tone slimed with innuendo, "You *should* know, darling?" His pouchy, powdered face cracked into a filthy leer and he gave out a vulgar laugh like an acoustic belch. He reeled in front of me, bumper of champagne spilling over the polished parquet deck. Bald and gross, his drag had a huge, rubber, candy-pink phallus protruding from the farthingale.

"You've changed, Jack."

"Too sodding right, I've changed, darling! Made a fucking mint out of Moreau." A kadet passed with a tray of drink. With an unsteady hand, Tubbs pinched the kadet's bottom. "Whey-hey-*hey*! That's fuckable!"

"What do you do for Arthur when you're not enjoying yourself, Jack?"

"Arms dealer, dear! Fucking license to print money." He slobbered champagne over the tip of the phallus, "I'm a Defence Consultant if you want to be posh, dear."

"The lowest of the low."

"Whoops! *Meow!* You wouldn't soil your wet little hands, would you, Debrett? That's why you're nothing and I'm rich. Self-righteous cunt!" He spat at me, but the gobbet missed its mark and dribbled down the phallus, "Useless prick!"

"Talking of pricks, I think yours is coming adrift. Hadn't you better go to the Gents and tie it back on?"

I saw Arthur's bed. He was half conscious, propped on pillows, attached to various drips and five monitors. His wig was adrift, his make-up smeared. The polka dot silk pyjamas and matching dressing gown gave a pathetic affect of the tragic clown. A glass of champagne was being gently tipped between his bluish lips by a compassionate male nurse. I watched the unswallowed wine dribble down Arthur's trembling chin. For a moment - no matter what - I was sorry to see him so reduced.

♠

Jeff, Nina, Ramona, the Captain, members of the crew invited to the party, kept glancing surreptitiously at their watches. Seventeen-fifteen, a quarter of an hour to go and no sign of Kyla, Thomas or Panno. I was also concerned that Stotz was absent.

"Shall I go below and find out what's happening?"

"Stick to plan, Johnny. It'll be pretty hairy when this tub goes down. We need to be on deck where we can keep together." Nina waved an open sandwich about, "Did you try the sword fish? Don't! It's been doctored, the Captain told me. They're high as kites on the stuff. Something real bad's going to happen if Moreau kicks the bucket. Real creepy."

"Mass suicide?"

"Too right. I was thinking the same. Hey, Johnny, something's happening down the other end." Nina grabbed my hand and lead me towards the centre of the saloon. "We have action, Johnny."

Nine chefs wheeled a large table into the centre of the Saloon floor. It was covered in a white damask cloth swagged with Passion flowers. A gigantic, seven-tiered cake rose from the centre of the table and four gold basins of punch were placed at each corner. Medals were lined round the perimeter of the cloth. There was going to be a ceremony. The guests gathered round the edge of the Saloon twittering, eyeing Arthur's bed expectantly. The bed was manoeuvred nearer to the table and Arthur, amazingly restored by a shot of amphetamine, was sitting up, looking down the list of those to be honoured. A microphone on a pivot was angled near his mouth, a kadet shouldered a television camera.

Jack Tubbs took the centre of the floor holding a remote mike, "My lovely pals! It isn't often we have the penalty of looking at our wonderful leader in her hospital bed . . . are we weeping buckets? . . ." A falsetto chorus of, "We are *not*, dear!" . . . "Of *course* we're not! We're happy as sand-girls to see Arthur, bless her, in the pink of health!" Applause. Screams of, "*Bless* her!" Lots of whooping and girlish giggling. "So to waste no more time, luvvies, I'll ask our darling Arthur to say a few words and . . ."

The noise of the helicopter powering-up above us drowned all sound. The expression of officious fury on Tubbs's face changed to terror as a central section of the parquet deck reared up, Tubbs with it, to be folded over by a pivoting mechanism and sink out of sight. Tubbs, pop-eyed, plummeted into the hydraulic controls five decks down - where his body was crushed to pulp.

As the stupefied queens screamed and surged back towards the walls of the Saloon, many vomiting or urinating with fright, the helicopter noise became a frightful thrumming. We saw a platform rise into view with majestic, surging velocity. Upon it, glittering and evil, supported by the bronze bier, was the glass casket. Standing to attention round the casket in grey battledress were Kyla, Thomas, Didier, Hans and Conrad. In their dignity and resolve, the young men looked like saints in a cathedral window.

Arthur guessed it was the end. His screaming face became a study by Francis Bacon. Kyla approached him as he writhed down the bed sheets, tubes and wires pulling and disengaging from his bowel. Kyla upturned the monitors and swept from the bed its covers, grasping the leads and wires still attached to the twisting body to wrench them away with force. With one sweep of powerful arms, Kyla plucked the screeching old man from the bed, trailing cables and guts as the operation wound opened horribly and spilt the large intestine over the polka dot pyjamas.

The four men round the casket lifted its twinkling lid and held it to one side as the watching revellers moaned and screeched and the helicopter pounded and rose. We saw the vision of Arthur, now a lump of brown-red gore with its screaming head, chucked by Kyla into the crystal maw of the awesome sarcophagus, as a man might chuck a piece of decayed beef into a skip. The lid was slid into place. It engaged with a terrible, glassy clunk. We saw brown sludge spattering up the ice-blue sides.

We felt a violent vibration as four timed explosions went off down one side of the ship's hull at exactly seventeen-thirty hours.

The charges were moderate, enough to create a fifty meter split in the hull plates, similar to the notorious gash of the Titanic. Slowly, the ship began to heel to starboard. A second, terrible bang went off, and a ball of fire shot up the port side of the ship. The chaos was uncontrollable.

Nina grabbed Jeff, Ramona grabbed Didier, I grabbed Thomas and hailed the Captain who motioned us towards the bow where two life boats were swung-out on their derricks, manned and ready to lower. Ramona shouted, "Louis Mayer would've paid a million dollars for this scene!"

The ceiling of the Saloon shattered and sections of leaded glass plummeted onto the squealing crowd. Plates, tables, chairs, falsies and phalli swept over the drunken deck towards the lowering side of the Saloon. Arthur's followers were forcing something into their mouths, maybe tablets or poison from phials. They began to drop like stones, rolling towards the Louis Quinze pilasters, hands and feet twitching like mad acrobats.

Hundreds of crystal goblets smashed off a buffet that wrenched from its moorings. Lobster mayonnaise, cold salmon, crab salad, truffles, trifles, strawberries and cream vomited over the debris and the corpses. Two thousand bottles of vintage champagne cascaded from a series of refrigerated cabinets, smashing into bodies, skulls, and falsies. A steam pipe ruptured, boiling a huddled group alive. Musical instruments clattered and slid towards the walls followed by a waltzing chaos of dainty gilt chairs.

We turned, Thomas and I, just before leaving the Saloon, to make certain nobody in our group was trapped. We saw the casket begin to move, as the bier, on its wheels, gathered momentum down the sloping deck. Arthur writhed within the casket as it smashed through a pair of elegant French doors. The bier was stopped dead by a steel stanchion, and the casket sheered off it, vaulting over the deck rail to plummet, almost gracefully, to the surface of the sea that it hit with a resplendent splash of foaming, heavenly silver brine. We saw it, for a second, the lid still in place, pause. Then it sank, its monstrous contents wed for eternity … to the Deep.

"That's it, Gov'ner! That's the end of it!"

"Not yet, Mate. Get your arse into one of those boats, and fast!"

♠

We were dogged by the huge helicopter circling low overhead, the down draft from its swirling blades impeded our efforts to distance the boats from the sinking liner. Looking up, I saw a remote camera panning the scene. They were filming us!

Thomas wailed an animal, despairing cry. "Kyla isn't with us!"

"Are you sure?" He was in tears, "We have to go back for him!"

"We can't! The ship will plunge any second now. You can't do anything for him."

"I'm going to swim over!" I held him round the waist, "You can't! You'll die!" I made him look at the Eocratic. The promenade deck was no more than ten feet above the sea. "She's filling with water like a colander. You must give him up!"

"I *can't!*" He tore himself from me, leaping over people to Captain Zanetti who was directing the helmsman with professional calm. They talked, Zanetti looked at his watch, I joined them. Thomas was shouting, "You *have* to!" to which the Captain firmly responded, "She has about six minutes to live, ten at the most. If we go back we risk being sucked down with her, or overturned." I looked again at the foundering superstructure, ringed now with cascades of frothing, agitated seawater. By one of the funnels I saw a man waving a white mess jacket. It was Jock.

"We have to go back, Captain! Jock's by the aft funnel." Zanetti looked through his binoculars, snapped out an order to the helmsman, took up a megaphone and hailed the second boat to move away. With full power of the marine engine, we were soon rocked amongst the terrifying cascades of escaping air. Standing up in the boat, the rail of the Promenade Deck was easily grasped. I swung myself aboard and hauled Thomas with me. Against the Captain's orders he would not stay put. We raced up to the Shade Deck where Jock waited in his life jacket, shouting above the noise of the ever present helicopter, "I cannie budge him, Sir!"

"Who?"

"Kyla." He threw open a steel door and we saw Kyla crouched in a ball on the floor. "He cannie swim, Sir. He won't wear a life jacket." I grabbed the kadet by his head and made him look into my eyes. Thomas shoved me brutally to one side, dragged his friend from the floor, slapped his face hard, and gave him a kiss on the mouth. Jock pulled the life jacket over the Kadet's wondering head, and we linked arms round the slim waist, bundling ourselves down the companion way to the Promenade Deck that was now awash to our knees with sluicing seawater.

"She's going, Sir!"

The helicopter came close enough to catch our plight on video. Too close. The craft lurched against the forward radio mast and for a horrifying five seconds, time we did not have to spare, we watched. The craft tore itself free, making a gashed dent in the side of the cabin. Thankfully, it rose and veered into the sky.

Groans of tortured steel boomed from the depths of the disintegrating hull. Zanetti called through the megaphone, expertly guiding our choreography as we waded towards the prow of the waiting life boat. The strongest of the crew held out hooked staves. Thomas held Kyla in a fearless grip: only a hatchet could have parted the pair. Jock was first aboard. He turned to help me shift Thomas and Kyla over the submerged rail.

There was a massive explosion. A sea green curtain closed as the auditorium of my mind went black.

♠

Terry drove Alice Kingston out of Wisbech at ninety miles an hour. Following the Jaguar they flew over the flat roads of East Anglia towards The Wash. The smell of burning rubber went unnoticed.

Kadet Precinct Outfall Four was their destination. Blocked in mountainous silhouette against a dawn-spun sky, the complex was awesome.

"Fucking Hell!"

"Soap and water, Terry! Drive through the arch before they close the gates."

"How did it get here?"

"*Drive*! . . . Left! ... Over there!"

"It's supposed to be the village of Long Sutton, Alice. My auntie lives in Long Sutton."

"It probably still is, dear. They're going into the building on the right. Pull up! We'll wait." She opened her window, relishing the cool, early morning summer air, looking at the kempt lawns round a large, white villa. "Listen to the birds, dear. Isn't it lovely!"

"What's going on, Alice! This place is bigger than a nuclear power station and nobody knows about it."

"I could murder a cup of tea."

"Why don't they see us?"

"The arrogance of power, Terry. They don't see anybody but themselves." She looked at her watch, "Time check, please."

"Three-fifteen hours. Saturday, July twenty-third."

"A quarter past nine at night in Minneapolis. Friday to you and me. A little bird tells me that's about right! I'm going in." She handed Terry Charley's locket, "Keep this by. Be ready to show it me when I get back."

"What do you mean, Alice?"

"I mean, Terry dear, that what I'm about to do is risky."

"I'll come with you!"

"No you damned well won't, young man! You'll stay put here and you'll pray to God I finish the bastard off once and for bloody all!"

He grinned, boyish; "Soap and water, Alice!"

♠

215

She went through the open front door of a white villa and walked down a brown marble corridor to where lamps were on in an office. Here, seven or eight kadets lounged on chairs playing cards and smoking. Their shirts undone, their boots off, greasy wine glasses dotted over the floor, they seemed to Alice like a pack of rag-tag teenagers with the parents out of the way. None of them noticed the stranger.

Alice crept towards a silvery, flickering light. She walked into a large room and faced a multiple television screen that covered the opposite wall. The arrangement would seem old fashioned now, at the time it was the last word in audio-visual technology. In front of the screen, in silhouette, like a cartoon film, a long desk was outlined. Standing at the desk, facing the multiple screen, was her quarry. The upper body rose from the desk as one shape, topped by powerful, broad shoulders, a bull neck and sharply chiselled head. Light from the screen shone through the man's lawn shirt an x-ray picture of his animal, brutal, lithe torso.

It was he! A kadet appeared, standing by him holding something that was difficult to make out. A weapon? She needed to be certain before she made her move. Alice took a step nearer, as far as she dared without the kadet seeing her. The man took the objects from the kadet and placed them one by one in a row on the desk. Alice saw the shimmering reflection of Friedemann's 'Mind of God' disks. She backed away to the wall and felt for a chair. She sat down to wait, giving the man a few more minutes.

The screen showed a large, modern room. It must have been designed by an architect, Alice thought, because it looked so uncomfortable. Slots in the white walls contained potted cactus plants, but the zany item was a huge bird cage constructed on a concrete podium. The cage was the height of the room, a Cubist creation in black and white steel angles. Perched in a line, along a fake branch, were five white ravens.

Suddenly, in this strange room, Alice saw a door open. An insignificant looking man appeared. He had thinning hair and wore a dull business suit. Was this Stackton? Could the interior be somewhere in Gracewood? . . . The building with a smoking steel chimney that had so infuriated the Burdets? Was this Stackton's control room? Stackton's lair?

The cut-out figure in front of Alice snapped a command to the kadet and was handed a microphone. He began to speak to the man on the screen. Alice listened to a voice she knew so well: smooth, Public School vowels curled with menace.

"I have the five disks, Rick! You should hand-over control to me now, before I make trouble for you." Stackton jumped, then stared wildly towards what must have been an identical screen that Alice could not see. Taking up a microphone himself, Stackton shouted, "You fucking, treacherous shit! Traitor! You bloody, fucking cunt!" The words were a high pitched scream, as of a man

216

who has already lost the battle and knows it.

"Oh dear me, Rick! What sharp teeth you have when you squeal. Control yourself. Acting like a hysterical woman won't do you any good, not in your situation. Hear my terms; it could work out well for you if you listen carefully to what I have to say."

They were going to argue. She might as well listen-in for a while, they might give something away. Surreptitiously, Alice illuminated the dial of her watch; zero-three-forty hours. "I'll give them five minutes."

At the back of the room on the screen, the door opened again. A group of people entered, following what looked like a Stage butler. Alice couldn't believe her eyes.

♠

At eight-fifteen Minneapolis time on the same night, safe at the Burdet's home, Ramona handed round a plate of cookies and bawled that if anybody wanted another cup of coffee they'd better make it themselves, "Because, boys, Nina and me have had *enough* of that beautiful kitchen!" She helped Kyla manage his cookie, his right arm neat in a gauze sling, "There you are, darling, Momma's here!" She kissed the top of his head, catching my eye as I stood by the stone Indian, gin and Italian in hand.

"To think the kid was made in a bottle, Johnny."

"Technically speaking, Ramona, he was made in a womb."

"Technically speaking, Johnny darling, he's so damned handsome I could bed him this *minute*." Jeff glanced at a clock, "Talking of minutes, isn't it time we got inside Gracewood? We're all pretty much rested now, injuries on the mend."

For a set of shipwrecked mariners we weren't in bad shape. We'd managed to reach Minneapolis by Thursday, July 21st, and spent Friday relaxing. The plan was to get into Gracewood, find Stackton, hopefully with Stotz, then - in Nina's words, "Rope 'em up!"

Ramona clapped her hands for attention, "Listen, everybody, and listen good! It's half past eight on a lovely evening and I venture to guess that the folks in Gracewood will be having dinner."

"Stotz is serving boiled cabbage at this very moment!"

"Thomas, darling, you're cute and I could kiss you, but, please Sweetie, this is no time for schoolboy repartee!" She winked at me, "I know how to get into Gracewood without going through the front door."

I groaned, "Don't tell me! There's a secret tunnel connecting the house to the Catholic church round the corner."

"*Johnny*! . . . You read the book! . . .Absolutely right!"

"Please, my dear! Spare me another Hollywood adventure movie. I've had enough of playing Cary Grant to your Ingrid Bergman."

"Now there was a duo! They'd have had Moreau trussed up in . . ."

". . . the time it took Alfred Hitchcock to make a movie." I took a slug of my drink, "Take us down your tunnel, if it isn't full of rats."

"When and why was it constructed?"

"My grandmother was a Roman Catholic, Jeff. They built St. Margaret of Cortona along with Gracewood, and connected the house by a tunnel so they wouldn't get involved with anybody. They just turned up in the family pew, heard Mass and left without anyone but the priest knowing they were there."

"Do you think the tunnel will be accessible after eighty years?"

"If we don't quit talking and get up off our asses we'll never know."

♠

Jeff and Nina, wardens of St Margaret's, had keys to the church. In the well preserved Blaisedale family pew Saint Anthony of Padua's plaster robe concealed a bronze door handle. The saint, on his gold-leafed panel, swung open, and a musty smell of basements fronded from the cage of a private elevator . . . that worked.

The seven of us arrived somewhere below street level in a well ventilated tunnel lined with scenes from the life of Our Lord painted on ceramic tiles. Electric lights were in working order, and though there was a layer of dust on the paved floor, there was no sign of vermin. We walked for two minutes and came to a lofty vestibule.

"Where are we now?"

"Under the terrace facing the lake. Those doors go into the cinema, and that's the elevator into the house. Boy! It's a long time since I was down here."

We rose in a huge car, a spaghetti of gilded, fake Rococo frond-work embellished with tortoise shell. The doors slid apart. Facing us was Stanley. By him was a most attractive blond girl with her arm round Panno's waist.

Stotz was dressed in his butler's uniform, standing at a teak sink in a bee-striped waistcoat washing tea cups, his shirt sleeves rolled to the elbows. His tail coat was hung on a hook at the back of the olive green pantry door.

"You wish for me to terminate the tom-foolery?" His accent was now thickly German, as if he were disassociating himself from Gracewood and America.

"In Toledo you told me you will help us, you told Johnny the same on the Eocratic."

Silencing Stanley with a hand, I cut-in sharply, "Stackton is in the next building. Am I correct, Franz?"

"Correct."

"He is Arthur's chosen successor."

"He is not."

"Then who is?"

"I cannot tell you."

Nina slapped the deal table with the flat of her hand, "Baloney, Franz! You're playing your old tune again. You know everything, Franz. You've been in this circus from the start. Now help us, or I'll cut your throat with this carving knife ..."

"Nina, cool-it, Honey. Franz, we'll make sure you live comfortably if you assist us now. Johnny has promised you that."

"There is one other in Moreau's hierarchy of the first intellectual rank."

"Is he here, in Gracewood?"

"Please, be patient, I need to prepare some coffee." Stotz gave a cinder dry laugh as he walked to an oak dresser and opened a cupboard, taking out a silver coffee pot, reaching for a cream jug, cup, saucer and a tray.

"I presume, everybody, that you wish to dispense with Stackton completely?" Panno came into the pantry carrying a white box. Stotz unlocked the brass padlock of the box lid and took out an ordinary looking bottle with a screw cap, then a glass measuring vessel. "There it is! What you have all been waiting to see. Friedemann's serum! Enough in this little bottle to radically alter the personalities of the inhabitants of Texas, New Mexico, Oklahoma and Louisiana within the space of one month, provided . . ." he wagged a grey index finger, "it is mixed precisely according to the directions on the label. Simple, Ladies and Gentlemen, (the cinder dry laugh) *ven* you know how."

He rummaged about in the white box, bringing out a glass phial that he immediately cracked open, pouring its contents into the coffee pot. "I will modify the serum with a recipe of my own." He unscrewed the cap on the bottle. We smelt almonds and curry powder. "Kyla, my dear, open the window please, we do not want our guests to feel ill before the pleasure of observing our little party trick." He poured a tiny amount of serum into the measuring jug, then rolled-down his shirtsleeves, and put on a pair of gold cuff-links. Panno helped him into his Butler's tails.

Fishing in the inside pocket of the coat he drew out a straw of paper, tore the end off it and gently shook some grey powder into the coffee jug. There was a smell of mice. Panno poured steaming coffee into the silver pot from a Cona, and Stotz emptied the contents of the measuring jug over that. He snapped the silver lid down with a finicky movement, put on a pair of white cotton gloves, took up the tray, had Kyla open the pantry door, and turned to face us, "Follow me, please."

♠

We heard Stackton screaming abuse well before we reached the door of his control room. He was almost incoherent, as if the man were in a sort of uncontrollable rage with somebody. There was also desperation in the voice.

"What's the time, Johnny?"

"Twenty minutes to ten. Be careful with that shoulder, Thomas. No dramatics." Kyla gently took hold of the nape of Thomas's neck with his free hand, steering him forward as Stotz beckoned us into a huge, strange room.

I saw the wall of multiple television screens before anything else. The man on the screens was twice life-size, in sharp focus. He wore an expensive lawn shirt without a tie, widely open at the neck. His brutal, handsome face, the groomed hair, could not be mistaken.

"What's up, Johnny, you've gone white?"

"Peter Tyndale! . . . Sir Frederick's right-hand man! . . . . My Brother-in-Law." Of course, the handwriting on the four items was that of Peter's pert P.A., Liz.

"The Labyrinth, Thomas. There is our Minotaur."

Peter: paragon, hero, business mogul, ideal husband, wonderful father, all round sportsman, chairman of charities and golf clubs, church warden, school governor, high in the Boy Scout movement, friend of Royalty, valued by senior government administrators in five continents, confided-in by Heads of State . . . . Peter Tyndale; a modern saint. Trusted, revered, respected . . . a legend in his own lifetime.

"How could Frederick not have known?" I grabbed Stotz by his tales before he could move further into the room. "Is that Moreau's successor?" I pointed at the screen like a maniac.

"You know him?"

"Of course I bloody know him! I'm asking *you*, Franz; is he Moreau's successor?"

"He is The First Eocrat. Since five years. Hidden amongst you all, at the heart of the Establishment, as clear as day."

"But that's *impossible!*"

"That, Herr Johnny, is terrorism."

♠

Alice decided to make her move. Creeping up behind Tyndale, Alice heard me shout, "But that's *impossible!*". She gauged Stackton was so disturbed that he would not see her approaching Tyndale. She saw Stackton freeze for a second, as he registered our presence, she saw him reach down to a desk and uncover a black box.

Her gun aimed, she walked towards Tyndale's powerful back. She heard Stanley's crisp cry, "Hey! Johnny, there's somebody behind him." Tyndale whipped round to face Alice as we advanced past the enormous, Cubist birdcage.

"Stay where you are, Peter!"

Wired tense like a puma, Tyndale regarded the woman through narrowed eyes, "You bitch, Alice! You bloody *bitch*! I'll kill you for this!"

"Give me the disks." She continued to advance, steady, cold, professional. She knew this man, she knew the type - when faced-up to, they were nonentities. He leapt to the desk, fingers fanning to gather, like ears of corn, the disks.

Stackton marched from his desk, stood in front of Stanley and slapped his face, "You *dare* come in here! Fuck off! . . . *Stotz*! Clear these shits out of here!"

Stanley socked his jaw, sending the man sprawling. We heard a shot from the screen and saw Tyndale reel and swerve. Jeff and Ramona picked Stackton from the floor and sat him in one of the chairs in front of the desk, holding him by the shoulders. Stotz placed the tray of coffee on the desk and turned to a black box where a suspicious control knob stuck up.

Tyndale tried to fix his jaw back on his face. Alice shot twice, severing his spine. His legs parted and he collapsed like a flung raincoat. Merciful, she shot him three times through the skull. The body twitched and was still.

Stotz pulled the old fashioned, Space Ship style lever of the black box.

The kadet attending Tyndale began to melt. It was a horrible sight but Alice let the process happen, not looking. She gathered the disks from the desk, we saw her doing this in full focus. I grabbed Stackton's mike, "The last disk, Alice! The fifth! Take the fifth!".

She snatched Tyndale's mike from the floor, "How do I know, Johnny?"

Stotz went to a podium, neatly adjusting his white tie, "They are numbered, Madam. It has the number 'five' in large red print, Madam. And please, Madam, try not to scratch the surface."

Stackton screeched like an owl, "What are you *doing*, Franz?"

"Calm yourself, Master Rick. Drink this coffee and calm yourself. The work is complete. I am drawing to a close the first act of our little drama." He pronounced 'drama' like barbed wire ripping through a silk scarf. He handed Stackton the cup and saucer.

"Johnny ..."

"What is it, Alice?"

"They've put gas in here. I don't think I can get out in time. Can you stop it there?"

Stackton took a mouthful of coffee and was able to wriggle out of Jeff's hold. Before I could prevent him, he nipped to the black box and pulled the knob further across the arc of its brass bound slot. We heard a hissing sound.

I turned to the screen. The room Alice was trying to escape from was disintegrating. "Hey! Grab Stotz! He's getting through a panel!" Jeff and

Ramona grabbed the butler's tales, Panno the belt. They hurled Stotz to the floor and sat on him. In German I shouted, "If I pull that lever back, will this stop?" But he only whispered, *I cannot tell you.* The air smelt of mice …. the serum …. pumped through ducts? No time for questions. On screen I saw Alice take the final disk as the space round her was enveloped in a sheet of flame. We heard her scream, "I'm at the door! Johnny, it's locked!" We could not see her but the fire was a strange colour, unreal. Thomas wrenched my arm, "Like Friedemann's lab, Johnny. I'm going to shout those numbers, see if Alice gets free."

Stackton finished his coffee. Ramona pointed, "He's melting!" Stackton emitted a rasping sound from the base of his throat. His arms ran through the grey jacket in a stream of black fluid. Thomas shouted down the mike, "Nine, eight, six, seven, zero, zero" Alice cried, "I don't think I can make it!"

"The floor's vibrating."

"The screen is going pale."

Stackton was propelled towards the bird cage. His remains smashed through the steel mesh as his lower body became a slug. His mouth twitched and jerked, the tongue licking amongst the white ravens' buttery droppings. The room made cracking sounds, the high level window frames fell away and night air rushed in, cool and pure. We heard Alice cry, "There's an earthquake!" Thomas blurted, "What was that Shakespeare line?" I grabbed the mike, Stanley stood at the podium. Taking my cue we bellowed, *Now is the winter of our discontent made glorious summer by the sun of York.*"

The screen went cobalt blue. We heard Alice say, "I'm sorry, Johnny. It's going to kill me!" Then we saw her running, "I'm through!" We saw her running towards an opening that expanded into sunlight. We saw her running through rose beds towards a car where a young man in a chauffeur's uniform took Friedemann's fifth disk and put it in a wallet. We saw him show her a locket. We saw her smile. We saw an English village, a church, a row of quaint, brick cottages . . . We saw Alice's car drive-off down the main street.

Stackton made a sound like a bassoon. Nothing was left but a stinking pool of liquor and his maggot infested skull. The white ravens sedately pecked his eyes out.

There was complete stillness.

Through the gap in a clipped laurel hedge where the door to Stackton's control room had been, Sir Frederick Appleby appeared, immaculate in a Prince of Wales check suit, silk bow tie and gold-topped, malacca cane. In his button hole was a Gloire de Dijon rose. Dabbing his blind eye with a cream silk square he surveyed the bird cage, then looked at us as we sat in a circle on a lawn golden with early morning light.

"Ramona Delano! What a delightful pleasure to find you amongst my friends, and here, of all places! . . . Time has not altered your beauty." He made her a chivalrous nod of his dignified head. "I saw one of your films only last week, *'They Named Her Jezebel!'*. Frederick looked about him, "What I find here rather reminds me of the final scene."

EPILOGUE

Franz von Stotz lived out his last years in America under house arrest by the tranquil west shore of Bantam Lake, Litchfield, Connecticut. He had repented of his terrible life but he could never be trusted. Round the clock, discrete guards patrolled the steel fenced domain of Woodville House, an elegant, two storey clapboard residence built for the Hartford born pianist, Emeline Craig-Lewis.

New friends were made, mostly Quakers, and Franz entertained them in a spacious drawing room, or - in Summer - on a rose-clouded terrace backed by green oak woods. Every morning he worked in his laboratory with an assistant, converting information on Friedemann's fifth "Mind of God" disk to balance a fraction of Moreau's evil with good.

Two beings benefited from the completion of Friedemann's work, Kyla and Panno. Though there were many who demanded the Kadets' execution, Frederick would not hear of it. They were all that remained of an extraordinary period in our history. Stotz had given us the formula to make the necessary drug that kept them alive, but nobody could be sure what would happen to them when their accelerated aging process turned them into decrepit old men by the normal age of thirty-five. The thought of watching these nobly ideal creatures age in days, decompose alive and die in agony, was more than most people could stomach.

Moreover, Panno and Kyla were sterile, though their genitals were perfectly developed. I gathered from a communication from Stotz that the sterility was technically reversible. He also told me that there was a chance to give the two kadets a normal life span and aging process by adjusting some of their genes in tandem with their immune system. He could make no promises, but he was working on the problem. In the Autumn of 19..., I received a telephone call from Frederick.

"He's done it, Johnny!"

"Who's done it?"

"Stotz! The old devil's done it! We can bolt the balls back on our two Kadets." For all his gruffness, I knew that Fred was very fond of Kyla and Panno. He had arranged for them to live in a secluded part of Yorkshire, attended by a mansion full of staff as if they were young lords. Although he would not say as much, Fred had virtually adopted them.

"What happens now?"

"He wants you and Thomas to get over to Woodville House. I have arranged transport. You can be there today, noon their time."

"That's not very convenient. I have a book fair in Moscow. Thomas is fell walking in the Lake District with his girlfriend."

"I have decided that you will give Moscow a miss this year, Johnny. As for Thomas, he is now on a special flight to RAF Northolt. The young lady waits her beau's return at a guest house in Keswick. There is nothing more to be said."

Nine hours later, Thomas and I were cleared by security at Woodville House.

♠

Stotz sat in a chintz upholstered armchair by the elegant Sheraton-style fireplace of his begonia decked drawing room. Between us, on a mahogany occasional table was a large silver tray bearing a generous afternoon tea. We had spent some time dawdling with cake and bread and butter - that the Security man sitting in the background had refused. We talked of Friedemann's silly codes, particularly W M D O.

"Ah, Gentlemen . . . it was no joke. Puerile, but no joke."

"I got all the numbers correct!"

"You did, my little English friend!" He smiled at Thomas, avuncular and kind; one might never have guessed he had been personally responsible for the murder of sixteen million people. "But what you could never have unravelled, even with your boyish charms," his laughter was like an ebbing tide, "was the Atomic numbers Tonio concealed in those ridiculous letters." He asked a guard to bring schnapps. We sipped it from Eighteenth Century Bohemian crystal glasses.

"Atomic numbers?"

"Yes, Johnny. The double-U, the twenty-third letter of our alphabet, is Atomic Number twenty-three. This is Vanadium. And so we have the 'M', is thirteen, is Aluminium. And 'D' is Beryllium, and 'O' is Phosphorus. Add the numbers together, we make fifty-five: and that is Cæsium."

"A recipe?"

"Precisely, Johnny! A recipe."

"What does it make?"

"Human misery, gentlemen. Fortunately for us, Tonio's cook book is destroyed." He sat still, breathing noisily, gazing into the fire, his glass of Schnapps held at an angle, his mouth a melancholy line. Then he looked up, and smiled radiantly so that I saw how good looking he had once been. "All in the past! Silly, silly men and their silly secret societies, hmm? Let us talk of the future. Of my children, Kyla and Panno."

We discussed a surgical operation that involved Thomas as the donor and required a special theatre fitted with three linked stations. I was dubious, but Thomas, because he loved Kyla and Panno, wanted the scheme to go ahead.

"It's easy, Johnny. I'll do it!"

"Provided Franz is present to direct the surgeons . . ." I glared at Stotz, severe, ". . . and that we can trust you."

He took up a piece of bread and butter, curled now with the heat of the fire, "Trust me? Because I have the blood of millions of souls on my hands you do not trust me? I am to make my children live! Thomas is to provide the splendid link that sets their beating hearts at one with God's Own Blueprint." He put half the piece of bread and butter into his mouth and took it out again, "Trust me? . . . *Ha!* You would trust your sister not to take a knife and slit your throat?" He snapped a knarled finger and thumb, the security man shot forward to re-fill our glasses with Schnapps.

"Listen, Johnny Debrett, to a wise old murderer. I have enjoyed so much, in the past, to liquidate those millions. Now, I shall delight in saving but two." He looked at me, amused, messily chewing the bread and butter, speaking with his mouth full, "Did not Jesus Christ say something of the sort, Johnny?"

"From a different viewpoint, Franz."

His laugh was a moonlit sonata.

♠

The operation lasted for seven hours, and was performed by nine surgeons. Thomas was brought in first, lain on his front, and an instrument designed by Stotz cut into the nape of his neck, inserting two needles into his spinal cord. A device was taped over his pituitary gland.

Anæsthetizing Kyla and Panno was extremely complex, even Stotz appeared nervous as a unique anaesthetic was injected into their arms at exactly the same moment. They went out like lights, breathing calmly. Kyla was placed to the left of Thomas, Panno to the right. A different instrument, again designed by Stotz, was placed over the base of each kadet's spine and a strange needle was inserted into their livers. Their three hearts were connected and various innovative instruments were wired to a computer. Stotz sat in a chair, without notes, and directed every move with meticulous, verbal instructions. Frederick, myself and a team of International Observers watched through a glass window.

Finally, Stotz pronounced the operation successful. The team in the theatre sighed with relief. The three young men - for this was now the status of Kyla and Panno - were wheeled to a special ward.

The senior surgeon took off his gloves and walked over to Stotz's chair. In our glass fronted booth, Frederick nudged my arm, "What's the betting the old bastard's dead, Johnny?"

The senior surgeon beamed at Stotz who sat in his chair bolt upright, his grey face smiling, his narrowed eyes expressing mild superiority. "Mr. Stotz, this operation has been a first for America! I guess a first for Mankind. We could not have achieved this feat of technology without you, even though my team has an aggregate of ninety years top rank experience between us . . . Mr.

Stotz? . . . Mr. *Stotz*?" He bent down to peer closely at Stotz's face, "Are you OK?"

"He's dead, Alec!"

"*What*?"

"Look at his eyes. Glass cold. He's dead."

"He can't be!"

Sir Frederick's commanding voice boomed over the intercom, "Oh yes he can! His one good deed for the day, Gentlemen! Bury the bugger and let's have done with it!"

"Sir Frederick is correct, Alec. He's taken poison." With two rubber-gloved fingers the assistant surgeon expertly felt round the inside of Stotz's mouth, "Here's the capsule under his tongue. The guilt factor, I guess." A nurse took a slip of paper from the old man's cooling hand. Franz's last pencilled note read; *Scatter my ashes in Lake Konstanz, by Langenargen; the town where my dear Mother was born.*

And so we did.

♠

A few years have passed since Kyla and Panno were brought into the world as men. Weeks after recovering from the operation, they began to show every sign of mature, adult normality. They were subjected to innumerable psychological tests and physical examinations, but nothing of their delinquent root could be traced. Their sexuality, that in Kyla's case had been distinctly aimed at his own kind - less so in Panno - proved explosive. They couldn't stop thinking, talking, dreaming - about girls! As for Thomas, the three young men could have been brothers. Many people remarked that they looked like triplets.

Frederick formally adopted the kadets as his sons, the news was splashed over the media worldwide. He was careful that they were not exposed to publicity, arranging for private tutors and a band of what Fred called, "Suitable young friends.".

It was during a Summer holiday at La Breuse, while watching Kyla and Thomas play polo, that I asked Corinne to marry me. I write these memoirs now - looking from my study window in the circular south-west tower of my wife's beautiful château - as the Comte de la Breuse. The book business continues both in Aylesford and New York, where it is run by my business partner and lifelong friend, Stanley Casper.

Our wedding was discrete. The chapel of La Breuse set the scene; Thomas was my Best Man while Corinne was given away by her Uncle, the Duc de Lussac. There was a sumptuous lunch to follow when some of the greatest French wine was consumed with a reverence normally reserved for divine worship.

Stanley and Daisy's three daughters, the triplets Nissa, Gilda and Zona, planned to join our house party two days after the ceremony. Gilda was working in Cologne at the time and when her sisters joined her from the States, she drove them to La Breuse in her little German car - and a very giggly car-load those three young women were.

Having sped through the gates of La Breuse, they were awed by the majesty of the château. Its silver-cream walls, its circular towers with conical, blue slate roofs, the green-gold skein of lawns, the fountains and cascades filling five manmade lakes. It was like a castle from a fairy tale, they said.

"Stop the car, Gilda. Let's get out and soak it all in." Gilda pulled-up near a statue of Venus pestered by Cupid and a bunch of sex-crazed cherubs.

"It's better than Disney."

"I told you it was amazing."

"We're goin' to *stay* in there!"

"Hey, girls! There's three horsemen coming over the grass."

"Look at those stallions!"

"Look at those *guys*!"

"It's Panno!"

"They're *gorgeous*!"

"They're a *dream*!"

"The one on the left's mine!"

"I'm nuts about the one in the middle!"

"Panno! . . . He's *mine*!"

Kyla, Thomas and Panno dismounted. Graceful and strong, they wore riding breeches, polished boots with gold spurs, and short-sleeved white shirts open at the collar perfectly displaying their muscular, bronzy arms and powerful necks. They came over to the car as the three girls shyly walked towards them: six hearts beating hard. The men stopped, caught in a hail of arrows from Cupid and his platoon of cherubs. The girls took their fill of beautiful male eyes, the dark lashes as long as poems. Transfixed and speechless, the three young men stared . . . and stared.

And that - as they say in the storybooks - was that!

♠

The announcement of their engagement was made after lunch two days later. Daisy and Stanley agreed with Ramona, Jeff and Nina that a Triple Wedding would be the sensational way to proceed. Where and when posed a problem, but Frederick stood under a sizeable Louis Seize chandelier and clapped his hands for silence,

"As I am the foster father of two of the happy six, I'm telling everybody that Stanley and Daisy can sit back and relax! This wedding, in fact the entire bloody shooting match, will be paid for, and organised, by me!" His wife piped up, "Darling! Suppose Stanley and Daisy would like a say in the matter, and what about Thomas's parents?"

"They'll all damned well do as they're told, Vera! I'll fix your Father, Thomas, he and I are old friends. Johnny, where shall the ceremony be? I fancy an English cathedral! Which one?"

"As you have turned every English Cathedral into a jam factory, Frederick, that is a difficult question!"

"Nonsense! The priesthood is back on the road, where Christ intended them to be! Now *think* man!" Thomas piped-up, "You made the universities into foundries."

"Listen to the impudence of the young fool! Steel and iron does the soul of a nation good, Thomas. Besides you know very well how you love roaming the country in student bands, finding your teachers in the forests and by lakes. Learning in the beauty of Nature: an excellent combination! I won't have a word said against it."

"Darling, aren't we rather getting off the point?" But he only snorted. Ramona poured Fred a glass of champagne, "Freddy darling, grab this bubbly and hear me out!" She put her arm round his waist seductively, "Listen good, Babe. I have a property in Switzerland near St Gallen. Kind of a Swiss chalet, frilly roofs and heaped-up balconies. It's on a mountain with great views of the Alps and the place is big enough for two thousand folks. Why don't we do the reception there and marry our dream-team in the fabulous Abbey of St Gallen?"

"Marvellous! I'll telephone them now!"

"I already did. What's more, Corinne has a gift for the girls." Corinne opened a Sixteenth Century *cassone*. Inside was a bolt of ivory-cream Alençon lace, by it was a second bolt of quartz-white Florentine silk brocade. "If you agree, you can have identical wedding dresses made from these. There is enough lace to trim the trains and make beautiful veils over your lovely blond hair."

Tears!

"And! . . ." bawled Frederick, "I will have the three young men in that uniform Kyla sports. White military tunics, blue silk sashes, black trousers with scarlet braid down the sides. Diamond stars over your hearts. What do you say to that, lads?"

"It sounds like a chocolate box to me, Fred!"

"It is a bloody chocolate box, Debrett! That's what a bloody wedding's all about!"

♠

Thousands of people came to St Gallen, most saw the ceremony on giant

230

screens set-up in the park above the abbey. Over a billion watched it on television. I need not describe what you can well imagine, except to explain Frederick's idea to have the three couples married by a representative of every religion that looks to God. He said, "You see, Johnny, two of our boys came from nowhere, so now they will belong everywhere. Quite simple!" It was a problem arranging the combined final blessing, but the production was seamless.

"The Kiss" sent every woman into floods of tears. Men could not restrain a tear, myself included. It seemed in a single movement, Nissa, Gilda and Zona turned to their new husbands who each drew up the lace veil of his bride as candle light shimmered through the love-enfolded fronds. Lip met with lightly parted lip in a triple, solemn kiss, the boys tall and handsome, betraying gentle male devotion in the exquisitely curved nape of each manly neck.

Standing by Sir Frederick at the front, I looked up at the Rococo ceiling of the abbey church. I saw an inexplicable light forming, descending onto the three couples. I nudged Frederick and signed upwards with my eyes. After gazing up for a second he whispered, "They always put on a good show for me." He paused, then murmured, "The Light of the World, Johnny."

♠

The banquet that followed the wedding was held *al fresco*, amid a profusion of Swiss wild flowers. Two thousand people were well served and drank their fill. Eventually, it was the turn of Sir Frederick to make his final speech. Jovial, larky in parts, his jokes delighting the young men present and producing matronly smiles from the ladies, he was ever sharp and to the point. He ended with the following words;

"This so happy occasion terminates a grim saga in the annals of Human affairs. Who was to know that Kyla and Panno would be the only survivors of a dismal era? A pack of evil men hunted the World and ensnared us. A generation of soulless youth was made to beguile us, to lead us beyond common reason to a point where we became callous, selfish and heedless of our inheritance: the Earth.

"So blind were we made that we could not see their vast concrete pyramids of perversion towering amongst us. Nor could we understand the searing plague that was designed to rage in our neighbourhoods, towns and cities. This plague was concocted to damage our minds so that we became selfish and treacherous, so that we devoured each other in a blighted race to revel in a life of tawdry luxuries and ineffectual superficialities.

"Yet the worst of it was not so much in destruction. Humanity can cope with destruction. We rebuild. The worst was in the fact that the leaders of Arthur Moreau's empire were not to be found abroad, sitting in caves, fashioning their bows and arrows. The leaders were amongst us! They were the chairman of great companies and banking houses, they were influential men and women in high public office, they were our politicians, even our Heads of State. They were the priests in our churches, they were the moguls of the Media, the heroes of our Recreations, the owners of supermarket chains and of manufacturing concerns. They belonged to respectable Country Clubs and lived in grandly bedecked homes.

"How well these people knew their role! How artfully they acted their parts. Sinister beyond belief, they lived amongst us as friends and colleagues! These charlatans flattered, lied and wormed their way to prominence and fame. Their slick words, their sham gestures, their cunning ploys, fooled even the most discerning.

"I thought my friend Johnny Debrett had been taken for a lifelong ride by Arthur Moreau. How ghastly it was, finally, to realise that my own deputy, my own man! that I considered Honour personified, held in his hands the black keys to the Gates of Hell.

"My own man! Married to Johnny's sister, my Goddaughter! A fellow who stood at my side, who knew me so well, who understood the supreme nature of my power. Yet he had the gall to deceive me in my own realm.

"We faced Moreau's tyranny square-on and the walls of his sordid citadel fell before us. A dynasty of fakes vanished into thin air because we had the Will to make the destruction happen. Was it real? Oh yes! it was real. Because we made it so. All of us. We played Existence as a gambler plays Roulette. But the instant Moreau's iniquity was challenged, his fantasy slid into the Ditch of Fate like a shovelled heap of dung.

"Thomas, a young man armed only with the Sword of Innocence. Kyla and Panno, who had the courage to defy their unspeakable conception. Three young women who wish to make these men happy. Their loving union is our reward.

"Their weapon? Invincible Truth."

He raised his wine glass so that the sunlight caught the jewelled claret and the reflection of distant Alpine peaks was ruby-hued.

"My blessing be upon the three couples, and upon the Peoples of this Earth, our unique World. The World that has borne us, and that cherishes us.

"Elect now honest authorities that value our World. Drive out from the High Places those that exist in the shadow of Corruption, the charlatans and deceivers who make our lives a troubled, dark dream when Truth, in Truth, is the Bright Wakefulness of Creation."

The End

Lightning Source UK Ltd.
Milton Keynes UK

177973UK00002B/5/P